A TRAITOR'S WAR

THE METAFRAME WAR:
BOOK 2

Graeme Rodaughan

Published by System Zero Productions Pty Ltd, 2017

Trade Paperback ISBN-13: 978-0-9945952-3-2

Kindle Edition ISBN-13: 978-0-9945952-4-9

EPUB Edition ISBN-13: 978-0-9945952-5-6

Cover art by Huw Jones

For Linda, for her unfailing love and support that always leaves me in awe.

I would like to thank a number of people who have assisted with my progress as an author, including Alex, Tim, Lisa, Lena, Marie, Eldon, Michael, Christopher, Perry, Nick, Andrew, Laura, Daniel, Ginger, Jody, and the regular crew of Beta and ARC readers at the Castle Dracula group and my many friends and followers on Goodreads. You have all contributed more than you know to my craft and your support and encouragement are invaluable for this journey.

Books by Graeme Rodaughan

The Metaframe War Series

A Subtle Agency
A Traitor's War
The Dragon's Den
The Day Guard
The Crane War
The Key of Ahknaton
The Metaframe Adept

Omnibus Volumes

A Subtle Agency Omnibus (includes A Subtle Agency, A Traitor's
War, and The Dragon's Den)

Dramatis Personae

The Ancients

Ahknaton, Ruler of the Southern Realm, High Priest of the Temple of Thoth. Master Architect. Ramp Master.
Hakron, Second prince of the Southern Realm. Master Scribe. Ramp Master. Ahknaton's brother
Mekra, Princess, Ahknaton's wife.

The Vampire Dominion

Cornelius Crane, King of the Vampire Dominion
Chloe Armitage, General, The Americas, ex Order of Thoth and Crane's chief enforcer
Haras Mosule, General, Middle East, ex Red Empire warrior of the 3rd rank
Dieter Franz, General, Western Europe
Clayton Maze, General, Africa
Shen Zhen, General, East Asia
Marcus Drake, Chloe's aide de camp
Rawlings, Centurion, praetorian

The Order of Thoth

Ramin Kain, Head of the Order of Thoth
Samuel Luther, Ramin's chief of staff and aide de camp
Deon Lamar, Order Traveler (Spy Catcher)

The Exiles

Arthur Slayne, (Exiled) Master Strategist, Force Leader, Weapons Grandmaster, Speed Talent.

The Mirovar Force Team

Francis Mirovar, Force Leader, Weapons Master
Juliette Mirovar, Loremaster, Netmaster, Combat Surgeon
Yvette Mirovar, Operative
Jay Creeley, Operative, Weapons Master

Peter Lamb, Operative, Armorer, Strength Talent
Chiara Romano, Operative, 2nd Combat Surgeon
Anton Slayne, Order novice
Li Wu, Order novice, Weapons Master

The Red Empire

Shabbah al Ahmar, aka 'The Red Ghost,' aka Dalien Morte. Head of the Red Empire
Al Ghurab, aka 'The Raven,' Operative inserted into the Order of Thoth
Al Far, aka 'The Rat,' Operative
Thueban Kabir, aka 'The Great Serpent,' aka 'Taipan,' Weapons Grandmaster, warrior of the 3rd rank
Nasr al Dam, aka 'The Blood Eagle,' Fist team leader, warrior of the 2nd rank

Shadowstone

James Haley, Head of Operations, United States
Louise Wesson, Operative

Other Players

Jean Philippe Allemande, Metaframe Sorcerer

Justin Blake, Force Leader (South West) Weapons Master, Strength talent. Former student of Gang Wu

Dillon Browne, Gang Leader
Caleb Moore, Dillon's enforcer
Aaliyah Williams, Dillon's girlfriend
Gabriel Williams, Aaliyah's younger brother
Ethan Jones, Gangster,

John Tilson, Captain, US Special Forces
Smith, Sargent, US Special Forces, Tilson's 2IC.

Prologue

Port-au-Prince, Haiti, December 24th, 1857, 20:25

The scent of aniseed laced rum filled the air as drunken revelers spilled out of the port tavern. The foul odors of sweaty, unwashed bodies clashed with the salt tang of the ocean and fought battles with the reek of bales of goatskins and mahogany stacked in piles along the docks of Port-au-Prince. The lush warmth of the night fed the ambiance of celebration as children carrying oil lamps sang carols in the street, and people sang, danced, drank and feasted.

Pools of light from taverns, shops and warehouses illuminated the packed earth of the street, and the people moved through the soft lights and dim shadows as they mingled, shouted in semi-delirium and loved wildly.

The people of Port-au-Prince celebrated Christmas Eve. Above them, an entirely different ceremony was well advanced in the top floor suite of the Ivory Moon hotel. The hotel's staff had cleared the rooms of furniture the week before, the bare floorboards lay exposed, and thick black curtains draped the windows.

Jean Philippe Allemande, Voodoo Sorcerer, and his student sat opposite each other within the confines of a magic circle. The circle was three yards across and drawn in fresh human blood. Both men had stripped to the waist, wearing simple dark cloth trousers. They were wet with perspiration. A fine sheen that glowed like gold in the candlelight covered the student's pale skin, long limbs, and lean musculature. Jean Philippe's mahogany skin, burnished in the candlelight, dripped sweat onto the floorboards where it soaked into the dry wood. The air was thick with the scent of black candles wrought from the fat of human cadavers. Flat copper bowls of slowly congealing blood lay at the eight cardinal points around the bloody diagram on the floor.

The student had arrived in the winter months of 1846. They'd struck a bargain. They'd swap power for immortality. In the following years, the student had visited, time and time again. Participating in training his mind, body, and soul to confront the Divine Engine of Thoth and draw from it a tiny fraction of its true power.

The student's agents had delivered Jean Philippe to the Americas, the Far East, Turkey, Europe, and England, where he'd aided the student in the acquisition and binding of a circle of five servants of great power. Tonight's service would be the last one that he would provide, and it would bring him a step closer to the fulfillment of his greatest desire.

Jean Phillipe's craving for the Key of Ahknaton threatened to break his deep concentration. The wondrous artifact that granted full access to the Divine Engine was often in his thoughts. It was why he sought immortality, a gift the student bore within his blood. With immortality, he would have the time to find the Key of Ahknaton, and with the Key in hand, he could remake the world in his own image.

Jean Philippe had explained the ceremony to his student. The protections were necessary to defend themselves from the raw power of the Divine Engine. It was only with strict adherence to the rules that the precautions would work. The slightest misstep would bring utter catastrophe. The student had insisted that despite the risks, they should proceed, and finally, the time had come to complete the greatest sorcery that Jean Philippe had ever attempted. From bitter experience, he understood the boundaries of what he could ask of the Divine Engine. He'd brushed against those limits once before and had spent many months cowering in madness before a semblance of sanity had returned.

Jean Phillipe watched his student intently. He speculated on the power the student had asked for. He wondered what might happen if the powers of the Divine Engine were set against each other. Would an irresistible force meet an immovable object? He admitted to himself that he no longer had the courage to attempt such a thing. He thought it best to keep his concerns to himself lest the student leave without making payment.

The student was ready – residing in a place of perfect stillness. Jean Philippe tightened his concentration to a single point. The air shimmered within the confines of the circle, like summer heat rising off sunbaked stones. An awesome presence filled the room. The candles dimmed, the shadows thickened, and a glimmering rainbow flickered in the center of the magic circle. The rainbow solidified, resolving into a swirling mass of multi-colored lights the size of a melon hovering two feet off the floor.

He uttered a single phrase, "Grant the power of foresight."

Gleaming dust motes halted in their flight before Jean Philippe's eyes and time itself seemed to pause, then the Divine Engine disappeared.

Intense disappointment cut him like a knife. The promise of limitless power remained tantalizingly out of reach. Without the Key of Ahknaton, all he could practice were petite sorceries, and he could never satisfy his lust to consummate a union with the Divine Engine and become one with the gods.

He glanced at his student. A terrible wonder lit the vampire king's face, his eyes focusing on empty space a yard in front of him.

"Mr. Crane, what do you see?"

"The many future paths before me."

"That is a potent gift."

"Agreed."

"I have delivered what I promised, five binding curses and an unlimited sorcerous power for you."

"You shall have your reward."

The student's mouth trembled. He smiled hungrily, fangs gleaming wetly in the candle light. He lunged forward, sinking his razor-sharp teeth into Jean Philippe's throat.

With his blood rushing out of his body, Jean Philippe's gaze lit upon the lone spectator to the ceremony. A young woman, her body warm and luxurious, struggling frantically against her bindings, her eyes wide above the cloth gag filling her mouth. Her companion lay dead on the floor, his blood used to draw the magic circle and fill the copper bowls. She would be his first true meal, the fruit of the earth, destined to satisfy his immortal needs.

A succulent fruit, the first of many he would savor on his island home.

Chapter One

Progress Report – The Day Guard Program Phase V

Report#: 134
Date: June 11th

Summary begins:

The development of the Day Guard serum has now entered its final stage. The success rate is now more than 50% (50.4%), with enhanced effects proving persistent beyond thirty days without degradation. We conclude that administration of the serum will produce permanent enhancements without side effects within 3 hours in one of every two healthy, adult subjects.

Current averaged measured results across the twelve successful test subjects are as follows,

- Strength increases by 304%
- Motor speed increases by 315%
- Agility increases by 294%
- Endurance increases by 515%
- Reflex speed increases by 324%
- Pain tolerance increases by 312%
- Healing rate increases by 524%
- Motor skill increases by 378%

These results represent a doubling in activation of the System Zero epigenetic factors when compared with the Phase IV subjects, yet still fall about 50% short of the theoretical maximums.

The symptoms of serum failure continue to manifest as berserk rage, followed by progeria, and catatonic depression with onset 24 to 48 hours after the administration of the serum with inevitably fatal results within two days of the onset of the symptoms.

All test subjects have been terminated using the TEF-4 neurotoxin. Final wrap up of this program has commenced and can be expected to be completed within two weeks. All technical details for the design and production of the Day Guard serum, the TEF-4 neurotoxin, and their associated delivery systems have been committed to secured data vaults on the Panopticon cloud.

The primary active ingredient of the Day Guard serum is derived from the *Ophiocordyceps diabolicus* fungus. A substantial quantity of the fungus has been harvested from the Amazonas region of Brazil – sufficient to compose five hundred doses of the Day Guard serum.

The fungus has been sent by secure courier to Shadowstone Research Facility #19, Fort Dix, New Jersey.

Summary ends:

– Quantum encrypted email from Shadowstone Research Facility #34, Brazil.

* * *

Boston, June 11th, 20:53

General Chloe Armitage ran her fingers through her damp hair.

She glanced into the police cruiser's rear-view mirror. The heavy bruising on the right side of her face had disappeared, her eyes were clear, and she glowed with health. Feasting on a young Boston police officer would do that for a vampire. She drew her hand down her face and nodded – pleased with her perfection.

Her wounds from the pair of .50 caliber bullets, katana chest thrust and the nightfalcon helicopter crash occurring less than half an hour before had healed completely.

Exiting the car, her smartphone vibrated with the arrival of a text. Drawing the phone from her pocket, she read the message, 'Ramin Kain – quantum signature attached.'

Only one person could have sent that message: the Raven.

Chloe grinned broadly, filled with exhilaration. She put the phone away. With the quantum signature of Ramin Kain's phone, she could penetrate his information defenses. She was certain it would not be long before she would know everything there was to know about the Head of the Order of Thoth.

She determined to ensure that Shabbah al Ahmar's agent within Francis Mirovar's force team never discovered who she was. The Raven was too valuable a prize to lose and finding out the supposed second agent of the

Red Empire in North America was general Chloe Armitage of the Vampire Dominion would do exactly that.

Chloe took in her surroundings. She was standing in the first level parking garage of the Boston Risk Investigation Security Consultants building. There were two stairwells, one elevator, another lower-level parking garage, and eight cameras, two of which pointed straight at her.

The nearest stairwell echoed with the quick footsteps of men rapidly descending toward her. Pausing next to the police cruiser, Chloe sardonically saluted the nearest camera. The stairwell door burst open, three Shadowstone operatives dressed in suits and carrying FN P90 submachine guns fanned out into the parking garage.

"Halt!" shouted the lead operative.

The second operative demanded, "Put your hands up."

The third operative moved sideways. The barrel of his gun aligned perfectly with the middle of Chloe's chest. His gun's red dot sight sitting steady on the matte black of her battered and scarred chest plate.

Chloe turned toward the lead operative, arched an eyebrow quizzically, and inquired sardonically, "Which is it, halt or put my hands up?"

The men suddenly recognized her, a flash of confusion shadowing their faces like clouds passing over the sun. They quickly lowered their weapons.

The lead operative stepped forward; his face stiff with fear. "My apologies, Ma'am. We didn't recognize you wearing combat armor and with all the chaos tonight—"

Chloe frowned. "Don't justify your overreaction, I expect better from Shadowstone operatives."

"Yes, Ma'am. What are your orders, Ma'am?"

"Do you have a nightfalcon?"

"No, Ma'am. We have a light transport chopper."

"It will have to do," Chloe conceded. "Order the pilot to begin immediate pre-flight checks, I need to be back in New York as soon as possible."

"Yes, Ma'am. It should be ready for take-off in ten minutes."

"Let's make it five."

"Yes, Ma'am," he replied, tapping his earpiece and giving urgent commands to scramble the R.I.S.C helicopter.

"One other thing," Chloe noted, glancing back at the car.

"Yes, Ma'am?"

"Dismantle that police cruiser and dispose of the two bodies in the trunk."

"... Two bodies? ... Dismantle a police cruiser?"

Chloe pushed her shoulders back and glowered at the lead operative. "Are you going to make me repeat myself?"

"Ah, no, Ma'am," the lead operative averred, his Adam's apple bobbing as he swallowed nervously. "I will make sure it's done."

"Tonight – no delay."

"Yes, Ma'am."

Chloe dismissed the men with a nod. Turning she entered the stairwell. Once out of sight, she blurred upward before any of the operatives could follow her. In moments, she reached the top of the R.I.S.C building and stepped out onto the helipad. The helicopter rested in front of her, a sleek, black, civilian model, with R.I.S.C written in bold white letters on its side. The letters sat beneath a red lightning bolt that arced to the nose of the craft. The helicopter's pilot was sitting in the cockpit, rapidly flicking switches. The single turbine switched on, started to spool up and the rotors began slowing spinning. She bent low, jogging over to the open cabin door, climbed in and sat down directly behind the pilot.

She tapped him on the shoulder.

He jerked half out of his seat, twisted around and yelled, "HELL!"

Chloe tilted her head slightly, smiling at the pilot with quiet amusement. "New York – The R.I.S.C Tower."

The pilot slapped his chest a couple of times. His eyes wide, he managed to state, "I assume you're the VIP Carter told me to scramble for."

"You assume correctly."

The pilot hesitated for a second, clearly perplexed. He turned back to his controls, muttering under his breath, "How did she get up here so quickly."

Relaxing back in her seat, Chloe strapped herself in. She considered her options, composed a brief message on her smartphone, and sent it to Cornelius Crane.

* * *

The boardroom dominated the north side of the 101st floor of the R.I.S.C Enterprises Tower. It was here that Cornelius Crane, King of the Vampire Dominion, played the part of the mysterious and reclusive owner of the privately-owned R.I.S.C Enterprises Corporation. The public face, hidden amongst thousands of ordinary corporations, that masked the Vampire Dominion and Cornelius Crane's Citadel.

Cornelius stared out of the boardroom windows at the brilliantly lit skyscrapers of midtown Manhattan and the dark swathe of Central Park beyond them. The windows resembled regular commercial glass but were composed of transparent armor that could stop a direct hit by a 30mm anti-tank round. The windows were slightly darker than normal, hiding a broad-spectrum electromagnetic shield laminated within the armor. An information cloak proof against any known method of spying encapsulated the boardroom.

He blinked and sighed, pressing a button on a hand-held remote as he frowned at the vibrant city laid out before him. It had been decades since he'd witnessed such losses in the west. The Red Empire had killed four praetorians, and destroyed the Shadowstone facility in Jerusalem. An agent or agents unknown had killed two more praetorians in Brazil, and now the Order of Thoth had slaughtered six of his best in Boston.

Cornelius turned and studied the large monitor and multiple screens filling the far wall. He watched the wreckage of a suddenly hot war burn in silence. He'd muted the sound to help himself think. He glanced at the bottom right-hand screen, dominated by several digital timers. There was one in red, just ticking over eighteen minutes. An hour ago, it was registering over nine years of continuous, uninterrupted operation of the Panopticon.

Cornelius cursed out loud, "How the hell did they haze all the nearby cameras and the satellite over Boston. I've got a seventeen-minute black hole three miles wide centered on that damn warehouse, and during that time everything goes to shit!"

For the first time in decades, an unsettling sense of creeping chaos wormed its way into his mind. The sudden and severe loss left him staring incredulously at the screens. The initiative had clearly shifted to his opponents, and he vowed silently to get it back.

The door into the boardroom clicked open, and Cornelius inhaled the familiar scent of a subtle perfume.

"Sir?" A feminine voice asked.

Cornelius looked toward the voice. His executive secretary stood in the doorway; petite, blond, beautiful and superbly efficient.

"Ursula, organize the immediate recall of the Orange-2 spectrum team to Fort Dix. Violet-7 must remain on deployment at research facility number thirty-four in Brazil until the current phase of the Day Guard program is complete, then they are to return to Fort Dix as well."

"Yes, Sir. Should I liaise with General Armitage?"

"No. Pass my orders directly to the Shadowstone troop commanders on the ground."

"Yes, Sir. Is there anything else, Sir?"

"Has Ramin Kain arrived at our meeting point?"

"He has signaled that he expects to be there at 21:15."

Cornelius nodded. "Good, ten minutes from now. That will be all."

Ursula smiled briefly. "Yes, Sir."

Cornelius watched her slim form depart the boardroom, the door closing behind her. He turned back to face the muted screens on the wall opposite from where he stood.

Multiple real-time drone and satellite feeds of the Boston warehouse site dominated the main screen. All the important objects on the monitor had streams of Panopticon metadata associated with them. Flashing red star and stable white cross markers littered the warehouse and dock. The Order of Thoth had killed six vampire praetorians and over sixty Shadowstone operatives. The wreckage of four nightfalcons lay in piles around the site, two were still burning, the other two had almost cooled to the level of the background environment. A fifth helicopter lay under the surface of the Mystic River, its vampire pilot also dead. A Shadowstone RHIB burned a half mile along the Mystic River, destroyed by the Order of Thoth after using it to escape.

One screen showed a civilian R.I.S.C helicopter rushing toward his Citadel. Crushing the remote in his bare hand, Cornelius slowly shook his head and declared, "How did this happen? I'll have her head if she is responsible for this!"

A row of picture-in-picture views along the bottom of the main screen remained dedicated to events off site. Two nightfalcon helicopters were inbound from Cornelius' Citadel, each carrying eight fully armed vampire praetorians with an ETA at Boston of 21:50. Another nightfalcon from Fort Dix was circling to land at the Boston warehouse with half the Yellow-3 spectrum team. The rest of the Yellow-3 team raced from Fort Dix to Boston in Shadowstone OPSEC vans; they would arrive in another three hours, just after midnight.

Three vans sporting the livery of major news channels were racing along the I-91 highway from New York City to Boston. Shadowstone PSYOPS crews were due to arrive on site in less than an hour to shape the public news feeds. Their colleagues in the Shadowstone PSYOPS directorate were already hard at work in the offices of a Manhattan public relations firm, wholly owned by R.I.S.C Enterprises.

There was a view showing two Shadowstone operatives still alive on site, the metadata next to the blue markers read James Haley and Louise Wesson. The woman's vital signs indicated she was suffering from a concussion.

Cornelius shook his head again, disgusted at the waste of good, useful men. He didn't care about them individually; it was the fact that they would have made excellent candidates for his Day Guard program that hurt the most. The sixty men would have provided thirty loyal fighters he could have used in daylight operations against his enemies.

Cornelius smacked his hand down on the table. "What the fucking hell has she done? I explicitly told her not to waste my Shadowstone men against the Order."

Cornelius looked down at a printed email resting in an open buff-colored cardboard folder on the boardroom table. It described the final results of the Day Guard Phase V program. His own initiative, designed to produce an enhanced super-soldier, capable of engaging the Order of

Thoth and the Red Empire in daylight. They would provide the edge that he needed. His opponents would not be able to rest. Pursued by the Day Guard during the day and his praetorians at night. It was the one bright spot in an otherwise disastrous night.

His lips curled into a sneer as he silently vowed to wipe the Order of Thoth and the Red Empire off the face of the Earth.

Cornelius flipped the folder closed. Noticing the crushed shards of the remote that littered the boardroom table, he used the folder to sweep the fragments into a nearby waste bin.

He put the folder into a disposal chute on the wall, where with a slight whirr, the paper and plastic turned into confetti and dropped down to a basement incinerator. He strode over to a rack in the corner of the boardroom and selected a hat and a light coat. He spoke a sixteen-digit alphanumeric code. There was a brief hum, a seam appeared along the long axis of the boardroom table, and it separated into two perfect halves. They glided apart to reveal a hole a yard wide in the floor, its interior a blend of chrome and shadow.

Cornelius stepped forward, disappearing down the hole.

* * *

Cornelius Crane wore a light weight, dark-gray coat over his suit, and a matching fedora with a barely discernible white and gray feather in the band. He glided on his long legs up the stairs toward the East Balcony of Grand Central Terminal. As he came onto the upper level, the doorman of the Gilded Tea Club greeted him.

Unknown to everyone in the discrete and fashionable Gilded Tea Club, Cornelius owned the establishment through a set of front companies, and Shadowstone swept the site for surveillance systems on an hourly basis. It was a public place where he could hold a secure and anonymous conversation without revealing the location of his citadel to whomever he was talking with.

Cornelius nodded politely to the doorman; a sudden bead of perspiration appeared on the man's brow as Cornelius strode past him. Entering into the warmly lit interior of the cafe, the rich aromas of premium tea and coffee, aged oak, fine leather and the sharp, coppery scent of the blood of more than thirty humans surrounded him.

He moved amongst the people like a force of nature. A pathway leading to where he wanted to go opened up. People paused in their conversations, suddenly lost for words. Others stumbled aside or mumbled confused apologies. In moments, he reached a sheltered cubical in a back corner of the room farthest from the entrance.

Behind him, the room rushed back to normal, like a ship righting itself after a rogue wave.

Cornelius sat down opposite a man of above average height and solid build. The man could pass for early forties in age with a sprinkling of gray in his dark hair. He had the charismatic face of a successful politician and wore a dark-blue suit. They stared at each other for a couple of seconds as the background noise of the cafe returned to its usual modest volume.

Ramin Kain nodded in greeting, and said with a note of irony in his voice, "I heard on the news that a counter-terrorism exercise in Boston has devolved into catastrophe. Apparently, a helicopter had a major weapons system malfunction and shot down four other helicopters before plunging into the Mystic River with massive loss of life." He tilted his head slightly. "Or so I'm led to believe."

"Indeed," Cornelius noted, his mouth tightening into a grimace.

"The Boston Police Department are also missing two officers. Apparently, they went rogue, killing two of their colleagues and absconding with a cruiser." Leaning forward, Kain arched a quizzical eyebrow. "And you know what? They're still missing. So, what happened? Is the Red Empire now operating in North America or was it a masterful display of Shadowstone incompetence?"

Cornelius stared at the man impassively. He'd met men like Kain before; intelligent, vain, ambitious, overconfident and – in the end – dead. He always outlived them, and he fully expected to outlive Kain.

"The Order of Thoth as it turns out," Cornelius stated, watching carefully as Kain's grin evaporated from his face. "Combined action by the Wu family and the Mirovar force team."

"The Wu family? They opted out ..." Kain rubbed his top lip and then snapped his fingers. "Two decades ago! They must have been associated with the Slaynes." He spread his hands wide. "But this is a small price to pay for what I give you."

Cornelius kept his face impassive as anger and disgust flared in hidden depths.

The two men stared at each other; one with studied patience, the other with feverish ambition.

"Why did you call this meeting?" Cornelius asked.

Kain leaned forward, and demanded conspiratorially, "I need a new coven of vampires, I need to get results to impress the force leaders and keep them in line. I provided you with the Slaynes, you owe—"

"I owe you nothing," Cornelius snapped. "Our arrangement exists at my pleasure, should I recall my forces from the rest of the world and bring them here. I could easily extinguish the Order of Thoth once and for all."

Slapping the table with the palm of his hand, Kain leaned forward and asserted forcefully, "And you would have the Red Empire at your back. I gave you the Slaynes. I virtually gave you the Papyrus of Hakron the Scribe, all you had to do was send someone around to pick it up."

"… Yes, and now you have much less to offer me," Cornelius observed disdainfully.

For a long moment, Kain looked up at the ceiling before flicking his eyes back toward Cornelius. "The detente has served us well. You have a quiet front here in the west, and you keep your senior vampires alive. While I rule the Order of Thoth without challengers."

Cornelius leaned over the table, his hands apart on the dark wooden surface, his face a thin veneer of control over restless passions. "Served us well, has it?" he shook his head, pointing a long finger at Kain's face. "No — not at all. You will fix it, and you will fix it soon. Get your force leaders in line. I tell you now, Mirovar must die."

Kain blinked uncertainly, his mouth moved as if he was about to speak, but he remained silent.

Cornelius sat back and remarked matter-of-factly, "I will provide a new coven. Allow two months for the fruit to become ripe."

Kain nodded.

"One more thing. Two survived the battle on the dock. One was the Wu girl, who was the other? I must know who the other person was and you will find out for me."

"Yes, of course," Kain vowed.

Cornelius straightened out of his chair, stepping away from the table. "Excellent, I believe we're done here."

"Yes, we are."

Cornelius turned and walked briskly out of the cafe without looking back.

* * *

Cornelius blurred out of the hole in the floor, appearing in the middle of the R.I.S.C Enterprises boardroom. He spoke the code words again, and the two halves of the table glided back together to form a seamless whole. He returned his coat and hat to the rack in the corner of the room.

He turned to the windows, extended his senses to their vampiric maximums and silenced his mind to a still point of concentration. He became a tall, lean statue, preternaturally still while passions flowed through nearly a thousand years of memory. He began the process of activating the precognitive power sourced from the Metaframe sorcery of Jean Philippe Allemande.

Mekra; her touch had been pure electricity, her passions like storms as powerful as they were unpredictable. She'd found him in the Levant in 1096, Baron Cornelius de Grue, a noble of Brittany and a General in the first Crusade. She'd told him she wanted a military leader to stand at her side and quell the chaos of the vampire world. Her offer had fallen upon fertile ground. Cornelius had grown weary of the internecine struggles between various factions of the Order of Thoth and the Red Empire. The constant wars to gather together the three artifacts of the Metaframe to a single hand. He'd forsaken his oath to the Order of Thoth and Mekra had made him a vampire.

Memory continued to unfurl, rolling past the diamond-like focus of his mind. The chaos of centuries of war of all against all, his eventual rebellion and assassination of Mekra, and the destruction of the cult of her devotion. The discovery of the voodoo sorcerer Jean Philippe Allemande in Haiti. The realization that magic was very real, and based on a partial, incomplete access to the Metaframe. Training with Allemande and using the sorcerer to bind five generals to his service during the 1850s. Four exceptional men and one unique woman who were unable to harm him, and unable to defend themselves against him. With the generals in place, the Vampire Dominion had become the unquestioned power amongst the surviving vampires, and the time of chaos had ended.

Chloe Armitage flooded his mind. They shared a common heritage; both born into the Order of Thoth, both Ramp masters before their conversion into vampires, both heirs to rulership. Desire, admiration, and regret flooded his soul, warring amongst themselves without resolution. Of the five generals, she was the best, and the closest to what he'd sought in a protégé.

The power of prevision bloomed within him. The near future came into view, as the momentum of past events spread out into a multi-dimensional matrix of possible events aligned to his own life. Bright lines anchored in the certainty of the past, whipped through the nodes of the matrix, linking the most probable future paths. Other lines, fading from bright to dull, indicated the less probable through to the least likely events.

There were no nodes where Chloe could attack, or kill him. The curse of Jean Philippe Allemande continued to bind her and the other generals, making it impossible for them to harm him. It was an inescapable trap, born from the same source that gifted him his precognitive ability.

He noted a new line, barely illuminated, leading directly from the events on the Boston docks to spear through a new node of his own death. There was a small chance that within a year, his long life would end. A new threat had been born on the docks, closely associated with the Wu family and now waiting to grow to realization. Cornelius had foreseen such events before and had taken action to thwart them. He noted the possibility and anticipated he would again be victorious. He would watch the event gain form, he would identify who was shaping it, and he would kill them before the possibility of his death could become a certainty.

He searched through the matrix for pathways leading to the acquisition of the Interpretive Codex. A line of moderate strength led through General Haras Mosule. Chloe was now absent from all pathways that would bring the Codex into his possession. He emerged from the previsionary meditation and reflected upon what he'd learned.

Something has recently changed, her growing ambitions blind her, she is no longer looking for the Codex. It is slipping away from me. First, we must quell this petite rebellion and then refocus our efforts on recovery of the Codex. Chloe will be the key to both goals, I must restore her motivation to the tasks at hand, she is the most valuable piece on the chessboard. And now there is a new threat, Chloe has messaged me of her victory over the Order grand master Gang Wu, but what of his daughter and his apprentice? Either of them could be the origin point of the new threat line. I need to know more about what happened tonight.

Cornelius paged his secretary. A moment later the boardroom door opened and Ursula inquired, "Sir?"

"Any news?"

"Sir, General Armitage has just arrived on the external helipad in a R.I.S.C helicopter."

"Bring her here, I'm not meeting her in my private quarters tonight." Cornelius shook his head emphatically. "But first – bring me my sword."

"Yes, Sir," Ursula replied and left.

Cornelius continued to watch the details of the recovery and cleanup of the Boston warehouse site, the main screen illuminating his face with colored lights and shadows.

He mused out loud to himself in the empty boardroom, his voice filled with dreadful intent, "I've spent centuries mastering information and knowledge. I built my library, mastered more than a dozen languages, I commissioned the Panopticon and even acquired a secret Metaframe inspired pre-cognitive ability, and yet I couldn't see that it was a trap. Someone set a trap, and caught us in it – but a trap set by whom, Francis Mirovar, Arthur Slayne or Shabbah al Ahmar? Chloe had better have an exemplary excuse for tonight, or by God, I will bathe this room in her blood and take the Interpretive Codex from the dead hand of Shabbah al Ahmar myself."

* * *

Chloe stared at the smooth chrome of the doors as the elevator descended from the external helipad to the 101st floor. Crane had never asked her to attend an audience in the corporate boardroom. That was where Crane dealt with humans, not with his generals. He was deliberately insulting her. Chloe sighed once; her lips pressed into a thin line as she considered the possibility, she'd misjudged Crane's response.

She'd taken off her body armor in the R.I.S.C helicopter, stripping down to her form-fitting black jumpsuit. The nanotube suit was already dry, she stood comfortably in her bare feet waiting for the elevator to reach Crane's public executive suite. There was no point in trying to protect herself from her king; Allemande's curse ensured that she would not be able to defend herself should Crane choose to attack her. In her left hand, she carried her chest and back plates by their straps; the puncture marks and bullet holes clearly visible on them. The body armor damage matched similar blood-stained holes in her jumpsuit.

The body armor was her primary evidence to explain what had happened and to drive home the risks that Crane now faced.

Chloe considered her tactics. *A bold approach is best. The truth is my ally, the more he knows, the better to demonstrate my loyalty and competence in the face of a tactical defeat. There is but one key fact I must keep secret – the existence of Anton Slayne.*

The elevator pulled smoothly to a halt, the door swishing open. Chloe walked into reception, approaching the main desk. Sitting primly behind it was Crane's executive secretary Ursula Zielinkski.

Ursula smiled coldly, her blue eyes lighting up with anticipation. "General Armitage, you're expected. He is waiting for you in the boardroom."

Chloe ignored her, walking confidently into the boardroom. Closing the door behind her, she dropped her body armor onto the top of the boardroom table where it clattered against the fine wood and leather.

"Six praetorians you gave me – I needed twelve!" she declared forthrightly.

Crane blurred across the room toward her. Chloe reflexively stepped back, there was neither room nor time to avoid him pushing her hard up against the wall. The point of Crane's broadsword punched through the fabric of her jumpsuit, slicing through the skin over her sternum and grinding through the bone beneath. For the second time this night a sword blade rested inches from her heart.

Crane's left hand clamped down on her right shoulder, holding her against the wall. He held his sword flat and level as he leaned in, his face inches from her own.

A cold fury erupted deep within Chloe, she stared hard at Crane as he straight-armed her up the wall, her feet dangling half a foot off the floor.

Crane glared at her with tightly held rage, and demanded, "The truth Chloe."

Chloe blinked, for a second the world closed in upon her. The hand holding the sword in her chest was rock steady, terrifying in its stillness, matching the resolve writ large in Crane's eyes.

The urge to fight flowed strong and clear through her soul and Chloe's hands clenched into fists. She conceived the attack in a moment, she would take a deep cut as she pushed Crane's blade out of her chest with her left hand, while her right broke his hold upon her shoulder.

Chloe dropped into a supreme ramp and blurred.

Lightning crackled through the boardroom, playing along her skin, icy fire ripping along her nerves.

"Allemande's curse!" she gasped past gritted teeth, her limbs as limp as a rag dolls. The lightning ebbed; her mind raced, *I'm trapped, but the truth is still my ally.*

Crane barked a single harsh laugh. "Tell me the truth!"

Chloe looked steadily into Crane's eyes, and explained around gasps for air. "The ground proved more treacherous than anticipated. The Order used the river to advantage and approached with stealth. Our forces failed to discover them."

Crane shoved her hard against the wall, the plaster cracking behind her. "I warned you about giving your opponent the choice of ground for the battle. It was clearly a trap, and you walked into it like a novice."

"Mirovar would never have appeared without the ground, he is not stupid," Chloe observed; managing to hold onto her composure. "I had to give them the ground to draw them out, and it worked – they showed up in force."

"Well, we lost. So, someone was stupid," Crane said, glaring at her. "I wonder if it was me for trusting the promise you made in Jerusalem."

Chloe shook her head. "We needed the extra praetorians. If we had twelve, we would have won."

"I've always respected your integrity," Crane said, his voice silky soft, "You've always kept your word."

A wet patch spread out from the cut in her chest as blood oozed past the blade. She braced herself, she'd seen Crane in this sort of mood before where he would praise quietly before—.

Crane twisted the sword blade a quarter turn, speaking with tightly controlled fury. "But now you falter, now you fail."

The metal grinding against raw bone sent jagged bolts of pain through her body.

Chloe gasped out past gritted teeth, "I asked … for twelve … you insisted … I go with six."

"Six would have been enough if you had not lost our Shadowstone forces before the battle started," Crane snapped.

Chloe's eyes widened. "You advised me to keep Shadowstone out of it – and now you claim that they were essential for victory?"

Dragging his sword clear, Crane threw her down to the floor.

Catching herself before she fell flat, Chloe crouched and looked up at him, her face an unreadable mask.

Crane frowned, shaking his finger at her. "Do not dare put this on me. We have worked together for more than a century – I know your tactics – you should have won."

Chloe stood up, the wound in her chest began to close. Nodding contritely, she said, "Normally I would have. This time was different."

"I wonder if you held back. I wonder if your heart is still in this fight. Are you still willing to take the battle to our enemies or," Crane said, then thrust his long index finger at her, "are you playing your own game?"

Chloe tilted her head and declared incredulously, "I am stunned that you would ask that of me."

"Something happened in the last twelve hours that cost us victory tonight. You are the most powerful piece on the chessboard. What happened? Why did you fail?"

Chloe shook her head.

Crane stared at her. He remained silent, forcing her to continue.

"We underestimated Gang Wu, he was a genius with the sword," Chloe attested, pushing a finger through the sword cut on her jumpsuit. "He nearly killed me; his blade was against my heart." She thumped her chest. "I only just managed to get my hand down in time to prevent him dragging his sword out and cutting it in two."

Crane's face twisted into an incredulous leer, he stepped close, pushing his fingers through the hole in Chloe's black jumpsuit.

"He would have been fully ramped," Crane observed decisively, his eyes darkening with suspicion. "You're very fast, but that is extraordinary, even for one of us."

"I was lucky, I started moving as he thrust."

Crane sniffed skeptically, stepping over to the boardroom table, he fingered the bullet holes in Chloe's chest plate. ".50 cal if I'm not mistaken."

"Depleted uranium, hurt like hell and pushed me out the side of the helicopter."

"You didn't see them firing at you?"

"Not this time."

"I don't see how someone, as experienced as you are, could miss a machine gun firing at them."

"I'd just been stabbed!"

Crane pursed his lips, dropping the chest plate on the table. Turning away from Chloe, he looked out the windows at the metropolis shining in the night.

"Then what happened?" he asked irritably.

"Machine gun fire struck the engines of the helicopter, and it followed me into the Mystic River. It crashed on top of me, knocking me unconscious and pinning me in the muck on the bottom."

"… Clearly, you got out."

"The nose cracked open on impact with the river bottom. Luckily, I was off to the side and not directly underneath it. I was able to wriggle my leg free and get back up to the surface before I drowned or bled to death."

Crane turned back from the window. He stared hard at the wrecked body armor, frowned, and studied it closely.

He is listening — success.

* * *

Cornelius stroked his chin thoughtfully.

Chloe had almost died. If his best warrior was almost overwhelmed, he must have underestimated the threat. Obviously, Kain did not have enough control over the force teams and especially the Mirovar team. Was the Order resurgent? The shift in probable outcomes could easily have resulted from actions by the Order. Was it the doing of Mirovar, Gang Wu, or the new fellow from Boston? He decided he'd relied too much on the secret detente with Kain.

"We have become complacent but not anymore," Cornelius declared. Reaching out, he flicked a switch on a console in the middle of the table. The room filled with the open communications from the praetorians at the Boston warehouse site.

Cornelius and Chloe looked up at the main screen. He manipulated the console and one of the satellite streams on the screen expanded to fill it. It showed a floating crane positioned about sixty yards away from the dock. Thick black cables ran down from the crane into the Mystic River, they snapped tight, the barge tilting under the load.

A tall praetorian stood on the dock, blond hair escaping from underneath his tactical command helmet. Looking up at the Vampire Dominion drone hovering two miles above the site, he tapped his comm link and inquired, "Sir, are you watching this?"

"Yes, Centurion, give me your report."

"We're in the process of recovering General Armitage's nightfalcon and her equipment."

"Can you confirm casualties?"

"Yes, Sir. I can confirm Spengler, Hendricks, Smithson, Calley, Senna, and Hato are dead. We have also recovered the pilot's body from General Armitage's nightfalcon."

"Were the bodies sanitized?"

"Yes, Sir. The Shadowstone lead operative has used grenades to keep our secret."

Chloe said quickly, "James Haley cleaned up the evidence."

Cornelius' eyes flicked toward Chloe, and he whispered, "So he knows."

She nodded once.

"And the status of the site, what of the humans?" Cornelius asked.

"Sir, we have secured the site and bagged the bodies. Shadowstone PSYOPS are providing media coverage."

"Good. Ensure full handover to Shadowstone by oh four hundred and return to the Citadel."

"Yes, Sir," the Centurion replied. The audio dropping back to mute as he turned away and began giving orders to his troops.

Cornelius frowned, turning back to Chloe he directed, "It is clear that Haley knows our secret, and even though he has done the right thing, he and the Wesson woman must be dealt with."

"Yes, Sir. I've watched Haley closely over the last eight years, and I would recommend him for advancement into our ranks. He has highly intuitive combat skills and would make a fine vampire warrior."

"Haley's conversion is approved but what of Wesson?"

Chloe's eyes flicked back to the main screen, and she suggested, "From the data, looks like she's got a concussion, I will confirm what she remembers. If she doesn't know our secret, she will assist us with rebuilding Shadowstone. She is a highly capable operative and excels at forming teams. I will need time to assess how best to induct Haley, and I will verify Wesson at the earliest opportunity."

"Be careful how long you take with Haley."

"We will need to allow time to provide an effective cover story and to groom a replacement for him. I would recommend holding off for now – especially given the current state of the Shadowstone organization, Haley is critical to rebuilding it."

Cornelius frowned. "You will be held accountable for his actions."

"I can guarantee his discretion."

"See that you do."

"Yes, Sir."

Confident of his safety and the effectiveness of Allemande's curse, Cornelius turned away from Chloe. Stepping toward the broad windows, he surveyed the city before him. The boardroom lay reflected in the transparent armor; to his right Chloe moved up, and stood a couple of yards back from his shoulder.

Cornelius studied the city-lit nightscape and said confidently, "I believe that the Red Empire has commenced operations in North America. The attack in Jerusalem and this event in Boston have occurred too close together not to be part of a coordinated plan."

"I agree," Chloe conceded. "It would not surprise me to discover that Shabbah al Ahmar has a secret agent in Francis Mirovar's force team – it would allow for a coordinated action just like this."

Cornelius stared at Chloe's reflection in the boardroom windows incredulously. "You suggest that the Red Ghost has co-opted Mirovar."

"Not with Mirovar's knowledge, just someone on the inside who he trusts. Someone who is able to provide information at the right time and make Mirovar a cat's paw for the Red Empire."

Cornelius stared out the window, his voice thoughtful as he said, "Well as unlikely as that may seem, if you live long enough, you will see all manner of improbable things come to pass."

"Yes, Cornelius – our enemies surround us on all sides."

"The Order have lost respect for our power and we must teach them a sharp lesson. You have carte blanche for operations against the Mirovar force team in North America. Fulfill the promise that you made in Jerusalem and bring their heads to me. First, we must quell this pathetic rebellion and then refocus our efforts on recovery of the Interpretive Codex. Never forget, securing access to the Metaframe remains our primary goal."

"Yes, Sir, understood."

"Set Haley, and Wesson – if we can trust her – to rebuilding Shadowstone, and do it quickly. I want Shadowstone back to full strength within three months. Focus on recruiting special forces, we need warriors more than we need intelligence operatives. The state of play between the Ramp Masters and the Vampire Dominion is evolving rapidly."

"Cornelius?"

Cornelius stared at her reflection in the window. "You know what you need to know."

"Yes, Cornelius, and what of the praetorians?"

Cornelius smiled grimly. "I will personally select and recruit them. I will call on you when the time is right. I will need more than one vampire to help me convert as many as I need."

"Yes, Cornelius." Chloe smiled slightly. "Of course, I will render every possible assistance."

Cornelius turned to her and said without hesitation, "I am sure that you will."

Or else you will discover that my patience with you has worn out.

* * *

Carte blanche, Perfect. Chloe thought triumphantly.

Crane believed the might of the Red Empire was on the move. Chloe determined to leverage that belief in full. She mastered the impulse to smile broadly, keeping her face calm and her expression alert. Her body completed healing itself from the trauma of Crane's recent attack and the ripping forces of Allemande's curse. She waited patiently for the meeting to end.

Crane stroked his chin contemplatively, tapping his index finger against his lips. He pointed his finger at Chloe and declared, "There is one more thing."

"Yes, Cornelius?"

"There were three Order of Thoth operatives in Boston; Gang Wu, his daughter Li and someone else. I've reason to believe the Wu family were closely associated with the Slaynes. I need to know who that other person was. Whoever he is, he survived a battle with six praetorians and yourself, and he has appeared from nowhere. It's imperative we find out precisely who he is and determine the risk he presents to our operations."

Chloe's heart froze. Crane was so close to the truth. The smallest misstep and her plan would come undone.

"Cornelius, the Panopticon identified him as Anton Smith, he is young, he must have been trained in secret by Gang Wu."

"I want a comprehensive report on my desk by tomorrow night."

"Yes, Sir. I will start immediately."

"Good work, you are dismissed."

Chloe nodded, bowed respectfully and departed the boardroom.

James Haley had best be awake, she thought furiously. *He has work to do. And what of Ramin Kain, if he is the traitor in the Order, he could reveal the truth to Crane. I can't let that happen.*

Chloe entered the elevator, ascending to the external helipad on top of Crane's Citadel. The pilot and the R.I.S.C helicopter were still there.

"Move it! Now!" Chloe shouted, running over to the helicopter cabin. The pilot started the engine. In moments the sleek, black and red helicopter was aloft. She gave him directions to her Manhattan penthouse; they would be there in minutes.

She had to move quickly. There was too much evidence in the Panopticon. They would have to hide it immediately.

* * *

Chloe rushed into her penthouse suite. She sat down at her desk, opened her personal laptop, and logged into the Panopticon.

She opened her smartphone, dialed Louise Wesson's phone and set her phone down on her desk with the loudspeaker on. She expected James Haley would still have Wesson's phone. James was essential to her plan. She needed his knowledge of Shadowstone and his ability to act in daylight.

James will respond to trust with loyalty, she thought. *I must exploit that weakness.*

The phone rang three times before James answered it. "Ma'am?" James asked, a slight tremor tinging the edge of his voice.

"James, I have a critically important task that only you can do."

"… Yes, Ma'am. What is it?"

"We need to reset the history of Anton Smith away from his parents and his family home in Jamaica Plain. There can be no connection between the Anton Smith in the Panopticon records and the identities of William and Anna Smith. They must become childless, and Anton must have a new set of parents. We should also position him as close to the Noodle House as is practically possible."

"The identity of Anton Smith is already a fake."

"Indeed, it is, James. Well done. We'll have to take this another step forward. It will be a fake of a fake, the second level of misdirection."

"This will be messy," James warned. "There will be physical records, such as photos, that we will not be able to reach."

"That doesn't matter, we simply need to ensure that the Panopticon does not link Anton Smith to his real parents in any way, shape or form – is that clear?"

"Yes, Ma'am. When do you want it done?"

"Immediately. You must complete this work before dawn."

James paused for a long moment. "That's impossible."

"No, it's not – don't disappoint me – use the R.I.S.C building in Boston. It's only minutes away from where you are. You can access the Panopticon from there without interruption."

"I don't have the right privileges to do this. I'm going to have to dig through a multitude of systems."

Chloe tapped her keyboard. "You do now – I've elevated you to my level for the next eight hours, make the most of it."

"… Yes, Ma'am," James paused again, his voice steadying. "There is a way this could be done."

"Yes?"

"No parents at all, we can make him a foundling orphan, a ward of the state. I can easily access all the state records. All the public elements of his life will remain untouched: schools, sporting teams, online accounts, everything. We just insert him into the right records, it will do the job, a lot less complicated than putting him into another real family."

"I knew that I could rely on you James, now make it so."

"Yes, Ma'am will do."

"… While I have you – what of my sword – has it been recovered?"

"Yes, Ma'am. The praetorians have it. I asked them for it, but they would not release it to me," James answered, his voice betraying his disappointment.

"Don't worry about that. The praetorians will bring it to me, that task is complete. I need you to focus on the new mission."

"Yes, Ma'am," James confirmed, his voice steady for the first time in the call.

"Send me a text when you are done, and get a new phone, I can't be calling Louise Wesson all the time."

"Yes, Ma'am."

"By the way James, how is Ms. Wesson? I am a little surprised she is still alive."

"She is concussed; she has no memory of the battle or knowledge of vampires."

"James," Chloe said warmly. "I am sure you will manage the risk. You are on a new path now, embrace it, and all will be well."

"Yes, Ma'am … yes, Ma'am, I will."

"Send me a text when the work is done."

"Yes, Ma'am."

Chloe hung up the call and put the smartphone down.

The Panopticon system data streamed down her laptop monitor. Chloe accelerated her mind, her fingers flashing over the keyboard faster than a human eye could follow. The computer responded, the images and command line text becoming a blur. After thirty minutes of dedicated work, she'd erased all evidence that could personally link Anton Slayne (alias Smith) to herself. Especially the conversation recorded the morning before in the garden behind the Wu residence, where Gang and Li Wu revealed so much about the Slaynes. Now there was only the task of restructuring the false identity of Anton Smith, which James would complete before sunrise. She relaxed, leaning back in her chair and allowing her mind to float freely.

She surprised herself with an unladylike snort of laughter.

Anton Smith 2.0 is about to be born.

"Now to focus on dismembering the schemes of Ramin Kain," she whispered to the empty room.

* * *

It was a cloudless night, the sky was crystal clear, dominated by a full moon and a massive river of stars.

Anton stood in an open field, a short distance in front of him was a wooden fence, painted white like the ones used to corral horses. There was an awful insistent murmuring behind him, and a dreadful feeling crept through him. His breathing was suddenly shallow, his lungs tight; he forced himself to turn around.

A writhing mass of naked humanity lay before him; the crowd of people seethed and heaved, stretching away into the distance as far as the eye could see. Above the people, hovering mere yards away from Anton, was a creature beyond nightmare — his eyes widened, instinctively taking a step backward and lifting his arm up as if to ward off an attack.

Its body was leech-like, easily thirty yards long and about two yards across. Its pale, translucent skin glistened wetly in the moonlight. The creature's internal organs were dark shadows, visibly writhing beneath its skin. Its large, saucer-shaped eyes were blood red, with vertical irises like a cat. Its lipless mouth reflexively gaped open, revealing rows of needlepoint teeth. Its tail ended in a foot-long sting; scalpel sharp and slick with venom.

The creature glided over its host, its head bowing low over one particular specimen, a healthy young fellow who moved with more vigor than the rest. Slit-shaped nostrils flared, the monster's tail quivered, lashing forward, the sting plunged into the man's back. A pouch directly above the sting violently contracted, injecting venom, and inducing a sudden lethargy in the man.

In plain sight of Anton, the man slumped to the ground. His plight ignored by the crowd of humanity instinctively moving away from him.

The head of the creature swung lower, red eyes gleaming with wet hunger, it fixed its mouth onto the man's abdomen with an unbreakable grip. The man's eyes stared blankly, venom coursing through his veins, he was unable to grasp what was happening to him.

Anton froze with terror — panting — unable to move.

The parasite extended a proboscis from within its throat into the man's abdomen, flushing his body with digestive fluids. The corrosive liquids rendered the man's organs into a dark mush, rapidly drawn up into the hovering monster. Anton watched in horror as the monster consumed the man from the inside out. In a handful of seconds, his body collapsed into a dried husk, the crowd surged back, and he disappeared beneath the living, his loss unnoticed by those around him.

Anton rose high into the night sky as if lifted on the hand of a giant. The air rushed past him until the curve of the Earth stretched before him. Beneath him, the surface of the world lay crisscrossed by white fences, and within each corral, there was a mass of humanity attended by a hovering parasite.

To the east stood a single tower, rising high above all else. It gleamed in the moonlight, on top of it floated the largest of the leeches, surveying the world below with a tireless intelligence.

Anton flew helplessly toward the tower with tremendous speed, and in a moment the tower filled his vision. It was taller than it first appeared and he rose upward until he reached the marble platform of the ruler of the world.

The monster turned to face him, its baleful gaze boring deeply into his soul.

Anton shivered as the creature's insatiable hunger flowed over him in an icy wave. Its mouth gaped open, its fangs gleaming in the bright moonlight, its harsh voice cracked through the air like thunder.

"You are mine!"

The monster lunged forward.

Anton awoke in a cold sweat, his throat dry, and his heart pounding.

A hand with fathomless strength grabbed his shoulder, and a deep voice asked, "Hey buddy – are you okay? You were screaming like a girl."

Anton's eyes focused, and he recognized the burly form of the man named Peter. He sat opposite Anton in the van as it drove smoothly through the night. He glanced around the dim interior of the vehicle. The rest of the members of the Mirovar force team sat in their seats looking at him with quizzical expressions on their faces, only Li and Peter evidenced any concern.

"We're farmed like cattle," Anton muttered.

Peter snorted, slapping Anton on the shoulder. "You've woken up – good."

Anton gave him a dark look.

"We're almost home," Peter enthused. "You'll feel a lot better once you get something to eat."

A wave of nausea gripped Anton's stomach.

Everything is wrong, he thought. He swallowed hard against a sudden reflex to vomit.

* * *

The wheels of the van crunched over a gravel yard before pulling to a stop.

An athletic young man with dirty-blond hair and a close-cropped beard slid the side door open and leaped out of the vehicle. In moments, most of the team followed him, leaving Anton and Li in the cabin.

Seconds later, the rear doors of the van opened, and the bearded young man directed, "Bring his body out now."

Under the interior lights of the van, Anton looked down at Gang's body, now wrapped in a black, plastic tarp. Li maneuvered over to the other side of her father's corpse, and he nodded when she caught his eye. Together they gently lifted Gang's body and carried him out of the back of the van.

Once clear of the van, Anton adjusted his hold, lifting Gang's body by himself. Li let go, ducking back into the van to retrieve their dragon swords.

The cool night air struck Anton like a jolt of caffeine. He took a deep breath and a small surge of energy sparked along his limbs. There was not much left to draw on, the last thirty-six hours had taken their toll. Someone switched off the van's engines and killed the lights. An ocean of brilliant stars lit the sky. He paused, drunk on their beauty in stark contrast to the mute sadness of carrying the lifeless body of Gang Wu.

In the distance was a very faint glow, a small rural town a handful of miles away. The yard was big, easily a hundred yards across, the boundaries dominated by a pair of large wooden barns that stood opposite each other, and an even larger haystack. At the head of the yard, a large two-story house loomed, several ground floor windows lit by interior lights.

Peter and Francis flicked on flashlights, and Li returned with their swords.

Francis waved his flashlight toward the far barn and commanded, "Peter, take them into the main barn and set Gang's body on a table. We will bury him tomorrow afternoon."

"Sure, Boss. Anton and Li, follow me," Peter called back over his shoulder, as he strode toward the barn.

They followed him. In a minute, they were inside the barn, and Peter was clearing a space on a large wooden table with easy familiarity.

"You've done this before?" Anton asked.

"There are occasional casualties, we always have a place to put people before burial."

"Right."

Anton placed Gang's body onto the table. Adjusting the tarp to ensure there were no gaps leading into the body. Li put her hand on the tarp and bowed her head. Anton did the same, feeling flat, drained, and numb. The adrenaline from the battle at the Boston warehouse had completely worn off, leaving him mentally and physically exhausted.

Peter stood back from the table, waiting patiently. When they looked up, he said, "Time for our debrief. Hopefully, the Jorgenson's have catered for our arrival."

"The Jorgensons?" Anton asked.

"This is a working farm, John and Mary Jorgenson are order helpers who live here. The farm makes a small profit, pays taxes and provides a perfect cover for what we really do here."

"Order helpers, like the two guys that were with the van back in Boston?"

"Yes. Not everyone in the Order is at the tip of the spear."

Anton nodded.

"Follow me," Peter directed. He led them from the barn. Once back out in the night air, he shut the barn door behind them and strode toward the house.

Anton and Li fell in beside him, and Anton asked, "No locks?"

Peter smiled. "Not needed. We have some sensors. He'll be safe tonight."

"Oh," Anton grunted.

They approached the house. It rose out of the darkness, a large, two-story affair with a pair of wide wings left and right. Warm light leaked through curtained windows, spilling in soft pools in front of the house. The building was a classic and well-maintained rendition of New England architecture dating from a previous century.

Peter led them inside. Voices murmured mere yards away; in moments, they joined the rest of the Mirovar force team in a large room. An oval table, surrounded by a dozen, mostly empty chairs, dominated the chamber. A pair of trays laden with sandwiches, bottles of water and glasses sat in the middle of the table.

The room held a lot of empty space and four thick wooden columns supported the ceiling. Peter leaned toward Anton and whispered, "Ex-dojo. We replaced it with the barn. You'll see where we train tomorrow."

Anton nodded.

Peter smiled, sitting down opposite the trays of food and declared gustily, "Perfect."

Anton and Li followed, sitting down next to him.

Francis stood in front of a large whiteboard, jotting down notes with a blue marker. There was a list of abbreviated bullet points on the board: penetrate police lines, capture RHIB, attack Shadowstone on the dock, kill nightfalcons. Juliette sat nearest to him, a laptop open in front of her, her fingers occasionally flashing over the keyboard as she took notes.

The serious-faced young man with roughly cut, dirty-blond hair from the van reported, "The stingers just dropped dead like hitting a wall about thirty yards back from the black helicopter."

"Electronic warfare; must have been her personal nightfalcon," Juliette Mirovar noted.

Peter snorted. "Definitely not standard issue tech."

Francis frowned at him, and Peter adjusted his position in his chair as if he could not find a way to sit comfortably.

A young woman with long coppery hair tied back into a ponytail and warm blue eyes, sitting next to the first speaker reported, "We fired as we landed on the dock and managed to hit one of the praetorians." She glanced at Li and continued speaking matter-of-factly, "The one that Li was fighting froze, and she took his head off."

A smile flitted across her face. "A praetorian came out of the river, catching us by surprise, and then one of the Shadowstone operatives fired a grenade and emptied his clip, but everyone evaded, and no one got hurt."

"Ahh…" Peter uttered, scratching the side of his head. "I beg to differ; I caught a piece of shrapnel."

Juliette looked up from her laptop and inquired with a frown, "You didn't mention this before."

"Well, I thought it would be okay – it's really just a scratch."

"I'll be the judge of that," Juliette declared, reaching for the medical kit bag at her feet.

All business, Juliette stood up and walked briskly around to where Peter continued to squirm uncomfortably in his chair.

"Where were you hit?"

"… In my butt."

Juliette blinked, raising her eyebrows she asked, "Which side?"

Francis sighed. "Okay everyone – take five minutes."

While Peter submitted to the attentions of Juliette, the rest of the team started on the sandwiches and water. Anton realized how hungry he was, helping himself, he bit into a ham, cheese and tomato sandwich with gusto. Anton thought to himself, *I need some names here, everyone already knows Li, and I'm at a loss.* Finishing the sandwich, he determined to introduce himself.

"Hi guys," he stated. They all stopped talking amongst themselves and looked at him. "I'm Anton Slayne."

Silence dropped over the room, and everyone stared at him.

Okay – what? Have I suddenly grown a second head?

* * *

Jay Creeley dropped his half-eaten sandwich back onto his plate. Putting his hands on the edge of the table, he pushed his chair back hard and stood up. He smacked the table with an open hand, and it shook fit to break.

"Jay!?" the copper-haired young woman next to him half-shouted in sudden alarm.

"If I'd known we were picking up a Slayne tonight," Jay ground the words out with barely restrained fury. "I wouldn't have bothered."

"Steady on Jay, he's not committed a crime," Juliette asserted as she closed her medical kit bag.

"Not yet. But why should we give him a chance?" Jay asked incredulously.

"He's fought bravely against vampires, he is one of us," Li declared.

"He's not a member of the Order," Jay spat the words angrily, "and neither are you."

"Not yet, but we both will be," Li promised, fire igniting behind her eyes.

"I've got nowhere else to go. I know too much. What do you expect from me?" Anton asked, his face filled with shock and dismay.

"I'm sure a second grave can be dug tomorrow," Jay declared with a sneer.

"Enough!" Francis roared – his voice cutting through the room like a knife. "Jay Creeley, I have invited Anton to join us and prove his worth to the Order, and that is the end of it."

Francis looked directly at Anton. "I realized who you were as soon as I met you, you're the spitting image of your grandfather when he was younger."

Jay stared at Anton, his face flushed, his mouth a grim slit.

Francis looked at Li. "I was a little mystified as to why your father didn't mention Anton's family name in his communiques."

Li shrugged her shoulders.

Francis turned to Jay and said, "Now I know why. Jay, I understand your feelings, but you have to let this go. Anton is not his grandfather."

Jay's eyes flicked back and forth between Anton and Francis, and Francis stared back – a hard uncompromising light behind his eyes.

Jay lowered his gaze. "… Yes, Sir," he conceded flatly. His face rigid, his mind burning with righteous anger. He would rather die than see a Slayne confirmed in the Order.

* * *

Maybe I should just leave.

A sudden nausea gripped Anton's guts; his emotions churning chaotically.

Francis called the meeting back to order. Li sat down on Anton's right and Peter on his left.

Francis addressed the young woman with coppery hair sitting next to Jay, "Yvette, please continue your report."

"Well, there were two vampires left on the dock – both wounded at that point. I saw Jay clean up the one that you had slashed as you ran past him, then Juliette and I killed the blond one that came out of the river. They were all dead, except for a Shadowstone operative who disappeared back into the warehouse."

Anton wondered what happened to the suit leading the Shadowstone forces. He hoped he'd stepped on a mine as he escaped back through the warehouse. But there had been no explosions.

He probably got away. Anton thought bitterly.

"Thanks, Yvette," Francis said. He turned his attention to another young woman with lustrous dark wavy hair, olive complexion, and large brown eyes. "Chiara, what have you got to report."

Chiara reported, "I was first on the RHIB. I manned the MGL and later the .50 cal. I was the one who shot Armitage. I watched her helicopter drop into the river. I'm sure that it landed on top of her."

Francis nodded. "Very good, Chiara."

"Did she die?" Anton asked hopefully.

"Without a body – we can't be sure she's dead," Francis observed.

Anton murmured in pain, and everyone in the room looked over at him.

"Anton, you have something to add?" Francis asked.

"No … nothing," Anton noted. His heart sank, certain that against all hope – Chloe Armitage was still alive.

Jay snorted disdainfully.

Francis looked around the group, and addressed the team, "Thank you for your work tonight. We lost a great warrior in Gang Wu, but we have won a victory against the Vampire Dominion. Get some rest, we start a new training cycle tomorrow at 08:00. I expect to see all of you in the training barn fit and ready. Is that clear?"

"Yes, Sir," the team members chorused. Anton and Li assenting a moment later.

"Peter and Chiara. Anton and Li can share your rooms. That is all – good night."

The team dispersed around the house. Li smiled briefly at Anton before she got up to leave with Chiara.

Peter tapped Anton on the shoulder and directed, "Hey, Anton, follow me."

Anton followed Peter down a hallway and up a flight of stairs. At the back of another hallway was their shared room. Inside the room were a pair of wardrobes and double beds.

"Our bachelor pad, not much to it. The bathroom is down the hall on the right, just before the stairs and your bed is that one over there," Peter instructed pointing to a neatly made bed with a simple, gray cover. He pointed at the wardrobe nearest to Anton's bed. "You can put your stuff in there."

"Li and I have nothing, just our swords and the clothes we are wearing." He thought of Gang lying in a pool of blood on the dock and sighed quietly. "We lost everything in the fight."

"We have spare clothes here, I'm pretty sure we will find some that will … kinda fit you. Li and Chiara are very similar in build; Chiara will have some clothes to share. As for equipment, we can always get more, that's not a problem."

"Thanks," Anton said, slumping down on the bed. His shoulders sank forward, and he asked, "Do I belong here?"

Peter cocked his head, sitting down on his own bed opposite Anton. "That depends on you."

"Are you sure of that?"

"I'm certain."

Anton looked down, brushing his right hand through his thick dark hair and rubbing the back of his neck.

"Trust me – things will improve," Peter said.

"I can't help who my grandfather is."

"Precisely – which is why Jay will come around. He's not stupid. Besides which, Francis more or less endorsed you. He would not have invited you to join us if he didn't believe that you could make it."

"Why would he endorse me? He doesn't know me. Why would he care?"

"Francis has never said a bad word about your grandfather, mind you, he has never said a good word about him either, but Arthur Slayne was his force leader and his weapons instructor. There must be some sort of bond between them. Given that you look just like your grandfather it's no surprise that he recognized you. Now I've never met Arthur Slayne or even seen a photograph, so who you are was news to me. But I don't care about your past. I'll make my own judgments based on what you do, and you fought vampires tonight which is good enough for me."

"Thanks, but you know what? I don't think I killed any vampires tonight. I think at most, I chopped half a foot off."

"Better than me, I didn't hit anything." Peter shrugged his broad shoulders and grinned broadly. "I just got hit in my butt."

Anton half grinned.

The room fell into silence. Peter looked thoughtful for a moment, then said, "It kinda begs the question you know, who else is going to recognize you? Anyone who knows your grandfather will see the similarity and are likely to draw the obvious conclusion that you're related."

"Not much I can do about it."

"Except be prepared for more reactions like Jay's."

Anton nodded. "Sure."

"Look, you're probably feeling a bit lost with everything that has happened, so I'll fill you in with a bit of history about us all. The Red Empire killed my parents when I was ten years old. Francis and Juliette took me in and raised me as a member of their family. I still remember my parents well, and of course, I still love my parents and miss them, but the Mirovars are like a second set of parents to me, they're family."

"What of the others?"

"Well, there's Jay Creeley, his father has been dead for a long time, his mother was killed at the same time as George Madison – apparently by your grandfather."

"So that's why he's so pissed off at me," Anton said quietly.

"Yep, then there is Yvette Mirovar."

"Their daughter?"

"Adopted. Unknown assailants killed her parents when she was eleven. She has been with us ever since; she is a year younger than I am."

"How old are you?"

"Twenty, and you?"

"Eighteen."

"We're a young crew. Jay is the eldest at twenty-four."

"So, he would have been about five when his mother died – and his dad was already dead. It's harsh, no wonder he's angry, I get it."

"Everyone has lost someone they love."

"What about the last one, Chiara?"

"Ahh... the lovely Chiara Romano. Italian-American heritage, a runaway from an abusive family. She started her training late. She would have been about nine when she arrived, which is pushing it to start Ramp training. But she has progressed really well, a quick study, a strong talent. You wouldn't know she only started at nine. She is very good, especially with edged weapons, almost as good as Jay."

"How good is Jay Creeley?"

"Every force team has a premier warrior, someone who is the best, baddest, most dangerous fighter – in our team – that is Jay Creeley."

"He's better than Francis?"

"Just a touch better, he will be a force leader one day, and a great one at that. The Order is grooming him for the role."

"Great. I have really dangerous people wanting me dead."

Peter shrugged. "Look, Jay's a good man. Give him time, he'll come around."

Anton muttered dejectedly, "What if he is right? What if my grandfather was a murderer and a traitor? I don't know what happened back then."

Peter paused contemplatively for a moment. "Why don't we set out to find the truth."

"Can we?"

"I'm sure of it. I will help you find out what really happened on the night George Madison died."

Peter put his hand out, and Anton shook it. Peter's handshake was powerful, there was clearly a reserve of strength within Peter beyond anything he'd met before. He assessed his roommate with fresh eyes; Peter was perhaps an inch taller, about six feet two with a shock of red hair adding another inch of height. Built like the proverbial brick wall. He was thick of calf and thigh, with a low center of gravity through the hips, broad shouldered, deep chested, with long muscular arms that ended in big powerful hands. However, there was no hint of being musclebound or overdone in the easy, confident way he carried himself.

Peter chuckled. "So, you noticed."

"Just how strong are you?"

"Sometimes you will find someone in the Order who has a capability beyond what is normal for a Ramp master, some are faster, some are stronger. I'm stronger – a lot stronger."

"You look like you could go hand to hand with a vampire."

"Yes," Peter smirked. "But it's not recommended."

"Is there anyone else like you?"

"Just one, Justin Blake. He's the force leader covering the South West of the US. He's a true badass. You will meet him when we get to the Order conclave for your confirmation."

"Cool."

"Look, it's been a long night. Time to get some sleep, we have a big day tomorrow."

"Right, thanks for filling me in."

"No problem."

Anton and Peter made their preparations for going to sleep. Anton managed a quick, hot shower in the bathroom down the hall and in minutes was lying in his bed in a darkened room. He sighed, no longer tired. He tossed and turned for close to an hour, his head buzzing with thoughts before he finally began to drift off. His mind ebbed away with a fading sense of indignation, unfairness, and loss.

Gang is dead, and she's alive.

These thoughts continued to disturb him as he fell into a restless sleep.

* * *

James looked at the clock, it read 06:30. He'd been awake for over a day, and there was still work to do. Yawning fit to dislocate his jaw, he rubbed his eyes and stared harder at the large computer screen a foot in front of his face.

He tapped fluently at the keyboard, hesitated, backspaced with a flurry of clicks and tried again.

"C'mon, almost done," he whispered.

James hit the enter key, and the computer responded with a stream of command line outputs across multiple windows on the screen. He glanced at the large coffee mug to his left, its interior stained brown from use. There was no decision to make, he stood up, walked to the nearby kitchenette and refilled it from a pyrex jug filled with lightly steaming filtered coffee. When he got back to his desk, the computer windows were still scrolling text output.

He blew gently on his hot coffee before taking a sip. He put the cup down and checked a written list of tasks on an A4 pad to the left of his keyboard; he'd ticked most of them off. Three tasks remained: verify the new Anton Smith ghost identity, purge the main physical backups at the Panopticon hub in Utah, and purge the offsite backups at Fort Dix.

James stared at the list, feeling decades older than his thirty-eight years.

The act of swinging his Glock 9mm up from behind his back and leveling it at his wounded men haunted him. He'd emptied the clip before they could properly react. Their expressions were vivid, the shock, the terror, the hate – some had lived just long enough to hate him. His years of training and specialized skills had meant quick deaths for them all, but he knew that he would never forget their faces.

Murderer, he accused himself.

The shocking self-accusation quickly succumbed to a wave of bitter acceptance. The light in his soul was fading, and in its place, a creeping darkness had begun to take hold.

He rubbed his scalp hard with both hands, his short dark hair was slick, grimy with old sweat. In front of his eyes, the screen continued to writhe with lines of output as windows opened, ran their programs and exited. The work recruited a tiny fraction of the quantum processors of the Panopticon. They processed their commands at the speed of light. Other, much older systems out in the world beyond Shadowstone responded far more slowly. The programs ran, traversing networks, subtly altering data, and transforming the original identity of Anton Smith in place.

The windows on the screen all came to a halt. James started a Panopticon verification program, and twenty seconds later it displayed a dashboard covered in green ticked checkboxes. The old Anton Smith had become a forgettable memory, in his place was a new doppelganger, a ward of the state of Massachusetts with no connection to Anna and William Smith.

He crossed off the third last task on the A4 pad, only the purging of the physical backups at the primary site in Utah and at Fort Dix remained to complete.

The image of shooting his men flooded his mind again, and he violently shook his head.

Slamming his fists into the desktop, he cursed, "Fuck it! The job is hard. I did what I had to do. How many more would die if there were no one to maintain stability? Millions? Billions? The world is a fucking nightmare."

The weight of recent events weighed heavily upon him, he momentarily shivered, and the darkness crept closer. He reached for options the way a drowning man would reach for anything to cling to. He could create a new ghost identity. Someone with money, not too much but enough. A ghost living a long way away – somewhere like New Zealand.

He lifted his coffee mug, taking a full mouthful, his eyes unfocused as his mind spun away.

I could escape and remain ... human.

He frowned, putting the mug back down onto the desktop. At the Boston warehouse, Chloe Armitage's sword had appeared in her hand faster than the eye could follow. Certain death had stared him in the face – she was a vampire, one of many, and sure enough, they would hunt him down and kill him.

He had courage to spare in any fight where his own skills could make a difference, but in a fight against the Vampire Dominion, there was no chance of victory. His eyes dropped, his shoulders sagged, and he sighed loudly as all vestiges of hope fled from his life.

Chloe Armitage's words echoed in his mind. *'You are on a new path now, embrace it, and all will be well.'*

He barked a single bitter laugh.

The light within him died. A spiritual candle snuffed out in a winter storm. The desire to serve his country that had inspired him to join the US Army, the CIA and finally Shadowstone, died silently. He'd wanted to make a difference. He'd wanted his life to matter. He'd dedicated his life to being the best at whatever he turned his hand to – now none of that seemed to matter – none of it at all.

The creeping darkness engulfed him.

James spent the next five minutes staring silently at the computer screen. Once the screen saver came on, he stood up. He looked around, spotted a long couch, walked over to it, laid down upon it, and was asleep in moments.

He screamed once in his sleep, his arms flailing wildly – but no one was there to hear it.

* * *

Chloe stood before the full-length windows of her Manhattan penthouse apartment.

The windows were composed of the same dark transparent armor of the nightfalcon canopies. The heavy shielding of the transparent armor, the only thing protecting her from swift death. She could see the ball of the sun, rising into the mid-morning sky. With a deep, longing to walk in open sunlight coiling quietly within her soul, she considered her options.

Chloe mentally ticked the items off in her mind. One, find out where the Mirovar force team's safe house was so she could keep an eye on Anton Slayne. Two, find out the details of the Crane-Kain detente, and three, do it quickly before events got away from her.

With the quantum signature of Ramin Kain's smartphone, she could make a single, full access call to his phone. As soon as he realized someone had compromised his phone, he would surely destroy it. There would be precious seconds where she could use the phone's own systems to record voice prints, take photos and video. A treasure trove of useful information she could give to James to seed Panopticon searches with.

Once found by the Panopticon, it would be a relatively simple matter to hunt him down and disrupt his plans, or even kill him. However, James would have to conduct all searches secretly. Chloe would not be able to justify how she knew who Kain was without revealing too much about her own capabilities to Crane. With the Crane-Kain detente almost a certainty, Crane would not forgive such a step against his own carefully cultivated plans. He would likely reward her with a suicide mission against the Red Empire.

Today would be Kain's final test. She would capture the information she needed from his phone. She would then use the Panopticon to track his location. She was sure that he would lead her to the current safe house of the Mirovar force team and Anton Slayne.

Chloe's eyes glittered like burning coals. Crane wanted to know who Anton Smith was. If Kain was the traitor, then Crane would have asked Kain to investigate from within the Order of Thoth. As soon as Kain found out that Anton Slayne existed, he would no doubt conclude that Anton Smith was a cover identity, but which name would he give to Crane, Smith or Slayne?

Chloe retraced the brief that she'd received for the recovery of the Papyrus of Hakron the Scribe. Her eidetic memory enabled perfect and certain recall. There was no mention of the name Smith anywhere in the brief, it was only about Anna and William Slayne and the residence in Jamaica Plain.

It was her own mission preparations that had revealed the Smith cover identity and the existence of Anton Slayne. It was an unresolved mystery as to why the Smith cover identity was not visible to the Vampire Dominion. A fact she was thankful for; if Crane knew that Anton Smith was really Arthur Slayne's grandson, her own plans would become next to impossible.

The only real possibility was that whoever informed on the Slaynes knew them by sight, and in their own mind never thought of them as other than Slaynes. Such a person would have reported the existence of Anna and William Slayne to Crane without mention of a cover identity that had nothing to do with the presence of the Papyrus of Hakron the Scribe.

It was clear that for some reason Kain had missed the existence of Anton Slayne.

If Kain told Crane that the other survivor was Anton Slayne, then her plans would be in tatters as Crane would seek out Anton and destroy him. Even worse, Crane could easily conclude that either the cover identity had duped her, or she'd deliberately lied to him. Most likely, he would decide that she'd deceived him and there would be a long wait in a silver coffin in her future or summary execution.

She stood in perfect stillness. Staring through her window, she stopped breathing. It would be necessary to put the knowledge of Anton Slayne's existence at risk to find out more – there was no other way. Her eyelids closed as she calculated the risks. She resumed breathing; the decision made.

Chloe opened her eyes. It was essential that she was able to track Kain's movements as soon as possible, and Anton Slayne would make the perfect bait. She picked up her smartphone and placed a call using the stolen quantum signature.

* * *

The beautiful Monday morning sunshine beamed out of a bright blue sky, gracing Midtown East Manhattan with a relaxing summer ambiance.

Ramin Kain adjusted his 24kt gold aviator Ray-Ban sunglasses for a slightly better fit on his nose. He used a fork full of the last of his Atlantic salmon to chase down the final bit of yolk from a pair of poached eggs. The rest of his plate held the half-eaten remains of rye toast, smashed avocado, grilled tomatoes, and mushrooms. He'd ordered an espresso instead of a cafe latte since recently committing to watching his waistline.

Opposite him sat Samuel Luther, his lean frame neatly attired in a new suit. He'd scraped his plate clean, and he was already drinking his second, long black coffee. Even sitting still, he always struck Ramin as a man possessed of excessive nervous energy or a mind-blowing coke habit. Ramin was thankful he'd found Sam. He was an excellent and able junior partner in his ventures. They shared the same values, politics, and predilections. If Sam had been a woman of even average good looks, Ramin would have seriously considered marrying her.

Pushing his breakfast plate back, Ramin sipped his espresso. He savored the flavor of an exclusive Costa Rican blend and soaked up the pleasant ambiance of an early summer Monday morning.

Ramin's smartphone rang. He waited for it to buzz to one less than the maximum six before it would divert to voice mail. He looked at the screen and picked up the phone. He realized at the last moment that the caller was unknown and he stabbed at the answer button.

"Hello, who's calling?" he asked brusquely, curiosity flooding through him.

"A friend," declared a wonderfully modulated feminine voice with a dash of upper-class English polish.

"A friend, eh?" he said skeptically. "You must be a genius or insane to ring this phone."

The woman laughed briefly. "Is there a difference?"

Ramin tapped his fingers impatiently on the table top, and he asked in a low tight voice, "Who the hell are you and what do you want?"

"It's not who I am that matters, it's what I know."

"Don't play games with me girly. This is a private number; how did you get it?"

"Let's just say that a little bird told me and leave it at that."

Ramin growled, and snapped, "I told you not to play games."

"No Games. There is something that you should know."

"What?"

"Anton Slayne is with the Mirovar force team."

Ramin froze. The fine breakfast he'd just enjoyed, suddenly a dead weight in the pit of his stomach. A moment later the call disconnected.

Ramin looked at his phone with horror. He stood up, moving briskly outside he smashed it to pieces on the sidewalk. Sam rushed after him.

"Who was that?" Sam inquired urgently.

"I don't know?" Ramin replied, frowning as he ground the phone into fragments with his heel. "Get the valet to bring the car around."

"Sure, RK, where are we going?"

"Maine – but first, I need a new phone."

Oh hell, Ramin thought with growing dismay. *The other survivor at the Boston warehouse was Anton Slayne. How did I miss the fact that Anna and William Slayne had a son? I'll have to deal with this immediately.*

* * *

Chloe mused, *should I assassinate the Head of the Order of Thoth?*

She lowered her smartphone. She'd only spoken with Ramin Kain once, and already she didn't like him. He'd made her wait as long as he could before he'd picked up the phone, he was clearly self-important. Studying the images stripped from his smartphone while he was speaking, she noted his gold sunglasses, the expensive suit, the upmarket cafe. His vanity and pride were on full display. He'd arrogantly called her 'girly.' She smiled ruthlessly, Kain had some obvious weaknesses that she would enjoy exploiting as she crushed him.

She grasped and rubbed her jaw. She considered killing Kain tonight. Just to be sure he couldn't interfere with her plans, and damn the risk of discovery.

Looking at the rack on her wall that held her swords, the Red Dragon was conspicuous in its absence. A pang went through her soul. She missed her favorite blade. She consoled herself with the knowledge the praetorians would return it soon.

Staring at the gap where the Red Dragon normally rested. A realization struck her. Kain's recent words roared through her memory. His pride, vanity, and arrogance would not allow him to ever admit he'd done anything wrong. No one else knew his darkest secret, not even the flunky who was having breakfast with him. She hummed with satisfaction. The only option that Kain had was to tell Crane that it was Anton Smith who was with the Wu family on the Boston docks. Kain would confirm her own story.

Chloe went to her desk, opened her laptop and logged into the Panopticon. She pulled up all the available data on the identity that matched the photos of Anton taken by CCTV outside the Noodle House. She quickly accessed the new cover constructed by James Haley. Anton Smith's parents remained listed as 'unknown,' and had abandoned him days after his birth. The local authorities made him a ward of the state of Massachusetts until his eighteenth birthday on April the twenty sixth of this year. He'd then left the orphanage and lived on the streets for a short while before Gang Wu took him in. His history matched the new identity, his schools, and sports teams remained the same, even library cards, bank accounts, and social media all reflected the new identity, every reference to parents pointed back to the state, the home address was always the orphanage.

Chloe considered the problem of Anton's Ramp skills. She reasoned Gang Wu must have used the pressure point technique for Ramp activation. She knew Crane would accept it as an explanation for Anton's skills and his sudden appearance from nowhere.

She ran a second search on Anna and William Smith. Anna came back as deceased, a victim of an unsolved murder. William was still missing, and there was no reference to a child. James had scrubbed Anton from all online photos, and then extrapolated and filled in the backgrounds as if he'd never existed. Even subtly modifying gestures and body language to ensure the images still made sense. He'd then followed with inserting pitch-perfect images of Anton into relevant online photos from the orphanage.

Chloe was impressed; the work was without flaw.

She returned to the previous query on the doubly fake identity of Anton Smith. She drew down what she needed to compose a report for Crane. The report would be perfect and just as she'd promised, would be on his desk tonight.

She picked up her smartphone and dialed Louise Wesson's phone. She knew James had Wesson's phone, his own destroyed during the battle in Boston. The phone rang out and went to voice mail. Chloe tried again with the same result.

Chloe frowned and remarked disdainfully, "Humans – what's a vampire got to do to get something done?"

* * *

James woke up. Someone was shaking his shoulder.

"Sir. Wake up, Sir," the operative said, almost shouting in his ear.

James opened his eyes; he was lying on a couch in the Boston Shadowstone offices at the local R.I.S.C building. He blinked, swung his legs down and sat up. The man shaking his shoulder stepped back as James rubbed his face with both hands. He looked up at the man standing in front of him. The operative wore a fresh suit, was clean shaven, bright eyed and thoroughly energized.

James wanted to vomit. The taste of stale coffee filled his mouth. He desperately wanted a cigarette but had run out the night before. This day was starting as badly as the previous night had ended.

"The boss rang," the young operative reported. "She wants you to ring her ASAP."

James rubbed his ears and his cheeks. His head clogged up and fuzzy, seemingly stuffed full with mush. He sniffed once and muttered, "Yeah, Okay. I got it."

"Yes, Sir."

"Dismissed Rose. Good job," James stated, blinking and frowning.

The young man quickly left the room.

James got off the couch, went to the kitchenette and drank a couple of large glasses of water. He returned to his desk, picked up Louise Wesson's phone and dialed Chloe's smartphone, it rang once before she picked it up.

There was a moment of silence before James inquired, "Ma'am, you asked me to call?"

"Yes James, you owe me a text," Chloe reminded him.

"My apologies Ma'am. The lapse is inexcusable."

"I'm going to overlook it this one time."

"Yes Ma'am."

"I've checked your work. It is precisely what I was looking for, immaculate, very well done."

"Thank you, Ma'am."

"Now that task is completed, I need you focused on a new mission."

"Yes, Ma'am," James replied. "What do you need?"

"I have a new target for you named Ramin Kain, I want you to track his whereabouts, and if possible, record his communications. However, I also want this done off the Panopticon record. Make immediate offline copies of the material and scrub the online records."

"I will need your level of security access to be able to do that."

"Granted – the privileges that I gave you last night have been extended indefinitely."

James paused for a moment digesting the implications of her words. Chloe Armitage was trusting him enormously.

"Is the target using quantum technologies?" James asked, his interest flaring like a new flame.

"Yes."

"Do you have his quantum signature?"

"No, but I have excellent photos, his voice print, and I know he will be traveling from New York today. I've just sent you the details, if you act quickly, you should be able to pick him up."

"When do you want reports?"

"Daily – by physical drop at this address," Chloe instructed, providing a dead drop location in Manhattan.

"Yes, Ma'am. Why is this target so important?"

"Kain is the Head of the Order of Thoth," Chloe declared.

"… Yes, Ma'am," James replied with quiet intensity. His heart surged with new life. Here was a real purpose that he could sink his teeth into.

"You are the only person that I can trust to get this done," Chloe said, her voice glowing with approval.

James' chest swelled with pride.

"Yes, Ma'am, I will see it done."

"I'm sure that you will," Chloe declared confidently.

"Is there anything that I should be on the lookout for?" James asked.

"The Mirovar force team safe house. I expect that Kain will lead us to it."

"That's fantastic, operational safe houses have been extremely difficult to find."

"This opportunity is the best we've had in years. That's why I'm entrusting it to you – I know you will not fail me."

"I'm your man, Ma'am," James attested.

"Indeed, you are," Chloe said.

The phone call disconnected, and James put the phone down. He logged into the Panopticon and began searching for Ramin Kain, the Head of the Order of Thoth.

* * *

The morning sunlight streamed through the open windows of the barn. Hay bales lined the walls and packed earth comprised the floor. Whereas the main barn opposite was a real working farm barn, this one supported the training of a small specialized team of fighters.

Peter nudged Anton's arm. "We work with time-honored principles such as, 'No Pain, No Gain,' better get used to it."

"I know how to train," Anton declared confidently, arching his back with his hands held high up in the air. There was a loud click behind his shoulder blades. "Geez, I feel like crap."

"You're new to the Ramp, and you spent a lot of time ramping in the fight last night. I overheard your conversation with Juliette on the RHIB, your body must still be adapting, it's no wonder you're hurting."

"Humph," Anton grunted. Turning his head left and right, he tried to loosen up.

Peter grinned. "But it's a good hurt you know."

"How's your butt?" Anton asked with a wry grin.

Peter laughed and replied, "Almost healed up."

Anton considered the injuries he'd sustained eleven hours earlier. A sword cut to the right shoulder and a ball bearing through his right foot. Juliette Mirovar had expertly cleaned and stitched both wounds, and in half a day they had shown the healing progress of five days. They were nearly ready for the stitches to come out.

The foot wound was the more serious of the two, but the steel ball had miraculously missed the bones and passed straight through. Anton tried jumping lightly up and down, testing the foot and everything seemed to hold together nicely. He felt ready for anything that the team could throw at him.

Everyone was kitted out in loose, light clothing and had runners on. Anton had borrowed his own, very loose clothing, from Peter. He was barefoot, as he didn't have shoes that fit him yet and his combat boots hadn't survived the fight at the warehouse. Peter had promised him that he would go into the nearby town of White Hill and get all the necessary essentials. When Anton had pointed out that he didn't have any money, Peter had told him not to worry as the Order would pay for it.

Yvette and Jay were pushing against each other to warm up and studiously ignoring Anton's presence. Li had dropped into the splits and was touching her right shin with her forehead. Chiara was hanging from the ceiling of the barn, suspended twenty feet upside down on a rope. Francis and Juliette walked into the barn carrying buckets filled with crushed ice and towels.

Peter nudged Anton again and grinned. "The ice is for injuries, and to cool us down – high intensity – it's the name of the game."

Anton shook his head. "How long are you going to keep up with these clichés?"

"We never give up – we make the other guy give up."

Francis addressed everyone in the barn, "Listen up team, we have new members in Anton and Li. So, we will start a new training cycle to embed them into our ways and means. Is that clear?"

Everyone chorused, "Yes, Sir."

"Excellent," Francis declared. He cast his gaze up toward the ceiling of the barn and commanded, "Chiara, drop down and lead us in a warm up. One of your specials to iron out the kinks of battle and freshen us up."

Chiara let go of the rope. Twisting acrobatically through the air, she landed perfectly on her feet in front of the group. "Okay everyone," she ordered. "Form a circle around me with a spacing of ten feet between you and your teammates beside you."

The team moved, and in moments they were ready.

"Let's start," Chiara directed. "Please follow my lead."

Chiara began with short sequences of standard exercises, each one running for twenty or thirty seconds before she replaced it with a different exercise focused on different muscle groups. All the exercises were dynamic, there was no static stretching.

Anton's body loosened up. Then the exercises got harder, squat leaps, one armed pushups, and inventive exercises that Anton had never seen before. This continued for another fifteen minutes without rest.

Chiara stopped and instructed them. "Shake it off, folks."

The break lasted fifteen seconds.

"The next move requires a partial ramp," Chiara explained, expertly assuming a handstand which she held with perfect poise.

Everyone did a handstand and held their form steady.

"Hold it," Chiara commanded.

Chiara had positioned herself directly opposite Anton, and they spent the next five minutes facing each other in silence. Chiara had plaited her long wavy hair into a thick ponytail that snaked down to the ground beneath her head. Her eyes were large, brown and filled with hidden depths, her body was an exquisite balance of sensuality and athleticism.

She stared at Anton with quiet intensity.

Anton stared back. He held his position. He could feel the perspiration rolling over his face before disappearing into his hair. The partial ramp required to hold his form created a slowly intensifying burn in his torso, shoulders, and arms.

Chiara appeared to hold her position with ease, Anton started to feel the strain.

"Fingers now," Chiara directed. Pushing off her palms and balancing on her fingers.

Anton followed suit.

"Right hand," Chiara directed. Shifting her weight slightly, she supported herself with one hand.

Twenty seconds later she directed, "Left hand."

Everyone shifted to their left hand.

Another twenty seconds passed, and Chiara grinned and commanded, "Right thumb and hold."

Anton lifted his focus. The ramp increased, a line of heat flowing from his thumb through his whole body before exiting out of the soles of his feet. A drop of sweat ran into one of his nostrils, and a sudden urge to sneeze made him squeeze his eyelids tightly shut for a second.

"Control," Chiara urged. Her eyes crinkling slightly as if she was laughing inside.

The Ramp burned through his body.

"Left thumb and hold," Chiara commanded.

Anton shifted his focus, transferring his weight to his other hand, supporting himself on his left thumb.

Chiara watched him with a slight smile.

The burn continued to mount, he wanted to gasp but controlled his breathing.

"Release," Chiara instructed. Flexing her thumb, she returned to an upright position on her feet in a single graceful movement.

Anton collapsed onto his face, before rolling out and back onto his feet.

Chiara stepped forward and whispered, "We will have to work on your dismount."

"Yeah," Anton agreed sheepishly, brushing straw and dust off the front of his body.

"Take five minutes and re-hydrate," Juliette instructed, and the team walked around, drinking water and talking in quiet tones.

The time flew by.

Francis stepped forward and commanded, "Okay team, time to move onto sword drills."

Everyone got a metal training sword from a pair of racks. Jay and Yvette paired up, and Anton nodded toward Li, who stepped toward him.

"You four," Francis declared, indicating Jay, Yvette, Li, and Anton, "can swap."

"Huh?" Jay grunted, then moved to stand opposite Li.

Francis moved over to him. Took his left arm and pulled him into position in front of Anton, and directed, "Get used to it, you're on the same team."

"This is a mistake!" Jay said incredulously.

"No arguments."

"… Yes," a hard grin flashed across Jay's face, "Sir."

What's he thinking of doing? Anton questioned silently, staring into Jay's blue eyes while preparing to defend himself.

Francis and Juliette stood to the side to watch the combat form of the team members.

"Open sparring, normal sparring rules apply, no ramping," Francis instructed.

Anton threw a quizzical glance at Francis. Jay immediately attacked, Anton barely managed to get his sword up, but Jay's blade went through his defense like a hot knife through butter, nicking his chest. Jay stepped back; the very tip of his sword smeared with Anton's blood.

"You're dead," Jay noted, a touch of relish creeping into his voice. "You need to pay attention."

Anton's eyes widened with momentary dismay.

"Why don't you give it your best shot," Jay taunted.

Anton began a series of attacks. Jay danced aside, batting his blade away each time, after the third deflection, he riposted and again nicked Anton on the chest, an inch away from the first cut.

"You're dead again, how the hell did you survive last night?"

"I was trained by a master."

"You're kidding me."

Anton lifted his focus without ramping. "Gang was a genius."

Jay slashed left and right. Anton deflected the attacks away, but when Anton riposted, Jay's blade met his early and easily deflected it aside.

"Gang was a true master, everyone knows that. Too bad you didn't learn anything."

Jay launched an attack high, which Anton moved to defend against, then Jay went low with his body, sweeping Anton's legs out from under him. Anton found himself on his back. Jay's blade nicked his throat, no worse than a shaving cut. Anton leaped back to his feet, his sword ready, but Jay was already out of reach.

"Once more you're dead," Jay remarked with a mirthless grin. "Gang wasted his time on you."

Anton glanced at Francis and Juliette, who were watching all three pairs train.

Jay tracked his gaze and said darkly, "They're not going to save you – no one can. Sometimes people die in training."

Both men paused for a split second. Silence overwhelmed Anton. Suddenly Jay was moving, the tip of his sword thrusting toward Anton's heart at full Ramp speed. Jay's blade was set to skewer him like a piece of meat.

Anton's Ramp blossomed as he stepped aside, turning, bringing up his sword in a desperate defense. His Ramp echoed his experience fighting the blond praetorian the night before and against the last of the gangsters in the Noodle House kitchen. The Ramp was wild, time slowed, Jay adjusted his movements, automatically tracking Anton's defenses as the two swords clashed and ground against each other in a shower of sparks. Anton barely pushed Jay's blade aside.

Jay continued to attack, too close now to use his sword effectively, his right fist flashing forward at Anton's face, a killing blow at such speed.

Anton's right hand appeared before it, catching Jay's fist inches in front of his nose. There was a loud clap as Jay's fist stopped as if it had hit a brick wall.

Jay's right leg jack-knifed like a machine, his kick catching Anton on his left ribs and propelling him thirty feet across the barn.

Anton landed hard, slid across the dirt, and rolled on the ground, winded and struggling to breathe.

Jay grunted with pain and dropped his sword. He twisted away and plunged his fist into a nearby bucket filled with an ice slurry.

"Stop!" Francis shouted. He stepped between the two men who were too busy hurting to put up any more fight. Juliette, Chiara, and Li all went to Anton. Yvette went to Jay, who dragged his fist out of the water long enough to groan at the damage before plunging it back into the ice.

Anton started to sit up, and firm hands pushed him back down.

"Lie still, Anton," Juliette commanded, expertly assessing him for damage. "I saw that kick."

Anton winced as she prodded his abdomen and his ribcage. He could see for himself a wide bruise already spreading on the left side of his chest.

"Li, bring me an iced towel from my bucket," Juliette ordered.

A moment later, a freezing cold towel was soothing the pain of his ribs.

Anton looked around him, there was the professional concern of Juliette as she held the ice-cold towel in place. Li and Chiara kneeled beside him to his left and right. Both girls looked at each other with the same quizzical, annoyed, 'what are you doing?' expression on their faces.

Juliette hauled Anton to his feet. "Up you get, soldier."

Francis, stepped back so that he could see both men at the same time. With tightly checked anger he declared, "You were both warned not to Ramp. What are you trying to do – kill each other?"

Jay and Anton looked at each other, a dark promise passing silently between them.

"The vampires would love this dissension in our house. That is who you are serving with this behavior. You're a disgrace, the pair of you," Francis declared coldly, giving them both a withering look. "Well, neither of you are fit for training now. Show up ready tomorrow. Li, stay here and work with Peter."

Francis looked at his wife, and she nodded with understanding.

Juliette ordered, "Okay you two, come with me. Chiara, I will need your help."

"Yes, Ma'am," all three replied, following Juliette from the barn. Jay hugged a bucket of icy water with his left arm, his right fist resting in the slurry. Anton walked gingerly a few yards to his right with an ice-cold towel pressed to his ribs.

Anton and Jay glanced at each other. Looking at Jay was like staring at an unyielding glacier.

What a mess, what a great big mess, Anton thought despondently to himself.

* * *

Anton lay face up and stripped down to his shorts on a padded table in a well-lit room.

The Order had converted two former ground-floor bedrooms into a clinic for Juliette to practice her medical skills in. She was tending to Jay's broken hand in the room next door.

The sharp medicinal odor of herbal balm cut through the room. It was the same balm Gang had used. It brought back sad memories that cut through the residual resentment of the fight. Anton had no desire for a war with Jay Creeley. He understood how Jay felt, he was increasingly familiar with the desire for revenge, and could not condemn in another what he felt so strongly himself.

Gentle, careful hands dabbed the balm onto the skin of his chest. They brushed it down the left side of his torso from just below his chest muscles to the top of his hip, gliding over his smooth skin in confident strokes.

It never felt like this when Gang slapped on some of his healing balm.

Chiara had a focused look on her face, which broke into an easy smile when she realized Anton was watching her. Her touch had an unreal quality about it. Her fingers stroked his skin, applying almost no pressure, and yet they were touching an inch beneath the surface.

It was mesmerizing and unlike anything he'd experienced before.

Chiara completed the application of the balm and directed, "Please sit up, I will strap your ribs."

Anton sat up, expecting stabbing pains across his chest, but only a muted ache remained.

Chiara approached him with a rolled-up bandage and strips of strapping tape. She gestured for him to raise his arms. Anton lifted his arms up and out. Chiara moved in carefully, and efficiently applied the strapping tape, following with the bandage.

With each loop of the bandage, she reached around Anton's torso, getting up close and almost hugging him. Anton couldn't help but notice how good she smelled. They had been working out for nearly an hour, and yet she had a fresh, delightful scent.

She applied the last of the strapping tape to hold the bandage in place and advised, "Keep that in place for two days, and you will be ready to go, but no training for the next forty-eight hours."

"Two days."

"Three cracked ribs, two days to heal, the wonders of the Ramp in action, all we have to do is strap and bandage."

Anton moved to get off the table.

"Not so fast," Chiara warned, placing her hand on his chest.

"What?"

"Show me your hand."

"Oh." Anton held out his right hand.

Chiara took his hand. Turning it over, she squeezed it. Anton squeezed back.

She shook her head. "That's amazing. Jay's broken half a dozen bones in his hand and will be out of action for a week, and you got off Scott free – how did you do it?"

"I honestly don't know."

"I don't think anyone knows how you did that, and I'm not the only person here who noticed it. Your hand didn't move when Jay hit it. I've never seen anything like it."

Chiara sniffed quizzically, then patted him on the shoulder. "Well, all done here."

She watched him as he dressed and then shooed him out of the room. She called to his back, "I have to write notes for Juliette."

Anton paused at the door and looked back over his shoulder. "Thanks for all your help."

"Not a problem," Chiara said with a smile.

Anton nodded and left the room.

* * *

Anton sat on an ancient wooden porch seat next to the front door.

He was resting while his ribs healed, and waiting for the rest of the team to complete the preparations for Gang's funeral. He watched calmly as a car emerged from the lane leading from the main road to the safe house.

The silver Bentley sedan rolled smoothly over the yard before pulling to a stop in front of the safe house. The driver exited first. He was of medium height with a lean build, and short dark hair. He stared intently at Anton through a pair of sunglasses. He held his face still, impassive, like a poker player but his taut stance screamed raptor ready to attack.

The passenger exited the other side of the car and walked purposefully around the front of the Bentley. He was taller and heavier than the driver, with a hint of gray sprinkled through his dark hair. Both men wore finely tailored dark suits, Italian shoes, and sunglasses that gleamed in the late afternoon sunlight slashing across the yard.

The passenger grinned as he approached Anton and the driver fell into step behind him.

Who are these guys? Can't be vampires in daylight, Anton thought warily to himself.

Smiling warmly, the passenger walked toward Anton. He extended his hand to shake and asked pleasantly, "Hi, and you are?"

"Anton," Anton replied, lifting his hand to grasp the stranger's hand.

"The resemblance is striking," the stranger observed, dropping his hand before making contact with Anton. "You really do look like your grandfather when he was young." He stepped adroitly to his right. Behind him, the driver held a Glock 9mm pistol aimed for the center of Anton's chest.

Anton automatically began to ramp. His senses snapping into razor sharp overdrive.

The driver's finger pulled the trigger.

Anton shifted violently to the right.

The muzzle flashed. A spent brass casing flipping away to the left. The bullet ripped through his left lung before punching a hole out of his back.

Anton jerked backward with the momentum of the hit. A second bullet followed the first, smashing through his ribs a couple of inches to the left of the first wound. He started to build up speed as a third bullet crashed through his left arm, breaking the bone before exiting.

The driver began ramping hard, his pistol tracking Anton's movements.

Anton ducked low and blurred to the right. The first three gun shots echoed across the yard. A fourth bullet slashed through Anton's shirt from behind, taking a chunk out of his right shoulder. Blood splashed from his chest, back, and arm, and he could feel his lung begin to collapse, but there was almost no pain, just a growing sense of pressure. He leaped hard over the porch rail. He flew twenty feet out into the yard, landing near the back of the Bentley and rolling on his left shoulder.

The driver fired twice more, the bullets zipping past Anton's head as he ducked behind the car.

Anton twisted around, lifting his head up just enough to stare through the car's windows at the front of the house. He needed to get sight of his enemies if he was going to find a way to defend himself.

The front door burst open, a fully ramped Peter Lamb blurred past the passenger, tackling the shooter and taking hold of his gun arm. There was a loud crack as the shooter's pistol arm snapped like a twig. Grunting loudly with pain, the shooter dropped the gun.

Peter turned in an instant, throwing the disarmed shooter directly at the passenger, knocking him to the ground.

The shooter rolled away with a moan. The passenger leaped back to his feet and shouted, "How dare you interfere with Order business – stand down!"

Francis and Juliette appeared on the porch, poised to fight.

"Ramin Kain?" Francis asked, mystified.

"He's shot, Anton!" Peter yelled.

"Everyone stop," Francis commanded.

"Where is he?" Juliette demanded, stepping off the porch and scanning the yard.

"Here … I am," Anton called out between gasps. He waved his left hand just above the trunk of the car. His legs gave out, his shoes slipped across the gravel, and he sank back out of sight.

Juliette rushed around the rear of the car and appeared at Anton's side.

Kain stepped around the front of the Bentley, drawing a silvered Glock 9mm from a shoulder holster under his jacket. "Step back everyone," he commanded, waving his gun around, "I'll finish this cleanly."

Jay, Yvette, Chiara and Li rushed into the yard from the training barn.

Anton slumped back against the side of the car and wheezed a question at Juliette. "Who … are they?"

"The Order," Juliette said in tight hard tones, staring up at Kain. She assessed his wounds in a moment. Grabbed his right index finger and jammed it straight into the first bullet wound in his chest, and ordered him, "Hold this still."

Anton gasped. Li and Chiara appeared next to him, crowding in, applying pressure to his wounds.

Juliette stood up, facing Kain across Anton's splayed legs. Her voice cut through the air like a sharp knife as she stated with absolute conviction, "I declare sanctuary on Anton Slayne."

Everyone stopped, and all Anton could hear was his own wheezing.

Kain staggered back a step as if slapped. His pistol hand dropped to his side, and he objected, "You can't do that."

"Whoa," Peter declared from the front of the car. "She just did."

Kain spluttered. "This is outrageous. It's the law."

Francis promised in cutting tones from the porch, "Harm my wife, and I will have your head on a platter."

Juliette put her hand on Anton's head, and a sad peacefulness swept through him. Li looked at him, her face filled with horror. Chiara's face was serious and tense. His breathing was horribly labored, his heart racing. He coughed hard, blood spraying in a pink mist. Broken ribs, a ruptured lung, and his broken arm erupted into fiery agony. It was like someone had pulled a pin. A floodgate loosed and pain washed through his body. He gritted his teeth and attempted to bear it, but a low agonized groan escaped his lips.

"Peter come here," Juliette ordered. "We need to get him into my clinic now."

Peter appeared next to Anton. Lifting him effortlessly, Peter carried him inside the house and down the halls to the medical rooms. He put him gently onto a table. The lights were already on, they were terribly bright, and Anton clenched his eyes shut.

"Stay with us Anton, I'm going to have to operate, and fast," Juliette directed.

The world closed in, and he fell away into darkness.

* * *

The Bentley was brand new. Its sophisticated onboard electronics allowed the car to drive itself. Its powerful headlights cut through the night as the car raced along the I-95 toward New York City.

Ramin sat in the driver's seat deep in thought. There was a movement on the edge of his vision. He looked across at Sam, his partner was carefully cradling his right arm close to his chest. The break had been a simple one, Ramin had set it, and used Sam's tie and his Glock pistol as a simple splint.

Sam looked at him and declared incredulously, "He's faster than anyone I've ever seen."

"It's not your fault, Sam."

"He's faster than anyone has any right to be, he ramped straight out of the blocks."

Ramin nodded. "Yes, he is very fast and very lucky."

"Then there was Lamb, he broke my arm – who are these people."

"Dinosaurs."

"RK?"

"On the way to their own extinction."

"Well, he's probably dead."

"Maybe, maybe not – we can't assume that."

"Oh, I hope he's dead. The Slaynes are such a threat to what we're trying to achieve."

"Unfortunately, Juliette Mirovar is a crack combat surgeon."

"I got him twice in the chest," Sam said despondently. Attempting to poke his own chest with his right hand. He winced, lowered his broken arm, and swore under his breath.

"And good shots they were too, Sam."

"Surely, he's dead, he would have bled out."

Ramin frowned in the shadows of the cabin. "Until it is proven otherwise, we have to assume that he has survived."

"I screwed up. I should've put the first one in his head."

"Don't worry Sam, there will be another chance to put this right."

"What are your plans?"

Ramin smiled briefly. "Oh, I'm sure that another opportunity will present itself soon enough."

"We can't just go and shoot him again. Juliette Mirovar has declared sanctuary on him."

"Yes." Ramin paused for a long moment. "Direct action is off the table. We will have to ... do something else."

"Is she crazy, why did she do that?"

"She's a traditionalist, just like her husband."

Sam shook his head. "Madness."

"Quite so," Ramin said sagely. "Attachment to the past is a form of insanity, and in the end, it will get them all killed."

"I hope so."

Ramin faced forward, staring into the distance. He let the conversation lapse, there was nothing new to speak of. Sam understood his plans to transform the Order of Thoth and bring it into the twenty-first century. It was good to have a loyal confidant who fully understood the need to centralize power and control with a single capable leader. If the Order was truly united underneath a single commander, he could wield it as a real force against the vampires.

Once the transformation of the Order was complete, then Crane would discover just who was playing whom.

Ramin's face froze as he burned with old resentments. *Mirovar. Mirovar! MIROVAR! He's a dinosaur. He's everything that has to change in the Order if we are to move forward.*

Ramin rubbed his right temple, he could feel a headache coming on. Today's events had gone badly. He'd lost the opportunity to kill Anton Slayne under the remit of protecting the secrecy of the Order. Possibly, the young Slayne was still alive, a living threat who could undermine his rulership of the Order. While everyone continued blaming Arthur Slayne for the deaths of Mary Creeley and George Madison, no one was looking for the truth, but Anton Slayne could change all that – if he survived.

Anton Slayne was now sheltering underneath Juliette Mirovar's wings. He must do something about that, but first, he had to give Crane a name. He couldn't tell him about Anton Slayne, Crane would wonder why he never mentioned him to start with. Ramin had recognized William Slayne at a public lecture at Boston University. He'd found out that he was calling himself William Smith, but Ramin always thought of him as a Slayne, and that was what he'd reported. After all, it had always been the Slaynes who possessed the Papyrus of Hakron the Scribe and that was what Crane was really interested in.

If Crane knew that Arthur Slayne had a living grandson, he would investigate him. He would be very interested in Anton Slayne, after all, Arthur Slayne was still out there, and the last thing that Crane would want would be a return of the Slaynes to leadership within the Order.

There was already an identity in play – Anton Smith – he decided to give Crane that name. Most likely he would look no further. It would be a disaster to have someone with Crane's powers look too closely at his past relationship with the Slayne family. Crane's investigations could lead him back to Ramin, and he couldn't let that happen. The last thing he wanted was for anyone to find out he'd killed Mary Creeley and George Madison. No one must ever know what really happened.

Oh my God! The leverage Crane would have if he knew the truth.

Ramin opened up his smartphone, held it so that Sam could not read the screen, typed in a message and sent it to Cornelius Crane.

* * *

The smartphone's screen lit up with a message, 'The other survivor at the Boston dock was Anton Smith.'

Cornelius' lip curled skeptically. Both Ramin Kain and Chloe Armitage claimed that the other survivor was Anton Smith.

He sat by himself at his desk in his library. In front of him was an open folder holding a freshly printed copy of Chloe Armitage's report. Turning the last page, he closed the folder.

There was a laptop on his desk, he used it to log into the Panopticon.

Cornelius ran searches on Anton Smith, Gang Wu, Li Wu, William Slayne and Anna Slayne. After twenty minutes of careful work, there were several clear conclusions. Gang Wu and Anna Slayne were dead. According to the Panopticon, William Slayne was missing, but Cornelius knew that William Slayne was a vampire interred in silver at the secret facility on Rikers Island. Li Wu and Anton Smith had disappeared. Crane surmised that they had gone to ground with the Mirovar force team at a safe house. He hungered to know where they were now, but the Order continued to evade the Panopticon.

Cornelius glanced at the closed report next to his laptop.

There was no connection between Anton Smith, and Anna and William Slayne. Gang Wu had likely switched Anton Smith on with the pressure point technique. It was a risky process, and he was lucky to survive it. However, it was the explanation that best fit the facts.

Cornelius sat back in his chair, slowly stroking his chin.

Everything seemed to check out, there is no way that Chloe and Kain could be colluding on anything. The Panopticon confirmed that Anton Smith was an orphan who had recently been closely associated with the Wu family and now he'd disappeared with the Mirovar force team.

The story, around this young man who had appeared from nowhere, checked out neatly.

Cornelius paused mid-thought. *Perhaps too much so.* There was a single thought, like a splinter in his mind, working its way deeper and deeper into a festering wound. *Chloe Armitage and her ambitions.*

Leaning forward, Crane opened the intercom and instructed his executive secretary. "Ursula, please recall General Clayton Maze from Nairobi. I want him back in New York City within three days."

"Yes, Sir," she responded.

It was unsafe to assume he'd mastered all the information. Boston had taught him the dangers of complacency. It would be best to bring in another set of eyes of proven loyalty. He would set a wolf to watch a fox and make sure that Chloe Armitage was not playing any games.

* * *

Louise Wesson lay in her Massachusetts General hospital bed, with her eyes closed and her ears open.

While she appeared to be sleeping, she was wide awake, her mind on fire, processing the events of the previous night. She was fully aware of the young, armed, Boston Police Department officer sitting outside her room. The city had assigned him for her protection. The Boston police force saw her as an agent for a Federal Government anti-terrorism task force, but she knew better.

She was expecting a visitor, someone who would tie off loose ends. She'd secreted a dinner knife under her sheet, it wasn't much, but in her hands, it was far more dangerous than it appeared. There was a rustle outside her door, the slight scrape of a chair across a linoleum floor as the BPD officer stood up. There was a brief conversation followed by a light knock on the door.

"Ms. Wesson. May I please come in?" queried a voice she immediately recognized.

Louise pushed herself up into a sitting position and replied, "Of course, General Armitage, please come in."

The door opened, and Chloe walked into the room. She nodded at Louise, indicated a nearby chair and asked, "Do you mind if I sit?"

"Please, make yourself comfortable."

"Thank you," Chloe said. Repositioning the chair so that she could sit within easy reach of Louise.

The two women looked at each other calmly for a moment, neither giving anything away.

Chloe leaned forward slightly. "I wanted to personally thank you for your service last night. It is clear that you have acted with honor and bravery under the most trying circumstances, and it has not gone unnoticed."

Louise drew upon a decade of specialized training to master her autonomic responses. She harnessed her sympathetic and parasympathetic nervous systems and put pupil dilation, heart rate, perspiration rates, capillary response and breathing under conscious control. Her long history as an elite CIA spy hunter and assassin equipped her perfectly for this moment.

"I only wish the outcome had been different," Louise declared earnestly.

"Don't we all. However, every defeat is an opportunity to learn," Chloe replied sagely.

"That's true."

Chloe leaned further forward, resting her hand lightly on Louise's wrist, her face lit with concern. "I'm glad you survived, I was impressed with your work at the Noodle House, you're very insightful, and Shadowstone needs you." Chloe looked into Louise's eyes. "… We need you. We need someone who is sharp and decisive as the head of the North American arm of Shadowstone, and I believe that is you."

"Are you offering me the job?" Louise asked with surprised interest.

Chloe smiled. "Not yet. Mr. Haley still has some work to do. But I believe the position will become available in the near future."

"I'm honored," Louise acknowledged.

"You've earned it."

"Thank you."

Chloe's smile faded away.

"In the meantime, there is much work to do. It's a shame you're still here," Chloe noted, frowning with concern. "How is your concussion?"

"Good," Louise answered. There was the slightest increase of pressure on her wrist under Chloe's hand. "I should be out of here tomorrow morning."

"Excellent, and your memory?" Chloe asked, watching Louise steadily.

Louise shook her head and replied, "I still feel like I've been on the wrong end of a Shadowstone sleeper dart. All I've got are flashes of the nightfalcons arriving in the early afternoon, after that – it's a black hole."

Chloe nodded and said, "Perhaps it's for the best. You don't want to be carrying all that ... slaughter with you for the rest of your life."

Louise nodded and said, "Yes. It's a memory I don't need."

Chloe let go of Louise's wrist. Standing up, she directed, "Thank you for your time. When you discharge tomorrow morning, go to Fort Dix and report in. Shadowstone needs rebuilding, and you will play a critical part in that process."

"Will do, Ma'am."

Chloe nodded once, turning away, she left the room. The BPD officer poked his head into the room with a quizzical look on his face. Louise tilted her head, he backed away and closed the door.

Louise reflected on her experience at the Boston warehouse, she remembered everything up to the point where James Haley had pushed her aside and shouted 'incoming' and the grenades had starting exploding through the troop of Shadowstone operatives. She remembered throwing up on Haley's shoes and watching him walk away while fitting a silencer to his Glock 9mm. She remembered everything with the trained precision of a highly experienced CIA black-ops operative at the top of her game.

She bit her bottom lip pensively. *I'm working for vampires, and they don't know that I know.*

Louise was suddenly sick to her stomach and almost gagged before her training mastered the automatic responses. She took a couple of slow, deep breaths as determination nourished from deep within herself welled forth. With razor sharp clarity she began to plan her response to the existence of vampires. A small smile caressed her face. She always felt at her best when she believed in her mission.

Chapter Two

"Behind every unquestionable belief is a system of control." – Juliette Mirovar, loremaster of the Order of Thoth

* * *

White Hill, Maine, June 12th, 22:30

A dull light leaked through Anton's eyelids.

He blinked a couple of times, before squeezing his eyes shut again. He was lying on a table. There was a nearby machine whispering away, and there was something hard and uncomfortable in his throat.

There's a tube down my throat.

Anton tested his fingers and toes; he could still wiggle all of them. There was a dull ache across his chest, especially on the left side and his left arm was in a cast. There were people nearby speaking with quiet voices.

"He only just made it. I had to repair a mass of blood vessels just to the left of the heart. It was a mess in there, it's a miracle he didn't bleed out. The first bullet did most of the damage. The second was almost as bad. The third broke his left arm in the middle of the humerus, but that will heal up fine. The fourth was just a superficial wound on his other shoulder."

"He would have needed blood, how much have we got left on site?"

Anton realized that the speakers were Juliette and Francis Mirovar.

"We're out," Juliette noted. "We had to give him multiple transfusions. Fortunately, he's progressed far enough through the physical transformation to be a universal receiver, and some of the team helped out with live donations."

"Who supplied it?" Francis asked.

"Jay and Peter."

"… Well, Jay would have liked that," Francis observed ironically.

"He didn't complain," Juliette said calmly. They approached his bedside. "He's waking up."

Firm hands held his head steady as someone pulled out the tube in his throat. He almost gagged as it slid out of his mouth, the nauseous feeling passed immediately, and he started breathing without the tube.

"It's been five hours since he was shot," Francis stated.

"Equivalent to two days healing, he's doing well."

Anton opened his eyes.

Francis let go of his head. Moving to stand next to his wife. He asked, "How are you feeling?"

"Smashed … but I'll live," Anton replied, his voice quiet and raspy.

Francis smiled slightly. "Good man."

Anton lifted his head to sit up, thought better of it and rested back down. Juliette put a cup of water with a straw in it near his mouth, he tilted his head slightly, sipping the throat soothing water in careful swallows.

Anton looked at Francis and inquired, "What happened? Who were they?"

"Ramin Kain, and—"

"His lackey, Samuel Luther," Juliette interjected. "What?" she glanced at her husband, her eyes flashing. "You know I've never liked either of them."

Francis nodded. "The Head of the Order of Thoth, and one of his staff."

"They tried to kill me, why?"

"That's a good question," Francis sighed. "And I'm not sure what the answer is."

"He shouldn't have shot Anton, it's outrageous," Juliette declared fiercely.

Francis said, "Yes – attacking someone who is already training with a force team – it's just not done. Any disciplinary matter is always referred to the force leader." He shook his head. "Never has the Head of the Order attempted the blatant assassination of an unconfirmed member of the Order."

"So, why?" Anton asked perplexedly.

"Technically he is entitled to defend the secrecy of the Order." Francis said.

Juliette titled her head, her lips curling skeptically. "And it's what he claimed he was doing."

Francis frowned. "Yes, he went on about it at length."

"I'm no threat to the Order?"

"Of course, you aren't," Juliette agreed, placing her hand calmly on his forehead.

"Are they still here?"

"Long gone," Juliette smirked. "Kain stormed off, with Luther scuttling along behind him."

Francis put his hand gently on Anton's left shoulder. "Don't worry, they know better than to try something like that again."

Memories flashed through Anton's mind, and he asked, "Sanctuary – what is it?"

"The heart of our tradition," Francis declared seriously.

"Anton, you're a guest with us until the Conclave," Juliette stated serenely. "There is no way that I would allow a guest to come to harm, not while I draw breath."

Francis' mouth worked momentarily, and he looked away. When he looked back, his eyes were glistening. "You're under my wife's protection, that means that you are under mine as well."

Francis' emotion washed over him in a wave. Its power shocked him to his core. Two things were crystal clear, Francis Mirovar loved Juliette more than life itself, and he hated the fact she'd taken on the risk of protecting Anton.

Juliette put her arm around her husband's shoulders. Leaning in, she kissed him on the cheek and whispered, "Always the emotional one."

Anton was embarrassed by the display of private intimacy between Francis and Juliette and glanced up at the ceiling.

"Harrumph," murmured Francis. He fixed Anton with a steely glare. "Don't imagine that our protection is a pass on training, combat or acceptance by the Order. Get well soldier, I don't want you falling behind."

"… Yes, Sir. Thank you, Sir."

Francis nodded, squeezed his wife's hand and left the room. Juliette continued to work with Anton, adjusting equipment and monitoring his vital signs for another fifteen minutes. She gave him an injection to help him sleep. As he started to drift away, a question gnawed at his mind.

The Head of the Order of Thoth wants me dead, and I don't know why. What the hell is going on?

* * *

The afternoon sunlight cut through the glade, dappling the grass and freshly turned soil. A solemn quiet ruled the spaces between the trees on the hill. The members of the Mirovar force team stood around the open grave. There was no music, no fanfare, only the silence of the woods near the safe house farm.

Li lifted the flask that contained the last of her family reserve sake and poured it over the grave. She shook out the last drops, turned away in silence, her face streaked with tears.

Francis stated softly, "May his heart be as light as a feather."

I've had enough of this, Anton thought.

He nudged Peter's thigh with his right forearm and whispered harshly, "Give me a hand."

Peter leaned down and supported Anton as he lurched out of the Vietnam war vintage wheelchair, he'd been sitting in. He stood on unsteady legs for a second or three, wobbled a bit, and then straightened up.

"Gang was the best man I ever met. The best teacher and the best friend. I will never forget him."

The group murmured their assent.

"The world is poorer for his passing. I'm not going to sit in a damn wheelchair feeling sorry for myself when I'm damn sure that Gang wouldn't do the same. Goodbye … Gang … you'll always be in my heart." Anton's voice caught on Gang's name. "… I'm done here."

Turning, Anton pushed past Peter and started walking the half mile back to the safe house.

Juliette appeared beside him, and declared hotly, "Don't be stupid Anton, it's been less than twenty-four hours since you were shot."

Anton faced her. Wearing a reckless grin and glistening eyes. "This world is hard – I'm going to be harder."

"Well, don't waste my efforts dying on the way back," Juliette insisted in nettled tones.

Anton turned away, declaring, "I won't," over his shoulder, and led the team back to the safe house. He walked slowly and steadily. About halfway there, Li came up and nudged herself in under his right arm.

"You're really starting to wobble," she whispered.

"I'm going to kill her," Anton vowed.

"Not by yourself."

Anton looked down at Li, her face was still, her gaze was intense.

"Agreed."

Anton pushed on but had to admit to himself, it was only the presence of Li that got him the last fifty yards to the safe house.

* * *

Li found Francis alone in the library. A cozy room on the lower floor, opposite the briefing room. Bookshelves filled with an eclectic array of books and folios covered the library's walls. She hesitated for a moment at the doorway, pensive with a rare indecisiveness. She carried the White Dragon before her with hands that threatened to tremble.

Francis looked up; his eyes widened. He put aside the book he was reading. Indicating another lounge chair next to his own with a wave of his hand, he said, "Please sit with me."

Li walked over to the chair and sat down. The White Dragon resting in its scabbard across her knees. She looked directly at Francis for a moment, then lowered her eyes. After a moment, she looked at him again and declared baldly, "I want you to have the White Dragon."

Francis' eyes glistened. "Are you sure? It's a family heirloom."

Li paused for a long moment. "I am the last of my family."

"You may have children one day."

Li smiled wanly. "Perhaps, but who knows when."

"If you keep the sword, you can pass it down when the time comes."

Li stood up decisively, presenting the White Dragon to Francis. "No, the time is now. There is no one else who is more deserving of this sword. No one else who shares the same commitment to the goals of the Order as my father did."

Francis stood up and bowed toward Li. Receiving the White Dragon, he said sincerely, "You honor me with this priceless gift."

Li shuddered as grief, and helpless longing coalesced within her. The gift of the sword carried with it the final acknowledgment of the death of her father. With the memory of his burial fresh from the morning, tears rolled down her cheeks, and she sobbed once. Francis put the sword aside. He wrapped his arms around her. She buried her face against his chest.

Francis tenderly stroked the back of her head. She sobbed again and again. There was a timeless moment when she felt protected and safe. Taking slow deep breaths, her sadness retreated enough to allow her to speak.

"Thank you," she whispered.

"Thank you, dear child," Francis said softly, loosening his arms.

Li pushed back and looked up into Francis' face. There was only acceptance and fatherly love there. Her heart overflowed. Her breath caught for a second, she stepped back further, bowed formally and left the library.

* * *

The sun was peeking over the horizon, its light washing across the farm yard.

Anton had been up for fifteen minutes, it was a week since Gang's funeral, and he hungered to start training. Juliette had finally given him a medical release. He'd healed up enough to join in without risk of doing any more damage. The scars remained, puckered marks and suture lines running across his ribs just below his left nipple. His arm was free of its cast, and he rotated his shoulders to loosen up. The team waited in the training barn. Someone had thrown the doors wide open and a light morning breeze washed steadily through the building.

Francis ordered, "Peter, lead us in."

"Sure, Boss. Okay everyone, form a line. It's time to feel the burn."

Someone had arranged a set of stations throughout the barn. Tractor tires, thick ropes attached to the ceiling, heavy kettlebells, and thick rubber bands.

Peter stood in front of Anton, leaned forward and grinned. "I'm going to introduce you to the concept of active rest."

"Right, sounds like fun."

"That's the spirit."

Peter stepped back and addressed everyone, "Okay – we're just getting older standing around, Francis and Juliette, start with the tires, Li and Chiara on the ropes, Yvette and Jay on the kettlebells, and Anton and I will start with the bands. One-minute rotations, no stopping."

Peter checked his watch, set a timer and got into position next to Anton. He picked up the thick rubber band, stepping onto it with both feet shoulder width apart. He grabbed it with both hands palm down, lifted and pushed it up as if lifting a barbell. Anton watched Peter and did the same.

"Okay. No ramping – Go!" Peter shouted.

A familiar competitive urge rushed through Anton's soul, he desperately wanted to match whatever Peter could do.

The exercises continued without rest. Peter's watch pinged loudly every sixty seconds, and the pairs would swap to another station. Anton and Peter rotated through the kettlebells, lifting the twenty-kilo weights repeatedly up to their chests. Followed by climbing the ropes as fast as they could hand over hand and then reversing back down them. Then it was the tractor tires, flipping them over, running around them and flipping them back. After four minutes, each pair returned to their original station, and the cycle began again and continued throughout the morning. Peter spiced up the cycle by adding sprints up and down the length of the barn and then added squat jumps, pushups, and burpees as well.

At two hours and fourteen minutes into the workout, Anton pulled to a halt at the end of a sprint, doubled over and repeatedly dry retched for about fifteen seconds.

Peter paused next to him, and looked down at the bare ground at Anton's feet. "No blood, that's a good sign. Now try and keep up."

The session continued for another sixteen minutes.

"Good work everyone," Peter called out. "Get some water and come back in five."

Anton picked up a water bottle, and it shook in his trembling hands. He concentrated on stilling them and took a long swig of water. He stretched his chest, his ribs on the left were tight and raw. He breathed deeply, sure that his full powers would come back in time.

Li patted his shoulder. "Are you okay?"

"Yeah, sure."

"Good."

He followed her back to where Peter stood. Peter led them through twenty minutes of stretching, demonstrating that he possessed amazing flexibility for a big man. The session ended with a gut-busting plank where they held a position face down, supported on their toes and elbows for ten minutes. Anton made it to the seventh minute and then began collapsing onto the ground.

Peter appeared beside him, his finger just beneath Anton's chest. Peter pushed up slightly, supporting Anton's body weight. He whispered into Anton's ear, "C'mon Anton, you can make another couple of minutes."

Anton drew on every resource that he could call on and lifted himself back off Peter's finger.

"Awesome. C'mon Anton keep it going."

Sweat dripping from his face, his body trembling, Anton wore the pain and moved deeper into the intensity of the effort.

"Thirty seconds."

Anton vowed to go harder.

Anton's body dropped a fraction of an inch, brushing Peter's finger, and immediately jerked back up into position.

"Ten seconds."

White noise roared through Anton's body.

"Stop."

Anton refused to stop.

Peter's hand pressed into the middle of his back, and he collapsed forward onto the hard-packed dirt of the barn floor. He rolled over and lay there, sucking air into his lungs. Peter and Li stood over him, grinning.

"First session back – not bad," Li observed.

"Awesome work, Anton," Peter said. He hauled Anton back to his feet and handed him a fresh water bottle. "Time for a shower and breakfast."

Anton nodded and started walking slowly toward the house with Peter and Li. Before they left the barn, Francis called them over. Juliette was standing next to him, smiling happily.

Francis put his left hand on her shoulder. "Li, we need an understudy for the roles of loremaster and netmaster, Juliette will help you with that."

Li looked shocked. "I'm honored."

"You're a natural," Juliette said. "It would be a terrible waste not to train you."

"Thank you," Li said.

"Li and Anton," Francis directed. "You need driver and flight training. Peter will teach you."

"Sure, Boss," Peter agreed. He looked at Juliette. "Is it okay if I get them both into the simulations after breakfast."

"Yes, Peter, that will be fine," Juliette replied. "Li and I will start together this afternoon."

"Good. Then everyone knows what they're doing," Francis declared with a short nod.

Peter, Li, and Anton made their way across the yard to the safe house.

Anton looked across at Peter and Li, and asked, "What's a loremaster?"

"Someone who keeps all the recorded history of the Order of Thoth," Peter explained. "Juliette is a loremaster, there are only six alive in the world. The Order operates on tradition and precedence. The loremasters know everything there is to know about the Order of Thoth, they keep our traditions alive. They maintain the soul of the Order."

"How do they do it?"

Li grimaced. "By oral history and severe memory training – I think."

Peter looked hard at Li. "Yes – there is a lot of hard work involved as I'm sure you will soon find out."

Anton nodded. "Li, I'm not surprised they picked you. I'm sure you will do well."

Peter laughed, grabbing them around the shoulders and pulled them in with a hug as they walked toward the safe house. "Yeah, she'll be great, now let's get something to eat. My stomach thinks my throat's been cut. Then we can see how many helicopters you can crash before lunchtime."

"Helicopters?" Anton asked.

"Flight Sim – very realistic. I hope that you don't get airsick."

"I should be okay."

Peter chuckled. "I'll make sure that we have a mop and bucket handy, just in case."

"Right," Anton drawled as he followed Peter and Li up the steps and into the safe house.

The smells of the kitchen reached him in the hallway. His stomach growled and his mouth salivated like a broken faucet.

Eggs, bacon, toast, mushrooms, tomatoes, and sausages – great.

* * *

The classroom was located in the basement of the safe house.

There was a simple wooden table with a laptop on it in the middle of the room. There was a white pull-down screen, a projector, half a dozen desk chairs, and a pair of dual-sided whiteboards on stands. Soft downlights in the ceiling lit the chamber.

Juliette sat opposite Li, and inquired, "Was there anything worth noticing as you came down here?"

"There are metal contacts on the door," Li noted.

"Indicating?" Juliette asked.

"There's a Faraday cage around the room."

"Good, why would we build a room this way?"

"Electromagnetic shielding for security."

"Is it perfect?"

"No. But it is much better than nothing."

"Correct. This is the most secure location for a conversation on this site, and that is why we're here."

Li nodded, ready to hear whatever Juliette had to say.

Juliette paused for a long moment, looking steadily into Li's eyes as if probing her character.

Li relaxed, confident in herself.

"There is no obligation to accept the role of loremaster. If you wish, you can remain a warrior with full honor," Juliette noted, smiling softly. "In addition, loremasters are excluded from the roles of force leader and Head of the Order. If you go down this path, you'll never be in either of those two roles."

"Are any of the others training with you?"

"No. They were all offered the role, but they all turned it down."

Li hesitated for a second. "What's the issue?"

"I must share with you enough information so that you can make an informed decision about this," Juliette declared seriously. "Anything less would be unacceptable. I'm not interested in a student who doesn't understand the commitment they have to make to be loremaster."

Li was uneasy for the first time at the safe house.

"I overheard your comment to Anton and Peter earlier this morning. Yes, the loremasters maintain an oral history and undergo severe memory training. It is clear that your memory is excellent, in time, it will become perfect."

"You can train for an eidetic memory?"

"Yes. Furthermore, we can elevate your use of memory to become a powerful tool for integrating diverse information and finding obscure, but real, patterns. Using your memory this way, is known as a 'mind palace.'"

Li was intrigued and leaned forward. "That sounds cool."

Juliette glanced down at her hands before looking back at Li. "It comes at a price; I haven't spelled out the full role yet."

"Oh."

"We use technology too, and a nanotech implant right here," Juliette explained, indicating a location on the inside of her right forearm about three inches back from the wrist.

Li sighed softly, anticipating that the downside was coming up. "What does the implant do."

"It hooks through software on your laptop to quantum encrypted storage on the Cloud with a wetware interface directly into your nervous system."

Li's eyes widened. "… Oh my God. What does that feel like?"

"Both glorious and terrible. The loremasters can communicate with each other using quantum communications via the implant, and it feels like someone is talking inside your head."

"That could get weird," Li noted. "Can they read your mind?"

"Only what you're willing to share."

"Well, that doesn't sound too bad," Li conceded with a frown. "There must be something else."

"There is. This is critically important," Juliette instructed. "The quantum communications networks work alongside the regular networks, and—"

"Of course," Li interrupted, her mouth forming an O of surprise. "You can see everything on the regular networks, everything would be available."

"Yes."

"How do you filter it, there must be an enormous amount of junk data of no relevance to us."

"Through training, you learn to filter, but it's not the junk that is the issue." Juliette reached across the table and gripped Li's hands. "The darknet is also open to you, you will see every horrible, evil thing that human beings can do to each other and post online."

Li looked at Juliette in silence.

"There will be things you will see that you can't unsee," Juliette said emphatically. "It's corrosive. It can get to you and destroy your willingness to put your life at risk, or see your friends and loved ones put their lives at risk to protect humanity. It can make you give up. It can make you despair."

Li shook her head and stared at Juliette. "That won't stop me."

Juliette stared back. "There are loremasters that have killed themselves, two in the last decade. One in four loremasters have committed suicide."

Li shrugged her shoulders. "Suicide is not my thing."

Juliette looked hard at Li, as if peering into her soul. She remarked in a low voice, "There is one more risk, which is ... difficult to explain. If it eventuates you can always remove the implant before you are damaged."

Li arched an eyebrow and queried, "Hard to explain?"

"Yes. You have to experience it to know what it is. Not many become affected by it. You can still back out if you want to."

Li thought of her father, *what would he do?* She nodded and declared firmly, "When do I start?"

"Now."

* * *

It was an hour and a half before midnight.

Dillon Browne was just about as happy as he could be. He had a nice wad of cash and good quality Colombian cocaine in his shirt pocket. His crew was with him, it was the fourth of July in Boston, and it was time to party. Like every Friday night, they would walk half a mile to the Four Corners/Geneva railway station. They would catch the next train into Boston city. The nightclubs were their playground. They could have some fun and do some business hooking people up with whatever they needed. He liked the train. Cops didn't stop trains to test people on them for drugs like they did with cars. In the twenty-five years of his life, no cop had ever pinned Dillon for anything more serious than a parking fine, and he intended to keep it that way.

The night sky was clear. The air was fresh. Dillon walked with a jaunty air of confidence bred from total familiarity with the rules of how to get by in Dorchester. He was a big deal in the suburb. No one dealt drugs on his turf without his say so, and if anyone broke the rules, then his crew would punish them – permanently.

The sidewalk they were on curved past the entrance to a forested park. Streetlights normally lit the trees, but some idiot had vandalized the lights over the entrance. Now, shadows cloaked the park in a near impenetrable gloom.

As he approached the stone archway of the park entrance, Dillon's left hand slid over the rounded hip of his latest girlfriend. She wore a tight leather skirt, a see-through net top, high heels and little else. She was hot, hot, hot and he wondered if she would last more than the typical three to four weeks. He kinda hoped that she would. She responded to his touch by pushing in close underneath his muscular left arm.

A deep voice behind him declared, "I love fireworks, we'll see some great fireworks tonight."

Dillon looked over his left shoulder at Caleb Moore, his chief enforcer. Caleb was scary big and wide, a coulda, shoulda, woulda been NFL forward who never quite made it out of Dorchester and who was the longest serving member of Dillon's crew.

Dillon scrunched up his nose, grinned broadly, and swore happily, "They'll be fu—"

His left arm jerked hard, and his new girlfriend vanished.

Her younger brother, Gabriel Williams, who was tagging along for the night, pointed into the park and screamed, "Aaliyah."

Dillon whirled, his left arm ached like it was nearly dislocated, he reached behind his back with his right hand and dragged a Colt .45 automatic from the back of his pants.

He stared into the park. He could just see the outline of a tall, slim man gliding backward into the enveloping darkness. He was carrying Aaliyah like she weighed nothing, her feet dangling a foot off the ground. One of his pale hands was over her mouth. She was struggling but couldn't make a sound. A moment later they disappeared into the shadows.

A shiver of nameless dread prickled the skin at the back of Dillon's neck. He couldn't process how fast Aaliyah had vanished into the dark. It didn't make any sense. A part of his mind sat dumbfounded by what had just happened, the rest boiled with fury.

Ethan Jones, the third member of his crew, pulled a MAC-10 9mm from within his coat. He stepped up beside Dillon and snapped, "Some cracker stole your girlfriend."

Caleb Moore grunted in agreement, pulling out his own MAC-10 which looked tiny in his big fist. He waved the barrel toward the park, looking expectantly at Dillon.

Dillon growled, his anger boiling away the dread. His fist tightened around the pearl handled grip of his .45. "That fool is going to be in a world of hurt. No one takes what's mine."

He walked confidently forward, leading the other three men into the darkness.

* * *

Cornelius Crane cinched the heavy belt tight and locked it.

The young man, little more than a boy, stared at him wide-eyed without really seeing him. Cornelius stepped back from the boy to survey his handiwork. There was a faint diffuse light amongst the trees. The park was a night lit wonderland of luminous colors, rich scents, and faint rustles. Cornelius was perfectly aware that for the five young people trying to see him, he was little more than a dark nebulous outline.

The boy's face gleamed with the sweat of fear as he struggled vainly against the thick belt.

This one is named Gabriel, how like an angel he looks behind his terror. Perhaps too beautiful and too innocent to condemn to this immortal life.

Cornelius sniffed, his eyes narrowing. The five humans, four men, and one woman reeked of the familiar stench of terror. He'd strapped them upright to the trunks of old trees, their mouths covered with gray duct tape. They struggled and wriggled but could not escape their bonds.

Before each of his candidates, he'd laid out a similarly trussed and silenced homeless man.

Cornelius went to a nearby black duffel bag and extracted a thick leather binder the size of an A4 folio. He placed it on the grass and opened it. Inside was a set of six syringes, and a razor-sharp nine-inch knife. He picked up the knife and slashed the inner thighs of the five candidates. The cuts were deep, expertly severing the femoral arteries. The candidates moaned and whimpered behind their silenced mouths. Air rushed through their dilated nostrils. Their hearts, already beating fast, accelerated toward their maximum capacity.

The blood sluiced down the candidate's legs, pooling at their feet. Selecting five of the syringes, Cornelius filled them in turn with his own blood. He approached the first candidate, plunging one of the syringes directly into the left ventricle of his heart and emptied it. He repeated the process with each of the other candidates. When finished, he neatly packed his gear back into the duffel bag and closed it. He cleaned the knife, tucking it unsheathed behind his waist belt and waited patiently with his long arms crossed over his chest.

Vampire conversion takes a variable amount of time, but typically around five minutes. The first to complete was the second candidate he'd injected: the young woman. She stopped writhing in agony, a few seconds later she burst through the heavy leather belt and tore off her gag. Cornelius appeared next to her, his hand on the back of her neck, guiding her down to the throat of the homeless man lying in front of her. She needed no further help, tearing into his flesh with her new fangs and instinctively wrapping her mouth over the gushing wound. The sound of her ravenous sucking was loud in the otherwise silent park.

A moment later, the second belt burst and Cornelius assisted the huge man named Caleb to his first victim. Caleb crushed the man's skull with one big fist in his urgency to get to his throat, but a second later he was gorging on the homeless man's blood.

In the next handful of seconds, the other three completed their conversions. Cornelius blurred around them, making sure they reached their designated victims. He stepped back and waited for their feasting to finish.

He did not have to wait long. Moments later, Dillon Browne and his crew stood to face him, their terror gone, replaced with shock and wonder.

"What the hell just happened? Who are you?" Dillon asked.

"Hey man, we're vampires. He must be that guy, ah, Dracula," Ethan asserted.

Cornelius stepped forward and said calmly, "I promise you; I am not the figment of someone's fevered imagination, but yes – you are now immortal vampires, you will not age, and you need not die. As for my name, it is not important, what is important is that you obey my rules."

"Obey your rules." Dillon shook his head, sneering incredulously. "Your rules, cracker? We don't have to do anything that you say. This is our turf, I rule here, I say what happens in Dorchester."

Dillon growled, lunging at Cornelius. Ethan and Caleb blurred forward, moving with him to tackle Cornelius.

With nearly a thousand years of combat experience, Cornelius easily evaded Dillon's forward rush. He trapped his arm and threw him hard, face first onto the ground. He dealt with Ethan and Caleb in the same manner, throwing them on top of Dillon. Cornelius blurred forward, slapping Aaliyah unconscious and trapping the young Gabriel in an unbreakable hold. He turned, holding Gabriel a foot in front of him as Dillon, flanked by Caleb and Ethan bounced back to their feet.

Cornelius stared at them, a ferocious light in his eyes. He growled softly, almost a murmur, but certain that they could easily hear him. He declared in cold tones, "You will obey me because I can do this."

Pushing Gabriel toward them, Cornelius whipped the knife from his belt. He passed it through the young man's neck with such violent speed that it splashed blood across the faces of the three shocked men a dozen feet away. Gabriel's body took another step forward on its own before crumpling to the ground. His head rolled forward end over end, coming to a halt, a foot in front of Dillon's boots.

The fight drained from Dillon and his crew. They were predators through and through, they respected strength, and they instinctively understood that they were in the presence of the greatest predator they had ever seen.

"Okay," Dillon muttered. "Your rules."

"Yes, my rules. They are simple. Stay in Dorchester. You can hunt Boston but do not leave this city. If I find you outside of Boston, I will kill you. Do not attempt to make more vampires or I will hunt you down and kill you. Do not move in daylight as sunlight will kill you."

Cornelius paused for a long moment to let his words penetrate their minds. "Are there any questions?"

"Why? Why us?" Dillon asked.

Cornelius' lip curled into a half smile. "It's your lucky day, someone has to be immortal."

Dillon and his crew watched him in silence.

Cornelius glanced at Aaliyah who was waking up and commanded, "Tell her what I told you." He pointed at the bodies. "And dispose of the trash, don't leave it lying around for anyone to find. Keep yourselves secret or else I will come back and kill you all slowly."

He watched as Dillon frowned, sucking indecisively on his lower lip.

Time to disappear — that will really put the fear of God into them.

Cornelius flourished his long coat dramatically, throwing a short-fused flash-bang grenade to the ground. It burst into blinding light with a crash like thunder. By the time the new vampires regained the use of their senses – he was gone.

* * *

Cornelius Crane drove his personal black Mercedes toward New York City.

He left the autopilot off. He enjoyed driving, confident his own enhanced senses and reflexes were superior to the technology delivered with the car. After all, he considered, sometimes the autopilots crash the car and kill everyone inside. He anticipated that maybe in another fifty or hundred years they would get the technology right – he could afford to wait.

He mused about the night's events. *What's a cracker? I will have to look that one up, sounds derogatory.*

Shadowstone had fitted the car with an array of communications technology. It was a simple matter to conduct fully scrambled voice calls, and send and receive encrypted text messages driven only by voice commands.

"Compose text message to The White Pawn," Cornelius stated in a calm, steady voice. The White Pawn was an alias for the quantum address of Ramin Kain's latest smartphone. The quantum address was the sub-section of the full quantum signature, used to connect any two quantum communication devices in a traceless call.

Cornelius said to the machine, "There are four targets in Dorchester, Boston. End text message."

The system responded with a ping as it delivered the message.

Now the ball was in Kain's court. He needed to deliver on the Mirovar force team.

Cornelius grinned, with the Mirovar force team caught between operations from Kain and Chloe, their doom was certain.

The car pinged with an automated message from the Panopticon.

Cornelius frowned and commanded his vehicle's console, "Display."

The car responded by projecting a translucent image of live satellite footage onto the interior of the car windscreen. Cornelius' eyes widened, and his jaw dropped. There was a smoking crater surrounded by burning buildings and thick Amazonian jungle. As he watched in growing horror, the center of the remaining buildings suddenly exploded, sending debris high into the air. Thick black smoke billowed in great clouds over the site.

A red message repeatedly streamed along the bottom of the screen, '*** Brazil-34 *** No Communications ***'.

Cornelius snarled. He was certain who was behind this attack. "Fucking Arthur Slayne!"

Cornelius paused for a second before speaking through gritted teeth, "Broadcast voice message, list alpha. Activate the war room and meet me at the Citadel immediately. End Message."

The vehicle's communications system instantly sent the message to a list of first responders in his force of praetorians. Cornelius put his foot down, and the car surged forward.

"Damn it, how much of the fungus do we still have? Enough for five hundred doses, that's not enough for my plans."

Cornelius Crane spent the rest of the journey considering options to recover his Day Guard strategy.

* * *

The stream meandered its way down the hillside. The warm mid-morning sunlight speared through the thick canopy of Maples, Beech and Birch trees, dappling the rough stone and dirt trail that followed along the edge of the stream.

Anton ran alongside Francis Mirovar. They were both kitted out in running shoes, socks, loose shorts and sports singlets; newly bought for Anton and worn down with wear and tear for Francis. Francis wore an old, black peaked cap with a French flag on the front of it. His long hair tied in a ponytail hanging out the back of the cap.

Anton dragged his hand down his face, and it came away slick. They kept a good pace; it had been uphill for over an hour, and he was still feeling good and strong. His breathing was even and his movement fluid. It had been over three weeks since the shooting, the physical trauma had fully healed, and the scars were beginning to fade.

The hill became steeper, and the path ended on a set of stairs cut into the rock. The stream became a waterfall, falling from about fifteen yards above them. Anton moved to go up the stairs, and Francis tapped his arm.

"No Anton, this is where we stop," Francis noted, stepping off the trail and taking his shoes, socks, and singlet off.

Anton did the same and followed Francis as he moved to the edge of the stream. They leaped onto a boulder, moving nimbly over a slew of rocks to a position a yard out from the waterfall. The spray of the waterfall caught the sunlight, reflecting a crisp rainbow for a moment before Anton got too close, and the bright colors melted away. After the run, he cupped his hands, filling them with water and slaking his thirst. The water was wonderfully refreshing, clean and crystal clear.

The two men stood on separate boulders, relaxing in front of the waterfall. Anton looked steadily at Francis, who was rubbing his hands dry on the back of his shorts.

Francis looked across at Anton. "Your Grandfather was my teacher before my confirmation in the Order, and he taught both Gang and myself this practice which I will pass onto you today."

"What's that?"

"Watch and learn," Francis directed with a brief smile.

Francis centered himself, dropping into the silence of the Ramp. His fists blurred forward in rapid combinations that twisted and turned in the waterfall, but there was no disturbance of the flow of water. As quickly as it started, it stopped. Turning toward him, Francis opened his hands and displayed them – they were dry.

"Now you try Anton, ramp and punch through the water without getting wet," Francis instructed, watching Anton intently.

Anton confidently expected that there was an easy trick to the technique.

He nodded, turned and silenced his mind. He dropped away from anticipation and memory, allowing himself to flow with the moment. The Ramp flowered within, time slowed, the waterfall started to break up into streams of separate droplets. Anton's fists blurred forward and immediately splashed through the waterfall. Frowning, he dropped out of the Ramp, shaking the water off his hands.

"It's harder than it looks."

"Yes," Francis observed. "And that surprises you?"

Anton looked sheepish for a second. "Well, yes."

Francis studied Anton for a moment and promised, "Master this technique and your combat ability will be a notch above what it is now."

"Yes Francis, but what am I doing wrong."

Francis tilted his head. "There's no snatching in this – you're snatching at the spaces between the drops."

"… I hope that you're not about to tell me to 'be one with the waterfall,'" Anton remarked, rolling his eyes.

Francis rubbed the side of his nose. He suddenly tapped Anton on the chest, just hard enough to make him lose his balance. Anton slid off the rock and into the stream. He twisted in the air but hit the water before he could recover, making a big splash as he disappeared beneath the surface of the water. A moment later his head bobbed back up to the surface, and he swam back to the rocks.

Anton shook his head, his eyes narrowing slightly. He put his hand up for Francis to help him out.

Francis put his hands up in front of his shoulders. "I'm not falling for that, you'll just pull me in. You climb back out yourself."

Anton clambered out onto the boulder. He stood up, running his hands back through his thick, dark hair to clear the water from it. "Okay, I suppose I deserved that."

Francis threw him into the stream again.

Anton's head broke the surface of the stream again, and he swam briskly back to the boulder.

How did he do that? I never saw it coming.

Anton climbed out of the stream, taking his position on the boulder next to Francis' rock. They stared at each other for a moment, and Francis arched his right eyebrow.

"Do I need to push you in again or are you ready to learn?"

"Ready to learn."

"Good, then start with learning that cynicism is not wisdom, there is no place for it in my force team, do you understand?"

"Yes, Francis."

"Good, do you have any questions?"

"Yes, how were you able to throw me in the water the second time? I get the first happened because I was surprised, but the second, there was no warning at all. You didn't telegraph anything at all, it just happened, and then I was falling back into the stream."

Francis paused for a moment, then leaned forward slightly. "Because I can punch water without getting wet."

Anton bit down on saying *right*, and instead stared at Francis for a moment and nodded his acceptance.

"So, let us begin," Francis directed.

An hour later, a thoughtful Anton was tying up his shoelaces. The waterfall skill was wickedly difficult. It almost seemed like magic the way that Francis could do it at will. He'd assured Anton there was no magic involved, none whatsoever. It was persistence, method, and correct instruction, followed by deep insight, and more persistence. He'd spent the session splashing water with every punch, and it seemed he'd made no progress.

Gang knew this technique, but Armitage still killed him, how easy would it be for Armitage to kill me?

Anton vowed to himself, *I must master this skill, and soon ... and then go beyond it.*

Francis nudged his shoulder and said with a half-grin, "It's ten miles back home, let's see if you can beat me."

"Are we allowed to ramp."

"Yes."

"What if someone sees us."

"They won't, not today. Juliette checked the satellite positions – we have an open window until lunchtime."

"Okay then – I'll be waiting for you when you get back old man."

Anton blurred away, Francis blurred with him, and the two men hurtled down the track.

* * *

The barn was set up for unarmed combat. The central space was dry packed earth, swept clear of dust and straw. There were buckets of iced water and wet towels. Chiara, Peter, Li and Anton stood in a loose half-circle facing Juliette.

Chiara glanced at Anton, and thought, *this will be interesting.*

Juliette caught Anton's and Li's gaze and said, "Li, Anton, the Order has been perfecting unarmed combat for thousands of years and what we have now has influenced, and been influenced by every style in existence. We have distilled everything down to two key principles; does it work, and is it fast."

Anton and Li nodded, Chiara and Peter were both familiar with Juliette's instruction and stood relaxed, waiting for the physical part of the lesson to begin.

"Li, I know you have benefited from your father's instruction for many years, and can be considered fully trained, but Anton, it's been less than three months since you started, so we're going to focus on progressing your skills as fast as possible."

"Sounds good," Anton noted. "I'm ready."

"Ready to lose," Peter observed, grinning.

"Boys!" Juliette declared sternly. "Pay attention. Anton, we're going to test you hard for the next two days. This is an immersive training system, and mostly it's done while ramped. It will be grueling, and I can guarantee that by the end of tomorrow you will not think it was fun."

Juliette stepped close to Anton, her face looking up, inches from his own. "It will be three against one at all times. Peter with his strength is equivalent to a vampire at close quarters, Li and Chiara are equivalent to Red Empire assassins."

Anton glanced at Peter and said, "Gang always told me that it was a good idea to avoid hand to hand combat with vampires."

"He was right," Juliette agreed. "You should avoid grappling with Vampires, their superior strength makes it a low probability option."

"Why do we bother?"

"We don't always fight vampires. There is also the Red Empire."

Chiara grinned, and declared, "Deadly assassins."

"And in actual combat with edged weapons," Juliette explained, frowning slightly at Chiara. "Unarmed combat skills remain an essential part of our fighting system."

"Okay – what do I need to do?" Anton asked.

Juliette guided him to the center of the barn and stepped back. Peter took a position a couple of yards in front of Anton. Li and Chiara stood a similar distance away from Anton on the other corners of a triangle.

"I've already briefed Li on this training form, so everyone is ready," Juliette stated. She pulled a black hood from her belt and handed it to Anton.

"What's this?" Anton asked, looking at the hood.

"Vampires don't fight in daylight mate," Peter said dryly.

"I'm doing this blind?"

"Yes. You will be blind throughout the training," Juliette acknowledged.

Taking a deep breath, Anton sighed and put the hood on, pulling it down over his face.

"Focus on the silence within, Anton, find the still point of calm in the midst of chaos, and you will know what to do," Juliette instructed from the sidelines.

The attack started without warning. Peter leaping forward with a combination of blows, that he pulled at the very last moment so that they would not be penetrating. Anton's hands flashed up, blocking the attacks and he started to move left toward Li, who promptly swept his feet out from under him, and he fell backward. Chiara helped him to the ground with a lightning-fast kick to his chest.

He jackknifed off the ground like a click beetle on a summer night. One outstretched hand almost catching Chiara's foot as she launched a second kick which she instantly pulled to avoid getting trapped.

My God, he's fast and intuitive.

Chiara paused for a moment, circling, as Peter and Li engaged with Anton, carefully watching his every move.

How attached is Anton to Li? She wondered.

The training continued in two-hour blocks broken with fifteen-minute breaks for the rest of the day and repeated the next day.

* * *

Jay walked along the corridor to the front door of the safe house, putting his hand out to push it open.

Something dropped onto the porch in front of the door with a heavy half-muffled clunk. On a sudden intuition, Jay pulled to a halt just inside the door, placed his left hand up on the wood, leaned his head forward slightly and listened.

Francis' voice came from the porch as he asked, "How's your training at the waterfall progressing?"

"Still getting wet," Anton answered with a sigh.

Jay stepped back from the door. He turned to face an oil painting of a revolutionary war scene on the wall and pretended to study it.

"It's only been ten days since you started," Francis said. "Not everyone progresses at the same pace. Continue to persist, you'll get there in the end. Focus on the silence, and arresting your attention in the present moment. You will discover that silence is a spectrum where there is no end to how deep you can go. It is there, in the eternal quiet, that you will find the mastery that you seek."

"Yes, Francis."

"I have something else for you," Francis noted. "We'll spend a week on wilderness survival skills. You'll learn about fishing and hunting, water and shelter, making traps and snares, and how to move stealthily to avoid detection."

"I can learn all that in a week?" Anton asked incredulously.

"You will learn enough to make a difference, consider it a crash course, and there will be a test in three weeks' time."

"Where are we going?"

"About fifteen miles, due west, toward Mount Washington."

"Great, when do we start?"

"Now."

"Oh, is my gear in that backpack?" Anton asked.

"No, that is my gear."

"Do I have any gear?"

"Just what you're wearing."

"Oh … Okay."

"Let's move it," Francis directed. "… Wait a second, you're the one carrying the backpack."

"Oh, sorry, ah, your gear and all … yes, Francis."

The floorboards in front of the door squeaked as the heavy backpack rose off the porch. Two pairs of footsteps tramped away from the front door. Squeaking porch floorboards replaced by crunching gravel before the footsteps receded into the distance.

Jay ascended to the upper floor and the room that he shared with Yvette. He kept a fully stocked backpack ready in his wardrobe at all times. After changing clothes to suit a wilderness expedition, he grabbed the pack and started downstairs.

Yvette stood at the foot of the stairs. Looking up at Jay as he descended, she inquired, "Where are you off to in such a hurry? We have a training session in just under an hour."

"I've gotta get away for a week."

"A week! Are you crazy? What for?"

"I really need time away, this whole thing with Anton Slayne showing up has thrown me for a loop. I need to get away and clear my head."

"Have you told Mom or Dad?"

Jay shook his head. "No, it's a spur of the moment thing."

Yvette frowned. "I hope this isn't about getting at Slayne? You know Mom has put a sanctuary on him."

"Yes, I know," Jay said, looking away. "This isn't about him."

"Well, I certainly hope so. I know how you feel, but going after Anton Slayne would be going way too far."

"Sure." Jay nodded. "I've just gotta get some time away and get my head around this."

Yvette moved to stand in front of him. They stared at each other for a brief moment. She reached up, throwing her arms around his neck and kissed him hard on his lips. Jay kissed her back.

"Don't forget that I love you, you big lunk."

Jay hugged her tight for a moment, whispering in her ear, "How could I ever forget." He kissed her again. "Love you too."

"So where are you going?"

"Just the forest, I won't be too far away," Jay said, gently moving past Yvette and making for the door.

"Okay, bye then," Yvette said, her voice betraying a mix of concern and annoyance.

"Bye," Jay said over his shoulder, and pushed the front door open. He strode across the porch and into the bright morning sunlight. He squinted for a moment from the glare, and then put a pair of sunglasses on before setting off for Mount Washington.

Anton's tracks would be easy enough to follow, and come the test – he would be waiting.

* * *

Old fluorescent tube lights attached to the ceiling illuminated the training barn in a soft pale light. The air was still and humid. The shutters along the walls lay open but gave little relief from the evening mid-summer heat.

Peter punched a pair of big steel hooks into a hay bale and twisted them so that they sat behind a slim rope that bound the hay together. He'd attached two ropes to the hooks. Anton held one of the ropes, and Peter joined him at the end of the other rope. Together they pulled on the ropes, dragging the hay bale across the floor of the barn. Once they got the bale to the other side of the barn, they worked together to flip it onto its long end. They repeated the same operation another nineteen times, constructing an eight-foot-high wall of hay around the barn, and leaving one corner bare.

Anton brushed the sweat off his forehead with his forearm. He pointed at the newly exposed door in the floor of the barn. "Hey, Peter, what's down there?"

"Our armory," Peter answered, brushing straw off the front of his faded New England Patriots T-shirt. "Now that you're finished being chased by bears in the woods, I've got some cool things to show you."

The door comprised two steel panels, clasped shut with a thick bolt. Peter dragged on the bolt which opened smoothly. Anton stepped around to the other panel, and grabbed hold of the handle opposite the one Peter held with his right hand. Peter nodded, and they lifted together.

Anton's panel barely moved, and he watched as Peter dragged his up and let it down slowly, so it didn't crash.

"Sure, you're not really a terminator from the future?"

"Yes, I'm sure." Peter shrugged. "Give it another go."

Anton repositioned to effectively use his thighs to help with moving the door, he also dropped into silence and activated the Ramp. Power flowed through his body as he pulled on the handle, the door moved up and over, and he quickly repositioned to guide it down to the floor.

"Good work Anton, we don't really need locks if a regular person has to use a winch to open the door."

Peter stepped into the open doorway and descended a stairway into the armory. Anton followed directly after him, his eyes wide open, taking in everything that he could see. By the time they were halfway down the stairs, a set of lights in the basement automatically switched on.

The space beneath the barn was huge. It was composed of cinder block walls and concrete floor, with a fifteen-foot-high ceiling, and long racks of equipment. Anton was amazed at the array of equipment. There were NBC and Ghillie suits, personal communication rigs, packs of dehydrated rations, water purifiers, combat armor, edged and blunt handheld weapons and long racks of military style guns. Peter led Anton between the racks, pointing out the equipment as they walked.

"Milkor MGLs are over here, next to the fire-retardant blankets and anti-smoke/gas rebreather masks."

"I've used the MGLs before," Anton noted. "What rounds do you have for them?"

"The usual. Silver flechettes, standard high-explosive shaped charge, thermobaric and unarmed training rounds."

Peter grabbed a pair of buckets, labeled M67 training grenades. Handing them to Anton, he said, "We'll need these later."

They came back down the other side of the rack. Anton read the labels on the equipment packing the rack: plastic explosives, detonators, live grenades, and rows of Heckler and Koch 416 assault rifles, and the larger H&K 417 Recon rifles.

Peter walked past the rifles and picked up a single H&K VP9 pistol and a couple of spare magazines loaded with 9mm rounds.

"I haven't seen that gun before," Anton said.

"It's very accurate."

"Don't we need two?"

"Nope, just one will do."

Anton stopped walking. "I have a sneaking suspicion about where this is going."

Peter raised his eyebrows and shrugged his shoulders. "I don't know what you mean."

"I haven't seen a gun in the last six weeks, and I hope that I'm not at the wrong end of target practice."

"Don't worry about it." Peter grinned wickedly and began ascending the stairs. "We'll mostly be playing around with the grenades tonight."

Peter and Anton picked up half a dozen variable lengths of five-inch rainwater downpipe. Someone had welded the pipes to foot-wide square steel plates.

Anton lifted one of the pipes and indicated the weld with a flick of his head. "Is this your work?"

Peter grinned. "Sure is. You know, everyone loves to practice their fighting skills, but someone has to know their way around a machine shop or absolutely nothing would work around here."

"I'm glad someone is looking after our gear."

"Thanks," Peter said and pointed to a location on the floor. "Now put that one over there."

Anton did as Peter asked, and moments later, they'd arranged the tubes in a wide circle around the barn.

"Okay, let's start," Peter directed. "Pass me a grenade."

Anton picked up a training grenade from a bucket and tossed it to Peter. He caught the grenade, dropped it over his shoulder, and kicked it with his heel. It flew in a loopy twenty-yard arc, dropping directly into a down pipe.

Anton burst out laughing and called out, "That's bloody awesome."

Dusting off his chest with his knuckles, Peter said dryly, "Stick with me kid, and one day, you too can be a certified genius."

Anton and Peter spent the next thirty minutes practicing trick shots with grenades. With each move, they would call out, "Three, two, one. Bang!" training reflexes to manage the timely throw of a grenade.

Peter clapped his hands together. "Time for some batting." He moved to collect grenades from the downpipes, putting them back into the buckets.

"Batting?" Anton asked, moving to help.

"Yeah. Stand over there," Peter directed, pointing to the middle of the barn.

Anton moved into position, surrounded by the circle of downpipes and the hay bale walls.

"Be prepared to Ramp – they will be coming in fast."

"Sure, okay, I'm—"

Peter blurred, a bucket tucked under one arm, he threw grenade after grenade directly at Anton. It was like a semi-automatic gun firing, there were three grenades in the air before the first one reached Anton.

Anton ramped, his hand whipping up to deflect the first grenade away. He swayed left and right, his hands blurring in front of him. Peter leaped into the air, throwing grenades straight at Anton. Anton stepped left, then back, then right, ducking and batting the grenades away. Landing, Peter ran out of grenades and came to a halt.

"Well, I started with twenty, how many are in the pipes."

"I counted fourteen in, and six out," Li observed.

Whirling around, Anton demanded, "Where did you come from?"

"Peter asked me to drop by about 9:30, he said you needed some extra motivation."

"Motivation?"

"Yeah. Next round of the game," Peter explained. He handing the now loaded H&K VP9 pistol to Li and picked up the second bucket of training grenades. "She shoots at you, while I throw grenades and we see how many you can get into the downpipes."

Li lined the gun up on the center of Anton's chest in a single smooth motion. He shivered, feeling sick to his stomach.

Anton took a deep breath. Li and Peter were watching him intently, both suddenly serious.

Get a grip, he told himself. *I've gotta deal with this, and better sooner than later.*

Anton grinned wryly. "Do me one favor, start with a grenade, and I'll ramp on that."

Li winked. "Got it."

Peter's hand blurred, and the first grenade flew toward Anton.

The H&K VP9 pistol barked, the bullet zipped through the space that Anton had just vacated.

The H&K VP9 had a fifteen-round clip. Li emptied the gun three times in the next ten minutes. After she'd fired the last round, there was a resounding cheer as all the grenades were in the downpipes.

Euphoria surged through Anton, and he grinned crookedly.

I'm back. I'm really back.

* * *

Francis handed Anton a hunting knife.

"The objective is clear," Francis declared. "Don't get caught. The rest of the team will be looking for you. You have an hour head start. Meet us back here in two days' time at sunset."

"What happens if I get caught?" Anton asked.

Francis frowned. "We send you straight back out for another two nights, and we start again."

"So, unless you like eating raw food and sleeping on the ground ..." Peter observed dryly. "You'd better get on with it."

Anton drew the knife from its sheath, turning it left and right. It gleamed in the early morning light, sharp and deadly. He replaced it back into its sheath and tucked it into his waist belt. He nodded. The force team had assembled in the forest clearing. Jay and Yvette both stood impassively, almost disinterested. Chiara looked back, her eyes twinkling with hidden thoughts. Peter and Li were both smiling like tigers about to go on a hunt.

Francis and Juliette would drive the van back to the safe house. They would be back late on Sunday afternoon to pick everyone up.

The rest of the team wore comfortable clothes and practical shoes. They carried small backpacks, filled with food, water, medical supplies, and other useful items. Anton had the knife, a pair of loose pants, a black T-shirt and was barefoot.

Five versus one, an hour head start, don't get caught … simple.

Anton studied the glade, it was deep in the White Mountain forest, a couple of hours slow drive from the safe house, there was an old, mostly overgrown track that disappeared deeper into the forest. It was the same territory that Francis had led him through during survival training two weeks before. He had a handful of ideas and options in mind for where to go and what to do.

He needed to stay hidden from just after eight on Friday morning to sunset on Sunday evening. He planned on not using the Ramp, it would be a marathon, not a sprint. Not wanting to give anything away, he jogged casually toward the overgrown track.

As Anton hit the edge of the glade, Peter called out, "Don't embarrass us by getting caught by tourists."

Anton called back over his shoulder, "Thanks, I'll keep that in mind."

"Just being helpful," Peter shouted.

Anton smirked for a moment as he ran, and then his smile faded. It was time to put some serious distance between himself and the team.

He moved onto the track proper, and in moments, the glade disappeared behind him. He accelerated his pace, narrowing his focus on gaining distance, and not leaving tracks. He considered his strategy as he ran. What would he have done if he was doing the chasing? Guard the water sources and wait for the target to show up. Water was a basic consideration for a sixty-hour stay in the forest. He didn't know if they would work as a coordinated team, or as sub-teams or singly. He knew that he would have to allow for any of those strategies.

The trees whipped past, and Anton made the most of his natural running ability to penetrate deep into the wilderness. He focused on using everything he'd learned from Francis nearly three weeks before about stealth and wilderness survival. With his mind buzzing with thoughts of what to do, Anton pushed toward the nearest mountain. The first hour flew past, and a single note from a gas-powered horn rang out far behind him.

It was time to mix it up. Anton changed course, making for a second mountain beyond the first.

The hunt had begun.

* * *

The waxing moon, just shy of being full, sailed on a river of night toward the horizon. Its pale light gleamed in the golden eyes of a Great Horned Owl. A mature female, her head rotated this way and that, watching the forest floor beneath her perch. She suddenly called out in high-pitched alarm, "Hoo, hoo, hoo, hoo, hoo." Then with a sudden movement, she spread her wings and swooped noiselessly away. Giving her territory to another predator who glided over the forest floor in near perfect silence.

Chloe Armitage, dressed in matte black combat fatigues, walked smoothly into the open glade. She paused for a moment in the center of the clearing. Listening carefully and sniffing the air. She stared at a mass of branches and leaves. Anton's camouflaged lean-to was directly in front of her. Anton's breathing was quiet, his heart beat slow and steady. His smell was distinctive and familiar to her senses. It was clear he'd been living and sleeping rough for more than a day.

Chloe had been in the forest for hours. She'd discovered the positions of five other Ramp initiates. She whispered, "I've found you but what are you doing out here?" she tilted her head quizzically. "Is the Mirovar force team hunting you? Hmmm, not quite. No, you're in training."

The nearest member of the Mirovar force team was more than six miles away. Too far away to help if Anton should scream. Chloe frowned, her eyes darkening. She whispered, "But why should you scream?"

She took a step closer to Anton's lean-to. She stared hard at the rough shelter. Anton lay beneath the branches. His chest slowly rising and falling. Hard muscle curving across his shoulders. The moonlight dappling his dark hair. He'd grown since the Boston docks. He was stronger, more powerful. Her nostrils flared, the scent of him was delicious. Ancient urges stirred in the back of Chloe's throat. A warm tingling rose from low in her body, filled her chest, and flared into urgent desire.

Chloe found herself on her knees, inches away from the edge of the lean-to. The air vibrated slightly with each of Anton's breaths. Her heart instinctively accelerated as she carefully and silently picked at the lean-to. She separated the branches and removed individual leaves. Her actions were quick and precise. In moments, there was a hole a foot and a half across in the lean-to. The moon was behind her, its light streaming through the hole and falling onto Anton's chest. She gazed longingly at his smooth skin, luminous with life, rich with throbbing veins filled with blood, energy, and power.

Oh my God, I have left it too long since I last fed. She shuddered with need; her eyes widened. Her blue eyes, dark as the ocean in the moonlight. Her fangs descended into their attack positions. Her left hand snaked forward through the hole and hovered over Anton's throat. Her thirst was a torrent. She could feed on him now. The beauty of his life, so rich and abundant, so succulent, so tempting.

Chloe's hand descended to an inch above Anton's throat. The warmth of his flesh radiating like a furnace. Her senses, alight and roaring in response to the life force she could feel within him. Desire sang through every fiber of her being. An urgent need to feed rushing through her. An exquisite agony that stormed and raged through her soul.

Her hand trembled slightly, she shuddered again, drawing in a quick breath. She had almost no time left before her thirst would overwhelm her.

Chloe stared at Anton, her eyes filled with intense purpose riding over rampaging need, she whispered passionately, "Crane is my enemy. Crane ordered the murder of my parents. Crane is my enemy."

Anton stirred, frowning in his sleep.

She exhaled a slow sigh. Her hand moving instinctively, sliding her index finger over Anton's cheek, from the edge of his full mouth to the corner of his right eyebrow. Her skin tingled with the touch, a current flowing from Anton, through her hand, and deep into her body.

Chloe blurred backward to the center of the glade, her eyelids fluttering, her mouth an open circle. She shivered with unfamiliar terror and desire. She shook her head once as if to clear it. Turning away from Anton and the distant Mirovar force team members, she faced decisively to the west. A distant flashlight flickered on the edge of her supernatural vision. Murder filled her soul, extinguishing all other lights.

"Tourists! What a dreadful fate! Dismembered by a bear!" she whispered harshly.

She vanished into the forest.

* * *

A quick seven-mile run and I will be back at the pickup point.

Anton ran at a brisk pace down a stone track, the late afternoon sun warm on his back. To his left, old growth forest composed mostly of red pine hugged the side of the mountain, to his right, open ground led to a cliff edge and a sheer drop.

I can use this track to cut past the glade and come in from the far side, I will be able to approach parallel with the vehicle access track. The rest of the team will be pulling back by now. We're going to crowd the pickup point. I will have to—

A shape blurred out from behind a thick tree trunk and tackled him hard from the left. The momentum of the hit carried both men to the cliff edge, pushing Anton into the open air. He reached back hard toward his assailant, but he deflected Anton's hand away. With nothing to hold on to, Anton began dropping down the sheer rock wall.

Surging fear ripped through him, freezing his mind. Fighting vampires armed with the Blue Dragon was one thing, falling helplessly was another.

His arms started flailing. Reaching wildly for the rock wall, his fingertips brushed over smooth rock which began to accelerate past him.

His fear morphed into rage. A diamond-hard light exploding behind his eyes. He ramped wildly. Time slowed to a crawl. His eyesight clarified, the rock wall a yard in front of him snapping into razor sharp detail. The rock face was smooth, his hands brushed over it, once, twice, three times without finding any purchase.

Beneath him stretched a long, deadly fall, hundreds of yards onto bare rocks.

A thin shadow appeared opposite his knees. A fine horizontal crack in the rock, rushing upward past him. There was a single chance. He punched forward with his right hand; his fingers hard and tight like a knife. They penetrated into the inch-high space to the end of the second knuckle. His body kept falling. Anton put everything into holding his grip on the rock face. Heat surged along his arm. His hand fixed in place within the rock wall. With a crack, he thumped into the sheer rock face. A jagged jolt of agony ripped along his arm, but his grip held.

Drawing a shuddering breath, Anton held onto the rock face with the four fingers of his right hand, he scrabbled about with his left hand for something else to hold onto, finding nothing.

"Damn it, you're still alive." Growled a voice above him.

Anton looked up.

Jay peered over the cliff edge at him. His face frozen with grim determination. He turned away and disappeared.

Anton glanced down and to both sides, the rock wall was almost completely sheer. The little hole he'd filled with his fingers, a rare imperfection. Footsteps approached, and he looked up. Jay launched a rock the size of a basketball directly at his head.

The stone rushed toward him with tremendous speed.

Anton ramped again, wild, powerful, fast. His left hand swept up, deflecting the rock harmlessly past him.

"Why won't you die?" Jay cried out; his voice filled with frustration.

"Jay, you don't want to do this, you're not a murderer."

A hard smile twisted Jay's face, and he snapped, "Don't speak to me."

"I know you think my grandfather murdered your mother."

Jay vanished, his voice lingering above the cliff edge. "I don't think it, I know it."

Damn it, he'll be getting more rocks or something worse.

Anton envisioned Jay returning with a thick tree branch. A solid branch would wipe him off the rock wall like a windscreen wiper cleaning off a crushed bug.

Jay reappeared at the edge, and a volley of rocks the size of oranges flew down at Anton. He ramped again, batting and deflecting, but his position remained horribly exposed, and the last stone got through his defenses, glancing across the side of his head. Pain flared through his skull, and he groaned loudly.

Jay laughed bitterly.

Yvette's voice called out from some distance away, "Jay, what's holding you up, we're running out of time."

Anton looked up. Jay's face was torn with indecision. He called out, "Jay, I'm not my grandfather!"

Jay's face hardened. "The Slaynes are murderers, you'll kill us all one day." He turned and moved out of sight. His footsteps ran down the track and faded into silence.

Blood trickled down the side of Anton's neck from the cut in his scalp. Since he couldn't do anything about it, he ignored it.

Anton looked around himself again. The stone wall above him was smooth, unscalable, there could be no escape that way. He looked below him, after a handful of seconds, he spotted another hole similar to the one he was holding onto with increasingly numb fingers. It was fifteen yards below him and about four yards to his left. He was beginning to lose his grip on the rock wall. He pushed with his left and swung back to get some momentum. Launching himself diagonally across and down the rock face, falling and twisting he struck out with his left hand and gripped the hole. He thumped hard into the rock wall with the left side of his body.

He flexed the fingers of his right hand, he had to rest them for half a minute before he could make his next move. As they recovered, he scanned the rock wall below him and spotted more handholds. He decided on his next move, twelve yards down and three to the right. He took it, leaping and catching the handhold and again thumping hard into the rock face.

He paused for a moment, breathing deeply. He could feel the blood running down his neck from the scalp wound. He took another huge breath; he could see his way out. Seven minutes later, Anton reached the bottom, bruised, sore, but alive. He judged the way back to the glade from where he was. He smiled, there was a way to sneak in from this angle that most likely remained unguarded. Jay had inadvertently done him a favor.

Anton took off his black T-shirt. Folding it diagonally, he made a rough bandage. He wrapped it around his skull, covering the cut on his scalp over his right ear. Pulling the knot tight, he loped off through the forest toward the pickup point in the glade.

Jay is going to be very surprised when I show up on time. But what on Earth am I going to do about him? He wants to kill me, even though he knows it's wrong. I've got to find a way to get through to him. I can't let this continue to fester, or one of us is going to kill the other one.

Chapter Three

Where are the homeless disappearing to?

By Ralph Crawley | Mercury Correspondent AUGUST 5,

Anecdotal evidence continues to mount that something is happening to the homeless of Boston.

We have empty rooms in our shelter, I have never seen that before, said Samantha Laney from the Lighthouse Center Homeless Shelter in a phone interview on Friday night.

Quite a few of the people that we normally help are simply no longer there, said Jordan Rumsey of the Boston chapter of Meals for the Needy in a phone interview Saturday morning.

There has been no increase in missing person reports, but we are continuing to monitor the situation, said Boston police spokesman, Harold Jacobs in a phone interview Saturday afternoon.

It remains to be seen if the homeless of Boston are simply moving on in search of better opportunities, or if something more sinister is occurring. Only time will tell, but whatever happens, it will be faithfully reported by this newspaper.

– Boston Mercury Newspaper article on the Internet.

* * *

Dorchester, Boston, August 6th, 23:00

It was eight weeks since Ramin Kain's meeting with Cornelius Crane, and just over a month since the arrival of the text message alerting him to the creation of a new coven of vampires in Boston.

Ramin had waited for the reports to begin. The rumors of missing persons on social media. The sober news reports of disappearances in the mainstream media and the hysterical accusations on the Internet of UFOs, alien body snatchers, vampires, bogeymen and government conspiracies. The atmosphere in Boston had taken a turn for the worse. There was an air of uncertainty. People would pause and hesitate. They would look a second time for a lurking danger. There was a loss of confidence. A reluctance to be out alone at night. A nervous fear of an unknown threat.

The fruit provided by Cornelius Crane had ripened and was ready to harvest.

Ramin glanced at his watch, it was an hour before midnight. He sat in the driver's seat of a nondescript, gray Ford sedan. A one-way dark film that made it difficult for anyone, man or vampire, to see into the interior covered the car's windows. Next to Ramin, sat Samuel Luther. They wore casual clothes, wrap-around light amplifying night glasses, and wireless headphone sets. Their heads slowly scanned left and right as they hunted for vampires in a neighborhood that was falling rapidly into ruin.

Ramin turned a knob on a black metal box sitting on the dashboard and inquired, "Did you hear that?"

"No," Sam averred. "Wait … yes, what is it?"

"Digging! We need to move."

Ramin kicked over the engine and took off slowly. Gently accelerating, he drove about four hundred yards before pulling to a stop at a crossroads. He turned the knob on the box again, listening intently.

"We got em."

The box displayed coordinates in green writing on a small LED screen.

Sam entered the numbers into a program on his smartphone and declared quietly, "They're half a mile from here."

"They could notice the car. We'll leave it here and approach on foot," Ramin directed. He killed the engine and punched a button to unlock the car's trunk.

Ramin and Sam exited the car and circled around to the back. Ramin opened the trunk, revealing an extensive cache of equipment. They put on broad-brimmed hats. Strapped swords at their waists. Fitted Glock 9mm pistols loaded with silver bullets at their belts, and put on long dark coats to hide all the weaponry. Sam picked up a solid black case and Ramin softly closed the trunk. They turned as one, crossed the road and headed off down the street.

Five minutes at a brisk pace put them two hundred yards short of their target location. They slowed down to a gentle walk. They wore stealthy padded-soled boots, their clothing was neat and tidy, with their equipment held close to their bodies. They moved with barely a rustle along the deserted street.

Abandoned houses and derelict apartment blocks littered the street. The flotsam and jetsam of a decaying suburb. Only one in three street lights still functioned, their wan yellow light barely illuminating the sidewalks beneath them.

Ramin went to put his foot down and suddenly halted. Pushing backward, he maintained his balance. Sam sidled up behind him. Ramin stepped around a handful of spray paint cans and a black tote bag lying on the sidewalk. He studied the wall briefly, an unfinished graffiti mural of ghosts rising from tombstones covered half of it.

Not half bad, Ramin thought. *Too bad you picked the worst place in Boston to practice your art.*

Ramin turned to Sam. He pointed at the artwork on the brick wall and then at the cans, before silently making a two-fingered stabbing motion at his throat.

Vampire attack!

Sam nodded. Frowning, he looked at a map displayed on his smartphone. Lifting his right hand, fingers stiff, he pointed across the street toward a large five-story apartment block. The target building lay shielded by a thick line of trees and a row of shorter two-story buildings facing onto the street. The target was a hundred yards away. Beyond it was the Neponset River and an expressway. It looked like it would be a maze of rooms and a difficult target to attack.

Ramin continued forward, looking for a good location to stake out the target. He ducked down a side street that passed the near end of the target building. He jogged toward a water tower rising over the suburb. Ramin and Sam reached the base of the tower. They could hear the faint hum of the pumps. The water tower was still functional. They checked the ground-level entrance and a thick padlock secured the door. Ramin examined the padlock for a moment, the hint of a smile curling the edges of his lips. The tower could prove to be very useful.

Three yards to the right of the door, a weathered set of metal stairs started ten feet off the ground and snaked upward around the tower. Ramin glanced at Sam, nodded once, ramped and leaped up onto the stairs. Sam followed and in a handful of seconds they were at the top of the tower.

The location was perfect. The top of the water tower was fifteen yards across, surrounded by a four-foot-high parapet. In front of them squatted the derelict five-story apartment block. Behind them was the expressway, running with sparse, late Sunday night traffic. The expressway bridged the Neponset River.

Ramin stared intently at the decrepit building. He was certain it harbored a fresh coven of newly turned vampires within its rotten bowels.

Sam placed the black case quietly on the concrete top of the tower and opened it. Inside was an array of high-tech surveillance equipment. Three minutes later he had a suite of sensors arrayed on the top of the parapet. In a handful of seconds, the microphones and spectrum analyzers had picked up noises in the depths of the apartment block, providing a visual representation of the noise locations on a small six by nine-inch screen. Sam twirled a knob and the image on the screen resolved into ghostly human forms. Metadata appeared next to the forms in small red letters and numbers that read, 'Sub-37 Vampire.'

Ramin whispered, "Map it."

Sam nodded, adjusting the equipment. A minute later he packed the equipment carefully back into the case. They descended the water tower with gentle steps and crept away.

A quarter of an hour later they were driving toward New York City, all their equipment stowed in the car's trunk.

"They're burying their victims in the basement," Ramin observed sagely. "We've found four vamps."

"Definitely four," Sam agreed.

"It's a big coven. We haven't had a find like this for over a year."

"You're a genius RK." Sam gushed. "Where would the Order be without you?"

"Quite so, Sam. If everyone had the wit to see it your way, my job would be a lot simpler."

"Who will you send?"

"Mirovar, it has to be Mirovar's team."

"It's about time they did something useful."

"Yes, Sam – quite so – it is time for them to do something useful."

A slow smile crept across Ramin's face as the car rushed away from Boston.

* * *

Ramin Kain locked the front door of his Manhattan penthouse. He glanced at his watch, it read 04:04. He rubbed his forehead, sighing deeply. It had been a long night driving back from Boston.

Kicking off his boots, he walked in his socks to a climate-controlled cabinet. He opened it and spent half a second making a decision. He selected a vintage Shiraz, pulled the cork and poured himself a large glass of wine. He went to a long lounge and sat down in the middle of it. Sniffing the wine deeply, he took a full mouthful, swished it around in his mouth and drank it down. He sighed again and drank a second mouthful. Setting the glass aside, he lay back on the lounge and opened his smartphone.

The old bloodsucker should still be awake. He dialed Cornelius Crane's smartphone.

"Ramin Kain," Crane answered, his voice carrying the barest hint of interest. "To what do I owe the pleasure at this late hour."

"I've found the Boston coven, and I will use the Mirovar force team to wipe them out."

"And this matters to me?"

"I am willing to provide you with the exact time of the attack by Mirovar's team."

"Indeed ... and what will this information cost me?"

"Nothing at all, this is pure mutual advantage. We both need Mirovar out of the picture. He is a thorn in your side and an embarrassment to me."

"Go on, is there anything else."

"Anton Smith, he is a favorite of Mirovar and a born troublemaker. He has to go."

"The boy who was at the Boston dock, why him in particular?"

"He's dangerous, he loves Mirovar and will take everything that Mirovar stands for forward. They both have to go at the same time. With them out of the way, I can disperse the rest of the Mirovar team amongst force leaders of proven loyalty, and the virus of Mirovar's traditionalism will die out."

"Ramin, I'm surprised. Surely you can clean your own house without my help?" Crane observed sardonically.

"This is not a matter of house cleaning," Ramin retorted.

"Then what is it?" Crane inquired; his voice laced with curiosity.

"Smith! ... Juliette Mirovar has given him sanctuary."

Crane laughed. "Oh, well, that does change things. Why did she do that?"

Ramin rolled his eyes and snapped, "Hell, I don't know. A moment of madness?"

"Well, he is out of range now, touch him, and you touch her. More than half the Order would be baying for your blood. She's a legend in her own lifetime," Crane noted, chuckling wickedly for a long moment.

Ramin scowled, drinking another mouthful of Shiraz, suddenly the wine tasted sour in his mouth, he grimaced and swallowed it quickly.

"How long would you last?" Crane asked rhetorically between chuckles. "What? Less than twenty-four hours I would think."

Crane burst out laughing.

The bastard. The fucking bastard.

"Can't we focus on the deal?" Ramin growled bitterly.

Crane continued to laugh as if captured by some great mania.

Ramin fumed as Crane slowly regained his composure.

"Okay, okay ... you've come to me to sort your problems out," Crane observed dryly, his voice filled with delight.

Ramin sighed, he knew this part of the deal was going to hurt.

"Shutdown your operations in the northeast, pull everyone back west of Michigan and south of Illinois."

"That's too much!"

"You can do this without me?"

Ramin paused for a long moment, thinking furiously about how he could sell such a large loss of territory to the rest of the Order. A desperate plan came to mind. There would need to be a rebuilding phase. A tactical withdrawal to consolidate forces after the tragic and untimely loss of Francis Mirovar.

Ramin's eyes widened. "I agree to your terms."

"Then, we have a deal. However, I will offer you a caveat."

"Yes?"

"Bring me the head of Arthur Slayne, and I will grant you back your territory."

"Done," Ramin snapped eagerly.

"Indeed – we have an agreement, now to tactics."

"I will send you details of the attack once they're known," Ramin said. "I will be in a position to directly tip off your forces."

"I will provide you with a quantum address to use to send messages to my praetorians," Crane instructed.

"Agreed."

"We're done. Goodbye Ramin," Crane declared, hanging up the call.

Ramin smirked, and declared to the empty room, "Well, that was expensive, but I'll be rid of Francis Mirovar and Anton Slayne. I can disperse the rest of the Mirovar team throughout the Order."

Ramin leaned back on the lounge and proceeded to finish the bottle of Shiraz, dreaming of consolidating control of the Order of Thoth within his hands. His desire for power and control was so fierce that he could taste it. He reached for a remote, and flicked a switch, a moment later, the crystal-clear sounds of Beethoven's Ninth Symphony, fourth movement filled his penthouse. He waved his hands to the music as if conducting an Orchestra, careless of the half-filled glass of red wine in his right hand.

Vintage Shiraz spilled across the carpet. Ramin, his eyes closed, swayed in silence, drunk on his ambitions.

* * *

Cornelius hung up the call and chuckled again.

He hadn't laughed like that for decades. What an ass Kain was. Such a temporary little man filled with vainglorious ambition.

Cornelius leaned back in his chair and stroked his chin. Kain was desperate over something. It had to be something critical to him to put a whole force team at risk. Was it about the boy from Boston? Kain had tried to hide the introduction of the assassination of the boy as if it was an afterthought – clearly, it wasn't. He'd worked up to the boy, asking for the lesser thing first. In fact, the boy's death was more important to Kain than Mirovar's death.

Why would Anton Smith be so important to Kain?

Cornelius considered his options. He reached toward a panel on his desk and flipped a switch. "Ursula, please place a call to Centurion Rawlings, I will need three praetorian sniper teams for insertion into Boston at short notice."

"Yes, Sir," his secretary responded immediately.

Cornelius grinned wolfishly. Here was the perfect opportunity to take out the whole of the Mirovar force team in one operation. It would balance the ledger after the losses at Boston. With surprise and tactical awareness of the ground on the side of the vampires, victory would be swift and certain. Kain had clearly failed to understand the shift that had occurred after the delivery of the Slaynes and the Papyrus of Hakron the Scribe. He'd warned Kain he had less to offer, but he hadn't adjusted his strategy.

Kain was a fool who expected the future to be like the past.

Cornelius was not willing to risk failure. He contacted his secretary again. "Wait, Ursula, ask Centurion Rawlings to take personal command of the mission."

"Yes, Sir, three sniper teams commanded by Centurion Rawlings, the message has been passed on."

"Thank you, Ursula, that will be all for tonight."

Cornelius pursed his lips, struck by a disturbing thought.

Anton Smith's secrets will die with him, but even a dead man's secrets can come back to haunt us all.

The uncertainty around Anton Smith remained unresolved. It nagged at his mind, draining his good humor at Kain's obvious discomfort.

Pushing back his chair, Cornelius stood up and stepped away from his desk. His gaze lingered on the array of books within his great library. He walked to the stacks, selecting one of his privately commissioned works. Over the centuries, he'd selected authors to write unique works. There would be a single copy, and he would be the sole owner. It was time to revise a masterwork.

Cornelius smiled grimly as he walked to his bedroom with 'The Discovery of Betrayal' by Sir Francis Walsingham, spymaster for Queen Elizabeth the First.

* * *

The early August pre-dawn light promised a bright day to come.

Anton walked to the training barn for the next session of physical conditioning. Juliette fell in beside him. She handed him a glass bottle filled with a dark brown fluid. Anton took hold of the bottle. It steamed lightly, stinking of rotting vegetables and burnt mushrooms.

"What is it?" Anton asked. Sniffing dubiously at the concoction. "I hope you're not going to ask me to drink it!"

"It's a restorative," Juliette asserted. She smiled, gesturing a 'bottoms up' motion with her right hand. "You've only had one night to recuperate from your long run. This will help a lot."

Anton scrunched up his nose. "It smells foul."

Juliette grinned. "It tastes terrible but is incredibly effective. Just drink it quickly."

Anton frowned for a second, shrugged his shoulders and drank the bottle to its last dregs. The fluid was hot, thick and sludgy, and a pervasive warmth began spreading out from his middle.

"Oh my God, that's disgusting!" Anton declared, handing the empty bottle back to Juliette.

Anton looked at his hands. "My fingers are tingling, is that normal."

"Sure," Juliette said, patting him on the shoulder. "That effect will only last a few seconds."

Anton shook his hands as if drying them. Licking his lips, he said with a shrug, "Yeah. It's gone now, and so is the taste."

"Excellent."

Anton moved to go into the barn where the rest of the team were limbering up. Juliette pulled him aside and said, "A quick word Anton, I just wanted to say that you have been progressing really well, which is great to see."

"Thank you."

"You know, you're much like your grandfather."

"Is that a good thing?" Anton asked doubtfully.

"Arthur Slayne was my teacher, he has skills that I haven't been able to master. He is an exceptional man, and the man I know is not a murderer. It is good that you take after him."

"You have a lot of faith in him."

"More knowledge than faith," Juliette said with a soft smile. She looked intently into Anton's eyes, speaking with quiet conviction. "Arthur Slayne is a great servant of the Order of Thoth. You have every right to be proud of him."

A long silent moment passed between them. She reached up, hugging him tightly, and whispered, "You'll be okay Anton, it'll all work out in the end."

Anton hugged her back, a soft warmth flowing between them. His eyes moistened. Letting her go, he stepped away, a crooked grin playing at the edges of his mouth. "I better get to training."

"Yes, Anton. That's best," Juliette agreed with a warm smile.

Anton walked into the training barn. He grinned broadly as he saw his teammates. A rush of euphoric joy exploded through his chest. They were all such great people, much more than friends, they were brothers and sisters in arms. He knew without a shadow of a doubt that he would rather give his own life than see any of them come to harm.

Anton looked at Li and really saw her beauty, grace, and wisdom. Peter was standing next to her, with his easy-going grin, courageous, generous and loyal. Jay, poker-faced, stood to the side, his mind sharp and fast like his sword work, a natural leader carrying a dreadful wound. Yvette, standing at Jay's side, lovely, purposeful, and protective. Chiara, next to Yvette, sensual, mercurial, and mysterious.

Anton's emotions surged, swirling around in a chaotic vortex.

I'm all over the place, why is that?

Suddenly his knees wobbled, the ground rose up to meet him, and his world faded to black.

* * *

Anton awoke into darkness.

It was pitch black. Someone had jammed cloth into his mouth and bound it there with gaffer tape. A thick hood completely covered his head. Strong hands dragged him across the yard. He could feel the gravel tearing at his feet. He tried to move, twisting and bucking against the powerful grips holding him. His feet and hands were bound with what felt like rope and try as he might he could not break free.

What the hell's going on? There are two of them, one on each side. I've got to do something quick.

Stilling the surging panic in his mind, Anton fell into silence. He tucked his feet under himself and ramped. Pushing hard, he jackknifed upward. The grip on his right loosened, his heart leaped with hope, but the grip on the left tightened like an immovable rock, and he crashed back to the ground. A third assailant grabbed his ankles, and lifted him aloft. Unable to gain purchase and leverage, his captors rendered him helpless.

Where is everyone? He screamed silently.

The trio carried Anton another thirty yards and threw him down. He expected to hit the ground, but there was nothing there. He kept falling for another couple of yards before crashing onto something solid. Sucking air into his lungs, the earthy scent of wet clay assaulted his nostrils. He thrashed about, the smell got stronger, a terrifying realization cut through him as he dropped out of the Ramp.

Oh, my God, I'm in a pit.

Something landed on his back. Shovels struck the ground above him, an unnaturally fast staccato rhythm. Great clods of earth fell on top of him, pummeling him like fists.

They're burying me alive.

More earth, clay, and soil landed on top of him. In moments, the weight of the soil became oppressive. He could feel the hood closing in around his face.

I'm going to suffocate. There is no time. I must break this rope!

Anton took a breath, the hood dragging in close to his nostrils. He knew it was his last breath inside the pit. Closing his eyes, relaxing his muscles, his heart slowed. Silence rushed into his mind. Cold silvery fire surged from a point three inches in front of the base of his spine and arced along his limbs. He rested deeper into the silence. Time gave way, slowing down as his mind accelerated to a level he'd never reached before. Energy flowed through his body. His skin tingling as power coiled like a thousand forged springs tighter and tighter. He relaxed further, and terror fled. There was only the present moment, the pressure of the earth above him, and the power of the Ramp.

Anton flexed, energy unleashing like a bolt of lightning throughout his body.

There was a thunderous crack, like a shotgun firing next to his ear – something had broken.

His hands and feet were free.

Staying deep within the Ramp, power flowed, inexhaustible and pure. He pushed hard against the earth, and the mass of soil above him rose up. He scrambled in that split second where the earth and clay, seemingly ignoring gravity, floated above him. Getting his feet beneath him, he kicked as hard as he could. Reaching up he pushed through the loosened earth. He struck out blindly, his right hand reaching the lip of the pit, his fingers clawing into the gravel and clay. A moment later, his left hand went past it and found purchase as it dug into the ground. Surging violently upward, the soil above him flew into the air as he burst out of the pit.

Dragging off the hood, he ripped away the gag. He landed in a half-crouch on the familiar gravel of the yard, facing away from the safe house. His eyes blazing, his nostrils flaring, sucking in air, he whirled around.

Anton's heart froze.

"Oh, no!" he moaned in anguish.

* * *

It was deep night, a full moon sailed high overhead. A single light globe over the front door of the safe house competed with the moon to illuminate the yard.

In front of the safe house, Li, Peter, and Chiara lay in pools of blood, surrounded by their weapons. Peter had the tail end of a crossbow bolt jutting out of his forehead, his face unrecognizable beneath the gore. Li and Chiara lay face down on the gravel, their clothes bloodied and torn.

Beyond them, stood two praetorians in full combat armor and tactical helmets. Their mirrored visors were down, cruelly reflecting the broken bodies lying on the ground. They were carrying FN P90 submachine guns, and swords strapped to their waists. The smaller of the two praetorians fired first. The submachine gun ripping into life, smoke issuing from its barrel in gray blooms as each round cracked through the night.

Already fully ramped, Anton twisted his right side back, watching the first rounds fly past. The vampire responded by tracking his movement. Anton blurred forward veering to his left, tracers and bullets zipping through the air on his right.

He ran to where Li lay face down in a pool of blood, the Green Dragon lying naked next to her. Voiceless rage flooded through his soul like a freight train from hell. Moving instinctively and beyond all reason. He cartwheeled over the Green Dragon, picking it up and throwing it at the vampires in a single motion.

The Green Dragon gleamed in the sparse light. A silvery whirling shaft of edged death spinning toward the vampires like a divine scythe. It cut through the gun smoke which eddied and swirled around it. The praetorians violently fell away to the left and right. Blood splashed in the grim light. The blade clipping the taller of the two vampires on the shoulder.

The wounded vampire recovered immediately. He dragged his weapon up, stepping forward he fired at Anton. The second vampire regained their balance, running further to Anton's right, straight-arming their submachine gun and firing single handed. Bullets were flying at Anton from both directions. He leaped, tumbling and rolling past where Peter lay. Peter's sword and battle axe were on the ground, dropped from his dead hands. Positioned between the vampires, Anton picked up both weapons and threw them in opposite directions at the same time. The shooting stopped as the vampires dodged aside. Anton blurred to where Chiara lay face down on the gravel, scooping up her sword in a single fluid motion as more bullets began to whip past him.

With Chiara's sword in hand, Anton blurred forward in an arc, ending back near the pit. The move put the smaller of the two praetorians between the other vampire and himself. Advancing upon the closer vampire, he realized from their body shape that they must be a woman. She dropped the empty FN P90, swiftly dragging out her sword. Anton pressed his attack, he only had a moment to defeat her before the second vampire repositioned to attack with gun, blade or both.

Ramp and rage combined, barely holding back a storm of grief. Anton couldn't think the words, 'Li is dead.' He hurled himself forward, silence flooding his torn mind like a tidal wave through a broken dam wall. Power surged through his body, Chiara's sword moving so fast it was barely visible. The vampire retreated, blurring backward, her sword dancing, blocking, parrying – defending with everything she had – it was not enough. Anton lunged through her defenses, his strike piercing through her sword arm, her blade flying away from suddenly nerveless fingers.

She took another step backward, her arm coming free from his sword. Anton stepped forward, his blade blurring again, lunging straight for her heart. She started a desperate, madly defensive open hand parry of the sword blade.

A second blade caught his sword in a shower of sparks, the two blades pushing up, high into the air. The other praetorian was between them, his armored fist flashing forward, expertly catching Anton on the side of his head.

Thrown to the side, Anton fell once more into darkness.

* * *

Anton snapped awake to icy cold water splashing on his face. He was lying on the bare ground of the training barn floor. He blinked for a moment, his eyes stinging from the freezing water and the sudden glare of the overhead lights. Wiping his face once with his hand, the horror came back with a rush.

Li is dead! The thought ripped through his soul.

His heart skipped a beat before razor sharp claws of outraged grief shredded it.

Not again.

He blinked, something big moved above him, shadowing his face from the lights, it resolved into a familiar form.

"Peter?!"

"Hey, Anton," Peter greeted him, grinning broadly.

Anton leaped to his feet and whirled around. Li and Chiara were standing side by side in torn clothes soaked in blood. They looked at him with concern written all over their faces. Peter grinned at him; his face edged with traces of blood as if he'd given it a half-hearted wipe with a wet towel. The back six inches of a crossbow bolt stuck out from the front of his forehead. Under the bright lights, Anton could see the thin, flesh-colored straps holding the bolt to Peter's head.

Francis stood opposite Peter; his face impassive.

For a long moment, Anton was speechless, his mouth opening and closing like a beached fish. His emotions swirled and roiled before relief won through and he pushed past Peter, hugging Li for all he was worth.

Li hugged him back, sweet silence filling the spaces between them, and he whispered, "Oh my God, please never do that again."

"Never, I promise," Li whispered back.

Anton let Li go, turning to face Francis he stated with quiet intensity, "A test?"

"Yes."

Anton sighed. He knew that he just had to deal with it. Whatever was necessary to take down Chloe Armitage, the Vampire Dominion and especially – Cornelius Crane.

Anton asked curtly, "Did I pass?"

A faint smile curled the edges of Francis' mouth. "That remains to be seen."

Anton shook his head. "Juliette gave me a drug, didn't she?"

"Yes," Francis agreed.

"It wasn't a restorative?"

"Correct. It was a psychoactive compound that makes it easier for you to believe in what you are seeing. The effect has worn off now."

Anton bit back a snark-filled comment. He took a deep breath, released it and said, "Okay. Okay, I get it. I'm the new kid, so this is just typical stuff that everyone has to go through."

Anton looked at the faces around him, they were quietly shaking their heads; even Peter was frowning, his face speaking volumes.

"Your kidding – this was just for me?" Anton asked incredulously.

"Anton," Francis explained calmly. "You're a special case, we had to do—"

"I'm a special case?" Anton interrupted, his efforts at remaining calm starting to fray.

Francis put up his hands and shook his head. "Yes. Few people are switched on with the pressure point technique. Everyone else here has over a decade of training and are well known to us, you're not."

Anton stared at Francis. "C'mon Francis, you know me! I'm not keeping any secrets, I'm an open book."

"I believe in you, Anton, but I don't know you fully. We had to test you before you go into combat with the team."

"I can fight."

"That's clear Anton, but that's not the question."

"What's the question?"

"Will you keep your head—"

"While those about me are losing theirs?"

Francis nodded. "Precisely."

Anton realized that Francis was worried about him cracking up under pressure.

"Now please take off your shirt," Francis directed, indicating Anton's clothes with his right hand.

Memories of Gang hitting his chest to switch on his Ramp capability flooded Anton's mind. He took off his shirt and was surprised to discover a dozen white dots the size of his thumb, stuck to his skin. They had tiny red lights in their centers that blinked steadily with the beat of his heart. He was starting to get the picture. He sighed and asked expectantly, "You had me wired?"

"Monitored," Francis corrected. Moving in, he peeled the dots from Anton's skin.

"Turn around please."

Anton turned, and Francis collected another dozen patches.

"Done," Francis declared, tapping Anton on the shoulder. "Now have a shower, drink plenty of water and get some sleep, it's past two in the morning."

Peter clapped Anton on the shoulder, and said, "You aced it mate, nothing to worry about."

Anton gave him a dark look for a moment, then sighed. "What the hell. I'm starving."

"We have some pork fillets I picked up from the White Hill butchers this morning."

"Of course," Anton looked hard at the traces of blood on Peter's face, "pig's blood?"

"Yeah. A couple of big buckets worth."

"I don't want to know," Anton noted. Reaching up, he ripped off the fake crossbow bolt, which came free with a snap.

"Hey!" Peter yelped.

"Suck it up, princess. I think you owe me one for this."

Peter laughed, pushing Anton playfully toward the barn door. Li and Chiara were already halfway across the yard with Francis. Anton and Peter followed them.

"Where's everyone else?" Anton asked.

"Jay and Yvette are getting patched up by Juliette," Peter observed.

"Oh," Anton grunted. "Jay's going to be pretty upset with me stabbing Yvette in the arm."

Peter shrugged his shoulders. "He knew the risks, he volunteered for the role."

"Probably enjoyed shooting at me."

Peter pulled Anton abruptly to a stop and declared firmly, "He's not allowed to shoot you. Remember the impact of the drug. They were deliberately shooting past you, just close enough to allow you to believe it was real. They both shed blood tonight to allow Francis and Juliette to test your responses under stress. I suggest you think about that."

Peter turned back to the safe house, and said with a lighter tone, "Let's get inside, I've a delicious Cajun spice that will be great with the fillets."

"Sure," Anton agreed, his stomach growling and his mind buzzing with thoughts. It was one shock after another. He felt stupid to allow himself to feel comfortable at the safe house. Could he trust Juliette and Francis? He had to, there was no one else. They would not have done something this extreme unless they believed it was absolutely necessary. The fact that they had done it said a lot about how bad the threat must be.

Anton stood still for a second. Struck by the question – *am I the risk?*

Nameless emotions overwhelmed him. He clenched his fists, then relaxed them, taking a couple of deep breaths. Peter was a step ahead, pushing through the front door and didn't see his reaction. He was suddenly very much alone.

Mom, Dad, Gang ... I miss you all ... I miss my old life.

* * *

Francis sat opposite Juliette in the briefing room. The doors stood closed and locked, ensuring they remained alone. Juliette's fingers flashed over the keyboard of her laptop, projecting a graph onto a white screen hanging on the wall.

"What have we got here?" Francis asked, frowning at the graph.

"It's extraordinary," Juliette declared, using a red laser pointer to indicate an early section of the graph. "Anton goes off the chart right here, when he's buried in the pit."

"Li confirmed that Anton was switched on by Gang on the fifth of May," Francis noted. "It's now the eighth of August, he's completed the physical transformations of the Ramp."

"This is more than physical transformation, there were over fifteen hundred pounds of soil on top of him, and he's pushed it aside like it wasn't there."

"Hmmm ... where does this place him relative to Order norms?"

"Top ten percent on a sustained basis, and top one percent on bursts."

Francis stared at his wife. "There is also the incident where he stopped Jay's fist in the first training session, what's that all about?"

"We don't know, and notice this," Juliette advised, replacing the graph with a video playing in slow motion. It was the point where Anton ran around Yvette to position her between Jay and himself. Even with the video running in slow motion, it was clear that Anton was moving visibly faster than Yvette.

"Yvette's got the best defensive sword skills in our team, and he cuts through them in the first engagement, if Jay hadn't intervened the test would have been a disaster."

"How is he doing it?"

"It's a very good question." Juliette displayed another graph. "These are his emotions, normally when ramping people get calmer, not Anton – not this time. Really strong emotion was flooding him. It's surprising that he wasn't screaming in a heap on the ground. I can't be sure what he was specifically feeling, the type of emotion is not measurable with our equipment, but given the context, I believe it was rage and grief, look at his face."

Another video replaced the graph. Anton's face stood frozen as he moved in slow-motion, his skin pale, his teeth gritted, his eyes fixed in an unblinking stare.

Francis watched the video play out in stunned silence.

"How stable is he?" he asked in dismay.

"I don't know. This is new, I've not seen anything like this before. It's not part of our Order lore. It looks like he has another way of doing a Ramp."

"A second way?"

"At least. Possibly more. Now, Anton's opened the door – who knows where it leads?"

An unsettling disquiet gnawed at Francis. "What happens if his emotions lead him somewhere else?"

"Anything could happen. He's unpredictable."

Francis sighed. "Yes, we will have to keep a careful eye on him."

"He reminds me of his grandfather," Juliette observed, then mused, "I wonder if there's a family trait, something that skipped a generation?"

Francis shrugged. "Unknown and probably unknowable."

"Honestly, Anton could become dangerous."

Francis nodded. "Very dangerous."

"It's a good thing he's on our side."

"Yes, very good. If we can manage him," Francis asserted doubtfully.

Francis and Juliette stared at each other for a long moment.

"Best invite him in," Francis suggested.

Juliette nodded. She pushed her chair back, stood up and opened the door leading to the hall.

Anton was waiting on a chair outside.

"Please come in, Anton," Juliette invited with a warm smile.

Francis thought to himself, *how best to phrase this? Hmmm, emphasize the positives, yes, that will do it.*

* * *

The supreme art of war is to subdue the enemy without fighting.'

Well, that would be a nice trick wouldn't it, Anton thought sourly.

Anton was resting on the wooden porch seat next to the front door of the safe house. It was late evening with the sun close to setting, and long shadows stretched across the yard. He was finding it hard to focus fully on what he was reading, still mulling over the meeting with Francis and Juliette that morning. He put down Francis' worn copy of Sun Tzu's, 'The Art of War,' and replayed the meeting in his mind.

I was right about it last night. They're frightened that I'll crack up under pressure.

Anton shook his head, a slow burn of indignation oozing through him. *That's crazy, I didn't lose it in Boston at the warehouse or on the docks. They know that I can fight, they were clear about that, no problems there, but I'm too emotional, they're not sure if I'm ready for combat operations. They think that I'm a risk to myself and the team.*

Anton shook his head again; it wasn't making any sense.

Francis made a special point that I haven't mastered water – does it really matter, I'm getting faster and stronger, and my skills have really improved. I'm sure I'm ready, but how do I convince them of that without having a chance to prove it in combat?

Something caught his eye, and he looked up. Sunlight glinting off metal flashed again. A car was coming down the lane leading to the safe house. Anton stood up to see what it was. A familiar silver Bentley sedan emerged from the trees surrounding the mouth of the lane, and rolled smoothly over the gravel, before pulling to a stop in front of the porch. Anton's guts tightened, his eyes narrowing as he stared at the car. Ramin Kain and Samuel Luther exited the sedan and started walking toward the safe house.

Anton prepared himself to Ramp at a moment's notice, keeping a careful eye on both men as they walked up to the front door.

Kain took off his sunglasses, catching Anton's gaze. A smooth smile spread across his face. "Mr. Slayne, I hope that you're ready for battle tonight, the Order needs you."

Anton did a double take. He was unwilling to trust a word that came from Kain's mouth, but his heart leaped at the thought that there was a chance to prove himself against the vampires. He stayed silently impassive as Kain shrugged, stepping past him into the safe house. Luther followed, giving Anton a cold glare and a grin that wavered between a fake smile and a snarl.

Before the front door could swing shut, Anton dashed forward, following the men into the main hall. They had already veered left into the briefing room, and he caught the edge of the conversation as he approached the doorway.

"—of four vampires," Kain explained.

"That's a sizeable coven," Francis observed. "The Vampire Dominion usually don't let that many vampires operate in the same location, so I presume they're young and haven't been there for long."

"They're new, but their existence was obvious."

Anton watched Francis stare at Kain for a long moment. Francis' eyes flicked over to Anton at the doorway, he frowned and directed, "Anton, please go find Jay and send him in, and close the door as you go."

Anton nodded, Francis, Kain, and Luther watched him as he pulled the door shut. He wanted to stay and listen to what they said but frowned briefly as loyalty overwhelmed his curiosity. He dashed up the stairs to the first floor. Walking up to Jay and Yvette's room, he knocked on the door. There was a brief rustle and steps approached from within the room.

Opening the door, Jay looked at Anton and asked brusquely, "What?"

"Francis wants you in the briefing room, Ramin Kain and Samuel Luther are here."

Jay smirked and said, "That must have been fun for you seeing them again."

Anton stepped back to allow Jay to get through the doorway, and said as Jay pushed past him, "There are vampires."

Jay's demeanor immediately shifted, a stillness came over him, a smile curling the edges of his mouth. He glanced at Anton and said, "Good, I'm getting sick of nursemaiding you."

The two men stared at each other for a second, before Jay turned away and strode down the hall.

Something stirred on the edge of his vision, and Anton looked back into the room. Yvette was lying on top of the bed, dressed simply in jeans and a white T-shirt. Her long coppery hair lay in a loose fan on the pillows. Her left forearm resting across her flat stomach was bound with a white bandage. She regarded him with curious blue eyes, quizzically arching her left eyebrow.

"Yes?" she asked.

Anton nodded toward her forearm. "Sorry about that."

"That's okay, the training was necessary," Yvette replied calmly.

"Oh, good." Anton nodded. "I'll be on my way then," he stated, pulling the door shut.

Maybe they're starting to get used to me being here, Anton thought as he walked back down the hall to the stairs. He needed to retrieve the book he was reading from the front porch, and wait and see what eventuated from Francis and Kain's meeting.

* * *

Francis, Juliette, and Jay, sat opposite Ramin Kain and Luther around the oval table in the briefing room.

Jay listened carefully as Ramin used his smartphone to display a video filled with ghostly images onto a white screen hanging on the wall.

Ramin said, "We caught them burying their kills in a basement beneath an abandoned apartment block." He locked gazes with Francis and declared, "The mission is clear, you must assault the site and kill all the vampires. There are four hostiles, you will need every available member of your team to ensure that none escape and you minimize the risk of casualties."

"Thank you for your concern," Francis said, a faint hint of irony in his voice. "But the last time I looked, I was in charge of the tactical disposition of my force team, not you."

Luther frowned sourly, Ramin smiled thinly and said, "Of course Francis, I was just making the point that the site is littered with tactical difficulties. As Head of the Order, I fully recognize your authority over your own team, I only seek to assist by providing the benefit of my detailed knowledge of the target environment."

Juliette leaned forward slightly and inquired, "How did you find these vampires?"

"He's a genius," Luther blurted.

Juliette inclined her head and said dryly, "Well, of course, he is. That makes all the difference."

Ramin's eyes flashed darkly for a split second. "I track Internet chatter and news feeds. The signs are obvious if you know what to look for. The mood in Boston has taken a turn for the worse, and the presence of a coven of vampires was a simple conclusion."

"Simple," Luther stated, glancing knowingly around the table.

Jay sat quietly to the right of Juliette and Francis, and opposite Luther. He kept his expression neutral while he wondered why Ramin put up with such a sycophantic prat like Samuel Luther. While admittedly arrogant, it struck Jay that Ramin was an effective and capable leader of the Order of Thoth.

"This is getting us nowhere," Francis observed, frowning. "We need a full copy of your data for analysis."

"Of course," Ramin agreed. He handed a data stick over to Juliette who placed it next to her laptop.

In moments, the data transferred across. Juliette scanned her screen and nodded. She pursed her lips and said, "It's a beast of a site." A 3-D schematic of the building projected onto the wall screen and rotated around its midpoint axis. "Five long floors above ground, and one below. At night, vampires could leave from any direction. This should really be a daylight raid to ensure they don't escape."

"Impossible," Ramin declared. "It has to be at night, we can't risk exposure of the existence of the Order."

"Our rules of engagement are clear," Luther declared pompously.

Juliette shook her head slowly. "It will increase the risk that one or more vampires will get away."

"That is why you must take everyone you have," Ramin observed sagely. "Including your novices, Li Wu and Anton Slayne, they have already proven their worth in Boston. They will allow you to close this mission out successfully."

Francis and Juliette glanced at each other, a silent question passing between them. Juliette nodded, and Francis declared, "We will take the mission, and we will commit our whole team."

Francis leaned forward, turning to Jay. He commanded, "Jay, prepare everyone for a raid – we go to Boston tonight."

"Yes, Francis," Jay responded, rising and striding from the briefing room. He mused to himself as he strode up the stairs to where the team members were resting, *maybe Slayne will make some newbie error and get himself killed – one can only hope.*

* * *

The dark-gray van stood in front of the safe house. Its engine idled as the Mirovar force team prepared for combat.

The team members were all dressed in combat fatigues. Slashes of dark grays and browns suitable for blending into an urban environment at night dominated their clothing. They wore hoods, belts, and webbing to hold a multitude of edged weapons and submachine guns. They checked each other's gear and climbed into the van.

Peter pushed his kit bag into an overhead locker and declared loudly, "Someone's gonna get spanked for making vampires, it's well known that Crane hates unsanctioned vampire creation. It's suicide for a vampire to do it."

"So why would any vampire do that – surely, they know the rules?" Li asked, taking her seat in the back. The Green Dragon resting in its scabbard between her legs.

Anton sat down in the seat next to Li. "I suppose we'll never know."

Peter laughed. "We usually don't spend much time chatting with them – maybe we'll make an exception tonight just for you Li."

Li stared at him, and Peter grinned as he stepped back out of the van and got into the driver's seat.

Chiara, Jay, and Yvette filed into the van, taking seats opposite Li and Anton.

Jay leaned forward and whispered, "Hey newbie, Kain insisted that you be a part of this mission, so please do us a favor and don't get us all killed."

Anton stared back silently. *Bastard!*

Jay leaned back; a smirk just visible on his face for half a second. Then all business, he opened a small case. He extracted five sets of tiny earbuds and handed them around the team. "Put these in your ears, you'll have secure comms and still be able to hear everything around you."

Anton put the earbuds into his ears.

There was a short hum as they booted up, powered by his body heat.

"Okay everyone, listen up," Juliette stated over their earbud comm links. "I can see that everyone is hooked in and green across the board. I will be conducting net overwatch from the safe house. I will be in the background monitoring the Panopticon feeds, providing situational awareness and blocking identification by the Vampire Dominion."

Anton looked across at Jay and asked, "You've hacked into the Panopticon?"

Jay pulled out his earbuds, leaned forward and snapped, "It's not all about you Slayne. We had missions before you showed up, we didn't sit around with our thumbs up our butts. Of course, we've taken action to disrupt the operations of the Panopticon."

Anton leaned forward, pulled his own earbuds out and snapped back, "Right! I got it."

Both men sat back against the walls of the van. Jay re-inserted his earbuds, and Anton followed suit.

The comms system came back online, and Juliette inquired briskly, "Jay, Anton, are your earbuds loose, you both dropped out for a couple of seconds."

"It's all good Ma'am," Jay responded quickly.

Anton's lip curled, and he said, "Yeah, we're good Ma'am. Ready to go."

The van moved off toward Boston. Francis directed from the passenger seat next to Peter, "Okay team, game faces on. We have good intel on a coven of four vampires operating out of an abandoned apartment block in South Dorchester. The target building is next to the Neponset River and the Southeast Expressway. Anton and Li, you're new, I want you working with Chiara throughout the operation. Stick close to her and stay out of trouble. Jay and Yvette will form the second team, and Peter will work with me. I will spell out the details of the mission and assess contingencies as we drive there. So please pay attention as there will be no time for repeats. Is that clear."

"Yes, Francis," the team chorused together.

Anton looked around the van, there was a palpable sense of tension and excitement within the team members.

Just like a championship game.

Anton loved it, he'd been waiting for an opportunity to kill vampires since Boston, and now it was here. Energy snapped and crackled along his nerves and excitement flooded his soul, but from the back of his mind, from a place beaten into existence by recent traumas came a voice of caution, *take care, Kain hates me. For some reason, he wants me dead, and he insisted that I be on this mission tonight. Gang believed that Kain is colluding with the Vampire Dominion. Where did these vampires come from? They're so close to the safe house. Of course, it would be the Mirovar team that would deploy.*

Anton looked at Li. She put her hand out. He reached across and gripped it. She stared at him for a long moment in the dim light in the van, smiled softly and nodded.

Yes, we'll fight them together, but I'm keeping my eyes open, it could be a trap.

* * *

Chloe Armitage's smartphone pinged.

She glanced at the screen. There was a message from the Raven, the Red Empire agent within the Mirovar force team. The message read, 'Ramin Kain has ordered an attack on a vampire coven in Boston. The whole of the Mirovar force team will be engaged tonight.' A date-time stamp, and a set of GPS coordinates followed the message.

Chloe opened her laptop and logged into the Panopticon. She entered the GPS coordinates into the Panopticon's map system and examined the site. She opened a Panopticon sub-system and retrieved a list of the current whereabouts of the praetorians. The system listed seven as en route to Boston from Crane's Citadel.

Chloe recognized the names and said quietly to herself, "Three sniper teams and Centurion Rawlings. Crane already knows about this operation, and he didn't invite me – I'm cut to the quick."

Chloe used the Panopticon to make further checks. A military satellite would be over the site in three hours. Whatever was going to happen, the satellite would record it with high quality broad-spectrum cameras, but no sound. The clock on her laptop displayed 21:11.

She thought quickly. *General Clayton Maze will be watching me like the faithful hound that he is. Crane is suspicious, and with all the overwatch, a helicopter is out of the question. A hire car is cutting it fine to be there on time, but a hire car will have to do.*

Chloe prepared a long, black duffel bag with some recently imported gear, including an electrically heated body suit. She looked across to a finely crafted wood stand that held the Red Dragon in its scabbard. The priceless katana retrieved by the praetorians from the Mystic River and returned three months past.

"Not tonight my thirsty friend," she stated with a wistful smile. "You're a little too recognizable."

She reached for two shorter blades of Red Empire design, flourishing them with practiced ease before placing them into the bag with the rest of her gear. Zipping the bag closed, she hefted it easily over her left shoulder before picking up her car keys and leaving the penthouse.

She descended in her personal elevator to the parking garage in the building's basement. She'd long ago fixed the internal camera on the lift to a continuous loop that hid her current activity. She opened the bag.

Beginning with the close-fitting powered body suit, she fitted her disguise. The lift reached the basement, quiet excitement stirring within her.

Filled with intent, she mused silently, *time to go hunting.*

In the parking garage below Chloe's penthouse, the Panopticon recorded a car hired to a Mr. Jason Harcourt, drive out of the building at 21:15. Mr. Harcourt appeared to be just under six feet tall, wearing a long dark coat, and a broad-brimmed hat that hid his face.

He had a long, black duffel bag on the car seat next to him.

* * *

Cornelius Crane sat alone. He was at the head of a long table, in his most secure command room on the 103rd floor of his Citadel. Unlike the operations center on the same floor, he'd dedicated the war room to the most secret operations of the Vampire Dominion. Multiple screens depicting direct feeds from the Panopticon, as well as views from the helmet cams of the seven praetorians engaged in the current mission dominated the opposite wall.

Cornelius sat in perfect stillness. He ignored the screens, his mind far away, contemplating the threads of probability that ran through the next few hours of his life. In his experience, short term prevision was the most accurate. He confirmed for himself that victory remained highly likely, bordering on a certainty. He checked that his generals in the United States, Clayton Maze, and Chloe Armitage, would have no impact on the outcome of the mission. Both showed dark lines, indicating zero probability to influence events. His prevision confirmed his expectations of his generals. They remained unaware of his secret mission against the Mirovar force team.

There remained a low probability line, glimmering just above darkness, passing through the Mirovar force team leading to his own death. He expected tonight's engagement would extinguish that line forever.

Cornelius dropped out of his previsionary meditation. He leaned forward slightly, pressing a touch screen built into the top of the table, he opened up a single, secure comms link.

Looking back up at the main screens, he inquired, "Centurion Rawlings, are your men in position?"

The Centurion responded with a crystal-clear voice, "Yes, Sir."

"Confirm your tactics."

"We have triangulated the site; two of three teams can cover each approach."

Cornelius checked Rawling's words against the Panopticon feeds displaying real-time satellite and drone data on the wall of screens.

"Good work, Centurion."

"Sir, we're waiting for the Order team to arrive."

"Expect a vehicle, such as a van," Cornelius instructed, glancing at the clock, it was nearly midnight. "Expect them to arrive within the hour."

"Yes, Sir. Once we have a clear shot, we will take them out. We will catch them in a crossfire from at least two SAWs and two sniper rifles."

"Wait – allow the Mirovar force team to engage with the vampires in the apartment block first. They should not exist, and if any are still alive after you have destroyed Mirovar and his team, kill them all."

"Yes, Sir. Anything else?"

Cornelius declared without hesitation, "No, Centurion. Nothing, except good hunting."

"Yes, Sir." Centurion Rawlings responded enthusiastically.

The line automatically muted itself. Cornelius sat back, steepled his hands in front of himself and focused on the screens on the far wall.

Now it is time to strike a blow against the Order of Thoth, he thought with quiet, confident anticipation.

Chapter Four

BODY

- -

SHADOWSTONE, PSYOPS DIRECTORATE ANALYSIS REPORT, FINAL ANALYSIS

- -

COUNTRY: (U) UNITED STATES (USA)

SPECIFIC OBSERVATIONS AND RECOMMENDATIONS:

A. (O) THERE HAS BEEN INCREASED CROSS MEDIA REPORTS OF PARANORMAL ACTIVITY SINCE THE LAST REPORT.

B. (O) THE BOSTON INCIDENT OF JUNE 11 THIS YEAR HAS PRODUCED HIGH LEVELS OF CONSPIRACY IDEATION.

C. (R) THAT TACTICAL OPERATIONS AVOID HEAVY WEAPON USAGE IN URBAN AREAS UNTIL CURRENT CONSPIRACIES OF WEREWOLVES, VAMPIRES, ALIENS, AND SECRET GOVERNMENTS HAVE BEEN DISCREDITED.

D. (R) THAT ADDITIONAL PSYOPS RESOURCES BE ALLOCATED TO ONLINE INFORMATION SUPPRESSION AND DISRUPTION UNTIL MEDIA REPORTS OF CONSPIRACY RETURN TO THEIR FREQUENCIES PRIOR TO JUNE 11.

~~TOP SECRET/FGEO~~
RQ
#5404

NNNN
CLASSIFICATION: ~~TOP SECRET~~, SECRET

– Content from a partially declassified Shadowstone PSYOPS analysis report.

* * *

South Dorchester, Boston, August 9th, 00:30

The dark-gray van slowed to twenty-five miles per hour as it crossed into South Dorchester.

A wary, nervous energy shadowed Anton's excitement at the impending raid. He worried about the possibility of a trap. He didn't want his new friends and teammates to get hurt or killed. Taking a deep breath, he sighed noisily.

"What's up?" Li asked, patting his thigh.

Balancing the Blue Dragon on the point of its scabbard, Anton nervously flipped it from hand to hand. "I just have a feeling this is a trap."

Li's hand paused on his thigh. She leaned closer, frowned and asked, "A trap. How?"

Jay sitting opposite Anton, overheard. Tilting his head quizzically, he declared, "A trap! The only people who know we're here are members of the Order of Thoth. What are you saying – there's a traitor in the Order, someone who would sell us out to the vampires?"

Anton shrugged his shoulders.

Jay rubbed his face with his right hand, and stated incredulously, "I can't believe I'm hearing this. Who are you to question us? You're not even a member of the Order. Why are you here? You don't belong—"

"Quiet!" Juliette commanded over the comm links.

"Ma'am?" Jay responded. "But—"

"You heard me. Focus on the mission."

"Yes, Ma'am," Jay agreed flatly, his eyes flashing with controlled anger.

Anton stared at Jay, and thought to himself, *keep calm, Juliette is right. Don't let Jay get under my skin before we go into combat.*

Anton leaned forward so that he could see out the windscreen of the van at the streets they were passing through. They almost lay completely deserted. They passed one corner where a trio of young men faced each other in a huddle.

Is that a drug deal going down? A couple of miles away are four vampires, and those guys are oblivious to what is happening.

He shook his head cynically.

Juliette directed, "Commence stealth operations, no talking unless absolutely necessary. Jay, please pass out the night glasses and ensure that Anton's and Li's fit perfectly. GPS logs indicate there is still vehicle traffic along the streets near the target building so we can approach closely without seeming out of place. You're twelve minutes to the drop off point."

Anton leaned back, stilling his nerves. He closed his eyes, his right hand on the Blue Dragon. His left resting on top of an FN P90 submachine gun loaded with a fifty-round magazine of high-velocity silver bullets.

Only a few more minutes, this waiting is the hard part, he thought silently to himself.

* * *

The late summer night was warm and sultry. The waning moon was pushing up into the night sky. A light breeze, occasionally gusting, matched the patchy clouds that drifted languidly across the sky.

The vampire adjusted his squat position behind the parapet of the water tower. From where he crouched, he could see a black van parked three hundred yards away on his left, up on the near edge of the southeast expressway overlooking the apartment block. His commander, Centurion Rawlings, and the Alpha team were in the van. Their position allowed them to cover the whole of the south and west sides of the target environment.

He scanned the north and east approaches, the night was alive with silvery moonlight, and soft shadows fell everywhere. There was a background hum from the laboring machinery of the pumps beneath his boots. Rustles, drips, and knocks drifted up on the cool, night air. He sniffed, there was a trace of the unmistakable stench of rotting corpses emanating from the apartment block. His mouth twisted into a sneer. He hated untidy vampires with a passion and considered the coven below to be nothing but low life scum he should eradicate like vermin.

As he squatted behind the parapet, he wondered who was stupid enough to violate King Crane's edict against vampire creation. He stared at the apartment block. The whole situation remained a mystery to him. Every vampire alive knew it was certain death to create another vampire without the express approval of King Crane. They all knew the praetorians and the generals would come for them and that there could be no survival against the military elite of the Vampire Dominion. And yet, the coven existed, and had apparently done so for months.

The vampire shook his head slightly, mystified by the circumstances of the mission. He scanned the approaches again, there was no sign of the approaching Order force team.

He opened his tactical comms link, and reported, "The northeast approach is still clear, Sir,"

"Roger that Beta One," Centurion Rawlings replied. "Keep your eyes open. We're expecting a dark-gray van. I'm broadcasting an image."

"Yes, Sir," The praetorian scanned his heads-up display. An image of a dark-gray van appeared. It rotated through three-sixty degrees and displayed the number plate. There would be no mistake made in identifying the vehicle. "Image received, Sir."

The comms link returned to silence.

Beta One hungered for revenge. He relished the thought of slaying the Order operatives who had killed so many praetorians in the recent battle at the Boston docks. He sighed, wishing they could simply drop a two-thousand-pound bomb on the site and be done with it. But the directive to only use personal weapons had come from Crane himself, and the vampire had not survived the last century by disobeying the king's orders.

Beta One's .50 caliber sniper rifle sat next to him, and his spotter, Beta Two, kneeling two yards away, carried a standard issue M249 light machine gun with an uprated two hundred round drum magazine. The two vampires of Beta team stared at the north and east approaches to the nearly deserted apartment block and waited for the Order team to walk into their carefully prepared trap.

* * *

Jay lifted up his open hand, thumb and fingers taut.

Five minutes, Anton thought to himself, adjusting the fit of his new night glasses. They appeared to be simple, wrap-around sunglasses, with an elastic strap around the back of his head to fit them securely to his face.

He leaned forward, looking out the front windscreen at the boarded-up buildings, and deserted streets. The night glasses provided by Jay amplified and filtered the available light, making the world appear as if it was still early twilight. They passed three cars, stripped and burnt out, standing in a line like a skeletal parking lot. The street lamps were a uniform sickly yellow. More than half stood shattered, leaving pools of deep shadow, resting like lesions on the asphalt and concrete.

The urban landscape breathed desolation and decay like a bloated corpse lying in an open sewer.

Anton shook his head with wonder, and thought, *how did Kain find these vampires? Important vampires don't live in slums.*

He remembered Gang Wu speculating that Kain had a deal with Crane. A deal for throw-away vampires Kain could find and kill for show.

And yet I'm here despite the risk this is a trap, as Kain insisted that I be on this mission. Anton pursed his lips, *and anyway, I jumped at the chance to prove myself.*

A digital clock on the wall of the van read 00:44. The van started to slow down.

A tight wariness surrounded Anton like a blanket, it didn't matter to him if it was a trap, he would fight anyway. There was no going back, there was nowhere to go back to. There was only the team, he pushed away his concerns and focused on the mission – killing vampires.

* * *

The two praetorians of Gamma team heard the approaching van before they saw it. They repositioned to the northeast corner of the two-story building, standing between the five-story apartment block and the north side street. From their position, they could create a crossfire with the Beta team on the water tower, but they no longer had visual contact with Centurion Rawlings and the Alpha team in the black van on the southeast expressway.

The vampire smiled as he watched the dark-gray van approach, it matched the visual image Centurion Rawlings had supplied ten minutes earlier.

"I have visual on the target vehicle, they're coming down the street from the east," he reported. His tactical helmet comm links broadcasting to the other two teams of praetorians surrounding the apartment block.

"Copy that Gamma One," Centurion Rawlings stated. "Maintain visual contact and keep reporting. The damn Panopticon can't see them. An Order netmaster is blocking it."

"Beta team should be able to see them any second," Gamma one declared. "Damn, the windows are covered in a reflective material – I can't see inside."

"Hold your position, Gamma one. Maintain visual contact and allow them to engage the vampires in the apartment block."

"Yes, Sir."

The two praetorians in Gamma team assumed prone positions on the roof of the two-story building, keeping their weapons trained on the slowly approaching van.

* * *

The lightly thrumming pumps of the water tower hummed in the darkness. Ramin Kain crouched next to the second-floor window overlooking the northeast approach to the apartment building.

Earlier, he'd shrunk backward, when two fully armed praetorians had mounted the stairs spiraling around the water tower. They hadn't noticed him, his presence masked by the background noise of the nearby pumps, and the heavy-duty construction of the tower's walls. He'd sighed with relief as they passed him by, moving to the top of the tower.

He adjusted the fit of his Order night glasses and stared at the northeast approach. He checked his gear as he waited, his sword was ready, and his Glock 9mm remained loaded with silver bullets. He didn't expect to use his weapons. No one knew where he was. Even Cornelius Crane would only know that he was able to view the site, but would not know precisely where he was. If he had to use his weapons, it would only be to save his life and would mean that his mission had almost certainly failed. He checked his smartphone and ensured that it was on full silent mode. He returned it to his chest pocket. He'd used it fifteen minutes before to send an image of the Mirovar force team van to the praetorians, using the quantum address provided by Cornelius Crane.

A thin edge of fear hovered in the background. Ramin took a slow deep breath and wished for the arrival of the Mirovar force team. He stared through the window, there was a glimmer of street lamp light reflecting off painted metal.

It's the van, they're here, he thought excitedly.

A dark-gray van paused at the mouth of the lane way as if teasing him. All it needed to do, was roll forward about a hundred yards, and it would pass directly in front of the water tower. A perfect position for an attack from above. If not taken there, the van would loop around an abandoned parking lot, and past the main entrance of the apartment block.

Please come down this side, he begged whatever gods might listen.

With his breath passing through gritted teeth; Ramin waited in nervous anticipation for the murder of Francis Mirovar and Anton Slayne to begin.

* * *

The van rolled to a stop. Everyone inside waited in silence for the spectrum analyzers mounted on the front dashboard to scan the target building.

Francis' voice came in over the comm links, he stated, "We have them, four hostiles and two civilians. They're on the ground floor. They've probably just hunted and are now about to feed. We need to move fast if we're going to save those two people."

Juliette reported, "There is heavy counter-cyberwarfare occurring, the window of coverage of the Panopticon on site is not more than fifteen minutes and could be less."

Jay got up, moving to the back of the van. He opened the rear doors and jumped lithely out onto the street. Yvette followed him, they carried swords, and FN P90 submachine guns.

Chiara nodded at Anton and Li, and directed softly, "You two with me, stay close."

Anton and Li followed Chiara out of the van and onto the street. Yvette and Jay were already on the move, walking stealthily along the sidewalk toward the apartment block. Chiara signaled with her hand, running across to the near wall of a two-story building, Anton and Li quickly followed her.

Francis' voice came over the earbud comm links, he ordered, "Our targets are currently in the middle of the building on the ground floor. There are building entrances out the front and on the back corners. Team one, Chiara, take the northwest corner. Team two, Jay, take the northeast corner. We will move the van to the front of the building. That will attract their attention and then you will hit them from behind on my command."

"Yes, Sir," Jay murmured.

"Yes, Sir," Chiara whispered.

Anton carried his FN P90 low, as he fell into position, jogging lightly just behind Chiara and next to Li. He'd slung the Blue Dragon across his back, the handle jutting up over his right shoulder so that he could easily draw and slash in a single movement. Now he was moving, the nervousness fled. He grinned, a pale-yellow street lamp momentarily illuminating their faces and giving them all sallow, jaundiced looks.

"Time for some karma," he whispered.

"Cut the chatter," Juliette broadcasted over the comm links.

Absolutely, Anton thought to himself. He shifted gears, lifting the intensity of his focus and plunged into silence.

In the distance, a stray dog barked dolefully. A breeze rallied into a gust, sending a half-crumpled coke can scuttling along the laneway, and the team froze for a moment before proceeding on.

Chiara led them past the two-story building, through a stand of trees, and along a path to the far corner of the apartment block. To their left, Jay and Yvette positioned on the near corner. The van trundled toward the front of the building, disappearing past the edge of the apartment block.

* * *

Someone laughed heartily in the gloom.

Dillon Browne exulted with unrestrained bloodlust and power. He flicked a wall switch, and the overhead lights came on. He enjoyed seeing the food realize what was really happening to them. Huddled together in front of him, were a young woman wearing gold hot pants, a silvery mesh halter top and impossibly high platform shoes, and a thin young man with a waxed mustache, wearing a dark brown pin-striped suit.

Dillon blurred forward, taking the young woman by the jaw and lifting her upright. Her dark eyes were wide. Wet mascara ran in dark streaks down her cheeks. She tried to lean away, moaning with terror. The thin man, backed away, his shiny black shoes tapping on the cold linoleum of the floor, his head whipping around like a child's toy. Caleb Moore loomed behind him; the thin man froze, his eyes darting left and right, a thin line of spit hanging from his bottom lip.

Dillon's eyes flicked left and right toward Aaliyah Williams and Ethan Jones, he nodded toward the thin man.

He watched as Caleb's hand lashed forward, grabbing the man on the left shoulder, holding him fast. The thin man whimpered, trembling with fear. Aaliyah grinned, baring her fangs. Ethan snarled like a wild animal, his long canines gleaming in the overhead lights.

Dillon twisted the girl around, holding her tight, forcing her to watch what was happening.

She screamed, a full-throated, high-pitched, keening wail.

Dillon clapped his left hand over her mouth. Pulling her close, he declared mockingly, "Hush now, that sort of noise could wake the dead."

"Wait!" the thin man pleaded. "I can get you things, I can get you anything."

Dillon laughed, and the other vampires joined in.

"I can bring you people, boys, girls, anyone you need," he said. His eyes darted desperately from face to face. "Please, just let me go." Pointing at the girl, he declared enthusiastically, "There are plenty more just like her."

Dillon's mouth curled into a grin and he asked derisively, "Do you think we need your help?"

"Everyone needs he—"

Dillon's free hand blurred forward. A straight razor slashed across the thin man's mouth, cutting deeply through both cheeks. The thin man squealed; his tongue split in two wriggled obscenely. Blood began streaming down the sides of his chin to splatter in fat drops on the floor.

"I don't like big mouths," Dillon observed flatly and nodded again.

The three vampires attacked, tearing the thin man to pieces. Blood sprayed wildly. The vampires latched onto body parts and greedily sucked on the open arteries. The thin man's entrails fell to the floor where the vampire's feeding frenzy kicked them around.

The young woman looked on. Dillon clasped his hand tightly over her mouth, muffling her screams. Above his hand, a look of horror overtook her eyes, like an eclipse of the sun, all hope vanishing into eternal darkness.

Dillon could feel the young woman's heart beating like a bird trying to escape its cage. Lust to feed rose within him. He leaned her head to one side to expose her neck, his canines descending into attack position. He started to rear back his head for the final plunge forward when he jerked to a sudden stop.

Dillon looked around for a moment, his ears wiggling as he searched for what had disturbed him.

"There's someone out front," he hissed.

"Huh?" Caleb grunted, dropping a leg torn off at the hip.

"It's a van pulling up outside, get your guns," Dillon ordered with a snarl, holding the young woman tightly in front of him.

The vampires pulled out MAC-10 submachine guns and turned to face the entrance of the apartment block.

* * *

"Stow your guns, there is still one human left alive – swords only," Francis commanded.

Grinning crookedly, Jay slung his FN P90 over his shoulder. Drawing his katana, he looked at Yvette who had done the same. They stood opposite each other at the northeast side entrance. One door hung half off its hinges, and the other was gone completely. Before them stretched a long corridor, unlit except for a pool of light close to a hundred yards away that flooded from a large room into the hall.

"Four hostiles and one civilian are still in the main room in the middle of the building," Francis whispered over the comm links.

Jay nodded once, standing ready to enter the ground floor of the apartment block through the side entrance.

"Go!" Francis commanded.

Jay sunk into an immediate ramp, blurring through the entrance and down the long hall. Yvette ran beside him, her naked sword held above her left shoulder.

They reached the lit area and burst into the main room. Opposite them were four vampires and one terrified girl. The vampires were already whirling about, raising MAC-10 submachine guns. The girl began to shriek, thrown hard through the air toward Jay and Yvette by the vampire who had held her. They both moved to dodge her, Yvette veering left, while Jay went low. He put his left hand down and started to slide underneath the girl's body, angling his sword away to the right to protect her.

9mm rounds started flying as the vampires opened fire. Yvette cursing in alarm as she twisted violently and blurred away.

Jay's left foot ran into something slippery, and he lost purchase on the linoleum. He watched in sudden horror as blue and gray-white pieces of gut looped around his foot and he slid on his hip through a puddle of blood and human entrails toward a pair of vampires, one a hulking brute of a man and the other a snarling gangster.

His mind raced as he struggled to regain his balance, *where the hell is everyone else?*

* * *

Centurion Rawlings watched the Order van pull to a stop outside the front entrance of the apartment block. Two men leaped from the van, equipped with slung submachine guns and drawn edged weapons. They blurred toward the building as gunfire erupted inside. He checked his Panopticon feeds, the van was not visible, hazed into invisibility on his screens. The rest of the site was in view. His teams clearly marked on the screens with steady red stars.

"Gamma team reposition to cover any escape."

"Yes, Sir," Gamma One responded.

"Beta team, prepare to engage with crossfire on the kill zone between the van and the building. We'll get them as they exit."

"Yes, Sir, we're ready!" Beta One replied enthusiastically.

"Watch my mark Beta team, I will open up with the minigun, and I want both of you firing from your position."

"Yes, Sir," the praetorians of Beta team chorused together.

Centurion Rawlings slid the side door of the van to the left, exposing a gap a yard wide facing the apartment block. He hefted the Dillon Aero M134D-H minigun and pointed it directly at a point halfway between the Order van and the entrance of the building. His ears twitched as gunfire stuttered in the lobby of the building. He expected the Order would soon win the little battle inside the building against the worthless trash vampires. He grinned broadly, all he had to do was wait, and a whole Order force team would soon cease to exist.

He was supremely proud to be the instrument of their execution.

* * *

A bellowing laugh split the air.

Anton rushed into the lit room. Chiara and Li fanned out to his left. In front of him, a female vampire charged toward Yvette, who was dodging 9mm gunfire from another vampire near the entrance.

He took another blurring step, twisting to his right. Looming before him was a huge vampire holding Jay a foot off the floor by his throat and his right wrist. The vampire's shoulders bunched, preparing to tear Jay apart. Jay's face twisted in agony and horror, his body spread-eagled, his feet thrashing as he attempted to break free of the terrible grip. His one free hand, blurring forward, again and again, to beat at the hand at his throat.

The vampire holding Jay bellowed again, his laughter booming through the room like thunder.

Anton drove the Blue Dragon through a short, deep arc. The big vampire's head toppled forward as bright red blood fountained into the air. His body crumpling to the ground, dragging Jay with him in a tangle of arms, legs and spraying blood.

Snarling, the second gangster vampire leaped forward, somersaulting over Anton's head, striding momentarily along the ceiling as he lined his MAC-10 up on Anton's head.

Anton's Ramp went wild, he twisted, blurring to the left, as the vampire's MAC-10 billowed gray smoke just above him and a line of bullets raked the floor. Linoleum puffed upward, and blood splashed as stray bullets ripped into the headless body of the huge vampire.

The vampire landed, his gun running dry. Turning, he fled.

Anton started to run after him. A gleaming axe tumbled past his shoulder, shearing through the back of the vampire's head before embedding in the wall. The vampire flopped to the ground, twitching, and jerking. He pulled to a halt, twisting back to face the room. Peter and Francis rushed through the open front doors.

To his left, the female vampire wailed once, falling silently to the floor.

Yvette stepped past her body, flicking her katana clean.

Everyone evaded as another volley of bullets raked the room. The final vampire's MAC-10 clicked on empty, and he cursed loudly, "Fuck you—"

Francis beheaded him from behind with the White Dragon. His body slumped to the floor, his head rolling to the nearest wall. Blood gushed forth in a spreading red pool from his neck.

In the sudden silence, Jay pushed the big vampire aside and stood up, vampire blood dripping down his face. Breathing heavily, rubbing the red, raw marks on his throat, he declared in disgust, "I'm covered in this shit!"

Jay stared at Anton for a long moment. His face clouded with strong emotion, then he broke eye contact and looked away.

* * *

"Less than ten minutes of Panopticon cover left," Juliette broadcast over the earbud comms.

"Quickly now, clear the dead," Francis commanded. "Li keep watch, Yvette help Jay clean himself up, and Chiara, check the girl."

Peter caught Anton's attention, nodding his head at the gangster vampire he'd killed with a throwing axe. They went to grab the body, and it twitched violently, starting to push itself upright.

"Damn!" Peter growled, twisting the skull and snapping the spine. His muscles bunched again, and he tore the head free of the body. Blood fountained from the headless body onto the floor.

"Make sure that you've got a true kill," Francis warned. He started dragging the huge beheaded vampire by his boots toward the front doors.

In less than a minute, Francis, Peter, and Anton cleared the room of the various vampire body parts. They lined them up on the ground, a handful of yards outside the main entrance to the apartment block. Sunlight would flood the south facing entrance at dawn, and the bodies would flame to ash in seconds.

They returned to the main room. Chiara was helping the girl stand on unsteady feet. She began hyperventilating and shivering, Francis stepped forward and waved a thimble sized vial under her nose. She immediately collapsed, Chiara, guiding her gently to the floor.

Francis picked her up like he was carrying a sick child and commanded, "Back to the van now! We can run past an emergency room and drop her off on the way home."

"Won't she remember everything that has happened?" Anton asked.

Chiara remarked, "No way. Not with a dose of 'Lethe.' She won't remember anything from the last twenty-four hours."

"Focus everyone, guns back on, keep your eyes open until exfiltration is complete," Francis instructed, striding through the doorway with the limp young woman in his arms. Jay a step behind him, his FN P90 held up, scanning the environment. Anton, Li, Chiara, Yvette, and Peter followed them, weapons up and on the lookout for any more hostiles.

The team exited the apartment block. They descended the front stairs where the bodies of the four dead vampires lay and headed for their waiting van.

* * *

The praetorian, call sign Beta One, sighted along his .50 caliber sniper rifle. The magazine held six rounds of high velocity, hollow point ammunition. He targeted the lead Order member carrying a young woman in his arms. He focused the crosshairs onto the center of the man's chest, a single round would blow a hole through the man's body that he could push his fist through without touching the sides.

Breathing slowly, he mastered his excitement. His spotter lined his M249 light machine gun on the center of the group of Order operatives behind the first two. The kill zone was only 150 yards away from the top of the water tower, almost point-blank range for their weapons.

"This will be a turkey shoot," Beta One whispered.

His spotter chuckled softly before whispering back, "Fucking A."

Beta One tapped his tactical communications link and broadcast, "Sir, I have the lead Order operative in my sights right now, ready to take the shot, waiting for your mark."

...

"Sir?"

* * *

Ramin Kain stared through his Order night glasses at the Mirovar force team as they exited the apartment block and made their way to the van.

Any second now, he thought, his mind seething with expectation, his fists clenching spasmodically.

One of the team members toward the back of the group looked up, directly at the top of the water tower, as if they had seen something that grabbed their attention.

Hell, one of them has seen the praetorians above me!

Hell, fucking hell, when will someone start shooting?!

Ramin's eyes widened as he watched the Mirovar force team walk into the sweet spot in the middle of the kill zone between the van and the entrance to the building. The one who had looked up, glowed in his amplified night vision, their body temperature rising rapidly.

They're ramping!

"C'mon!" he whispered with desperate urgency. "Kill them!"

* * *

Beta One sighted along his sniper rifle, let his breath out, waiting for the pause between heartbeats. The shot would be perfect; the lead Order operative was about to die. Beside him, his spotter was ready to simultaneously fire his M249 light machine gun into the mass of Order operatives in the middle of the kill zone.

Where's Centurion Rawlings? They're smack in the middle of the zone right now. Must be a communications failure, more Order cyberwarfare, his mind raced. *I'll have to take the shot.*

Beta One started to squeeze the trigger.

A searing pain burst from the base of his skull. A blood-drenched blade rammed out through the space between the bottom of his nose and his top lip. He shuddered, his nerveless finger trembling uselessly next to the trigger. The blade twisted to the right, before whipping down to the left, carving its way through his jaw, spine and a mass of blood vessels in his neck.

Whoever attacked him blurred away toward the spotter.

Beta One's body slumped forward, his helmeted forehead bouncing off the parapet before settling back down upon it.

A wet gurgle came from his right. Facing the parapet, he could just see the sole of one of Beta Two's boots. The boot twitched twice and then lay still.

He rested there, unable to move, his head barely connected to his body. Blood flooding from his throat pooled at his knees. Locked in a pose that resembled someone praying, he began the final death.

Before the eternal darkness claimed him, a vast regret for the failed mission washed through him. Behind the emotion rolled a wave of all-consuming nothingness.

* * *

Flicking the two Red Empire swords clear of blood, general Chloe Armitage shrank back into the shadows on top of the water tower.

She surveyed the area around her. The nondescript black van parked three hundred yards away on the southeast expressway brooded with a ghostly silence. Its interior painted with the blood of Centurion Rawlings and the Alpha Team praetorians. Recent memory flooded her mind. Flashing blades, punctured metal, and bloody flesh. The praetorians had died in silence. Their deaths so quick, they had no time to draw breath, let alone scream.

From where she crouched, she could see the squat two-story building between the apartment block and the street to the north. On its roof, lay the broken remains of the praetorians of Gamma Team. They had been the first to fall to her blades before she'd swung around the far side of the apartment block to take the vampires in the van from behind.

Chloe sheathed her short swords in their scabbards at her hip, pulling a dark Red Empire cloak around her. An assassin's hood covered her hair. A dark veil covered her face from the bridge of her nose down. Only her vivid blue eyes and pale complexion showed in a thin strip above the veil.

She sidled up to the parapet, glancing down at the Order van, the last door closed and it started to pull away. She watched it pass beneath her, rolling out into the street and disappearing from view. She waited until she could no longer hear the engine of the van, and the entire site lay reduced to the background noises of nature and the mechanical sounds of the pumps beneath her boots.

Chloe prepared to leave when something clicked unexpectedly beneath her. She looked briefly over the parapet, and the door at the base of the tower pushed outward. She stepped back from the parapet, her mind racing. Someone had been watching.

Her lips parted with a knowing smile. She wondered if she would be surprised by who the watcher was. She flipped over the edge of the far parapet and clung on to the outside of the tower. She blended into the shadows; her Red Empire garb perfectly suited to her needs. The parapet extended out from the tower by about two feet. With fingers like forged steel, Chloe hung onto the crevices between the bricks. Her core strength allowed her to hold her position flat beneath the parapet for as long as she needed. The external metal stairs gave slightly, as someone jumped up on them. As they advanced up the stairs, she scrambled silently around the tower and remained out of sight. She could hear his heartbeat, it was slower than normal, that and the ten-foot leap to the stairs told her that it was a Ramp Master approaching.

Chloe continued to scuttle silently along. Hiding in the thick shadows beneath the parapet, placing the tower between herself and the stranger as he ascended the stairs.

* * *

Ramin Kain stepped onto the top of the tower, faltering momentarily as he took in the scene.

He braced himself for a second on the parapet, then stepped forward, careful not to leave any marks of his presence. The first praetorian knelt upright. Face down on the parapet, positioned like a wax figure in a grotesque display. The nape of the praetorian's neck lay exposed, a blade had entered straight through the brain stem, before tearing out most of the vampire's throat. The second vampire lay spread-eagled on the floor, his heart separated from his chest and resting half a dozen feet away. Ramin skirted the pools of blood around the praetorians and made his way to the center of the tower's roof.

Whoever had done this, was very fast, stealthy, expertly skilled, and had taken the two vampires completely by surprise.

His scalp itched terribly. Ramin rubbed both hands through his hair beneath his broad-brimmed hat. He looked around, shocked, disbelieving what he was seeing.

"What the fuck happened?" Ramin whispered. His voice trembling, so much had hinged on this mission.

Ramin looked around again, his head jerking left and right. His night glasses gave him excellent night vision, but he could see nothing out of the ordinary, except for a brooding black van parked on the expressway and two corpses lying yards from him. He strained to hear anything, but there was only the silence of the night and the faint noises of the tower's pumps.

A shiver went up his spine, he was horribly alone and exposed. Whoever had slaughtered the praetorians could still be around. He pulled his Glock 9mm and drew his sword. A dreadful sense of malevolent eyes watching him shivered across his skin, but he could not see from where or by whom. He ramped, hard and fast. Blurring away from the top of the tower, he descending down the stairs in a flash to the ground below.

Ramin promptly disappeared north along the laneway to the streets of South Dorchester.

* * *

Chloe pushed herself away from the brick wall beneath the parapet, dropping lithely to the bottom of the water tower. For the benefit of any watching cameras, she sank into a deep crouch, before standing up. The drop was a decent jump for a vampire but a mighty leap for a Ramp master.

She stared at the fleeing form of Ramin Kain. Smiling beneath her dark veil, she whispered to herself, "The wicked flee when no man pursueth: but the righteous are bold as a lion."

So, you were watching, and now you are running away as if pursued by the devil himself. Well may you fear a pursuer but not tonight, for tonight you are safe. You and I will meet again and then you will discover a fate beyond the limits of your imagination.

Snorting once, Chloe shook her head. *This damnable heated suit is horribly uncomfortable, time for this fake Red Empire Assassin to disappear for good. After all, it is wise to never repeat a specific tactic.*

She blurred along the laneway to the north as if pursuing the fleeing Ramp master, and disappeared into the desolate slums of South Dorchester.

* * *

The van accelerated away from the accident and emergency entrance of the hospital and merged into the street traffic.

"All onsite cameras were offline for the drop-off," Juliette reported calmly over the earbud comm links. "We will have continuous cover back to the safe house."

"Good work everyone," Francis added from the front seat. "That's one more innocent life the vampires didn't claim tonight."

Relief surged through Anton, everyone had survived, not even a scratch. He'd been certain that there would be a trap, and he still had a lingering feeling of a narrow escape. He looked around the team, everyone sat relaxed in the van, comfortable, variously happy or calm, discussing the night's events and actions the way that victors do, with a natural confidence and ease.

He felt oddly out of place like he was looking at a big jigsaw puzzle and a single pivotal piece was missing. There was something, an idea or a notion, that was tantalizingly out of reach, just beyond the boundaries of his mind. He tried reaching for it, but it was like groping in pitch darkness for something that wasn't there.

The sensation of missing something became painful, and Anton remarked, "Wasn't that too easy?"

The team quietened down, and Francis replied, "I don't think so, Anton. Chiara, Li and yourself came in late, and Jay nearly died. We also didn't save all the people, there was one casualty tonight."

Jay tilted his head and asked, "Yes, what slowed you guys down?"

"What was your entrance like?" Chiara asked Jay.

"Our doors were shut," Li noted. "We didn't open them until Francis gave the call to go."

Yvette nodded and reported, "Ours were off their hinges, we had a straight path in."

"That's enough to account for the gap," Francis observed.

Anton frowned, sighed and stated uneasily, "Okay, there's a tactical issue there, but apart from that, it felt too easy. It still feels too easy, like there's something missing."

Francis directed, "Anton, we will debrief in full when we get back to the safe house, see if you can clarify your thoughts by then."

"Boojums?" Peter remarked from the driver's seat.

Anton shrugged and frowned.

Jay caught Anton's gaze and grinned tentatively at him.

Anton leaned forward slightly in the gloom of the van's interior.

Jay put his right fist up in a lazy loop. Anton did the same, and they gently fist punched.

Jay leaned forward and said contritely, "You saved my life tonight. This doesn't change how I feel about your grandfather, but I understand that you are not him. I apologize for how I've treated you; it was horribly unfair."

An intense wave of relief washed through Anton, and he replied, "No problem, forget it."

Jay looked at Anton quizzically for a moment, whispering tightly, "I tried to kill you."

Anton grinned crookedly. "Well, you're not the only one."

"You're taking it well."

"Jay, I'm just glad we're on the same side."

Jay nodded and declared, "For sure, we're on the same side."

Finally, some progress, Anton thought.

* * *

The Raven strove to understand the night's events.

They had seen the break in the silhouette of the parapet along the top of the water tower. The Raven was sure it was two praetorians, armed with a sniper rifle and a light machine gun. The Raven had ramped without breaking stride. Their senses going into overdrive just as a new figure appeared from the shadows on the tower top. Cold metal had gleamed for a brief instant in the moonlight, and then the slaughter had begun.

The action on top of the tower was over a moment later. The figure shrinking back into the shadows. The Raven had breathed in the night air, letting it out slowly, allowing their Ramp to die to a cool ember. The two short swords, cowl, and long cloak were unmistakable; the figure had been a Red Empire assassin.

The rest of the team had not noticed the fight, their attention elsewhere at the critical moment. As no one else had reacted, it was obvious that only the Raven had seen the two praetorians and their mysterious killer. The Raven was shocked, what were the praetorians doing there in the first place? Did they know about the mission? Or were they simply staking out the coven, waiting for any members of the Order to arrive?

Anton, Li, and Jay had talked about the mission being a trap. Anton had proposed the idea and Jay had dismissed it, but it had turned out that Anton had been right.

An uncomfortable feeling of disquiet crept through them as they considered what had happened. Anton was quite insightful to see a trap which everyone else had dismissed. The Raven added it to the list of odd abilities that Anton had. The hard defense that broke Jay's hand and his wild speed under desperate conditions. One day Anton may have enough awareness to see through the Raven's disguise.

The Raven shook their head gently, beset with uncertainty. The mission had been a trap. There were two options. The first was that the Vampire Dominion had created the coven as bait, and then the praetorians had staked it out until the Order of Thoth showed up, and the second was that there was a traitor in the Order who had betrayed the Mirovar force team to the vampires.

The only people who knew of the mission were the Mirovar force team, Ramin Kain, and Samuel Luther. The Raven had grown up with the other team members. They were much-loved, albeit faithless heathens, who had not yet seen the truth of the way of the Red Empire. The Raven believed that they would all come willingly to the Red Empire in the end. It was the Raven's sacred duty to guide them to the truth, and God willing, it would be so.

The Raven considered it impossible that any member of the Mirovar force team had betrayed them, that left only Kain, or Luther, or both, in the role of traitor.

What were the possible responses? It was safer to assume that Kain and Luther were both traitors until proven otherwise. Although, they couldn't rule out that the coven was simply a lure designed to catch and kill them all.

What about the Red Empire assassin? Who was it? Perhaps their childhood instructor Taipan, a true master of Red Empire Ninjitsu, or another who had come of age since the Raven's insertion into the Mirovar force team. The Raven concluded that the assassin had to be the Red Ghost's other agent in North America, the same person on the end of the messages that the Raven had sent. The only one the Raven had told of tonight's mission and they had intervened against the vampires.

Why had the other Red Empire agent broken their cover to protect the Mirovar force team? The Raven considered the possibility they had come to observe and fortunately discovered the praetorians before they could attack. Could they also be secretly protecting the Raven? They could ensure that the Raven would fulfill their own mission of rising to the top of the Order of Thoth. From that high position, the Raven could bend the Order to the will of Shabbah al Ahmar until the Red Empire absorbed the Order.

Then all the Ramp Masters would unite under one glorious banner against the Vampire Dominion.

The following conclusions remained: they could not trust Kain and Luther and they may have betrayed the Order of Thoth to the Vampire Dominion, and Shabbah al Ahmar's agent in North America was willing to risk all to protect the Mirovar force team.

The Raven's eyes hardened. The Vampire Dominion may be willing to create covens of vampires simply to bait a trap with. Anton was brighter than people gave him credit for and his ability to reach the correct conclusion before others did may one day be a threat to the Raven's mission.

The Raven smiled slightly, barely visible in the gloom inside the van. They would have to ensure that Anton could never suspect them of having a mission beyond the Mirovar force team. They would have to take special care to manage their relationship with him.

The van sped through the darkness, chasing the twin cones of bright illumination that lit up the trees beside the road. The trees loomed over the road like giant watchmen, silent guardians of the boundaries of the highway leading back to the safe house.

The Raven relaxed in their seat. Something teased at the edge of their awareness. They wanted to ignore it, but it wouldn't go away, so they reached for it, and it rushed through them like an ice-cold knife.

What if Shabbah al Ahmar's agent in North America was a double agent or worse a member of the Vampire Dominion?

A sick feeling bloomed in the middle of the Raven's gut. The question was shocking, the level of betrayal almost beyond imagining, and yet – it felt right. It would mean Shabbah al Ahmar's agent had been playing the Raven to achieve their own ends. But what could be their agenda? If they were also working for the vampire dominion, why would they intervene and kill the two praetorians waiting to ambush the Mirovar force team? It didn't make any sense.

The sense of truth faded away into the surrounding darkness. The Raven groped after it, but it was like trying to grasp mist and shadow. In the end, they had nothing left beyond an uneasy feeling of having missed something critically important.

The Raven worked hard to remember in detail what they had seen on top of the water tower. The masked figure was briefly visible while the Raven was ramped, time had slowed, the assassin's techniques were pure Red Empire Ninjitsu and executed with stunning speed.

The assassin wasn't Taipan. Not even the Raven's premier instructor was that fast. It could have been a lone wolf, someone with a rare talent for speed, and their own agenda. Someone who knew of the Vampire Dominion and the Mirovar force team's plans.

Hell, it could have been a rogue vampire warrior dressed up as a Red Empire assassin.

The thought sent a shiver along the Raven's skin, and they remained troubled by thoughts of betrayal for the rest of the journey back to the safe house.

* * *

General Clayton Maze leaped from the hovering nightfalcon helicopter to the top of the water tower.

He landed on his feet, in a minimum crouch, his vampire physiology absorbing the impact of the twenty-yard fall without harm. His nostrils flared. The air reeked with the scent of recently congealed blood, and the whiff of decay from the apartment block opposite the tower. His eye's widened as he took in his surroundings. He noted the precise methods used to kill the two praetorians.

"Clearly an expert," he observed without irony.

Two praetorians equipped with body bags, dropped from the helicopter, landing beside him. They moved forward to recover the remains of the Beta team.

Clayton had already seen enough to confirm the video record he'd watched in the nightfalcon. The Panopticon had harvested imagery from a US military satellite during the mission and the two praetorians had died at precisely 00:52:34. He was not surprised by his failure to detect any sign of the assailant. He'd spent over a century at war with their ilk. His lips curled with distaste. He hated the Red Empire with a passion bordering on fanaticism.

He went to the parapet and looked over. Better able to judge the distance to the ground from where he stood than by watching satellite images in a helicopter. It was quite a drop; not too difficult for a vampire, but a long way for a Ramp master – a very long way. Was the assailant human? Anyone could don the garb of a Red Empire assassin, but no one could fake the combat effectiveness on display.

A brief gust pulled at the dark suit jacket that he wore. The air was moist, the first hint of rain. He stood with his hands on his hips and surveyed the site. Another team of praetorians had commandeered the black van on the expressway and were driving off with it. A second nightfalcon hovered over the two-story building to the north, picking up the remains of Gamma team.

His final team was bagging the bodies of the coven vampires arrayed by the Order of Thoth in front of the apartment block.

Clayton was troubled. There was the telltale heat plume of the Ramp in the satellite view, easy to detect with an infra-red filter. It appeared there was a very talented Red Empire assassin conducting operations in North America. He shook his bald head slowly – the facts seemed to fit a Red Empire assassin. But he'd never encountered one this effective and that left room for doubt.

Clayton reviewed the video footage in his mind, the assailant had appeared out of the abandoned houses on the north side of the main street at 00:52:06. They had blurred across the road to the base of the two-story building where they had ascended the outer wall. They had surprised and promptly dismembered the Gamma team on the roof at 00:52:13. They had then moved on, descending down to the trees and the path that wound its way around the western end of the apartment block.

Cornelius Crane had issued his abort mission command to Centurion Rawlings at 00:52:19. Rawlings never got the chance to pass the message onto his teams.

The assailant had reached the expressway over the Neponset River at 00:52:20. The van's rear door had been torn from its hinges, and the assailant had entered the van, exiting two seconds later at 00:52:23. They had then covered the three hundred yards from the van to the tower top in ten seconds. The Beta team praetorians had died a second later.

Clayton leaned out over the parapet and saw there was enough room for someone to hide underneath it. Provided they could hold onto the edges of the bricks. A vampire or a Ramp master could do it.

The assailant had paused for a while on top of the tower, before hiding out of sight underneath the parapet while another Ramp master had ascended the tower and investigated the dead praetorians before disappearing away from the site. The assailant had dropped from beneath the parapet to the ground. They had paused briefly, and according to their infra-red heat signature had remaining ramped. They had blurred away, disappearing into the nearby abandoned houses bordering South Dorchester. For man or vampire, it would be an easy matter to break contact with the Panopticon and escape. The camera coverage in South Dorchester had decayed with the rest of the suburb.

"Who was the other Ramp master?" Clayton asked, there was no answer from the rising wind.

The praetorians completed bagging the dead and retrieving their equipment. The nightfalcon swung lower to allow them to leap on board. Clayton shook his head as he surveyed the site one last time. He sensed the distances involved and evaluated the speed of the attacks, especially the assault on the van. He touched his right ear, where a Shadowstone quantum communications earbud rested. It filtered out ambient noise and allowed for easy conversation even within the howl of the helicopter's downwash.

"Sir," he said. "I don't think we're dealing with a normal Ramp Master here. They're faster than anyone I've seen, powerful too, most likely some sort of super Red Empire assassin."

There was a brief pause on the link, then Cornelius Crane answered, his voice tight and controlled, "It's too early to draw conclusions. Wrap up your operations and return to the Citadel."

"Yes, Sir," Clayton replied. Closing the link, he leaped up into the nightfalcon. He took a seat, looking out at Boston as the ground shrank away from the soaring helicopter, a question hammering at his mind.

General Chloe Armitage, where are you tonight?

Chapter Five

> 05:45:12 Init Transcript Program..........
> 05:45:12 Init Source Anonymization..........
> 05:45:12 Init Traceless Call..........
> 05:45:13 Call...1...2...3...4...5...6
> 05:45:19 Init Redial
> 05:45:20 Call...1
> 05:45:21 Call Connect [Sergeant Detective Luke Walker] [LW]
> 05:45:22 [LW] "What? Who is this?"
> 05:45:25 [ANON] "An informant."
> 05:45:27 [LW] "I have to tell you that it's an offense to make a false report."
> 05:45:32 [ANON] "You need to hear this."
> 05:45:34 [LW] "Hear what?"
> 05:45:39 [ANON] "A ring of serial killers has been murdering the homeless in Boston for the last two months."
> 05:45:39 [PAUSE]
> 05:45:42 [LW] "You can back this up?"
> 05:45:44 [ANON] "Check out the basement at [REDACTED]."
> 05:45:49 [LW] "[REDACTED]?"
> 05:45:53 [ANON] "Yes."
> 05:45:55 [LW] "Who are you?"
> 05:45:57 End Call..........
> 05:45:58 Move Transcript to
../../../Investigations/ChloeArmitage/[datestamp]/Transcripts..........
> 05:45:58 Set Privacy for Generals Eyes Only [FGEO] [General Clayton Maze]
> 05:45:58 Init Erase..........
> 05:45:58 End Transcript Program..........

– Content from a partially declassified Panopticon transcript.

* * *

The War Room, 103rd floor, Crane's Citadel, Manhattan, August 9th, 05:00

Chloe was fascinated by a throbbing vein on Cornelius Crane's left temple. She'd seen such things many times before on her opponents or her prey, but never on her king.

She'd disposed of the Red Empire assassin disguise in the sewers of Boston. The evidence burned beyond recognition with a white phosphorous grenade. She smiled inwardly. The sudden appearance of a terrifyingly capable agent of the Red Empire, the deaths of seven praetorians and the subsequent disappearance of the agent would create a mystery that would further confound her king and aid her cause.

Chloe had just returned to her penthouse when she received the call from Crane to come to the Citadel for an emergency meeting. She attributed the gap in time between the events in Boston, and the call, to the necessity of Clayton Maze investigating the site and then returning to Manhattan. It had allowed her time to change into a fashionable black pinstripe pants suit, offset with a scarlet red chiffon blouse and red shoes.

Chloe stared at Cornelius as he shouted at Clayton and herself. She brought her attention back to his words as he continued to rant, sweeping a bloody helmet off the war room table to the floor.

"—it's outrageous! Nineteen praetorians killed in seven months. What the fucking hell is going on?" Cornelius shouted.

The praetorian tactical helmet bounced and rolled to a stop in front of Clayton and Chloe. They stood to attention, staring resolutely forward. Neither allowed the helmet and the stale reek of dried vampire blood to distract them.

Cornelius shook his finger at both generals and snapped, "The two of you will find out what is going on, or I'll put you both in silver for a year and see if that sharpens your ability to follow orders."

Turning back to the war room table, Cornelius punched a button on a console. The screens at the opposite end of the room displayed a composite picture of a world map. More than forty red stars blinked repeatedly, spread throughout Europe, Asia, Africa and the Middle East. There was a single red star in North America; squatting by itself in New Jersey. Praetorian losses over the last twenty years, each one marked with a date-time stamp and a name.

"The status at the end of last year," Cornelius stated irritably, punching another button.

The screens refreshed, the original red stars stopped blinking, fading to a dull orange. Nineteen new red stars flashed into existence, four in Jerusalem, six in a tight cluster in Boston, two in Brazil, the first in Rio de Janeiro, the second in the Amazon, and another seven stars blinked in a second tight cluster in Boston.

"Boston has become a death trap," Cornelius declared.

"Clearly, the Order is increasing its activity," Chloe observed calmly, pointing at Boston on the map. "I know of these deaths on the Boston docks, I was there, and Arthur Slayne is the likely Order operative in Brazil. But what of these last seven? Where were they killed exactly? Can we expand the resolution of the map?"

Cornelius stared at Chloe for a moment before silently pressing another button. The map expanded, Boston, spreading across the screen. In moments, the map displayed the seven dead praetorians in three separate clusters, three on an expressway, two on a water tower, and the last two on the roof of a two-story building. Each site was approximately three hundred yards from the other two, describing the points of a rough triangle centered on a large apartment block.

Chloe read the metadata next to each red star, did a double take, and asked incredulously, "Centurion Rawlings is dead?"

"That's what it says." Clayton sneered.

Chloe stared at Clayton for a moment, tilting her head slightly. She looked back at Cornelius and asked, "Why were they there?"

"They were on an operation under my direction against the Mirovar force team."

Chloe leaned forward on the balls of her feet. "I thought that I was in charge of operations in the northeast?"

"I grew tired of waiting for you to fulfill your promise to deliver their heads," Cornelius stated flatly.

"Sir, I could've helped," Chloe declared passionately.

"Perhaps, but you may have met your match."

"Why, what happened?"

"Watch this footage," Cornelius commanded. Tapping a button on the console.

The main screen displayed full satellite video of the attack of the mysterious assailant. Clayton stood impassively; he'd clearly seen it earlier that night. Chloe watched the screen intently. The video finished with the assailant disappearing into the desolation of the South Dorchester slums.

Chloe looked at Cornelius and arched one eyebrow quizzically in an unspoken question.

"It appears that the Red Empire have unearthed a talent," Cornelius observed, shaking his head slowly. "A new Ramp master with extreme speed, strength, and skill."

"The Red Empire are ruthless killers," Clayton declared.

Chloe smiled slightly, and remarked, "Just like us."

"Nothing like us," Clayton snapped. "They're vermin."

"Enough!" Cornelius roared. He paused for a moment then continued in level tones, "Your petty rivalry bores me. Focus on the task at hand."

"This is unprecedented," Chloe noted. "Are we sure it's not a rogue vampire pretending to be a Red Empire assassin?"

Clayton glanced across at Chloe and said, "It's not beyond the realms of possibility."

"What of the operative that emerged from the tower?" Chloe asked, frowning. "Clearly, he hid carefully and watched everything. He must have been there before the praetorians arrived. Otherwise, they would surely have seen him. Who was he?"

"Unknown, there is insufficient visual or audio evidence for the Panopticon to identify him," Cornelius explained.

"Clearly, he was another Ramp master, but of the Order or the Red Empire?" Chloe asked.

"Also, unknown," Cornelius noted.

"What of the helmet cams," Chloe inquired, "did they record any pertinent features?"

"There was a tenth of a second of video from within the van," Cornelius advised. "Centurion Rawlings turned his head just before a blade ripped through his helmet. It took out the camera on the way through. It's a blurred image. The agent was moving very fast."

Chloe frowned intently, and asked, "Can Shadowstone clean the image up? Perhaps we could get enough detail to get a match."

"It's already happening," Cornelius stated. "A team at Fort Dix is processing the video. Looks like a face shot, someone covered with a veil, and a hood."

"Classic Red Empire garb," Clayton observed confidently.

"Interesting. At least that's something. When will we have a clear image?" Chloe asked.

"By tonight," Cornelius advised.

"Excellent," Chloe said, smiling.

"What are you so happy about?" Cornelius snapped.

"I love a challenge – they're obviously good with a blade," Chloe observed. She glanced sideways at Clayton. "I don't often get a challenge."

Cornelius stared at her for a long moment before grinning fiercely. His fangs descended into attack position, and he commanded, "Both of you have two days to find out what is going on. I will have a full report here, on Friday at 23:00. I expect results, do not fail me."

"Yes, Sir." They chorused together.

"Now get out of my sight," Cornelius ordered.

The two generals bowed low, backing away before turning and exiting the war room.

* * *

Chloe followed Clayton through the door and into the operations center. Over a dozen vampires staffed the main operations room; all busily at work for the Vampire Dominion.

Clayton turned to her and asked suspiciously, "So, where were you five hours ago?"

"I was in my Manhattan penthouse."

"Can anyone back that up?"

"I was alone – am I under investigation?"

Clayton stared at her for a long moment.

Chloe hissed. "What are you going to do? Accuse me of the murder of seven praetorians – are you mad?"

Clayton wrinkled his nose, and declared, "I have to investigate all options."

"You think!" Chloe replied sarcastically.

They paused for a moment; the operations center had fallen into silence. All the other vampires were staring at them. Chloe's eyes tightened with a thinly veiled threat.

Clayton sniffed and said in a low voice, "I don't have time to bandy words with you, I have a mess in Boston to clean up."

Chloe's eyes momentarily flashed with seething hatred as she watched Clayton turn away and stride from the room. The other vampires in the room had quickly returned their attention to their monitors, and sheaths of paperwork. She waved at them and called out in steely tones, "Stop faking that you didn't notice anything. Now get back to work everyone, the show's over."

The vampires buried themselves deeper into their work.

Chloe assumed a neutral expression on her face and walked calmly over to the elevators, the night was getting late.

The doors slid apart, she entered the elevator and punched the button for the basement parking garage. As the elevator descended, she worked through the problem of the helmet cam video. The video would reveal her eyes, and Crane and the rest would surely recognize her. She determined to ring James Haley as soon as she was in her penthouse. He was the only resource she had positioned to intervene. The mission would reveal to James her role in the deaths of the praetorians. He would know enough to destroy her by revealing her actions to Crane. If she took no action, failure was inevitable, she had to use James, but she would need to ensure his absolute loyalty.

Chloe smiled briefly, calculating how much time remained before dawn.

A phone call won't do; I'm going to have to pay James a visit. It's a good thing that he lives in New York.

* * *

Cornelius dropped out of a previsionary meditation. He continued to sit in the war room. His generals had left the room ten minutes before. He remained troubled, although the meditation had drained his anger away. The probability line toward his own death had strengthened during the night. The failed mission against the Mirovar team had increased the risk from someone within the force team. The probability line went all the way back to the Boston docks, and anchored in Li Wu or Anton Smith.

Cornelius steepled his long fingers and rested his chin upon them. It was clear he'd lost the initiative on the night of the battle on the Boston docks. He'd attempted to regain it with the lure of the vampire coven, and the complicity of Ramin Kain but his plan had failed. The mission was a disaster. His lead praetorian, Centurion Rawlings, was dead, along with another six of his elite vampire soldiers.

And now the threat to my life has increased. The thought rolled around his mind like an alien artifact, strange and dubious.

Cornelius pressed his lips into a thin line of determination. He'd not survived nearly a thousand years by giving way to fear, doubt and uncertainty. The situation was fluid, but he'd survived far worse threats than that posed by two children of the Order of Thoth.

His fingers dropped, and he rested his chin on his clasped fists, staring silently at nothing, his mind far away. He mused on the fact that his prevision had shown victory before the mission had begun, and yet comprehensive failure had occurred so quickly once the mission had commenced. It was clear that the assailant, Red Empire agent or not, was a personage of true power. Able to shape events at will, and beyond his capability to anticipate with his ability to see the future.

In the long years since the ceremony with Jean Philippe Allemande, he'd discovered that the precognitive ability was tightly bound to the results of his own choices and actions. The interventions of others could shape the results with sudden effect. Anyone with a persistent ability to impact his life, he had either eliminated or co-opted, but life goes on, new people are born, and new threats could always arise. He'd adapted to the limitations of his prevision and maximized its value.

The disappearance of the assailant troubled him. It was as if they had simply ceased to exist. There were no probability lines leading from the events of this night to another encounter with the agent who had worked so effectively against his plans. He'd never seen anything like it before.

Cornelius determined that he would get to the bottom of the mystery of the assailant. The first attempt to recapture the initiative from the Ramp masters had failed, he would adapt his tactics and try again. He leaned forward and used the command console on the war room table to place an encrypted call to Kain's smartphone. The phone rang three times before Kain picked it up.

"... Oh, it's you," Kain answered.

"What did you see?" Cornelius inquired.

"Someone killed your two vampires. I saw the fresh remains – there's a third player – and they knew what was happening."

"There's a leak in the Mirovar force team. Likely from a Red Empire agent, and they have a friend, someone powerful who killed my praetorians."

"The Red Empire does not have an agent in the Mirovar force team! That's impossible!" Kain declared incredulously.

"I know that my praetorians didn't leak the information. That leaves an agent within Mirovar's team, or it was you."

"Well, it damn well wasn't me."

"Are you trying to screw with me?"

"Of course not. What would I gain? I asked you to help me get rid of Francis Mirovar and Anton Smith. Why would I sabotage my own mission?"

"Which means the leak came from within the Mirovar force team – accept it – it's the only option left."

There was a long pause on the line.

Kain said, "Damn, you must be right."

"Of course, I am," Cornelius stated matter-of-factly. "So, do something about it."

"Oh, I will." Kain hissed. "Don't you worry about that."

"Once you find your spy, keep them alive, and in place, we need to find their accomplice, the one who killed my praetorians."

"Obviously."

"Keep me appraised of your progress on this topic – it affects us both. It would be harmful to our agreement for you to start keeping secrets on this issue."

"Yes, of course."

"Don't take too long."

"Yes," Kain agreed impatiently.

Cornelius stroked his chin and declared, "We're done then?"

Kain said, "Yes."

Cornelius hung up the call and smiled slightly. He always enjoyed it when Kain was under pressure. It was clear that Kain had not seen the insertion of the Alpha and Gamma teams at the mission site. He must have been close to the water tower, or even inside it when the Beta team had positioned themselves on top of it. Obviously, Kain was the other Ramp master captured on video fleeing the site.

Cornelius speculated that Arthur Slayne had returned to North America, and was now in Boston. He'd witnessed firsthand Arthur Slayne's fighting ability in the secret vaults and passageways beneath Saint Peter's Basilica. Slayne was capable of the deeds done tonight. The problem with Slayne's involvement was explaining how he knew of the mission. Cornelius sighed, no, there was no evidence linking Slayne to the events tonight. It was most likely someone else, someone as powerful and dangerous as Slayne.

Cornelius admitted to himself that Kain had said it best – there's a third player. He got up from his chair and made his way through the operations center to his personal quarters. It had been a long night, and he needed to rest.

As he lay on his bed, Cornelius contemplated the option the assailant came from the Red Empire, and was not human. He had to admit the final possibility that there were one or more rogue vampires within his own organization. He vowed to himself to find out if there were any traitors within his ranks. He was certain that Hell would be a place of love and kindness compared to the fate that he would visit on any who had betrayed him.

* * *

Ramin Kain shook his head incredulously as the smartphone call disconnected.

It had been another long night, and it had ended in disaster. He remembered with perfect clarity the moment when one of the Mirovar force team looked up and saw the praetorians on top of the water tower. Was it by chance? Were they simply scanning for threats, or did they know what to look for? The options were dizzying, Ramin's stomach churned and knotted.

There was something deeply wrong with Mirovar's team. The idea, forcefully provided by Crane, that there was an active Red Empire agent embedded in the team had shocked him. Current events forced him to admit that it was the only viable possibility. He drew on his memory of who was in the team. The agent would be someone young. Francis and Juliette Mirovar were beyond question. Jay Creeley's history was well known. That left only Yvette Mirovar, Chiara Romano, and Peter Lamb as the possible agent unless somehow it was Li Wu or Anton Slayne.

Ramin snorted derisively. Anton Slayne in the guise of Anton Smith was a true nobody, it was clear why Arthur Slayne had hidden his grandson. There was no chance the Red Empire had co-opted the young Slayne. The same went for Li Wu, a traditionalist like Gang Wu would not have raised a daughter who would spy for the Red Empire. No, the Red Empire agent had to be one of the other three.

Then there was the problem of the Red Empire agent's accomplice, the one who had surprised and killed the two praetorians on the water tower. Ramin reluctantly admitted to himself, that he didn't have the skills to creep up on vampires and suddenly kill two of them. The accomplice was clearly very skilled, powerful and dangerous.

Ramin rubbed his face with both hands. Having to deal with all this scheming by other players was a right royal pain in the butt. Why didn't people simply defer to his obvious genius? He shook his head again, still incredulous at the sudden turn of events. Victory had been certain, the plan had been perfect, and yet Francis Mirovar and Anton Slayne were still alive.

It was as if divine intervention was on their side, and whatever gods there were, were laughing at him as they destroyed his plans.

"Fuck it." He swore. "I'm going to have to find this damn spy, their accomplice and destroy Mirovar and Slayne as well."

Ramin vowed to himself to find a way to cut through all these difficulties and seize victory. There was no other way to transform the Order of Thoth into an efficient fighting force. The Order must be under his direct and total command. It was the only way to win against the vampires.

He toyed with the idea of getting Sam to simply kill Anton Slayne and Francis Mirovar. He could say that Sam had gone mad, and acted on his own. A crazed lone wolf attack. It would be best for Sam to die in the mission so he couldn't have any second thoughts or tell any tales. Ramin weighed his options. He wrinkled his nose, sucking air through his teeth. Sam was just a little bit too valuable to burn in a suicide mission. He needed another way, and he needed it quickly. Anton Slayne was getting more powerful every day. How long would it be before he was as capable as his grandfather? Another loose cannon with the ability to split the Order of Thoth down the middle and not only threaten his own position as Head of the Order but also his life.

However, the assassination of his enemies would not solve the complication of the Red Empire agent or their deadly accomplice.

Ramin racked his brain.

The pathway forward became clear, he needed an Order traveler. Not just any traveler but one of proven loyalty to himself. Someone who was aware of what Ramin stood for, and was truly committed to the transformation of the Order of Thoth. There was one man he could trust to do the job, Deon Lamar. A man whose particular talent had required Ramin's utmost skills to cultivate and co-opt.

A slow grin spread across his face. Ramin picked up his smartphone and dialed Sam Luther. He knew Sam would be up at this early hour, training with weapons. The phone rang twice before Sam answered it.

"Hi RK, what can I do for you?"

"Do you know where Deon Lamar is?"

"Deon Lamar? He's in Australia, Sydney, I think. Evaluating a new novice with the local Force team. Why?"

"I need him in Maine."

"You want him to investigate Mirovar?"

"Not him. A member of his team."

"Anton Slayne?"

"Hold your horses, Sam. I'll explain."

"... Sure RK."

"It looks like there is a Red Empire agent within the Mirovar force team."

Ramin imagined Sam shaking his head in disbelief.

"... That's shocking."

"Yes, quite so. Now, I need my best spy catcher on point for this mission, and that's Lamar."

"For sure, Lamar is our best man. He's also very switched on politically."

"True, he's very intelligent – precisely the sort of man that we want on this mission."

"Do you want me to contact him?"

"Yes. Get him over to Maine at the earliest opportunity. Warn him about Anton Slayne, and Li Wu. They're likely accomplices of any Red Empire agent in the team."

"Anton Slayne, a Red Empire spy? ... Sure RK, will do."

"Sam, don't underestimate the Slaynes, they have their fingers in all sorts of pies. They're the very heart of deviousness. We have to be clever if we are to defeat them."

"Sure RK, I understand perfectly. I will instruct Lamar on what to expect. Is there anything else?"

"Yes. Most importantly, impress upon Deon the necessity to identify the spy without giving away the fact he's discovered them. We need to find the spy's accomplice in the US. Is that clear?"

"Yes, RK. Crystal clear."

"Good work, Sam. I knew that I could trust you to understand the gravity of the situation within the Mirovar force team."

"I wish we could disband them."

"Quite so."

"Is there anything else?"

"No Sam, just keep me in the loop as things progress."

"Yes, RK."

Ramin hung up the line and put down the phone. He smiled grimly. *I may be able to manage this so the same net that captures the Red Empire agent also captures Anton Slayne.*

His smile broadened into a wide toothy grin.

* * *

There were a pair of knocks on the front door of James Haley's apartment. At the same time, his smartphone pinged with a text message. He rolled out of bed and glanced at the smartphone's screen. The message was from Chloe Armitage and read, 'Knock, Knock.'

"Oh my God, what's she doing here?" James whispered to himself as he pulled on a pair of shorts and tracksuit pants. He didn't have a clean shirt handy, and he walked bare-chested down the hall from his bedroom to the front door of his New York apartment.

James opened the door. Chloe stood before him. She wore a black pinstripe pants suit, a scarlet red chiffon blouse, red shoes and a slight smile.

Tilting her head slightly, her smile broadened. "It is customary to invite a guest in."

James hesitated for a split second, wondering if the old myth that vampires could only enter your home if someone invited them in held any water. In the same moment, he decided, *fuck it*, and replied, "Yes, Ma'am, please come in."

Chloe stepped across the threshold, approaching to stand directly before him. She smiled again, put her finger gently on his lips. "Please, call me Chloe when we're alone together."

She stepped past him, walking slowly down the hall, looking at photos on the wall. One caught her eye, and she paused in front of it. "Looks like Afghanistan?"

"Firebase Cobra, Oruzgan Province," James noted. His mind buzzing with questions. The chief among them – *why is she here?*

Chloe looked back along the hall and stated, "US Army 3rd Special Forces Group, 1st Battalion, Captain James Haley, Operational Detachment commander. Awarded two silver stars during your tours in Afghanistan. Then you joined the 902d Military Intelligence Group within US Army Counterintelligence. You served another two years there, mostly based in Washington DC, before moving to the CIA."

James nodded; the personal history lesson meant nothing to him anymore. Those events had happened to someone else. Someone who had wanted to make a difference in the world. Someone who didn't know vampires ruled the world and treated people as disposable cattle.

Someone who hadn't murdered his own men.

"Then Shadowstone of course. Quite a distinguished career you have James, we will have to see what happens next."

"And what would that be?" James asked flatly.

For nearly two months James had been actively tracking the Head of the Order of Thoth, Ramin Kain. He'd picked up his close associate Samuel Luther. He now had physical data files an inch thick on both men. He knew where they both lived, what their habits were, and most importantly – the location of an active Order safe house in Maine. The rush of enthusiasm he'd felt at the beginning of the new mission had faded over time. The desolation after the defeat on the Boston docks had come back to haunt him. Only his professionalism kept him moving forward.

Chloe looked at him for a long moment. "I understand your pain, James."

James frowned but remained silent. They stood in the hallway a couple of yards apart, but seemingly separated by a million miles.

"Patience James, a very long game is being played here, and don't underestimate your part," Chloe advised. "I promise you; I have the solution for your suffering."

"What? Vampirism?" James asked in dark tones.

"No," Chloe answered. "Nothing as blunt as that."

"Then what?"

"The truth."

"The truth?" James asked doubtfully.

"Yes, the truth, the whole truth and nothing but the truth."

"So, help me God?"

"So, help me God."

James frowned, his face frozen with suspicion.

Chloe said lightly, "But first, a shower and a shave. We need to get you ready for work."

"Yes, Ma'am," James replied automatically. He'd never seen Chloe act this way, so informal, it was – unsettling.

"Chloe." She corrected him softly.

"Yes, Chloe."

She followed him into the bathroom, and James had a sudden and disturbing vision that she was about to join him. Instead, Chloe grabbed a double handful of white towels, and said, "Meet me in the kitchen in five minutes, and don't bother shaving."

James ran himself through a quick shower and dried himself hurriedly. Five minutes later, with a bath towel wrapped around his hips, he walked into the kitchen. There was a pot of steaming water on the stove, wet towels in the sink and one of his stools in the middle of the kitchen.

On the bench, glistening like a wet mirror in the overhead lights, was an old-fashioned straight razor. It looked brand new; he'd never seen it before.

"Please take a seat, there isn't much time, and I need to explain a few things," Chloe invited with a warm smile.

James approached the stool, turned and sat down with his back to Chloe.

She put both her hands on his head, he almost flinched but managed to stay still.

"Relax James," Chloe advised and began to massage his scalp.

James found the experience surreal. Why was the most powerful vampire on the planet massaging his head? Despite himself, he started to relax. She was really good at it. He closed his eyes.

A minute later she wrung out the towels, and gently placed a hot wet towel on his face. The heat was right on the upper limit of what was comfortable. She gently massaged his face through the towel. She followed the towel with the application of lightly scented shaving cream.

A moment later, there was the first touch of cold steel against his temple. Chloe expertly drew the razor down his left cheek toward his throat. She finished by wiping the blade against a towel on the bench and re-positioned the blade to make her second swipe.

"You mentioned the truth?" James asked dubiously.

"There is a lot to tell you about the Order of Thoth, the Red Empire, and the Vampire Dominion. You need to know everything. You need to understand that your life matters."

James jerked forward, and Chloe whipped the razor away from his face. His eyes flashed, and he declared incredulously, "Matters! How does it matter now?"

Chloe put her hands on his shoulders, guiding him back into position, she leaned forward close to his right ear and whispered, "Trust me, James. It will become clear soon."

James sighed, sat back and asked, "What about vampires?"

"Vampires have only existed for a little over five thousand years," Chloe explained, continuing the shave, moving the blade perfectly to ensure that James could speak without injury.

"How did they come about?"

"By accident," Chloe observed matter-of-factly.

"You're kidding me?"

"It's the truth," Chloe said. "There were two princes in Southern Egypt. They had access to a system they called the Engine of Thoth. One of them, Ahknaton, tried to use the Engine to resurrect his dead wife. She came back as the first vampire and killed him. The other prince, Hakron, survived and recorded what happened."

"What's the Engine of Thoth?"

"We call it the Metaframe today. It's at the foundation of reality. It defines the rules of the universe, such as gravity is an attractive force, time moves forward instead of backward, and that vampires exist."

"That's insane."

"You're used to the idea that the laws of the universe are immutable. It's always a shock to find out they're not."

"Do you have proof of this?"

"Is it that big a stretch for you? How long ago was it you didn't believe in vampires?" Chloe inquired, lifting the razor away from James' throat.

James frowned.

"I can provide proof in time but not today," Chloe advised.

"So, the Metaframe is what this is all about?"

"Yes, James," Chloe stated approvingly. "The Order of Thoth, the Red Empire, and the Vampire Dominion are at war over who controls the Metaframe."

"Who's winning?"

"No one. My boss, Cornelius Crane has organized the vampires for nearly two centuries but it hasn't made a difference. The war is in a deep stalemate between the three factions. In fact, there is an active, secret alliance between Crane and Kain."

"That's corrupt. From what I know of the Order, they would never ally with the vampires."

"True, they shouldn't. Kain and Crane are both traitors, but their respective betrayals are not the main issue."

"What is?"

"Who protects the Metaframe and for what purpose."

"Who does protect the Metaframe?"

"No one. The war protects the Metaframe by keeping the capability to access it separated amongst the factions. Crane is in the dominant position as he has the Key of Ahknaton and the Papyrus of Hakron the Scribe. All he requires now is the Interpretive Codex which is in the hands of his arch-enemy, Shabbah al Ahmar, the head of the Red Empire."

"The Red Ghost?"

"Yes. You know Arabic? ... Of course, I remember now ... it's in your file."

James nodded. "What's the Key of Ahknaton?"

"Honestly, no one knows. Ahknaton invented or acquired it. It allows absolute access to the Metaframe. Hakron described what Ahknaton did when he used it, and the Papyrus is the only guide we have."

"What's the Interpretive Codex?"

"Hakron encoded the Papyrus, the Codex explains how to read it. Hence why Crane wants the Codex."

"No one can break Hakron's code?"

"It's gibberish. The Codex is essential."

"You've read it?"

"Both of them."

"Then you understand how to access the Metaframe?"

"Yes. I just need the Key."

"What will you do once you have it?"

"Protect Humanity."

"From what?"

"Everything."

"What do you mean?"

"I mean everything. Overpopulation, global war, climate change, resource depletion, asteroid impact, plagues, famine." Chloe stepped back and waved her hands expansively, the razor gleaming in the kitchen lights. "Everything."

"How?"

"Through a single use of the Metaframe to empower the true rulership of vampires over this world."

"So, vampires would rule?"

"Yes. Vampires have an absolute vested interest in the survival and health of the human population. Our immortality provides stability. Our rule will usher in a new world order of lasting peace and prosperity balanced with the long-term survival of the planet."

A new vista opened up in front of James.

"James – I need people at my side who are committed to really solving the problems that have plagued humanity for thousands of years. I believe that you are one of those people. James, your life matters enormously, your choices and actions are absolutely critical to the success or failure of this vision. I know you better than you know yourself. Let me tell you what your true purpose is. It is to become an immortal protector of humanity, a guide, and shepherd of the flock. A man with the power and the will to ensure that humanity survives and prospers."

James could see the sense of Chloe's words, but he said, "You're still vampires, living off the lives of people."

"We'll eliminate war, crime, illness, starvation, all the usual sources of early death. In comparison, the small harvest that vampires make on the human population will be trivial."

"Do you know where the key is?" James asked, belief growing in the tone of his voice.

"Yes, I know exactly where it is."

"What's stopping you from taking it?"

"A sorcerer placed me under a magical curse that forbids me from directly harming Crane. An impact of the curse is that seizing the Key of Ahknaton would kill me. I can't touch it while Crane lives."

"Sorcery? Magic?"

"It's real, and associated to the Metaframe."

"You're trying to get rid of Crane?"

"Yes, the long game that I spoke of earlier."

"What do you need from me?" James asked, his eyes flashing with fresh interest.

"There's blurred video footage of me at Fort Dix that needs to be managed."

"In what way?"

"Doctored, so that it doesn't look like me. Shadowstone is working to clarify it today."

Chloe made the last swipe with her razor and swished it clean in the hot water in the sink. She placed a hot towel over James' face and gently wiped the last traces of shaving cream away.

James stood up and declared, "I'll get it done."

"Thank you, James. I will stay here today. It's too late in the morning for me to move around outside."

James nodded. "Of course."

"Once the task is done, come back here."

"Yes, Chloe."

Chloe moved in close, leaned up and kissed James once on the mouth. She stayed close and whispered, "You're special James. Never forget that."

James stared at her for a moment, stepped away and went to his bedroom to dress. Ten minutes later he was in his car and heading to Fort Dix.

James considered what had just happened. Chloe really trusted him. Her words rang true. She'd told him everything. There was a great war of powers underway, and it was time to choose sides. What Chloe was fighting for made sense. The world did need protecting, humanity needed protecting. There was a real chance to make a difference of historic proportions. Chloe's ideas and ambitions were compelling. The choice was clear and easy to make.

James made his decision, embraced his future, and there was no more doubt.

* * *

The video conferencing system of the war room displayed three of the generals. Shen Zhen from Beijing. Dieter Franz from Berlin, and Haras Mosule from Jerusalem. In the war room, facing the main screens, sat Cornelius Crane, flanked by Clayton Maze on his left and Chloe Armitage on his right.

Zhen, Franz, and Mosule had completed their reports. In the last three months, there had been an increase in Red Empire activity across all world zones. They'd wiped out a Chinese Shadowstone cyberwarfare unit and stolen their cyberweapons. They'd embezzled tens of billions of Euros from several Italian, French and German banks. A Russian submarine armed with nuclear demolition munitions had mysteriously failed and sunk beneath the Arctic ice. The nuclear weapons remained missing, presumed lost to the Red Empire.

Clayton had provided his report detailing the parameters of the assailant who had killed the praetorians in Boston. The Shadowstone team at Fort

Dix had completed their work on the fragment of video that captured the assailant's face. He was male, brown-eyed, with a small mole next to his left eye. Based on satellite footage. His physical capabilities for speed, agility, and strength exceeded the upper end of the scale of a praetorian vampire. Clayton finished his report by concluding that there were two likely options. The Red Empire had managed to convert one of their own elite warriors into a vampire and send them on a mission, or there was a rogue vampire of great skill and power operating against the Vampire Dominion.

Crane rubbed the bridge of his nose and looked to his right. "General Armitage, your report."

"Sir," Chloe began her report. "I spent last night scouting the sewers of South Dorchester. I focused on the area directly north of the battle site where the assailant escaped to. I discovered a day old white phosphorous grenade scorch and this," Chloe placed a congealed blob of metal on the table.

Crane frowned curiously at the scorched metal. "What is it?"

"Based on chemical analysis it corresponds to the remains of a power unit for an electrically heated body suit."

"Someone wore a suit to artificially raise their body temperature?" Crane inquired.

Chloe nodded. "To simulate the Ramp."

"It had to be a vampire," Crane deduced.

"Yes, Sir," Chloe agreed confidently.

Clayton declared, "This confirms my results."

"A vampire is working for the Red Empire," Chloe asserted. "I double checked the video footage. The assailant is a master of Red Empire Ninjitsu. There are no vampires in the Vampire Dominion with that skill set apart from Haras Mosule, and he's accounted for."

"And yet," Crane frowned, "they destroyed the heat suit."

"They must be planning to change disguises," Chloe advised. "It makes good sense not to repeat tactics."

"So how did they know about the mission?" Clayton asked?

Crane and Chloe exchanged a glance. Crane stared at Clayton. "There is reason to believe a Red Empire agent is operating within the Mirovar force team."

Clayton did a double take. "Sir, when were you going to share that with us?"

Crane shrugged his shoulders. "It wasn't confirmed."

"It is now," Clayton declared. "The agent within the force team would have tipped off the Red Empire operative, and they showed up and protected the team. The Mirovar force team must be a cat's paw for the Red Empire."

"It would seem so." Crane allowed.

"If I may continue?" Chloe asked with a touch of exasperation.

Clayton nodded.

"In summary," Chloe stated. "My report confirms that a vampire is working with the Red Empire and is protecting the Mirovar force team. The vampire's skill set indicates they originated from within the warrior elite of the Red Empire. I suspect that he is a volunteer, once his mission is complete, he'll walk into the sunlight and destroy all evidence of his existence."

Crane said, "Excellent work General Armitage."

"Thank you, Sir."

Crane studied his generals for a moment. "General Armitage suggested the possibility that the Red Empire have an agent in the Mirovar force team back in June. Events have proved her to be correct. She has demonstrated initiative, perceptiveness and an admirable ability to integrate diverse pieces of evidence. The rest of you would do well to emulate her methods."

The other generals kept their faces impassive, as they replied, "Yes, Sir."

"Humph," Crane grunted. "The policy is clear – regain control over your territories and push back hard on Red Empire operations."

"Yes, Sir." The generals chorused more enthusiastically.

"Dismissed."

The conferencing system automatically shut down the remote screens.

Crane turned to Clayton and directed, "You have a new mission."

"Sir? What of my current mission?"

Crane nodded. "Your current mission is complete."

"Yes, Sir."

"I will brief you in two hours. Take a break and come back then."

"Yes, Sir. Very good, Sir."

Clayton collected his notes and left. The door automatically closing behind him.

Crane leaned forward and gently held Chloe's left hand. "Chloe, we need to talk."

"Yes, Cornelius."

I wonder what he's got in store for me now?

* * *

Cornelius looked steadily into Chloe's eyes. His previsionary experiences demonstrated that she could have nothing to do with the recent reversals. The probability lines for her and the other generals were always dark. He was impressed by her recent identification of the threat of the Red Empire co-option of the Mirovar force team and the revelation that an elite Red Empire assassin had become a vampire. The Red Empire agent in the Mirovar force team was working closely with the vampire assassin. The Red

Empire was on the move around the world. He needed his best general at his side and well informed of current operations.

It was time to tell her about the secret detente with the Order of Thoth and his strategic plan. He declared matter-of-factly, "There has been an agreement between the Head of the Order of Thoth, and myself for nearly two decades."

"What?" Chloe asked incredulously. "You know who he is?"

"Yes. His name is Ramin Kain."

"What's the deal? It must be good to justify such a bizarre relationship."

"Chloe, I'm a practical man. The detente is a temporary convenience. It has allowed me to focus on operations limiting the Red Empire and to complete my Day Guard program. The Day Guard program is all but ready to execute. I have enough super-soldier serum to create a force of two hundred and fifty soldiers. Soon I will be in a position to conduct twenty-four-hour operations against the Ramp masters. The Day Guard will eliminate their key strategic advantage: the ability to operate effectively during the day. When I'm ready, I will crush the Red Empire and the Order of Thoth."

"Who will lead the Day Guard?" Chloe asked.

"I will assign operational command of the Day Guard program to Clayton. It will be his job to see it through to completion. We will start with the first group of two hundred and fifty this month and build our tactical methods."

"Will the Day Guard be integrated with Shadowstone."

"Yes. They already are, in the UK."

"Indeed." Chloe nodded. "I remember you assigning a force from the UK to Jerusalem about two months ago when I was there."

"The Phase IVs in the UK are an advanced prototype of what we have now perfected."

"You will need a human interface between Shadowstone and the Day Guard," Chloe said. "I would recommend Louise Wesson."

"You have verified her?"

"Yes. She checked out fine."

"What of James Haley's replacement?"

"Wesson again. Allow her to select her team. She has the capability to manage both organizations."

Cornelius paused for a moment. "Granted. I will instruct Clayton of the organizational changes."

Chloe leaned forward slightly and asked, "You always emphasized the need to acquire the Metaframe artifacts. How does that fit with this strategy?"

"As always, the artifacts remain our primary goal. I need to hold the dynamics of the conflict steady while I build the weapon that can crush our enemies once and for all. The Day Guard is the weapon, and once in play, it will prove decisive."

"So, what happens now?"

"We are at a late stage in my strategy. These recent reversals threaten it. Stability is the key to completing my strategy."

"What do you need from me? How can I help?"

"I need Ramin Kain kept alive and in place as the Head of the Order of Thoth until I'm ready to act. He is a self-obsessed fool who imagines he is a great strategist. In reality, he is a conniving schemer with very real political skills but poor military ones. The last thing I need is for someone who would be militarily effective, such as Francis Mirovar or Justin Blake to replace him. Kain has become unreliable. He's deeply attached to killing Francis Mirovar, and for some unknown reason, Anton Smith. To stabilize the situation, we need to destroy the Mirovar force team and ensure Kain remains safely at the top of the Order."

"I'm sure it can be done."

"It is essential. There have been further reversals. Someone destroyed my research facility in the Amazon five weeks ago, most likely Arthur Slayne. I've begun the process of rebuilding it. But it has put the Day Guard program back by at least a year, perhaps two. Two hundred and fifty soldiers are not enough, I planned on having ten times that amount. I need to ensure that we have another year to complete the new research facility in Brazil. Once we have more serum, we can build a force of two and a half thousand fully equipped Day Guards. With such a force we can destroy the Order of Thoth and the Red Empire."

"It is a stunning strategy sir."

Cornelius studied his best general. Was she being sarcastic? The moment passed, there was no trace of deceit in Chloe's face.

"Humph," he grunted. "Be that as it may, it's not done yet. There are other risks we must manage. The new Red Empire vampire assassin, chief amongst them. I want you to focus on finding and destroying him."

"I will need resources," Chloe stated, spreading her hands wide. "There are many threads here. Find and destroy the Mirovar force team. Find and destroy the Red Empire vampire. Keep Ramin Kain safe. I can't be everywhere at once."

"What of James Haley, have you converted him yet?"

"No. He is still too useful as a human, and for this mission, I would like to keep him that way. Instead, I need Marcus Drake to return, and I need a specialized Shadowstone combat team."

"Granted. I will replace Marcus once I've recruited new praetorians."

"When will that be?"

"Tomorrow. You need to feed tonight and prepare for a trip to Syria. We will leave in five hours' time."

"Targets?"

"A US Black Ops team is on the ground. A much larger Syrian government force is about to swamp them."

Chloe raised her right eyebrow quizzically. "Which side are you playing?"

"Both."

"How many recruits?"

"A dozen to start with. I'll get eight to ten after we account for loyalty issues. It will provide a new force with modern tactical and weapon skills."

"Where will you use them?"

"Jerusalem, they can back up General Mosule, and you can have Marcus Drake back."

"Excellent."

"You mentioned a specialized combat team. What did you mean?"

"A small tactical unit equipped with blackwidow gunships."

"How many, and for what purpose?" Cornelius asked.

"Three, and I will use them against the Mirovar safe house when I find it."

"That's the spirit of old. I like your confidence."

"I'm sure that we will find the safe house, there are some good leads that suggest it is up in Maine. Another two weeks and we will have it for sure. Once identified, I will vector in the blackwidows and destroy them."

Cornelius leaned forward. "You can only use the Widow's if the target is outside an urban area. We must not risk another Boston incident."

"Yes, Cornelius," Chloe agreed, smiling confidently. "I will make sure of that."

"Another thing."

"Yes."

"This secret is known only to Ursula, yourself, and me."

"Understood."

"Shadowstone cannot be made aware of this arrangement."

"How will I keep tabs on Ramin Kain without engaging Shadowstone."

Crane smiled. "I'm confident you will find a way."

Chloe frowned. "Yes, Sir."

"That's what I like to hear," Cornelius said. He reached forward and patted Chloe's knee. "Now go and feed."

"Thank you."

Cornelius watched Chloe rise, bow and leave. Throughout the meeting she'd been attentive, responsive, genuine – the old Chloe was back.

* * *

The Raven's smartphone vibrated silently beneath their pillow. They woke up on the second vibration, grabbed the phone and got out of bed. They glided silently over the floor, wrapped a bathrobe over their shoulders and stole from the room. The other person they shared the room with remained blissfully asleep.

The Raven had participated in the deployment of the sensors that watched the area around the safe house and the barns. They had ensured there was a single narrow path through them to the haystack. The Raven used all their Red Empire Ninjitsu skills to navigate their way past the sensors. They moved around to the far side of the haystack, out of sight of the safe house.

The Raven read the text message. 'Request Contact.'

It was the other Red Empire agent. The Raven sent the next check message in the list they had memorized as a child. 'A red blade flies in the shadows.'

A few moments later, their smartphone vibrated with the response. 'And finds its intended mark.'

Satisfied with the response. The Raven dialed the quantum address. The agent answered the call on the first ring.

The agent, their voice depersonalized and masked by the software declared, "I have two tasks for you."

"Yes, I'm ready."

"Ramin Kain is now in play. Bug his phone with a tracker at the earliest opportunity. It is critical you ensure that other members of the Mirovar force team are aware of the bug and are able to track his movements. Send me a text when you have done it."

The Raven considered their options. There was a way they could do it. "Understood."

"I need you to place an immediate conference call to Shabbah al Ahmar using your phone as a node."

The Raven realized the agent did not have the capability to contact the Red Ghost directly. The agent had to be a third party and not a true member of the Red Empire. A shiver crawled over the Raven's shoulders.

"Of course," the Raven agreed. "I will place the call now."

The Raven completed setting up the conference call. Their phone vibrated once and became silent, excluding the Raven from the conference call. The agent would talk with the Red Ghost in unbreakable privacy. Three minutes later, the conference call ended with another vibration.

The Raven stared at their smartphone for a long moment. What were the agent and the Red Ghost planning? How would the Raven be involved beyond the bugging of Kain's phone? What would be the impact on the Mirovar force team? Who was the agent?

Filled with unanswered questions, the Raven made their way stealthily back to their bedroom. Five minutes later, they were under the covers of their bed, their mind still buzzing with questions. One loomed over the rest, leaving the Raven feeling sick to their stomach. Was the agent a rogue vampire?

They had no answer.

* * *

Half a dozen or more AK-47s fired on full auto, the bullets ripping through the wooden crates in the Aleppo warehouse. Cemal, the team's Kurdish guide, rocked backward and slumped to the ground; the top half of his skull splashed across the crates.

Captain John Tilson and his team of special forces operatives crouched behind whatever cover they could find, pinned down by the Syrians in the warehouse. The Syrian Army had shown up ten seconds ago and had opened fire immediately. He was already two men down. The rest of his team dragging Carter and Woodstock back. They had come in by truck from the town of Reyhanli, forty-five miles away, across the border in Turkey. There had been rock-solid intelligence the warehouse held a chemical weapons cache. The mission was simple, identify and record the weapons, and then destroy them.

That mission had gone straight to hell. The new mission was equally simple – survive.

"Back to the truck," John shouted. His men didn't need any urging. They fought their way back to the other end of the warehouse where the truck waited, engine idling.

Sargent Smith, John's 2IC, pumped a grenade toward the Syrians and followed it with a burst from his H&K 416 rifle. The grenade exploded. Men shrieked and cursed, and the hail of bullets from the Syrians lessened for a moment.

"Call in a drone strike," John commanded. He loaded a fresh mag, and zig-zagged back past another crate, bullets whizzing overhead.

Smith ducked, ran beside him and swore bitterly, "Damn comms are down."

"What the hell?" John asked.

"We're being jammed," Smith declared, his face bleak.

"It's a fucking trap," John called out. He twisted up and over the crate next to him and emptied his clip at the advancing Syrians. Two collapsed, and the rest dodged to the sides.

Smith cursed, "What a clusterfuck!"

John shook his head with dismay. "Someone's trying to get us killed. The mission's compromised, we need to exfiltrate now."

The truck's wheels smoked as it lurched backward toward the team. It smashed through crates of dry goods, spilling bags of rice across the concrete floor.

"Quickly now," John called out, urging his team forward.

Two of his men carried the wounded over their shoulders to the back of the truck. The rest of the team covered their retreat. Smoke bloomed from the hot barrels of their assault rifles and grenades cracked and boomed. The Syrians paused in their advance, taking cover where they could. John and Sargent Smith were the last to reach the back of the truck.

A rocket-propelled grenade zoomed over them, striking the cabin of the truck which promptly exploded in a yellow glare, killing the driver instantly. Machine-gun fire erupted from the side of the warehouse and raked the back of the truck. John watched in horror as a stream of bullets cut his team to pieces. He turned back toward the approaching Syrians and fired again, taking out the nearest with a head shot. A hail of bullets returned, some hitting his body armor but three more went through his lower gut.

John fell backward onto the floor. Sargent Smith stepped over him, his H&K blazing as his bullets ripped through the Syrians. Smith jerked backward, slumping to the side, his H&K clattering to the floor. His hands gripped his throat where a round had slashed through it, blood pouring past his fingers.

The firing stopped.

The Syrians advanced, their boots making heavy footfalls over the warehouse floor. A Syrian Army officer crouched next to John, pointed a 9mm pistol at his face and asked in passable English, "So Yankee, what in Allah's name are you—"

A shining sword blade appeared through the officer's skull. The tip dripping blood for a fraction of a second before the blade disappeared. John could hardly believe what he'd seen. It had happened so fast. The officer's body started to fall toward him. It stopped in mid-air, a handspan above him, and then flew backward like a broken toy across the warehouse. Wild shooting and panicked screaming erupted nearby. The shooting stopped first, and then the screaming a couple of seconds later.

A stunningly beautiful brunette appeared over him. A guardian angel with cold blue eyes, dressed in black combat fatigues. She put her sword down and knelt on one knee beside him. She pulled a thick syringe filled with red fluid from her belt and thrust the needle into the side of his heart.

"What ... are ... doing?" John managed to ask.

"Saving your life," she declared.

Behind her stood a tall, slim man, armed with a longsword. Figures blurred in movement at the edge of John's vision. He took another breath. That was when the gut shots faded into the background, and the real pain began.

* * *

It was late on Sunday night when James Haley's smartphone rang. The caller ID indicated, 'Chloe Armitage.'

He picked it up and asked, "Chloe?"

"Yes, James," Chloe answered. "I have a new mission for you."

"What do you want me to do?"

"You need to pack your bags. I've organized a private jet for you out of JFK airport at 02:00 flying direct to Jerusalem."

"A R.I.S.C jet?"

Chloe laughed briefly. "No. It's off the books. I'll text you the specifics."

"Okay. What's the mission objective?"

"We're going to assist the Red Empire to capture General Haras Mosule."

James smiled; he loved the audacity of Chloe's plans. "Captured, not killed?"

"Captured. It is essential we keep him alive. I just need him on ice for a while."

"How do I contact the Red Empire?"

"The Red Empire will contact you via my associate, Marcus Drake. He is in Jerusalem and will be a key ally in this mission."

"Do we have any Shadowstone assets on the ground?"

"Yes. However, they must never find out what is really going on. There is a mobile Shadowstone annex in operation. We have four agents there right now. Your Shadowstone contact on arrival in Jerusalem is Gareth Nightingale. I will send through all the necessary quantum addresses, and I will ensure that all your contacts are aware of your arrival."

"Is there anything else?"

"After the capture of Haras Mosule, I need you to escort Red Empire assassins into the UK and the US."

James blinked with surprise. "… Where in the UK and the US?"

"There is a private airstrip outside of Whitby in Yorkshire, and the US site is Logan International Airport in Boston. You will need to manage customs and border controls in both countries."

"Sure. I have ghost ID templates in the Panopticon. I can use them to set up internationally viable identities that will pass inspection by any US or UK government agency."

"Excellent. That's why you're on this mission. You're perfectly placed to make it work."

"Why do we need these guys."

"For use against the Mirovar force team."

James nodded. "Understood. Is there anything else?"

"There are detailed briefing notes on the plane which should answer any other questions you may have."

"Yes, Chloe."

"Good hunting, James."

"Thanks, Chloe."

The call disconnected. James consulted his watch. The flight would leave in three and a half hours. Plenty of time to get ready and make his way to the airport. He relished the idea of getting into the thick of operations on the ground. It was what he excelled at. No more herding clean-up squads and conducting endless evidence suppression. In the last four days, he'd let go of the shame he'd felt over killing his own men. Their deaths now served a far greater purpose, the protection of humanity. It was a purpose he'd grabbed with both hands, like a drowning man clutching at a life raft in the middle of an ocean storm.

James got his suitcase out of his wardrobe and opened it up on his bed. It was time to pack.

* * *

The Red Empire assassin lay crucified on an X-shaped frame. The raw steel frame stood within a bare open space. The floor was polished concrete, the ceiling and walls lost in darkness. A single modern lantern resting a dozen feet in front of the frame provided illumination.

The assassin's eyes flickered open as he regained consciousness. He gasped in pain. Metal spikes pierced his feet, knees, elbows and hands, pinning him to the frame like an exotic butterfly to a piece of corkboard. But unlike an insect in a collection – he was still very much alive.

General Haras Mosule emerged from the shadows and said calmly, "I see that you have returned to us."

He carried a squat, gray, ceramic urn. It was fat bodied with a narrow neck. He placed it on the floor next to the lantern. "I've grown tired of hunting you and your ilk. You are the unlucky one caught just when my patience has become exhausted."

"Traitor! I will give you nothing," the assassin shouted.

Haras frowned at him. "We will see if an ancient pet of the Red Empire changes your mind."

The assassin's gaze focused on the urn. His skin paled, his eyes widened, and he whispered incredulously, "Olgoi Khorkhoi?"

"Yes, Al Far," Haras answered. "A Mongolian death worm."

Al Far shuddered on the cross. His hands clenching spasmodically. Fresh blood dripped from his wrists and splattered on the concrete.

Haras smiled briefly, shaking his head gently. "I've recently fed; you will not distract me with such a display."

Al Far rallied, his eyes flashing with a trace of hope. "It's a trick. That urn is too small to hold a worm."

"You are right," Haras agreed, nodding. His eyes gleamed in the lantern light. "It's too small to hold even a young juvenile worm."

Haras pulled a thick, black, rubber glove from behind his belt and stretched it over his right hand. The glove reached up to his elbow, he flexed his fingers in front of his face, making sure that the glove fitted perfectly and was free of holes. He knew exactly how dangerous a Mongolian death worm was to human or vampire. The venom of an adult worm could kill a man in seconds and a vampire in minutes. Just touching the skin of a death worm was hideously painful. The larval form was without deadly venom, but its touch was as agonizing as an adult. For the purpose of interrogation, the larval form was far more useful than an adult worm.

Haras unlocked the lid, lifting it slowly and carefully off the urn. His gloved hand blurred down into the urn's neck. His arm vibrated and thrashed as he hunted the worm with all his vampiric speed and ancient Red Empire knowledge. Fine sand sprayed across the concrete floor as he jerked his hand free. In his grip writhed a pale worm, an oversized maggot, two inches thick and nine inches long. Its maw gaped open, revealing a trilateral arrangement of curved black fangs. Lines of smaller teeth disappeared in rows down its throat. Its tail ended in a hard nub, the immature form of a deadly sting.

Haras approached Al Far, putting the worm a hand span in front of his eyes. The larva responded by straining in Haras' grip, repeatedly lunging at the man's face.

Haras leaned in and whispered, "A freshly hatched larva."

Al Far moaned, pulling his head back as far as he could.

"This one is hungry," Haras stated, staring at Al Far with an avid gaze. "He hasn't fed for days. I think he's quite starved, the poor thing."

"Tanin al Layl – you and the vampires will never win."

Haras snorted. "You know my old name. No one has called me the Night Dragon for more than a century."

Al Far ground out between gritted teeth, "The Red Empire never forgets."

Haras snorted. "And yet nearly two centuries have passed without reprisal. The Red Empire's memory is nothing but an empty threat."

Al Far stared at Haras, and vowed, "And we never forgive. We will punish you for your betrayal. You should have greeted the dawn on the first day you discovered you were a vampire, rather than live in shame."

Haras smiled grimly. "You should worry about yourself first." He pushed the worm closer, to within an inch of Al Far's eyes. "Where is the location of the Red Empire Citadel? Tell me now, and the worm goes back in the urn."

Al Far shook his head, his lips pressed tightly together.

"I will kill you quickly."

The assassin shook his head again, then snapped, "I do not fear death."

None of us fear death," Haras agreed. "It's the dying that's the problem." He hummed, shrugged his shoulders and took a step back.

Al Far glared at him in silence.

Haras ripped Al Far's tunic open, baring his chest and stomach. He dangled the worm in front of Al Far's abdomen and declared, "They like the soft flesh best. It takes a longer time to die when they enter there."

The worm writhed and twisted. Its powerful muscles rippling under its skin. It turned and snapped at Haras' fingers. He jerked his hand back. Grinning ruefully, he re-established a sure grip on the larva.

Haras promised, "You will tell me in the end."

"Never," averred Al Far.

Haras slapped the worm onto Al Far's stomach. In less than a second fresh blood splashed on the floor and the worm disappeared into the assassin's abdomen. Al Far's eyes rolled upward, and he screamed in agony.

Haras stepped away. The bare skin over Al Far's torso writhed, several ribs cracked loudly as the assassin's body bucked on the frame. The bloody head of the worm emerged for a moment, its maw working, clearing meat and gristle before looping over to burrow back into the man's body.

Haras allowed the worm to feast for another ten seconds as Al Far shrieked and cried out. His hand blurred forward like a knife through the first entry wound and with a loud sucking sound he pulled the blood drenched worm free from Al Far's body. The worm, slick with blood, whipped back and forth in Haras' iron grip, its maw snapping open and shut in abject lust for flesh.

Al Far gasped and moaned in relief.

Haras leaned in close and whispered. "Where is the Citadel or it goes back in?"

Al Far whispered a handful of words and then convulsed, blood pouring from his mouth. Haras grinned, a hard light in his eyes. He now knew where the Red Empire Citadel lay hidden. His long search was at an end.

He replaced the death worm larva back into the urn and closed the lid, carefully locking it tight. He reflected upon his mission. *We must act immediately before the Red Empire discover we have compromised the location of their citadel. It is time to use the newly recruited praetorians against them. We will see how their modern weapons and tactics go against our ancient foe.*

Haras picked up the urn and disappeared into the darkness. He left the pinned corpse of the Red Empire assassin dripping blood onto the cold concrete floor.

* * *

Al Far's handful of words had led Haras Mosule to the location of the Red Empire Citadel.

Months of fruitless searching of Jerusalem, both above and below ground, had left Haras with two things; a burning hunger to come to grips with his enemies and a very detailed map. Al Far's information had neatly filled in a blank space on Haras' map. A space near enough to a main sewer line to provide a remarkable opportunity.

It had taken sixteen hours to mobilize a team of workmen to cut a path through concrete and raw stone from the sewer into the Citadel's main air duct. The final breakthrough into the duct had taken an hour of careful work to muffle the sound and vibration.

Haras' eyes gleamed in the darkness, and he smiled. This was a rare instance where pure brute force was preferable to subtlety.

The breach in the main air duct bypassed the duct outlets. The outlets to the surface were too small for anything approximating a human to pass, and useless as a means to enter or exit the Citadel. Without doubt, the latest Red Empire technology would scan the pipes and lay traps against any feasible intrusion. Autonomous drones with motion detectors would randomly travel along the ducts, setting off alarms over anything larger than a mouse. The drones would also traverse the main air duct but with so much territory to cover the chances of meeting one this far into the Citadel was greatly reduced.

It was a calculated risk Haras was willing to take.

He'd donned the traditional garb of a Red Empire assassin, the better to confuse his opponents in the event of a fight. The workmen were all dead. The last drained of his blood to sate Haras' appetite and maximize his ability to heal from any wounds.

His ear bud communication device whispered in his ear. Marcus Drake and the new praetorians were heading toward the staging point within a secured warehouse. Haras turned from the hole and blurred through the sewers. It was time to organize a diversion to hide his stealthy mission into the heart of the Citadel. Soon he would have the Interpretive Codex in his hands.

* * *

Facing an array of computer screens, James Haley sat alone inside a shipping container and considered recent events.

The flight from New York to Jerusalem had taken five hours. Chloe's off the books plane had turned out to be a supersonic Spike 512 business jet. James had taken the opportunity to get a nap during the flight before landing at 14:00 local time. Gareth Nightingale, the local head of the Shadowstone annex had met him at the airport and introduced him to the mobile command center in a shipping container on the trailer of a Ford rig. Nightingale had familiarized James with the mobile command center operations and provided him with an initial brief on the tactical environment in Jerusalem. He'd then declared he had no further part to play in the operation and had left just before sunset.

The Ford rig had driven from the airport and pulled into a nondescript warehouse. The driver had exited the cab and made a beeline for the exit. The truck would remain stationary in the warehouse during the operation. Ten minutes later James had met with the Vampire Dominion force.

They had emerged from the sewers, ten of them, led by General Haras Mosule. They wore typical Red Empire combat attire, but most carried modern weapons. One who looked like he could have a role as Thor in a Hollywood blockbuster had introduced himself as Marcus Drake.

Drake had then introduced an eight-man combat team led by Captain Tilson. They were heavily armed with modified M249 light machine guns fitted with two hundred round magazines and an under barrel experimental X41 rocket launcher. They also carried an array of white phosphorus grenades and thermobaric rockets.

James had nodded to himself. The focus on area of effect weapons made sense against fast moving opponents. He'd looked closely at the men, one of them had grinned at him, his fangs clearly visible in the gloom of the warehouse. They were all vampires, and by their modern bearing and speech, newly recruited. James had helped fit helmet cameras and strapped tactical communications rigs to their heads. The command center would act as a secure communications hub and would provide a control point for an array of autonomous ground and air vehicles, and a pair of high-flying surveillance drones.

The General had given the team their orders and emphasized the necessity of acting quickly. The General's information would grow stale as soon as the Red Empire realized their enemies knew the location of their secret citadel. One of the new praetorians had remarked wryly about "Nuking the site from orbit," and the General had simply stared at him until the young man looked away. He'd ended the briefing by giving James his orders. The team then left the warehouse, blurring away to the sewers.

That was just under thirty minutes ago.

Marcus Drake's deep voice cut through James' headset, and he declared, "Our men are in position."

Unleash the drones, James thought.

His fingers flew over the keyboard and one of the screens divided into twenty smaller views. Each mini-screen displayed a feed from a tiny camera mounted on a scurrying autonomous ground vehicle. The views were green lit, light amplified data feeds of the sewers near the Red Empire citadel.

"Crawlers are away," James broadcast to the team.

"Copy that," Marcus replied.

The vehicles rolled along the access paths next to the sewers, scanning for threats, identifying cameras, traps and automated weapons. Whenever they found something, they would fire an infra-red laser at it. The laser was small, but so were the hidden motion sensors and cameras. The twenty machines converged in a rough circle through the sewers toward the target. The Red Empire would know they were under attack as they lost sensors and cameras, but they could not be sure who was attacking or what size the force was.

The circle of drones contracted to the point where it was a mile across. James waited for the inevitable response. A handful of seconds later sentry guns opened fire. Bright bursts of light bloomed in the green tinged views. The data feeds from the autonomous ground vehicles started to go dark as the defenses shot the individual drones to pieces. They'd expected sentry weapons. The ground drones were expendable. Every drone that 'died,' identified the location of an automatic weapon.

James flicked a switch and broadcast, "Fliers are away."

"Copy that," Marcus replied for the second time.

The second wave of drones, held behind the first wave of crawlers, swept forward through the sewers. Each of the second wave drones was a mini helicopter, the size of a tennis ball equipped with an explosive charge. The fliers flew erratically toward the sentry guns. Bullets flashing past them. A counter in front of James switched down from a 100 to 99, 98, 94, 91, 90, 86, paused for a second as three mini-views went dark in green flashes indicating successful detonations. The drones swarmed forward; the vampire assault team close behind them. The advancing drones came into contact with more sentry guns, the counter dropping rapidly into the 70s. The sound of gunfire came through the helmet comm links as the praetorians pushed up behind the drones. The circle contracted to a thousand yards across. The counter dropped past 50. The fire from the automatic sentry weapons intensified as the circle contracted past five hundred yards. In seconds, his drones advanced another hundred yards, and the flier counter dropped to 24. The praetorians pushed in closer. They wanted to be right on top of the front door of the Citadel when they ran out of drones. Their job was to kick it down, push in hard, kill anyone they found, and then draw the assassins out of the citadel by retreating back into the sewers.

James vectored a reserve force of fliers past the praetorians. The drones zipped past Captain Tilson's soldiers and threw themselves at the remaining sentry guns. The counter momentarily rose to 48 with the commitment of the reserves and then rapidly dropped back below 30. The circle contracted to two hundred yards across, and the praetorians pulled to a halt.

They were close enough to see the entrance of the Red Empire Citadel. The counter was down to 9 fliers. They died in the next two seconds, taken apart by a pair of belt fed M134D-H miniguns. The automated guns tracked left and right, searching for targets as gray smoke curled from their barrels.

Captain Tilson's soldiers blurred forward as a coordinated unit, eight thermobaric bombs rocketing toward the sentry guns. The men maneuvered backward as a well-drilled team. The explosions whited out all communications. James scanned the monitors. The head cams all came back online a second later. The team blurred forward again, rockets flying from the launchers under their gun barrels. The rockets exploded against the main doors, evaporating the entrance to the Citadel.

The force disappeared through the smashed doorway. Their head cams went dark. A single line of white text, 'No Signal,' appeared in the middle of each head cam view.

James frowned and demanded, "Captain Tilson, report in ... Marcus Drake, report in ... anyone?"

The only response was utter silence.

"Recording comms down at 20:16:34."

He shook his head with dismay. Every monitor viewing a location within a mile of the Citadel was dark. Only the views from the high-flying drones overhead were still working. It was as if everyone in the team had simply vanished.

He considered the mission's true objective and wondered if they'd captured the target.

Where was General Haras Mosule?

* * *

The air duct was three feet in diameter, and Haras had nearly flown along it.

He came to an abrupt halt. A foot in front of him spun a metal fan. He pulled a device from his belt. A very short-range industrial cutting laser, good for a single shot. He drew it close to the center of the blades and pressed the trigger. The laser gleamed like a living ruby in his vampire vision as it cut through the fans. He nimbly caught the blades as they separated from the hub and put them quietly aside. A moment later, he was past the fan and rushing along the air duct.

Haras came to a screened vent. He peered through it and listened carefully. His vampire senses extended to their maximum capability. He could hear the beating of six distinct hearts within fifty yards of his position. He crouched closer to the screen, the tip of his veiled nose an inch away from it. His brown eyes swiveled left and right. There were four Red

Empire assassins in the immediate vicinity. They were standing still, waiting in the typical assassin guard pose. Relaxed, alert, and neatly balanced on their feet. He could burst through the screen with ease, but they would be on him in a moment.

He frowned. He was confident that he could defeat any two Red Empire assassins at the same time, but four at once would tip the odds in their favor. He waited; the first phase of his strategy was due to start any moment.

The explosions at the entrance of the citadel reverberated through the complex. The guards in the room all became preternaturally still. The lights in the ceiling of the room switched to a slowly strobing red. The Citadel was under attack. Haras grinned, soon at least some of the guards would have to leave to deal with the soldiers attacking through the front door.

There was a soft whirr. A metal shield began descending over the vent.

Haras' mind raced, *a lock down system!*

His eyes widened, he thrust with all his might at the vent's screen. It exploded into the room. He quickly followed it, catapulting forward through the vent and landing on his feet in the middle of the chamber. The four Red Empire assassins immediately blurred forward, their curved swords gleaming wetly in the red emergency lighting.

Haras dropped into silence, ramped, drew his swords in a flash, and fought for his life.

* * *

The crawler adjusted its position. Easing back past the blast debris before the front entrance of the Red Empire Citadel. Its motion detector red-lined. Its tracks spun, and it whirred backward at maximum speed. Its light intensifying camera continued to face the dark entrance. Its microphone, at full sensitivity, registered an outrush of air through the doorway.

A tall, blond vampire was the first to emerge from the darkness. His left arm hung limply at his side as he blurred past the crawler. A moment later, another four vampire soldiers erupted from the gloom, rushed past it, and disappeared from its scopes.

A second later a pair of rockets zoomed out of the doorway, whizzing over the crawler and vanishing around the sewer corners. A fraction of a second later there were massive explosions, and fire rolled back through the sewer pipes. The crawler lay flat against the ground as the edge of the flames blew over it.

The crawler started to rise, then flattened again. Red Empire assassins blurred above it. Booted feet fell to the left and right of the crawler as it hugged the concrete floor. In a moment, the assassins were gone.

The sewer was quiet, then gunfire erupted in the distance. There was the crump of explosions, magnified in the confined space of the sewers.

The crawler rose slowly, pivoted 180 degrees on its tracks and rolled forward. Its communications with the command center had failed at 20:16:34. It had waited sixty seconds for the comms to come back online. The default protocol kicking in after the re-connect sequence had timed out. The crawler scanned the space in front of it for threats. It was time to preserve itself, leave the Red Empire Citadel behind, and find its way back to its origin point.

The crawler moved off into the pitch darkness.

* * *

There was a loud crack.

Haras let go of the fourth Red Empire assassin's throat, and the man collapsed limply to the floor. Haras winced and looked down at his waist. A polished hilt and leathered handle jutted out from his stomach. The blade had pierced all the way through, courtesy of the dying effort of the assassin. He flicked his remaining sword clean and sheathed it at his belt. With both hands, Haras pulled the short-bladed sword from his gut and dropped it on the floor. He held his fingers over the wound for a few seconds, he could feel it knitting back together.

Haras stepped over the fourth assassin's body. His second sword lay embedded in the skull of the third assassin. He pulled it free, flicked it clean and sheathed it next to the first. He walked calmly to the first assassin to die. An officer of the Red Empire. His head lay severed from his body, and Haras picked it up by the hair. With the officer's head in hand, he strode over to a large, steel door in the wall opposite the chamber's entrance. Next to the door was a retinal scanner. He pried open the head's right eyelid and positioned the eye in front of the scanner.

"This had better work," he whispered.

A green light appeared above the retinal scanner.

Haras could taste victory. The Codex would be on the other side of the door. The Red Empire never changed the architecture of their citadels. The Codex vault was always located at the geometric center of the building. Only the defenses around it had evolved over time.

Something slammed behind him. The lights switched from dull red to a bright white glare. Dropping the head; Haras whirled around, shielding his eyes with his hands. Gray spots danced in front of him. He blinked, the spots cleared and he dropped his hands. There was a great polished steel door across the exit. Another steel sheet covered the vent he'd used to enter the chamber. The vault door behind him remained still and silent.

Stones ground above him, a thin sprinkle of dust falling from the ceiling. Hundreds of tiny holes appeared above him, and a gleaming mist of metal dust puffed into the room. Haras' heart sank. The cold, sharp, stench was unmistakable. He coughed as the first particles struck his face. His mouth went numb. He collapsed face down on the floor before the full effect hit him.

In moments, his body lay paralyzed, but his mind remained active. *Silver!*

The far door slammed again. Footsteps, dulled by the paralytic effect on his hearing, approached.

A triumphant voice spoke, sounding as if it was a long way away, "Wrap him in the silver net and transport him to the real Citadel."

"Yes, Shabbah al Ahmar."

"Remove our honored dead from this illusion and detonate the charges. Erase all existence of this place."

Helpless rage burned through Haras as strong hands lifted him and carried him away.

Al Far managed to lie to me, Haras thought incredulously. *He was bait. This whole site was a trap.*

* * *

The mid-morning sunlight bathed the private Jerusalem airfield. Four black Chevrolet Suburbans sat on the tarmac. In front of them rested a dart-shaped white and blue, Spike 512 supersonic business jet.

James Haley stood at the base of the stairs leading up to the cabin. Beside him was a simple fold away table with a cardboard box on it. The last two men in the line moved in front of him. There was a single parcel left in the cardboard box. He looked at the assassins in front of him. One he recognized from the data Marcus Drake had provided him. Nasr al Dam, the Blood Eagle, team leader of the group destined for the USA. Marcus' data had listed sixteen Red Empire assassins organized into two teams. James had spent all his available time over the last two days preparing a cover identity for each of the men. He'd handed a package to each of them before they boarded the plane.

James gave the final package to Nasr al Dam and indicated the plane with a slight nod of his head. Nasr nodded once, mounted the stairs and disappeared into the body of the plane.

The final assassin moved forward to stand directly in front of James. The man was of medium height and athletic build, with a touch of gray at the temples and in his neatly cropped beard. He carried himself with the casual ease of a skilled operator. It was clear this was a man who stood high in the ranks of the Red Empire. They spent a long moment staring at each other. A slight smile of studied indifference curled the edge of the man's mouth, and he said, "I am Thueban Kabir. You may call me Taipan."

"Okay," James replied, arching an eyebrow. "You have something to tell me?"

"Yes. You have delivered us our traitor, and in return, we have kept our word. These men will serve your master unto death, or if she orders them to attack each other or the Red Empire – whichever comes first."

James nodded once.

Taipan turned on his heel and strode over to the closest car. He quickly got in, and the suburbans pulled away.

James made a note to himself to remember everything that he could about Thueban Kabir or given a literal translation of his name, the Great Serpent. He'd given James the name Taipan. A snake species with the most toxic venom in the reptilian world. A single bite could kill a hundred people.

James asked himself, *is Taipan the most dangerous assassin in the Red Empire?* He believed it was a question he would one day have to answer. He walked up the flight of stairs and entered the crowded interior of the plane. The first Red Empire operatives to board had taken all the seats, and the rest filled the aisle. He grunted, then shrugged. He could stand – it would be a quick flight. First stop would be Whitby in Yorkshire, where he would drop off most of his cargo and four of the assassins. Then it would be another quick flight over the Atlantic to Logan International Airport in Boston. The final twelve assassins were for a mission in New England.

Time was fast running out for the Mirovar force team and their safe house in Maine.

* * *

Haras Mosule sat in utter darkness. He extended his vampire senses to their maximum power. The susurration of air through a vent far above him was the only thing he could hear.

The floor was hard and smooth. It felt like polished glass, as did the walls. He'd measured the dimensions of his cell. It was a cylinder, three yards across and an unknown number deep. The Red Empire had descended with him via a rope ladder. They had removed the silver net and wiped off the silver dust. They had used the rope to climb out of the hole. The rope had disappeared into the darkness and minutes later the silver paralysis was gone.

He had no way to judge the passage of time, but given how famished he was, it was at least two days since his capture.

A thin green slit appeared above him. Haras blurred to the center of the cylinder directly beneath it.

The light disappeared for a moment, and a hard voice snapped, "Here you go bloodsucker."

The green strip appeared twice more. There was movement above him. Something was falling toward him. He stepped aside and adroitly caught a soft plastic bag. Moments later, he caught two more. His nostrils flared with a familiar scent. He plunged his face into the first bag. His fangs ripping through the plastic and warm blood splashed into his mouth. He gulped and sucked, finally twisting and squeezing the last drop of blood from the bag. He dealt with the second and third bag in the same manner.

"Shabbah al Ahmar wants to keep me alive," Haras stated to the empty cell. "But for what purpose?"

Haras' mind flashed back to the capture of Al Far. Marcus Drake had led him to where he'd discovered Al Far. Not obviously, but through hints during the night. They had captured Al Far together after a chase. The rising sun had nearly beaten them. Marcus Drake had knocked Al Far unconscious and grinned at Haras in triumph.

The whole sequence of events over the two days before Haras' capture stank of treachery.

Marcus Drake had captured Al Far, what if the Red Empire had deliberately given Al Far to Drake. That would mean that at the very least Drake was a traitor, and most likely so was Armitage.

The parts clicked together – Chloe Armitage and Marcus Drake had betrayed him to the Red Empire. He couldn't imagine any reason for the Red Ghost to keep him alive. His imprisonment must serve another's purpose. The only other person with enough power to deal with the Red Empire was Chloe Armitage.

Haras shook his head. Crane and the Vampire Dominion were in deep danger, and there was nothing that he could do about it.

Chapter Six

BREAKING: Explosion Reported in Jerusalem.

There are reports of a massive explosion south of the Old City.

Published 08/14 14:05 EST

Witnesses report that a massive crater has formed a mile south of the walls of the Old City. Initial reports from Jerusalem authorities attribute the explosion to a gas leak in the sewers. The explosion occurred minutes ago just after 11PM local time.

– Breaking News article for The New York World site on the Internet.

* * *

White Hill, Maine, August 19th, 17:45

Everyone lies.

It was a truism Deon Lamar lived by. Fate had seen fit to gift Deon with the ability to see through lies. To discern falsehood and unravel webs of deception. To uncover spies and traitors. It was a rare talent amongst the Ramp initiated, and Deon was a master of it.

He'd vowed to fulfill his mission to investigate the Mirovar force team. The identification of the Red Empire agent would only be the first step. He would follow with the co-option of their means of communication, the laying of traps and the capture of their accomplice. In the end, he would charge with treason all those who had betrayed the Order.

A fiery righteousness burned brightly within him. He visualized the agent and their accomplice bound in chains before an inquisitorial court. The judges would make their stern and immutable judgments. He would take the guilty to a place where he could easily dispose of their bodies. It would be his honor to deliver swift and impartial justice with the executioner's sword.

It was a joyous mission, a true exercise of his gift. It was his calling to be an Order traveler. A spy hunter reporting directly to the Head of the Order. A man Deon revered as a living genius. A man with the vision to bring the Order into a state of perfection. The one man who had always acted with perfect integrity in his presence. The only man who was the exception to the rule. The man who had never lied.

169

Ramin Kain.

The deep, low-throated roar of the motorcycle's engine was unmistakable. Deon's Harley-Davidson, downshifted through its gears, rolling smoothly into the safe house yard. Deon was a thick-set man of medium height. He kicked the bike's foot stand into place, parking the bike in front of the house. Taking off his helmet, he put it on the bike seat. The late afternoon sunlight gleamed off his silver rimmed sunglasses. Taking them off, he rubbed his short, tightly curled hair with his free hand.

He'd arrived unannounced. All the better to begin his investigation with a surprise first impression. The yard was still. A lone farm tractor chugged away in the distance. The Order team stood in the shadows of the barn, watching him, hands still holding training weapons. A smile curled the edges of his lips, and his dark brown eyes narrowed with concentration. Amongst the group of young men and women was a Red Empire assassin pretending to be a member of the Order of Thoth.

His heart swelled with pride. He relished the opportunity to root the spy out and crush them. Samuel Luther's instructions came to mind. Twinging inwardly, his smile vanished; such satisfactions would have to wait. He was in the service of the Order of Thoth, reporting directly to Ramin Kain. Luther had been adamant about Ramin's directives. He must first identify the spy and then leave them in place to allow for the capture of their accomplice. The sublime righteous joy of delivering punishment to the wicked would have to wait.

And so, it would be. No matter how much he might chafe at such restrictions, the day of satisfaction would have to wait while a longer game played out to its inevitable conclusion.

Deon walked purposefully toward the team. It was time to get to work.

* * *

The man approached the force team like he owned the safe house farm and they were his guests.

He smiled confidently and declared forthrightly, "Francis, Juliette. Good to see you are both well. How is everyone?"

"All good. Thank you," Francis replied.

Juliette half smiled. "You're just in time for dinner, Deon. I'm sure that Mary and John can set another place."

Who do we have here? Another Order goon? Deon ... who? Anton thought warily to himself.

Deon looked past Francis and Juliette. Catching Anton's gaze, he said, "I see you have some new members in your team."

Anton stepped forward slowly, his hand outstretched to shake Deon's hand. "Yeah, Li," he indicated Li with a quick nod, "and I are new. I'm Anton Slayne."

Deon took his hand and shook it firmly. He clasped Anton on the shoulder with his free hand and declared, "My God, you're the spitting image of your grandfather as a young man."

"Yeah, I get that a lot."

Deon stared at Anton for a second, then grinned broadly. He turned, offering his hand to Li.

Li looked at his hand as if he was offering her a stale fish. Nodding once, she stared hard at him, and said, "Hello, Mr. Lamar. My father spoke of you."

Deon pulled his hand back, scratching nonchalantly behind his right ear. "All good I hope."

Li shrugged.

"Well then, let's not stand on ceremony. Please everyone, call me Deon."

"Great," Peter said. "Pleased to meet you again." He shook Deon's hand quickly. "I can smell Mary's cooking from here, and you know she doesn't like people coming late to her table."

There was a general assent, and everyone started moving across the yard toward the safe house.

Anton tugged on Li's elbow, and she slowed down. Chiara dropped in on Anton's other side.

"So, who is he?" Anton asked in a tight whisper.

"A traveler." Li and Chiara whispered back at the same time.

"That doesn't help."

"A spy catcher," Li explained.

"A walking lie detector," Chiara said. "He's only a problem if you have something to hide."

Anton shrugged his shoulders. "So, no trouble then."

Deon cast a glance over his shoulder at the three of them. For a fraction of a second, he stared directly at Anton. A slight smile curled the edges of his mouth before he turned to enter the safe house.

Anton sighed. He was beginning to wonder if there was anyone in the Order beyond the Mirovar force team that wasn't out to get him. Mounting the steps before the front door he asked himself, *it's not paranoia when they really are out to get you is it?*

* * *

Deon Lamar had tested the Raven at the last Order Conclave.

Afterwards, Francis Mirovar had formally accepted them into his force team and confirmed them as a full member of the Order of Thoth.

They had met other travelers over the years within the Order. Each time they had mastered their sympathetic and parasympathetic nervous system responses and kept their cover intact. The presence of the traveler could mean only one thing. Ramin Kain was investigating the Mirovar force team.

But what had prompted the investigation? Only Ramin Kain could assign a traveler to investigate a force team. It was clear that Kain had it in for Anton Slayne. The purpose of the investigation could be to find something that would allow Kain to eliminate Anton while he was still an unconfirmed novice. Even with the sanctuary of Juliette Mirovar in place, an Order Inquisition could possibly trump her sanctuary and reach Anton. But given Juliette was a loremaster and her husband a senior force leader, pitting an inquisition against Juliette sounded like a poor strategy.

If Anton wasn't the target of the traveler, then who was?

The Raven sighed softly. Kain must suspect there was a Red Empire spy in the Mirovar force team. If they knew who it was, the Raven would be in chains already or consuming false information to disrupt the plans of Shabbah al Ahmar. Since no one in the Order had revealed anything important to them, their cover most likely remained intact.

Therefore, Lamar was on a fishing expedition. The task at hand was to avoid the cast of his net.

The Raven needed a decoy. Someone to throw into the path of the traveler, ensuring they would become the focus of his investigation and not the Raven. It would have to be something major to distract a traveler. But it couldn't be anything that would hint at the Raven's mission or current assignment to insert a tracker on Ramin Kain's phone. It would also need to be a crime that would easily stick to the target. And above all else, it needed to be believable.

There was no apparent solution. The Raven was momentarily at a loss as to how to proceed. They shook their head slowly. They would have to wait, watching carefully until an opportunity presented itself.

Then they could pounce upon it.

They shook their head again. The Raven loved the other members of the Mirovar force team as if they were family, as well as brothers in arms. Whomever the Raven selected as a decoy; it would not be an easy decision.

The bonds of loyalty lay twisted within them. A knot of anguish tightened at the thought of sacrificing one of the other members of the Mirovar force team to serve their own mission.

They pushed the pain away. Disappointed with the presence of such weakness. What would their master Taipan think? What would Shabbah al Ahmar think? They couldn't tolerate such feelings. If they must sacrifice an innocent to advance the cause of eliminating the curse of vampires, then they must accept the sacrifice.

It was the Red Empire way.

The Raven steeled themselves, vowing to do what they must to succeed. The one positive of the presence of the traveler was Ramin Kain would not be far behind in paying a visit to the safe house. Their arrival would allow the Raven to plant the tracking software on Kain's phone. That would satisfy the last directive from the other Red Empire agent. They could use the opportunity provided by the discovery of the decoy to ensure that Kain's phone was properly co-opted. The Red Empire software would hide itself and the phone would continue to operate perfectly.

No one would be the wiser. But it was essential that other members of the force team could find out how to track the phone. That would be trickier. How to provide that information without giving away that they were also the source of the tracking software.

It was an unsolved problem, but the Raven was sure they would be able to manage it. Time was short, events were pressing, and they would have to take risks.

The Raven always lived with risk.

* * *

Peter Lamb held out a fist filled with straws.

Yvette, Jay, Chiara, Li and Anton stood in a semi-circle in front of him.

"Pick one. Whoever draws the short straw gets sober duty."

Anton waited until there were only two straws left, Peter's and his. Everyone else had picked a long straw. He shook his head and picked one at random, it was the short straw.

Peter sucked air through his teeth and clapped him on the shoulder. "Tough luck, mate. We'll really miss you at the party, but someone's gotta stay sober and keep watch. Can't have everyone on their ear if a bunch of vamps show up."

"What's the chance of that?"

"Pretty much zero," Peter stated with a shrug.

Anton sighed. "Catch you later." Picking up a tall glass of orange juice, he walked outside to the porch.

It was nine o'clock on a Saturday night in the middle of August. It was a beautifully clear and moonless night. There was the lightest of breezes flowing through the farm yard.

Anton sipped his orange juice, made a face and put it down on the porch. He walked over to the training barn and pulled a bale of hay from inside the wall. He positioned it a dozen yards back from the barn, lay down on top of it with his hands behind his head, and looked up at the stars.

His mind drifted for a few minutes, before picking up a current like a small boat captured on the edge of a whirlpool. The fateful events of April the 28th circled around him. His mother's torture and murder, and his father's abduction. He hadn't done enough since then. Chloe Armitage and Marcus Drake were still alive. His father was now a vampire imprisoned in silver, an undeserved half-life of torment.

He knew he would have to kill him. There was no coming back from being a vampire. It was the only way to free him, but God only knew where he was. A terrible sense of dismay attacked him, corroding any experience of peace.

How do you kill your father?

It was a horrible idea. It was something that had been lurking in the background. He'd pushed it aside, focusing on the training, learning everything he could and surviving the Order's boot camp. But now, during a quiet moment in the most peaceful of settings beneath a beautiful New England night sky, it had all come rushing back like some dreadful curse.

Anton exerted himself. Drawing upon his training, he evaporated his thoughts, falling into silence. The baleful images of the past disappeared like banished ghosts.

There was the barest whisper of movement nearby. A cool, gentle hand came down over his eyes, and he sat up with a start.

"Not much of a watchman, are you?" Li observed wryly. She was smiling mischievously with an eyebrow arched in a mock query. She balanced a tray with her other hand, supporting a glass jug filled with ice and a dark colored drink, and a pair of tall glasses.

She declared with a wave of her free hand, "I've made some iced tea."

"Great," Anton said, mildly disappointed. "I could really use something stronger."

Li frowned. "… Bad memories?"

"Yeah. I just feel … like I'm not doing enough."

"You can't rush it, Anton. You … no, we'll only get one chance at this."

There would be no second chances in a fight with Chloe Armitage. Anton remembered what he'd glimpsed on the Boston docks. Gang was a genius with a blade and she'd still beaten him. He asked, "When will we be ready if not now?"

"We're not ready," Li answered.

"You're sure?"

"Absolutely."

Anton sighed and shook his head. "How do we beat her?"

"… I honestly don't know," Li declared. She put the tray on the hay bale and sat down next to Anton. "You know what Father would do right now? He would pour some tea, and think about it."

Anton sat up, and Li positioned the tray between them. She took the jug and poured a glass for Anton and one for herself. Anton picked up his glass and Li did the same.

"Tea?"

"Yes."

"Not one of Juliette's specials?"

"No. Of course not."

Anton nodded. "Thanks."

"You're welcome."

Anton and Li sipped their tea in companionable silence. A mild fragrance from the tea filling the warm night air.

They emptied the glasses and Li moved the tray aside. In the moonless night, the shadows were deep, almost pitch black. The lights from the house were far behind them.

They both reached for each other at the same time. The silence of the night enveloped them. Anton's arms wrapped around Li and she moved in close. Li put her head against Anton's chest. He rested his chin on top of her hair. They held each other for a while, neither moving.

Li suddenly sobbed.

Anton's eyes were moist.

"Father," Li whispered in trenchant grief.

"I know."

"I miss him."

"I know."

Anton held her tight and Li wept quietly into his chest.

* * *

A slight breeze tickled the rooster-shaped weathervane, and it creaked as it rotated a lazy quarter turn.

The weathervane sat on a miniature version of the barn atop the safe house working barn. The blocky support was two yards long, a yard high and a yard wide, and provided a marvelous hiding place on a moonless night.

At least, that was how Chloe Armitage judged it. She sat in the thick shadows at the bottom of the weathervane on top of the barn. She stretched her long legs out in front of her with one ankle over the other and leaned back against the thick wooden base of the weathervane. She had used information provided by the Raven to carefully infiltrate the defenses of the safe house farm and had been sitting there for fifteen minutes.

Anton had emerged from the house, setting himself up on a hay bale near the training barn. Li Wu had joined him. She'd watched with interest as they shared tea and then quietly embraced each other.

Chloe frowned. If they had sought temporary oblivion in sex, she would have been happier. Instead, they had comforted each other in their mutual grief and cemented commitment to a shared purpose.

Emotional intimacy was dangerous. Emotional commitments could drag Anton away from her purpose. She could not allow such forces to persist in Anton's life.

She needed to remove any supports in Anton's life apart from those that would advance his combat skills. Li was a pillar who was restoring Anton's balance by giving him someone he could care about and relate to.

Li Wu was dangerous, she had to go. Chloe's eyes hardened. *Li Wu must die.* Li Wu's death would drive home Anton's sense of loss, horror, and need for revenge. She needed Marcus to be involved in the process. It couldn't be a random death. Li Wu's death needed to reinforce Anton's focus on Cornelius Crane and his original orders to seize the Papyrus of Hakron the Scribe and destroy Anton's family.

Events were in motion. Forces were on the move. Soon Li Wu must join her father in an unmarked grave. She was certain Li Wu would be dead within days.

Chloe waited for Anton and Li to return to the safe house. Once she was alone, she dropped down to the ground on the far side of the barn. She used her perfect memory to retrace her steps past the sensors to the outer perimeter of the farm.

Well away from the farm lights, she looked up at the clear, night sky. She stretched her senses to full awareness. The stars above glowed in an achingly beautiful river across the sky. The night sang with the rustles, clicks, and chirps of insects and night birds. A faint breeze caressed her face, ruffling her hair.

The beauty of the world filled her to overflowing, her heart aching with it. She could not bear to lose such beauty. She could not allow risk of harm to her world. Chloe vowed to herself to save all the beautiful things.

She was the only one who could.

* * *

Early morning sunlight speared through the kitchen windows.

The weekend was over. It had been two nights since the arrival of Deon Lamar, the Order spy hunter. Francis and Juliette had gone around the team and quietly advised them to be themselves and allow the traveler to do his work. They trusted their team and were confident that any inquiry was groundless and that Lamar would eventually leave empty handed.

Anton speared a sausage with his fork, spread some mustard on it and wolfed it down. Workouts that involved the Ramp burnt calories like a freight train, and he needed fuel. The sausage joined four fried eggs, three slices of toast, fried tomatoes, spinach, half a dozen rashers of bacon, honey, jam, buttered crumpets, a big glass of fresh whole milk with the cream settling on top of it and a pair of fresh, ripe oranges.

Across from him, Peter pushed his second plate away and tapped his taut stomach with both fists. "Damn that was good."

"Peter Lamb! No swearing. Not in my kitchen," Mary Jorgensen commanded, her gray eyes flashing.

Dismay flashed across Peter's face. "Sorry, Ma'am."

"You will be. I need a new load of firewood cut. Please see to it today."

"Yes, Ma'am. I'll see it done after lunch."

"Good."

Peter sighed and turned his attention back to Anton. He stroked his chin, his eyes gleaming mischievously. "I think we should all have code names when we go on missions."

"Yeah," Anton said, "such as?"

"Well, I would be Axeman, Li would be Bladestrike and Chiara would be Deathtouch."

"And what about me."

"Oh, … I think you would have to be Tiffany."

"Tiffany?" Anton said, pulling a face.

"C'mon – what's wrong with Tiffany? We could call you Tiff for short."

Anton rubbed his face, and then stated baldly, "Go for it. I'll be the most," Anton dropped his voice to a whisper, "bad-assed," and then raised it again, "vampire hunting, Tiffany on the planet."

"Speaking of," Peter mouthed, *bad-assery*, "it's time for more helicopter sims."

"Boys," Mary declared in exasperated tones. "I'm neither deaf nor blind. You've had your fill, now get out of my kitchen."

"Yes, Ma'am," Anton and Peter chorused together.

Anton got up from the table and asked, "What's the point of these sims? We don't have any helicopters."

Peter tilted his head. "You've heard of thievery, haven't you?"

Anton grinned. "You've stolen a nightfalcon?"

"Not yet. But I'm prepared to at the first opportunity."

Anton smiled and remarked sardonically, "I can just see it. It will work really well," he waved his right hand through a pair of figure eights and then smashed it into his left hand. "Until you run into something."

"Well let's test that out. You either shoot me down today, or I'm calling you Tiffany for the rest of the week."

Anton grinned and punched Peter's fist. "Done."

"That's the spirit," Peter enthused, clapping Anton on the shoulder. "Let's get to it."

"Sure," Anton followed Peter from the kitchen.

Lamar watched them leave, his face impassive as he nursed a cup of coffee.

* * *

There are no vampires in New Zealand.

The members of Justin Blake's extended family kept the islands clear of any bloodsuckers. Those were his mother's brothers and sisters, and his cousins on the Maori side of his ancestry. A family for whom the Order of Thoth and Ramp mastery seamlessly integrated with their ancient Maori beliefs.

His father, a US citizen, had brought his young Maori bride back to the west coast, and Justin had been born a year later. He'd lived most of his life in the US. Initiated into the Order at seventeen years of age, he'd taken command of his own force team at the young age of twenty-eight.

Now ten years later, he was on a personal mission for an old friend. He carried with him, tucked in a pocket inside his leather jacket, a letter. A letter addressed to Li Wu from her father. Gang had charged Justin to deliver the letter in the event of his death.

The engine of Justin's Harley-Davidson motorcycle rumbled as he pulled the bike to a halt in the farm yard. Motion to his right caught his eye. There was a lithe figure practicing with a katana in the shadows of a barn.

He parked his Harley and pulled off his helmet.

There was a squeal of delight. "Uncle. You're here!"

Suddenly there was a young Asian-American woman spread across his chest with her arms around his neck. He'd first met Li when he'd spent time training with Gang. She'd shyly asked him his name and he'd said casually to just call him, 'Uncle,' because Gang was like an older brother to him, and the pet name had stuck.

He hugged her back, a broad smile spread like sunshine across his face and he said, "Li, you've grown so much since I saw you last."

Li wrapped her legs around his flanks. She was a bundle of fierce enthusiasm in his arms. He placed one broad forearm under her hips and rubbed her back with his free hand. He whispered gently, "I know what happened. I share your loss. Gang was a great friend."

Li turned her head so that she could see his face. "You've been gone so long; why didn't you tell me you were coming?"

"Because it's a secret," Justin answered, pulling his head back and staring at her seriously.

Li scrunched up her nose and slid off him like a puma dropping off a tree.

Wrapping an arm around his lower back, Li looked up at him and asked, "What secret?"

"Have you somewhere we can talk?"

Li frowned. "How secret do we need to be?"

Justin shrugged his massive shoulders. "Just needs to be private."

"The library. It's normally deserted this late in the morning. Let's go there."

"Lead on."

Li stepped forward toward the safe house. Justin following her, shedding his black biker jacket. He wore a black T-shirt like a second skin. His heavy muscles rippling beneath the fabric as he followed Li into the house. Ducking his head reflexively as he walked through the door, his thick, dark curly hair still brushed the lintel. In moments, they were down the hall, and Li was showing him to a comfortable lounge chair in the library.

Justin started to sit down. Li reached out, grabbing his arm and declared, "I'm a terrible hostess. Can I get you something to eat or drink? You must be thirsty after your ride."

He smiled. "Just some cold water for now. I'll join you for lunch later."

"Sure, I'll be back in a moment."

Li ducked out of the room.

Justin looked around the library. He'd been at this safe house many years ago, before he'd become a force leader. He'd helped stock the armory under the barn. Justin had trained with the members of the Mirovar force team. Ticking off names in his head, most of them had survived. There had been some attrition, but less than most of the other teams. Only his own team maintained a better kill/casualty ratio. He glanced at the shelves lining the walls. The books looked worn and he recognized most of the titles. There was only a handful of new books; not much had changed in over a decade.

Li came back into the room with a tray which she placed on a low table in front of him. On the tray were a plate of dry crackers smothered in smoked trout pate, thick slices of aged cheddar, a large pitcher of ice water, and a pair of glasses.

Justin grinned. "You can take the girl out of the restaurant ..."

Then he faltered. Li sat down in a second lounge chair next to his. He saw memories of Gang in her eyes. Her grief was still quite raw. He reached over, picking up his leather jacket from where it lay draped over the back of a desk chair. Opening it up, he pulled a thick, double-folded, buff-colored, A4 envelope out of an inside pocket and gave it to Li.

"Your father wanted you to have this," he stated simply.

Li took the envelope and sat quietly for a long moment, staring at it.

Justin waited patiently.

She opened the envelope and pulled out a sheath of typed pages. Pinned to the top of the sheath with a paper clip was a hand-written note. She flicked her gaze from the note to Justin and back, and then began reading it out loud, "'I hope this letter finds you well little one. I wish I could be there with you, but I know that if you have survived to read this note, then my life has not been in vain, and my death was not a waste. The letter is all my research on the comings and goings of Ramin Kain and Samuel Luther. I only told you a fraction of what I found out. I didn't want you to lose all faith in what the Order stands for. The bearer of this message is a man who I would trust with your life. He, like the Mirovars and the Slaynes, understands the true soul of the Order. He lives for the protection of the innocent and come what may I would be pleased if he is with you.

BTW, I know you had a huge crush on him at fourteen.

Always your father.'"

She faltered for a moment on the last line. "'Gang Wu. The luckiest father in the world.'"

A tear fell onto the page, smudging the ink of Gang's name.

Li thrust the papers away. Wiping her cheeks with her hands, she sniffed, squeezing her eyes shut for a long moment. Taking a deep breath, she shook her head, her long hair swinging across her shoulders. She took another big breath, sniffing once more and composed herself. She picked up the pages of the letter. Separating the hand-written note from the rest, she placed it carefully back into the envelope. As she did so, something caught her eye. It was a tiny data stick the size of her thumbnail inside the envelope.

She fished it out and quickly moved to the desk in the corner of the room. On the desk was an open laptop. She logged in and accessed the data stick. A program ran, and map after map flashed up onto the screen. All marked with red path-lines.

Justin stood up, moving to stand behind her. He asked, "What is it?"

"I don't know yet," Li noted. Turning to the body of the letter she began reading the first page.

* * *

The Raven recognized Justin Blake.

They had first met at the last Order conclave. Blake had been too young for the Red Empire to establish a file on him while the young Raven had still been in training.

Blake was a concern for the Raven. The young force leader's career had risen like a flaming meteor streaking across the sky. His ascension established on the foundation of the loyalty he inspired in his team mates and his personal abilities for strategy, tactics, and combat.

He was an obvious rival for the position of the Head of the Order of Thoth. One day, the righteous would sweep the Kain/Luther cabal and their soulless supporters away. If Francis Mirovar didn't take the position of Head, then Blake would be the next logical choice.

The Raven stood in the shadows of the training barn. Li welcomed Blake like a long-lost brother, and they whispered something the Raven couldn't hear. They made a decision and went into the house. The Raven moved closer, spying on them through one of the library windows.

Blake gave Li an envelope. What did it contain? Was this the opportunity the Raven had been waiting for? Li was by far the least well known of the Mirovar force team. Li would be the easiest to sacrifice.

Where was Lamar?

The Raven went in search of the Order traveler, passing Li in the hallway as she headed toward the kitchen.

They nodded to each other in friendly greeting.

She looked happy. She looked to be happier than the Raven had ever seen her. The Raven's guts twisted. It was wrong to tip off Lamar, they pulled to a stop near the end of the hallway.

They ground their teeth in indecision. Their mission could not fail. They would honor their sacred duty regardless of personal feelings.

There would be no more weakness.

They walked through the back door. Lamar was meditating in the backyard. It was a practice that he did each day before lunch. The Raven walked up behind him. In minutes, they'd ensure Lamar's whole attention was focused on Li Wu.

The Raven prayed silently, that whatever Blake had brought Li would cast her in the worst possible light before the Order traveler.

* * *

Li finished reading the last page, quickly turning back to the laptop.

"The letter is a summary and a guide," she remarked. "The real information is on the stick, and it's dynamite."

Justin squatted down beside her so that he could see the laptop screen clearly. "Like what?"

"Father spent time tracking Luther and Kain over the last decade. However, most of the data is more than five years old." Li sucked on her bottom lip for a second, her eyes narrowing. "He stopped after Mother and Qiang died."

"He wanted to focus on you."

Li nodded. "I suppose that makes sense."

"Hmmm, what did he find out?"

"Kain never made a mistake when he looked for vampires. Every time he searched for vampires, he found them."

Justin frowned and asked incredulously, "How does anyone do that?"

"Father tracked him fourteen times in six years. It's here on the maps. The red path-lines show exactly where Kain and Luther went based on

Father's own GPS as he followed them. Each time he went straight from New York to the lair of the vampires."

"Show me the maps."

Li flicked through the images, and Justin studied each of them.

"They're all over the United States, and even in Canada and Mexico," he said, his voice rumbling in his chest like distant thunder. "These three here," he pointed at the screen, "in Los Angeles, Phoenix and Mexico City. My team handled those targets. All three were small covens of new vampires."

"They're all new vampires, less than six months old. And there is no evidence of these new vampires spawning other vampires."

"Following instructions, were they?" Justin asked, half suspicious, half joking.

"… It's very odd. Young vampires are notorious for being undisciplined. They must have been frightened of something to keep them in line."

"Or someone?"

Li stared at Justin for a long moment and whispered, "Crane?"

Justin nodded. "Who else could get away with it. Unsanctioned vampire creation would have Chloe Armitage and the praetorians hunting the vampire down. All this evidence points to consistency and planning, and an ability to get away with it."

"There is nothing linking Kain to Crane. Father mentioned it several times. All the evidence is circumstantial."

"With quantum technologies, they could be communicating with text messages, and no one would know."

"Yes."

Justin shook his head. "This is bad."

"It's terrible. Kain's in league with the Vampire Dominion."

"That's not what I mean," Justin declared and shook his head once. "What I really mean is that there is not enough here to impeach Kain with. It paints a horrible picture, but it doesn't nail him to the wall."

A hurt look shadowed her face, and Li asked, "Why didn't Father tell me about this?"

"This is dangerous information, he probably wanted to keep you safe," Justin replied. "He's kinda tossed you a live grenade with the pin pulled out."

They looked at each other quietly for a long moment.

* * *

The door to the library burst open. Deon Lamar rushed into the room.

"Treason!" he shouted. "Conspirators! Traitors! Criminals!"

He blurred forward, reaching for the pages of Gang's letter lying on the desktop.

Li's heart skipped a beat.

Justin caught Lamar's hand before it reached the desk. He blurred to the side, dragging Lamar with him and away from Li. A moment later they separated, Lamar flying to the opposite side of the library.

Li ripped the data stick off the table, stood up and moved to the side. Lamar regained his feet. The air in the room crackled with menace as the two men faced off.

Lamar snarled. "Stand down. Force leader or not, you have no right to obstruct an officer of the Order."

Justin raised an eyebrow and moved into the center of the room. His eyes gleaming, his voice rumbling as he said, "You lack manners."

"Manners!" Lamar shouted, stepping toward Justin. "Sedition is at work in this room, and you talk of manners. Are you mad?"

Justin stared down at Lamar and declared flatly, "Are you calling me mad?"

"I'm not frightened by you," Lamar cried out, his eyes flashing. "The Order of Thoth stands behind me."

"Actually," Li observed with a nod of her head. "It's the Mirovar force team that's standing behind you."

The room shrank around Lamar as the Mirovar force team swarmed into the room.

"What on earth is going on?" Francis demanded.

Lamar's head swiveled left and right. He focused on Li, thrust his hand out, his finger pointing stiffly at her face and declared, "Li Wu is a traitor to the Order."

An incredulous murmur spread through the room.

Juliette laughed. "Poppycock."

"It's true," he declared with utter conviction. "I heard her incriminate herself."

"What's going on?" Anton growled, moving to stand next to Li. Peter and Chiara moved to join him a moment later.

"A false accusation I would think," Juliette observed with an arched eyebrow.

"Not false. And you," Lamar claimed, pointing a finger at Juliette, "a loremaster – should recuse yourself immediately. How else can you officiate at an inquisition?"

Lamar looked at Li and demanded, "Hand over the data stick and the letters. I know you're hiding them."

"Don't do anything Li," Anton advised.

Francis stepped forward and commanded, "Everyone stand down. You too Deon. This must be some sort of misunderstanding."

Lamar declared flatly, "The law will have its way."

"Indeed, it will," Francis said. "Juliette, please take everyone out of the room apart from Li, Deon, and Justin."

Anton squeezed Li's hand before he joined the others leaving the room.

Francis shut the door and turned back into the room. His face was flat and serious as he demanded, "Li first, what's going on?"

"Justin brought me a letter from my father," Li declared.

"A document filled with lies," Lamar snarled.

"Enough Deon. Let her speak," Francis ordered, his eyes flashing with tightly held anger. "Go on Li, what was in the letter."

"It was about Ramin Kain," Li said firmly. "It looks a lot like he's in league with the Vampire Dominion."

Lamar sucked air through his teeth and declared triumphantly. "Sedition from her mouth. She self-incriminates."

Francis looked at Lamar as if seeing him for the first time.

Justin stared hard at Lamar. "If you make a spurious accusation against Li," he rumbled. "You'll answer to me for it,"

"You can't threaten me. I'm an officer of the Order."

"The laws of the Order still maintain the right of challenge."

"You wouldn't dare."

"You think so … we'll see who makes the first bone to break and you know as well as I do that there is no limit on which bone gets broken."

Lamar's face twisted into a snarl. "And we can impeach a force leader. You're not above our laws. Be careful you don't find yourself in chains before this day is over."

Justin snorted dismissively. "Did you bring metal thick enough to hold me?"

Lamar stared up at Justin and declared hotly, "You will conform with the law or be outcast. The choice is a simple one."

Justin stared back, his eyes flat and steely. "The first thing you've said that makes any sense. It's always been a simple choice."

"What do you mean by that. Do you seriously place Li Wu's life over the Order? You're not fit to be a force leader."

Francis came to an inevitable decision and commanded, "Enough! There will be no challenges here." He turned to Justin and demanded, "Justin Blake, force leader of the Order of Thoth, do you accept the charge of inquisitorial guardian of Li Wu, novice of the Order?"

Justin looked like he would rather do anything else as he said, "Yes. I do."

"Deon Lamar, Order traveler, do you accept the charge of inquisitorial prosecutor?"

Lamar's eyes gleamed with triumph as he declared proudly, "Yes. I do."

"Li, hand over the letter and data stick to the prosecutor," Francis demanded.

Li looked at Justin, and he nodded his head once. She handed the papers and the data stick to Lamar and said, "Look at what's in there. It's damning."

Lamar's lip curled derisively. "Yes, I'm sure it is."

"Open your mind," she snapped.

Lamar took a step forward. "You presume to instruct me?"

Francis put his hand flat on Lamar's chest. "Call the Head of the Order. Do what you must."

Lamar turned, hurrying from the room.

Francis looked back at Li. "I hope your position is defensible."

"What have you done to me?" she asked.

"What I had to do as a force leader," Francis declared, his voice hard. He turned away and left the room.

"Uncle, what's happening?"

"An inquisition," Justin observed gloomily.

"You'll be my guardian though won't you."

"Not that way. I'm to guard you to ensure you don't escape."

The world seemed to shrink around her, the library suddenly becoming horribly claustrophobic.

She looked at Justin, her eyes large with worry. "How do I fight this?"

"I don't rightly know," he said softly. "Tracking the Head of the Order and accusing him of being in league with the vampires without rock solid proof of his guilt ... and you're a novice ... it's not good Li."

Li sat back stunned. Her father had never discussed the intricacies of an inquisition with her – they were so rare.

What was going to happen now?

She had no idea.

Chapter Seven

"Humility and wisdom walk hand in hand; there are no wise zealots." – Quote from The Way of the Faithful, a book of Red Empire lore

* * *

Boston, August 21st, 11:45

James Haley's smartphone pinged. A moment later so did his laptop as a Panopticon message appeared on the screen.

James scanned the text with a glance. Ramin Kain and Samuel Luther were on the move. Predictive algorithms presented their most likely destination. A red line snaked across a map from New York to a spot just south of a small village in Maine.

The Order safe house.

He vectored cameras along the route immediately in front of Kain's current position. He drove past in his Bentley, followed by a white Chevy Suburban with four male occupants.

The implications of the second vehicle were obvious. Kain had a security detail with him. James had never seen these operatives before, and he mentally noted the new information. He used the cameras to capture sufficient details to identify them again.

James backed up the new data onto a small, portable hard drive, and then purged the information from the Panopticon. The current search on Kain and his associates evaporated, the Panopticon screens vanishing like ghosts.

He pocketed the hard drive.

Opening his phone, he deleted the duplicate Panopticon message and dialed Chloe Armitage. She picked up the call before the first ring had finished.

"James?"

"Yes, Ma'am. The package is in motion toward the Order safe house."

"Any pertinent details I should know about?"

"Kain has a four-man security detail."

"… Initiate the plan. I will meet you at the staging location outside White Hill."

"Yes, Ma'am."

"Good work James. Tonight, will see an important step forward toward our goals. It is critical the Red Empire assassins are in place on time. Will there be any issues?"

"No, Ma'am. The plan is ready to execute."

"Excellent. I will see you after nightfall."

"Yes, Ma'am."

The call disconnected.

James sat back in his chair in his office at the Boston R.I.S.C building. His mind abuzz with thoughts, his heart filled with keen anticipation. A dozen Red Empire assassins waited in a set of suites on the floor below. He pushed his chair back, stood up, grabbed his coat and strode to the elevator.

Fifteen minutes later, three black Chevy Suburbans drove out of the building's parking garage and took off down the street.

* * *

Chloe put the phone down on the marble bench top.

In front of her rested six plastic bags of 'O positive' blood. She'd been so busy lately she hadn't had time to hunt properly. The bags came from an emergency supply she kept in her fridge. She'd warmed them up in a pot of water set to ninety-seven degrees Fahrenheit.

She picked up a bag, tossing it toward her guest.

Marcus Drake caught the bag and remarked glumly, "Thanks."

"Yes, I know. Not perfect, but it will do. Time is pressing, and we must make do with what is available."

Marcus cut the bag with his teeth, draining it dry in a second.

Chloe picked up a bag and followed suit.

A few seconds later, all the bags were empty, and Chloe put them neatly away into a bin.

She walked into her living room, Marcus following behind her. Elegant lamps lit the chamber with soft, indirect lighting. She'd drawn heavy curtains across her full-length windows against the midday sun. There would be no sunbathing in the presence of Marcus, or any other person. Her longing to walk in sunlight would forever be her secret.

They sat down opposite each other on a beautiful and elegant couch of modern design.

"And what of Jerusalem?" Chloe asked.

"It's a disaster for Crane. He is there now, personally supervising the evacuation with general Maze."

"And the target?"

"Captured by the Red Empire and disappeared."

Chloe smiled. "General Mosule is currently held in the Obsidian Prison. It's a holding facility for vampires the Red Empire constructed back in the late '90s. He cannot escape."

"What happens to him now?"

"Nothing. He cools his heels in that black hole until I see fit to free him."

"He will blame me for his capture. He'll link the assassin that passed on the location of the fake citadel to me."

"Don't worry about him. By the time he is free, you will be beyond his power to harm."

Marcus nodded. "And the mission tonight?"

"You have one objective, the safe abduction of Ramin Kain."

"And what of the boy?"

"If you have to kill him to defend yourself, then do it. If he can't survive tonight, he was never going to be any use against Crane."

"You know that I would kill Crane for you."

"Yes. But you know that I want it. Your knowledge is a hook that links you to me and Allemande's curse. If you attack him, you kill me first."

Chloe looked away from Marcus, her eyes growing distant. "The attack against Crane must remain hidden, unexpected, and utterly self-motivated. The young Slayne is growing in power. One day he will match his grandfather and then … we put them together. Anton Slayne and Cornelius Crane. I'm sure that will be the day that I will once again be free."

"And I will be by your side."

Chloe turned back to Marcus; her eyes warm. "Yes, Marcus. At my side forever."

Marcus smiled.

Chloe's eyes hardened. "But first we strike tonight. With Crane's attention focused on Jerusalem and the Red Empire, we will be able to act without interference."

Marcus nodded; his eyes fierce.

Chloe stared at Marcus intently. "Victory will be ours."

"Yes, Chloe," Marcus agreed. He moved closer, Chloe leaning into his embrace.

She rested her head on his shoulder, wondering how many more days he had left to live. She held him tight.

There was little time left with Marcus, and she'd spend none of it on regret.

* * *

James Haley pulled the Chevy Suburban to a halt halfway along the main street through White Hill.

The Red Empire assassins driving the other two cars pulled dutifully in behind him. He turned to the man sitting next to him and directed, "Keep your men in the cars."

Nasr al Dam, the leader of the Red Empire troop, nodded and touched his earpiece, speaking a short command in Arabic.

James exited the car, walking over to the nearest street corner. The local post office dominated the street, and he slapped a device the size of a postage stamp on the wall of the building. A quick glance assured him the device remained securely attached and his actions unnoticed by any of the locals attending to their personal affairs.

He turned away from the wall, walking casually back to the car. The bug carried a tiny fish-eye camera and a radio transmitter with enough power to run for another twenty-four hours. James had programmed it to watch for Ramin Kain's Bentley. Kain's car would have to turn on this corner to head toward the Order safe house. Once it did so, the device would alert him instantly without leaving a Panopticon trace.

James glanced at his watch as he approached his car. Kain should be passing through White Hill in about two hours. He still had plenty of time to secure the staging area and prepare for battle. He got back into the car and drove off to the local airfield.

His eyes were flat as he led the suburbans through the airfield's entrance. The Red Empire assassins would assist with the bloody work of clearing the airfield and locking it down. He'd guaranteed Chloe there would be no witnesses to the night's forthcoming action.

He could not afford mistakes or errors. The stakes were too high. He would do whatever was necessary to ensure the success of the mission.

The three Chevy suburbans pulled to a stop next to each other in the airfield's parking lot. The doors flew open, the assassins blurring out of the cars. They all carried a simple dagger for work such as this, and in less than a minute the only people left alive on the airfield were those who had arrived in the black SUVs.

James opened his phone, sending Chloe a text message which read, 'The airfield is secured.'

He surveyed the carnage. His eyes flat. All these people had died for a great purpose. At least their lives were not wasted.

* * *

Chloe Armitage's smartphone pinged.

James Haley had sent another text message, it read, 'Kain has just passed through White Hill.'

She replied with, 'Our ETA is two hours from now.'

"Time to move Marcus," she ordered.

Marcus flourished his Red Empire swords and plunged them back into their sheaths across his broad shoulders. The dark cape he wore had a pair of slits that accommodated the blades positioned in an 'X' across his back.

"You know I would prefer a mace, flail or axe," he said with a grimace.

Chloe smiled briefly, gave him a pair of sais, and adjusted the fit of his tunic. "Tonight, you need to blend in. Now don't forget your hood and veil. It's very important."

"Yes, Chloe," he replied, tucking the sais into his belt.

She stepped back from him. She wore simple dark-gray combat fatigues and a matching cap; the Red Dragon belted at her left hip.

The edge of a smile curled her lips, her eyes gleaming with anticipation. "Follow me."

Chloe turned, leading Marcus up the stairs in her penthouse to her private, shielded helipad. A brand-new nightfalcon, as black as night, stood in a covered bay just large enough to hold it. She slid the side door back and bounded into the cabin. In a moment, she was in the pilot's seat and flicking switches.

Marcus sat down in the seat beside her.

Above them, heavy steel doors rolled back into hidden recesses. The late afternoon sun slashed across the rotors of the helicopter. The engines roared into life. The rotors blurred, the nightfalcon leaping into the air like a caged eagle suddenly set free. It soared away. The sunlight glinting off the darkened, transparent armor of the helicopter's canopy.

Chloe booted up the nightfalcon's combat system and sent commands to a flight of blackwidow helicopters stationed at Fort Dix. The attack helicopters had been waiting on hot standby for the command and immediately took off. Their engines hushed with stealth technology; they sprang into the air with a low rumble before rapidly dwindling to specks in the sky.

James Haley would log the whole operation as an aerial attack on an Order of Thoth safe house. There would be no reference to a troop of Red Empire assassins, and he would carefully manage the Panopticon record of events to back up the story.

Chloe flicked on the autopilot and leaned back in her chair. All the pieces were in motion. There was nothing left to do but wait.

She reflected upon her plans. The abduction of Ramin Kain was in play. She would spirit him out of the country. She would squeeze him of all useful information on the operations of the Order of Thoth.

It would be an utter disaster for the Order. They would try to rescue him. The only team in position to act would be the Mirovar force team. With Kain as the lure, she could set a trap that would ensnare Li Wu and drive Anton further along the path toward the assassination of Crane.

Chloe frowned. It was a good plan, but nothing was certain. The battle at the safe house could see any of the principles killed. She had to take the risk. There could be no stinting on the forging of a weapon to bring down an adversary as powerful as Cornelius Crane, King of the Vampire Dominion.

Anton would survive tonight's battle, or he would prove himself unfit to fulfill the purpose Chloe had for him.

It was entirely possible Anton would die, perhaps even probable. There were many ways her grand plan could stumble this night. But she had hope, a bright, shining hope. Crane's entrapment of her in his cursed web would blow up in his face. She planned to be there when it happened.

She wanted to be at his side when he died. To watch the light fade from his eyes. To hold his hand, not in comfort, but in a final intimacy to let him know just how badly he'd failed against her.

It was only fitting for someone who'd completely robbed her of her liberty.

* * *

Ramin Kain stared through the front windscreen of his Bentley without seeing what was in front of him.

What the hell has Lamar done?

Ramin desperately wanted to talk with Lamar. Preferably alone, in a quiet room with a baseball bat, or even better, in a hidden location in a trackless forest where a body could rot away without possibility of discovery.

Lamar was supposed to identify the Red Empire agent and hold back so that they could discover their accomplice, and if possible, link Anton Slayne to the agent. What on earth had prompted him to accuse Li Wu of sedition?

Anton Slayne wasn't even in the frame.

Ramin was flabbergasted by just how pear-shaped Lamar's mission had become in just a couple of days. It was bizarre. In his near twenty years in position as the Head of the Order of Thoth, he'd never seen anything like it.

The Bentley barreled along the country road. A white, Chevy Suburban a handful of seconds behind it. Sam slowed the big car, turning into a laneway. They had arrived at the safe house.

Now was the time to find out what had actually happened to precipitate this disaster.

The Bentley pulled to a stop in front of the house. Francis and Juliette Mirovar stood on the porch. A half step in front of them and to Francis' left stood Lamar. His face lit with an enthusiastic excitement.

Ramin got out of the car, walking around the front of it toward the safe house.

Deon came down the steps to meet him and declared, "Sir. I have uncovered a plot to destroy you."

"Very good, Deon," Ramin stated smoothly, shaking Lamar's outstretched hand. "We must not jump to hasty conclusions. The inquiry will reveal all."

Lamar blinked. "But Sir. The evidence is irrefutable."

"Deon, I fully appreciate your endeavors and your commitment to the Order, but we must allow the inquiry to run its full course. We must ensure that justice is not only done but is seen to be done."

"Yes, Sir," Lamar agreed, standing aside. "Of course, Sir."

Ramin checked his sympathetic and parasympathetic nervous system controls – they were still in place. He radiated confidence, certainty, and maturity as he walked past Lamar and proceeded up the steps to where Francis and Juliette Mirovar stood patiently.

"We have a serious situation on our hands," Ramin declared with a frown.

"Yes, we do," Francis agreed flatly.

"The prisoner, where is she?"

"With Justin Blake," Juliette observed. "She is safe."

Ramin leaned forward a fraction. "We need to make sure that remains the case."

"Of course," Francis replied, frowning. "It goes without saying."

"Quite so," Ramin noted.

The Mirovars did not move aside, and the scuffle of feet across gravel sounded loud in Ramin's ears as Sam, and his personal security detail moved into position behind him.

"Do I need to be invited in like a vampire?" Ramin asked incredulously.

Juliette laughed briefly. "Of course not, that would be ridiculous."

Francis stepped aside, and swept his hand back. "Please come inside."

Juliette took a step back, making space for Ramin, Sam and their men to enter the safe house.

"The security detail," Juliette inquired as Ramin approached. "Is it strictly necessary?"

Ramin paused in front of her and declared, "I'm here in my official capacity. Of course, they're necessary."

"Are you implying that the Mirovar force team is a source of threat to your personal safety? That we would violate our oaths to the Order?"

Ramin blinked, frowned, and said, "Of course not." He glanced to his side at Francis who stared at him with a look of utter distaste that could've killed an ox at ten paces. "I mean no offense. There is no reason to impugn the honor of a loremaster."

Juliette smiled warmly, putting her hand casually on his shoulder. "I'm so happy to hear that. I would hate to see an 'honor challenge' made over an ill-considered insult."

Ramin's lips pressed together for the briefest of moments before he regained control of himself. Juliette Mirovar had just threatened him in broad daylight in front of witnesses, and there was nothing he could do about it.

He had no illusions. A single match between Francis Mirovar and himself would end in only one way. With himself gutted like a pig in an abattoir. He loathed the ancient traditions of the Order with a passion but there was nothing he could do about it; an honor challenge was a very real possibility.

Ramin grinned at Juliette like a politician who has just kissed a baby with a full diaper and declared forthrightly, "There will be no honor challenges while I'm Head of the Order of Thoth."

Juliette looked into his eyes, and Ramin quailed inside. The woman was unnerving. She was outrageously self-confident, it was infuriating. She could say more with a moment's silence than many could with a long speech.

Ramin drew upon every resource he had, every ounce of training in the arts of manipulation and control. Speaking smoothly with an air of mature professionalism he said, "Let's move this unfortunate situation forward. There is no reason to be standing on this porch."

Juliette nodded. "Yes, let's get this done."

Turning she led Ramin and his retinue into the safe house.

Francis followed after them.

Ramin walked a step behind Juliette, his mind racing. She'd just made it absolutely clear he must take care to avoid any opportunity to turn this into a personal challenge. Mirovar and his blade would be ready, and his personal security detail would stand down in the face of tradition and the Order's senior loremaster. He would be defenseless. Perhaps with the exception of Sam, but even he would not last long against Mirovar.

He must avoid an honor challenge at all costs. Damn Lamar and his precipitous actions. He still didn't know all the details of what Lamar had accused Li Wu of. Such knowledge would have to wait until the inquiry.

What have I walked into here? It feels like a trap. A damn ugly trap.

He had to find a way to prevail. Perhaps he could salvage the situation. He could provoke Anton Slayne into a rash action that even Juliette's declaration of sanctuary could not save him from.

A glimmer of hope remained; he could use Slayne's inexperience, youth, and attachment to Wu against him. All Ramin would have to do was keep pushing on Anton's need to protect Wu. He wouldn't be able to help himself. He would do something stupid and get himself killed.

Hope bloomed in his heart, as his plans turned on a dime. It was all he could do to avoid smiling as he entered the library.

It was time to up the pressure on Anton Slayne.

* * *

Li stood in the middle of the library. The door was open, Francis, Justin, Kain and his men stood in the room while the rest of the Mirovar force team crowded the hall outside.

"I relinquish my charge to the Head of the Order," Justin declared solemnly, stepping away from Li's side. He moved to the side of the room, his eyes watchful, his face a dark, inscrutable mask.

Kain's men moved forward, surrounding Li.

She put her hands out in front. There was a solid click as steel shackles locked around her wrists.

Kain approached with Luther a step behind him and stood before her. They stared at each other for a moment, Li wondering why Kain hesitated.

"Li Wu," Kain began in formal tones. "You are charged with suspicion of insurrection against the Order of Thoth."

The room was utterly silent.

Li's heart was loud in her ears. *How do I fight this?*

Kain didn't wait for a response. "You will be given the drug, Truther. You will be taken to a chamber of inquiry and put to the question. The truth or falsity of the charge will be laid bare by your own testimony in front of a panel of judges. If the charge is found to be false, you will be freed, and no record of the inquiry will be laid upon you. If the charge is found to be true, given your status as a novice, you will be taken from the chamber of inquiry and summarily executed. Is that clear?"

Li looked around the room. Impassive, serious men surrounded her. She wished she had her sword with her. The Green Dragon would give her a fighting chance of survival and escape, but it lay in her room.

I'm trapped! Li looked at Justin, his eyes stared at her, dark with pain. He frowned slightly and gave the barest of nods. She glanced at Francis who stood near the door. His jaw was tight as conflict raged in barely hidden depths.

If she didn't go along with this, where would Francis and Justin end up standing? Would they side with her against Kain and his men? Two powerful force leaders allied against the Head of the Order. It would tear the Order of Thoth apart.

There were currents far deeper than her own life at stake here.

Li nodded and replied solemnly, "Yes. I understand."

Kain nodded once. "Samuel, please administer the serum."

Luther reached into his coat, withdrawing a small leather folder. He flipped it open. Inside was a syringe filled with a clear liquid. He took the syringe, stepped in close and jammed it into the base of Li's neck, depressing the plunger slowly.

Li stared at him. Luther stared back; his eyes gleaming with something that chilled her heart.

A cold fire spread out from the injection site, racing along her veins.

Luther pulled the syringe clear and stepped back. A faint smile flitting briefly across his face.

Li's eyes flashed with sudden indignation. "Is he allowed to enjoy this?"

Kain ignored her and ordered, "The prisoner will be kept in this room for the next two hours to enable the serum to reach full effect. The Chamber of Inquiry will be made ready, and we will convene there at," he paused to consult his watch, "twenty minutes past eight."

Kain turned away and left the room. The others followed until only Li, and the four Order operatives remained in the library.

She assessed the men. They wore suits, in-ear tactical comm links, and from the bulges, in their jackets, they carried Glock 9mm handguns. Each had a katana sword with a scabbard belted at their hips.

Li frowned and sat down, her shackled hands in her lap. There was nothing she could do except wait.

She turned inward, calming herself and preparing herself to act.

You never know when an opportunity would present itself, and she vowed silently to be ready for anything. She was willing to die to preserve the true spirit of the Order, but she wouldn't lift a finger to preserve Kain's corrupt rule of it.

* * *

Peter Lamb and Anton Slayne stood opposite each other in their shared room on the first floor of the safe house. The last vestiges of sunlight drifting through the windows managed to lift the illumination in the room to a dull gloom.

"This is nuts," Anton snapped in a harsh whisper. "If anyone should be on trial, it should be Ramin Kain."

Rubbing his hand through his thick, red hair, Peter declared without irony, "Kain has all the characteristics of a Bond villain and none of the charisma."

"What the hell is Truther?" Anton asked.

"A truth serum. Li will spill her guts. She's going to write her own death sentence."

"You're kidding?"

"No. The Order will end up killing her."

"That's crazy."

"It's how it works."

"What do you mean?"

"She's still a novice. She hasn't been confirmed as a full member at a Conclave. Kain can order her killed to protect the secrecy of the Order."

"What about sanctuary? Couldn't someone offer her that?"

"Not during an inquisition. It's the one, and only time, sanctuary can't be offered. She's in a very dangerous position – she could easily be killed tonight."

Anton shook his head. "We can't let that happen."

"It won't happen," Peter averred.

Anton thought back to what had happened to his grandfather and his family. Being innocent offered no protection from injustice. He asked, "Are you sure?"

Peter paused for a moment, indecision flashing over his face.

Anton made his decision. "If Kain is going to kill Li, then fuck the Order. I don't want to be a part of it."

Peter frowned. "You'll get yourself killed too."

"I remember you promising to help me find out the truth."

"… Hell … that I did. I wasn't expecting that particular promise to get me killed or outcast."

Anton looked at Peter in silence.

Peter shook his head, smiling grimly. "Don't worry, I don't forget my promises."

"We have to stop this trial – the wrong person has been accused. It should be Kain that is stuffed full of truth serum and put to the question."

"Maybe we don't have to stop anything. She could be found innocent, Francis and Justin are part of the judging panel, surely sanity will prevail."

"I'm not taking any chances."

"Okay then, but we do this my way. We'll hide our weapons in the briefing room and keep some flash bangs handy. If we need to rescue Li and make a break for it, we will."

"And afterward?"

"Well, that's going to be a negotiation with the Order."

Shaking his head, Anton looked at Peter. "I shouldn't involve you in this. It's too much to ask."

"Not really. Kain got up my nose when he had you shot down like a mad dog. I've never felt anything good about him. He's a creep, and the fact that he is Head of the Order is a mockery of everything I stand for."

Anton nodded. "I'll get the Green Dragon from Li's room. She'll need it if we have to rescue her."

"I'll grab my axes. I've also got a bag of flash bangs under my bed."

"Under your bed?"

"Of course, where else would you keep a satchel of explosives?" Peter asked with a mock incredulous grin.

Anton smiled briefly, then turned to his wardrobe, the Blue Dragon rested on top of it. He pulled it down, it always felt like it belonged in his hands and he was certain he would need it tonight.

"I'll bring a blanket," Peter said. "We'll need to keep everything out of sight … you know what? Maybe I should get some guns."

Anton arched an eyebrow.

"Nah, probably overkill."

Anton nodded, and clapped Peter on the shoulder. "Thanks. I couldn't do this without you.

"Hey, I'm doing it for Li. She's real cute."

Anton stopped for a second, staring at him.

"Hey – that got a reaction. I know you're keen on her."

Anton shook his head. "It's not like that. It's complicated."

"Sure."

Anton sighed.

"Don't worry, your secret is safe with me."

"We have work to do," Anton declared, giving his sword to Peter.

"For sure – see you back here in a minute."

Anton nodded, he needed to see if Chiara was not in the room, she shared with Li. He had to find the Green Dragon. Li would need it when they escaped.

Sanctuary with the Order, Anton thought bitterly, *what a farce.*

* * *

The Raven walked casually along the hall. The briefing room was empty.

They ducked through the doorway, blurring to the far side of the oval table. There were three high backed wooden chairs behind it, the judges' chairs. Ramin Kain as Head of the Order would sit in the middle chair.

The Raven moved behind Kain's chair.

The device they held was tiny. Dome shaped, with a half-inch-long stem. The Raven drove the device into the back of the chair, halfway up on the left-hand side. They had observed that Kain was right-handed, and right-handed people often kept their phones on the left side of their body.

The Raven fully understood that it wasn't the best plan in the world, but it was the best they could come up with at short notice. The device would activate when Kain's phone was within a foot of it. It wouldn't need long, a matter of seconds to co-opt Kain's phone and insert the tracking software.

They assessed the plan as a fifty-fifty proposition.

They blurred to the doorway. Reaching the hallway, they dropped back to a stroll and made their way into the kitchen. They had one proximity bug left, and they started working on a plan B.

They poured themselves a drink of water and were shocked when they almost dropped the glass.

Their hands had never trembled before – why now?

The Raven sighed, a wave of confusion flooding through them.

Suddenly nothing made sense.

Nothing at all.

* * *

The dark of night washed across the sky, pushing the last vestiges of twilight over the western horizon.

Chloe Armitage's nightfalcon swooped into land at the regional airport outside of White Hill. She checked her scopes. The three blackwidow attack helicopters were still en route with an ETA of 20:10.

She smiled, she'd fifteen minutes to address James Haley and the Red Empire assassins before the helicopters arrived. That would be plenty of time to get the men organized.

She switched the engines off.

Marcus pulled the helicopter's side door open. She stepped lithely down to the ground. Standing well back from the helicopter in a tight semi-circle were the Red Empire assassins. They had already changed into their combat gear. Each one wore a pair of lightly curved short swords, and an array of throwing stars and daggers. She studied them for a moment, more than half were barely into their beards. The Red Ghost had sent her a young crew. People he wouldn't miss.

James Haley stood next to them, dressed in his usual suit.

All eyes were upon Chloe as she approached the semi-circle of men facing her.

She lifted her voice and declared firmly, "Tonight we take a decisive step against our mutual enemy – the Order of Thoth."

The men stared at her with avid attention.

"We will abduct their leader – the Head of the Order. We know for a certainty that he is at a nearby safe house. Protected by a single force team and a handful of guards."

A murmur spread through the assassins. The Head of the Order of Thoth was a target equal to the Red Ghost. His death or capture would bring great honor to their names.

"Your purpose is his safe capture. Kill all who stand in your way, but do not waste time pursuing the operatives of the Order. This is a lightning mission; speed is of the essence. Once we have the Head of the Order, we will leave this location behind. Shadowstone attack helicopters will cleanse the site. Do not fall behind or remain behind forever."

The men nodded. A few smiled grimly.

Chloe indicated James with a wave of her hand and said, "My aide will introduce your target."

James moved amongst the men with an open laptop, Ramin Kain's face displayed on the screen. Each man took a close look at the rotating pictures, memorizing his features.

Chloe indicated Marcus with a glance. "Marcus Drake will lead you in your approach."

The assassins variously nodded and gave their assent.

"Is it clear? Any questions?"

The leader of the Red Empire troop stepped forward and tapped his chest. "I am Nasr al Dam, the Blood Eagle, we of the Red Empire will do our duty against the weaklings of the Order."

Chloe nodded once and ordered, "Marcus Drake will lead the assault. I command you to obey your oaths and follow him."

Nasr al Dam nodded once. Chloe stepped in close and addressed him directly, "Take your best men to capture Kain. Use the rest to cover your actions and keep the rest of the Order away from your target. Marcus Drake will back you up."

Nasr al Dam grinned, indicating four men to his left. "These are the 'Fist,' the best of my troop. We will not fail in our mission."

Chloe studied him for a second. "Excellent."

She stepped back, nodding at Marcus.

Marcus moved forward. "We leave now," he commanded. "We have three miles to cover to reach the target."

The thirteen men turned away as a group, blurring from the airport.

James approached, standing patiently at Chloe's side.

In the distance, three lights resolved in the night sky. The attack helicopters were arriving from Fort Dix.

She turned to him. "You will fly in one of the blackwidows. Create a perimeter and watch my lead. The Order will fight back, take care and expect substantial losses." She glanced after the distant Red Empire fighters. "Did you notice how young most of them were?" She sniffed, not waiting for his answer. "Guard my exfiltration with Kain and allow the Order to escape."

"Ma'am?"

Chloe smiled briefly. "There is a larger purpose in play tonight beyond the elimination of a handful of Order operatives." She looked off into the distance. "... It's a shame the Head of the Order of Thoth is about to be caught up in the destruction of an Order Safe House by Shadowstone." She clicked her tongue and shook her head. "Who could've predicted such an unfortunate turn of events. Crane will be most displeased when he hears of this latest reversal."

Glowing with an ebullient mood, she turned back to James. "It's such a great time to be alive. So much is happening. Tonight, is a pivotal moment where we begin to seize the initiative from Crane and Kain."

James nodded, his eyes narrowing.

Chloe dismissed him with a look. No one could possibly understand the future she saw for the world. Not until she'd actualized it. It was too much for them to grasp.

The attack helicopters circled the airport, swinging into land around the black nightfalcon.

A familiar pre-battle excitement began to build within her. She looked toward the safe house farm. Soon she would have Kain; forcing the Mirovar force team to follow after him to a battlefield of her choosing.

A battlefield where Li Wu would die and she'd push Anton Slayne toward his inevitable confrontation with Crane.

She shivered with excitement. Everything was at risk. As it must be to achieve great things.

If Anton or Li died tonight, it would be disappointing, but she had time to plan anew.

Oceans of time.

The ultimate realization of her vision was inevitable.

* * *

The briefing room had become a chamber of inquiry.

The main table stood near the back of the room, clearing a wide space in the middle of the chamber for the prisoner.

Li sat in a simple wooden chair facing the table and Francis, Kain, and Justin who sat behind it. Her wrists remained shackled, with a second, thick chain looping around the metal braces and hobbling her ankles. She calmly, a side-effect of the drug coursing through her system. She knew she would tell the truth. She wanted to tell the truth. Her inhibitions and sense of self-control had vanished on the Truther's tide.

The world was bright and shiny. She tried ramping and failed miserably. The drug affected her capacity to be silent. Her internal voice chattering incessantly; she was losing all her filters. It left her feeling naked, vulnerable and somehow – clumsy.

She looked around the room, everyone was there. She ached with sadness. What would her father think of her now, chained and alone in an Order inquisition? The lights dimmed, the gloom settling in like a clinging shroud around her. Where was the light? How could everything be so dark?

Why did people have halos?

She could see auras. *This was new*, she thought to herself.

Nausea worked slowly through her system. *People had colors, who knew?* Was this another side effect of the drug or was something else going on?

Luther and the four members of Kain's personal security stood in a group near the judges. A dark cloud shot with swirls of murky greens and reds moving through them. Kain sat between Francis and Justin, covered with the same murk as his men, but also crowned with a ring of red fire.

Though separated by half the room, Francis and Juliette were wrapped in brilliant golden cords with flashes of silvery light streaming between them. More of the same covered Jay and Yvette.

Lamar stood alone, wrapped in turbulent yellow and black mists. Chiara, Anton, and Peter stood against the front wall. Chiara limed in a hot, red glow, while bright blue and green lightning played and sparked furiously around Anton and Peter.

Justin sat at the judge's table, a purple cloud around his head, his eyes boring into her soul. He lifted his right hand and golden rays speared forth.

A woman's voice cut through the air. The words ringing through the chamber like the voice of an angel. Li's head whipped around to face the speaker.

"—inquisition is called to order."

Kain declared, "The judges acknowledge loremaster Juliette Mirovar – keeper of our law."

"Three are met, force leaders true," Juliette declared. All eyes in the room turned to her. "May the great Thoth guide their judgment with wisdom and fealty to the law."

A bell tolled three times. Incense burned, filling the room with its musky aroma.

Juliette's voice rang throughout the chamber, "The guardians of the law are in place; may justice be swift and sure. The Inquisition of the Order of Thoth has commenced. May no man stand against it, rebuke its judgment or stand forsworn before the great Thoth."

Juliette stepped to the side. Her eyes dark with hidden emotions.

Kain nodded toward Lamar and declared, "The inquisitor shall stand and begin their inquiry."

Stepping forward, Lamar stood a yard in front of Li. He focused fully upon her, his eyes staring into her face.

"What is your name?"

"Li Wu."

"Who is your father?"

"Gang Wu."

"Is he alive or dead?"

"Dead."

"Are you a woman?"

"Yes."

"How old are you?"

"Nineteen."

"Are you a novice of the Order of Thoth?"

"Yes."

"Have you answered any of these questions falsely?"

"No."

Lamar stepped back and announced to the panel of judges sitting behind the table, "The Truther is in full effect."

"Continue your inquiry," Kain declared matter-of-factly.

Lamar turned back toward Li, a slight smile curling his lips. Mustard and charcoal clouds stormed around his head. Red sparks crawling like ants over smoldering embers, filled his eyes.

Li stared at him. She loathed him and yet desperately wanted to tell him anything, as long as it was the truth.

Lamar stared back at her. He reached inside his jacket and pulled forth the envelope in which her father's letter had arrived. His eyes glowed with a fevered light as he regarded Li for a long moment.

He started to circle around her, his voice asking questions about the providence of the letter.

* * *

The blackwidows zoomed off toward the safe house.

Chloe Armitage's nightfalcon flew twenty seconds behind them. She sat in the pilot's seat and flicked a switch to provide a heads-up display of her combat team. Ghostly images played across the windscreen. Metadata streamed next to GPS locations for each of her men. Her command links were open, the soft voices of her team whispering with perfect clarity in her ears.

"The safe house sensor arrays have been disarmed," Marcus reported. "We're in position."

"Hold your position. Our ETA is two minutes," Chloe responded.

She expanded the view from a helmet cam strapped to Marcus's head. He was facing a curtained window at the front of the house. The infra-red filter showed a room full of people. The arrangement of the glowing forms hinting at an ancient memory.

Chloe's mind raced.

Kain had arrived with a personal security unit. He was here on official business. Three people were behind a table. One sat in front of them while a fifth person slowly circled the seated person.

Was it a court? *Yes. An inquisition.*

"Marcus, Kain is the middle man of the three behind the table."

Marcus broadcast the details to the Red Empire assassins.

"Our ETA is ninety seconds. We'll cut the house in two. Time your move with our attack."

"Yes, Ma'am."

"Good hunting Marcus," Chloe whispered to herself.

The three blackwidows broke formation and began to circle the safe house in decreasing circles. Two were circling clockwise, the third, with James Haley on the gun controls, circled in the opposite direction.

Chloe brought her nightfalcon to a spot a little above the blackwidows and eight-hundred meters off to the side. All she had to do now was wait and hope that the Raven had managed to bug Ramin Kain's phone with a tracker.

If the bug failed, she would need a plan B for leaving a believable trail for the Mirovar force team to follow.

* * *

It remained a peculiarity of an Order Inquisition that the inquisitor would withhold the evidence from the judges prior to the event. Only the charge would be known. In this way, the judges would be free of prejudice when presented with the evidence against the accused.

A peculiarity Ramin vowed to get rid of once he assumed the absolute rulership of the Order of Thoth.

Deon Lamar pulled Gang Wu's letter, and the data stick from the envelope. He laid the pages down on the table with a flourish and declared, "Here is the evidence of the lie. A seditious lie designed to tear the Order apart. A lie propagated by traitors claiming Ramin Kain is in league with the Vampire Dominion."

Ramin stared at the pages and data stick in front of him. His heart froze with fear. His mind clouded with a storm of doubts. *What the fuck is this?*

"That's outrageous," Sam shouted, his eyes flashing with indignation.

Juliette called out, "There shall be order in the court Mr. Luther, or must you be removed?"

Luther's head rocked backward as if he'd been physically slapped and he took a step back.

Lamar waved his hand theatrically around the room, declaring loudly, "I have examined the data stick carefully. It is a series of maps where the traitor Gang Wu—"

Anton Slayne hissed. "Bastard."

"Order Mr. Slayne," Juliette declared. She captured his gaze with a hard stare, and his face paled.

Lamar studied the audience for a long moment and then said, "Outlined Ramin Kain's sterling work discovering covens of young vampires."

There was a long silence.

Francis leaned forward slightly and asked, "And?"

Lamar turned to Francis and stated incredulously, "He deduced that Ramin's one hundred percent success rate on searches could only be the result of collusion with Cornelius Crane."

Ramin's armpits and the small of his back became wet with fear. His face flushed as decades of self-taught training deserted him. He whispered hoarsely, "You idiot."

A look of puzzlement flitted across Lamar's face. A low murmur spread through the room.

Justin Blake's hand appeared around Ramin's left wrist.

Ramin looked at it with shocked incomprehension, and then shouted, "Guards!"

His personal bodyguards drew their katanas free as one, moving to stand opposite Blake.

Their leader leveled his blade at the massive force leader, and commanded, "Let him go."

"Make me," Blake growled. A dreadful smile curling his lips while his eyes were as dark and flat as river stones on a moonless night.

The room fell into absolute silence.

The Wu girl, her face filled with sudden intent, called out, "Quiet, someone's here."

"What on Earth are you talking about?" Ramin snapped.

A look of recognition seized her face. "Helicopters. Stealth shielded."

"What?" Francis asked.

Straining at her chains, she shouted, "We're sitting ducks."

The low rumble of dampened turbines filtered into the room.

"Oh, fuck," Ramin whispered.

Chapter Eight

"For those who die with honor, the touch of death is simply the unlocking of a door between this life and the next."

– Quote from The Way of the Faithful, a book of Red Empire lore.

* * *

White Hill, Maine, August 21ˢᵗ, 20:27

Peter dragged the gray blanket away from the cache of weapons.

Anton snatched up the green and blue dragons. A pair of double-bladed axes appeared, like a magician's trick, in Peter's hands. Anton blurred forward to stand next to Li, the twin dragon blades crossed in front of him, his face filled with frightful intent.

"This stops now," Anton declared to the room, his eyes scanning the boundaries of the chamber.

Peter moved to the other side of Li where he grinned at everyone in front of him while circling his razor-sharp axes back and forth.

Luther screeched. "How dare you come armed—"

"See! See!" Kain shouted, leaping to his feet. His left wrist, still immobilized in Justin's iron grip, left him half tilted to the side. He pointed at Anton with his free hand. "Slayne is the traitor. He—"

The front door burst in. Windows shattered. The back door crashed open. Tan and black-clad forms blurred into the chamber. Each wielded a pair of gleaming curved blades. The night beyond the windows erupted into a thunderous firestorm as stealth gunships opened up on the safe house and the surrounding buildings. Twenty-millimeter cannon fire tore through the side of the house, evaporating everything it touched.

Chaos overwhelmed the room.

* * *

The room went to hell.

Justin dropped Kain's wrist. The side of his wooden chair shattered into a cloud of splinters as he blurred toward the one door out of the briefing room.

There was a swish to his right, a hidden katana appeared in Francis' hands, its blade mirroring the golden lamps and flickering candles in the room. Francis, his face a white mask, blurred right, interposing himself between two Red Empire assassins who were rolling to their feet and his wife, Juliette. Man-made lightning flashed beyond the shattered window behind the assassins as cannons thundered overhead.

The four men guarding Kain, their blades already drawn, swiveled around to face the threats rushing in from all sides. Their faces stilled as they descended into silence. Kain stood behind them, his mouth agape.

Justin picked up the remains of his chair with his right hand, swinging it through a tight arc at a knot of Red Empire assassins heading directly toward Kain. In the crowded space, the closest assassin could not escape the path of the chair, taking one leg across his chest and the other across his face. He flew across the room in a cloud of splinters, crashing into the far wall.

Justin surged through the opening and the doorway beyond.

Behind him, the wave of Red Empire assassins who had come through the front door, hit the four Order operatives guarding Kain, blades clanging and crashing in desperate combat.

Weapons. Justin blurred into the front yard where his Harley-Davidson stood. Above him, blackwidow helicopter gunships wheeled through the night sky, streams of fire lancing toward any available target. Their hammering cannons and whirring miniguns cutting across the low rumble of their muffled turbines.

Justin only had moments before their crews saw him and turned their devastating weapons against him.

He tore open the saddlebag on the back of his motorcycle. He reached inside. Grinning tightly, his dark eyes flashing, he drew forth his weapon of choice.

A line of 7.62mm rounds from a minigun speared into the ground, racing toward him.

Justin dove into silence, blurring to the side.

The blackwidow shuddered through the air, wheeling toward him, hunting him with its cannon and miniguns.

Thunder and fire bloomed around him.

Fuck!

Was there no escape?

* * *

Shattered glass littered the floor.

A pair of Red Empire assassins leaped to their feet, swords slashing toward Jay and Yvette.

Stillness reigned in Jay's mind. He blurred forward at maximum ramp, stepping inside the arc of the first blade. His right shoulder slamming into the assassin's chest as his hands slapped together around the hilt of the second blade. The assassin had just enough time for his eyes to register surprise as Jay spun a hundred and eighty degrees, wrenching the blade free of his grasp.

Jay used his grip on the unbalanced assassin's right hand to lean him forward with his own momentum. Jay's left foot lashed out, crushing the man's right knee. He pivoted back the other way, plunging the stolen sword through the assassin's skull, painting the nearest wall with a thin ribbon of blood.

The man fell limply to the floor, his other sword sliding across the polished hardwood.

Jay spun around. Yvette was dodging the flashing strikes of the second assassin, the pair of them rotating through a blurred and deadly dance. He reversed the sword in his hand, throwing it toward Yvette.

She reached for the blade.

Jay dashed for the second blade on the floor.

Is there enough time?

* * *

"What the hell," Luther shouted, backing away and dodging the strikes of the nearest Red Empire Assassin.

A second assassin flourished his swords, advancing on Chiara.

She fell into silence, time slowed down. The assassin ramped, rushing forward. She twisted away to the right as he went past her. She took in the room as she turned. Justin had vanished through the doorway. Five Red Empire assassins were rushing the Order guards in front of the judge's table. Francis engaged two more on the far side of the room as Juliette sought safety behind him. Jay ran past a blood-soaked corpse for a fallen blade. Yvette caught a thrown sword, turning furiously toward her opponent.

Chiara leaned back hard as blades passed over her head.

Li remained chained to her chair. Peter and Anton blurring around her, a ferocious wall of bright metal and desperate intent.

Lamar stood in no man's land, outside Anton's and Peter's defensive ring, his head swiveling, his face rigid with shock. Kain disappeared beyond the swarm of blades and bodies as the four Order guards stood firm before the onslaught of the best of the Red Empire troop.

Chiara leaped, flattening herself face up on the ceiling as the assassin lunged beneath her.

Weapons?

The glass on the floor glittered in the lamplight. She pushed back off the ceiling to land near the front wall. A gray blanket lay crumpled on the floor. She snatched it up, sweeping it over the glass toward the onrushing assassin.

The glass came alive. A glittering mist of shards flying through the air. She let the blanket go. It flew toward the assassin, spreading out like a sail in the wind. The assassin began to dodge aside but the glass was moving too quickly, and the blanket was too wide. The glass struck first, then the blanket wrapped over his front, covering his face and torso from the waist up.

Chiara followed, both her feet striking him in the chest. She rebounded back, the man flying across the room, crashing into the far wall.

She grinned. He'd dropped one of his swords. She scooped it up, twisting around, the sword snapping up into a defensive position in front of her.

An assassin, his leather veil knocked away, blood streaming from his crushed nose, came at her from the front corner of the room. He ramped and lunged. Chiara ramped and defended. His first attack got past her defenses, scoring a cut across her shoulder.

She grimaced, giving ground. This one was a better fighter than the first.

Where was Luther? He'd vanished. There was no help from that quarter. She dodged again. A second assassin, the one who had first struck at Luther, advanced upon her from the opposite side.

It was two against one, and all she had was one Red Empire sword to defend herself with. She vowed to sell her life at a high price. She plunged deep into silence, becoming one with the moment, energy surging through every fiber of her being.

The assassins struck, whirling past her.

She was alone.

She fought.

Blades ground against her sword. Sparks flew, glittering as they drifted away in slow motion. Reflected in the mirror-like shards of glass remaining on the floor. Her dark hair floated around her as she moved through the narrow spaces between the assassins' shining weapons. Candlelight gleaming in her eyes. Four blades against one, her only hope was for one of her opponents to make a mistake.

The first to do so would die.

She held no illusions – she had to fight perfectly.

She'd had practice at that.

* * *

The shock passed, evolving into outrage.

His mind on fire, Deon Lamar took stock of his surroundings. Anton Slayne and Peter Lamb had brought weapons to an inquisition in clear violation of the law. Even worse, Francis Mirovar, a senior force leader of the Order of Thoth had hidden a katana beneath the judge's table.

The violation of trust was more than he could bear. He screamed in inarticulate rage. He stood in a pocket of space devoid of violence, except for the righteous fury burning within his soul.

"Criminals!" he shouted, pointing at Francis. His face flushed, pointing at Anton and Peter, he screamed, "Criminals! Traitors! Spies!"

He spun around.

A Red Empire assassin blurred into the doorway. A straggler, the only member of the troop to enter the house via the back door. Their eyes locked on each other. The assassin rushed forward, his swords flat edges of shining metal at chest height.

As an Order traveler, Deon's training emphasized unarmed combat against armed opponents. All the better to arrest a spy or traitor alive so he could interrogate them before the inevitable execution.

He had an unassailable belief he could survive this encounter. With exquisite timing he pivoted to the side, taking control of the assassin's right arm, he flipped him forward, face-first onto the floor. A sharp crack resounded through the room as the man's face caved in on the polished hardwood.

Deon stepped back, the assassin's limp body lying in perfect stillness at his feet.

The man's death was a deserved death. The Red Empire had split from the Order twenty-three centuries ago. A rebellion that could end in only one way – destruction and death. He thrilled with the knowledge he'd assisted, even if in only a small way, with the destruction of the Red Empire.

Slayne shouted at him, the words lost in the wild noise of battle.

His heart filled with triumphant exultation. He turned and shouted, "Victory is—"

A pair of blades, their points soaked with his blood, appeared in front of his chest. The blows picked him up, carrying him forward to the front wall. The points of the blades drove into the drywall, pinning him like a bug on a cork board.

The swords dragged down and out, shaving through half a dozen ribs on either side of his spine. The world turned, he slumped backward, crashing to the floor.

Deon looked up, for the briefest of moments, his assailant loomed above him.

He flailed feebly with one hand, once, twice.

The world grayed out, and darkness swept in.

* * *

The Blue Dragon flashed through the air, and sparks flew to the left and right. The chains binding Li's wrists dropped to the floor.

Li's eyes flicked between Peter, Anton and the chaos swirling through the room, she snapped, "I can't Ramp."

"It's the Truther," Peter said, his battle-axes held ready and his eyes searching for foes.

Anton shouted, "We've got to get her out of here."

"Where?" Peter asked. "There's helicopters everywhere."

"Damn it."

The Red Empire were all over the chamber. Only half the Order in the room had weapons. Francis wielded the White Dragon, Jay, Yvette and Chiara had managed to capture blades from their opponents, but Lamar, Kain, Luther, Juliette and Li stood unarmed or unable to fight.

A battle boiled mere yards from where Anton stood as the four elite Order guards held off the core of the Red Empire troop. Lamar slammed an assassin face first into the floor. The man's head caving in on contact with the polished hardwood.

The largest of the Red Empire assassins, hanging back from the fight with the Order guards, peeled away to his left. He headed straight for Lamar.

Anton shouted, "Behind you."

Too late – the big assassin plunged his swords through Lamar's back. Blurring forward, he lifted Lamar off the floor and pinned him against the front wall. Dragging his blades out with a downward draw cut to maximize damage, he stepped back to get out of the way of the falling body.

The assassin turned around and faced Anton. Their eyes met – it was Marcus Drake.

"What the fuck?!" Anton swore.

A sick feeling surged through his guts. His breathing stuttered. His father's words, *'I will make you pay,'* slammed like a freight train through his soul. The edges of his world whited out – there was only Marcus Drake and the memories of April the 28th.

Drake strode forward. His booted feet reverberating across the floorboards. His dripping swords snapping up into an attack-defense position, the forward one low, the rear one high.

Anton stalked forward, the Blue Dragon in his right hand, the Green Dragon in his left. For a brief moment, they stood ten feet apart, staring at each other in silence as individual battles raged throughout the room and helicopter gunships rumbled like fire-breathing dragons overhead.

"Where's my father?" Anton demanded through clenched teeth; his voice low with tightly-held hatred.

Drakes' eyes tightened, he snarled once then declared, "Beyond your reach."

"You know where he is?"

"Of course," Drake stated, grinning broadly.

"Tell me," Anton demanded.

Drake's face froze with hatred and he shouted, "Never!"

A red mist descended. Something snapped within Anton. Anguish surged up through his chest. His face paled, his hands stilled to stone-like immobility. Energy coruscated from the base of his spine, flooding muscles, nerves, and bone.

Silence rushed through him, swirling around a pillar of agony transfixed in the middle of his soul.

He ramped instantaneously.

Drake blurred, his swords arcing forward like the scythes of the angel of death.

Anton snapped his blades diagonally up and down, catching Drakes' strikes. The Red Empire metal ground against the genius-forged meteoric iron of the Dragon swords. Splintering in silvery shards, they shattered into thousands of burning pieces. Blooming into twin clouds of glittering metal.

Drake kept coming. Closing to grapple where his overwhelming strength would be a decisive advantage.

Anton's right foot lashed out. All the explosive power of his Ramp flowing through a simple front kick performed with perfect timing. Drake folded around it. All of his forward momentum arrested and reversed. He flew backward, smashing a hole in the wall and disappearing into the front yard of the safe house.

Anton followed him through the gap and into the night.

* * *

Justin leaped straight up the front of the safe house.

Streams of minigun fire ripped through the spot he'd been standing in. The two Harley-Davidson's parked in front of the safe house were torn in half, falling away in crumpled heaps of burning metal.

"Now that hurts," he remarked, landing on the roof in a crouch. He pointed the Milkor MGL he'd taken from his motorcycle's saddlebags at the blackwidow and pulled the trigger. The launcher chuffed, a bloom of gray smoke trailing the grenade arching toward the helicopter.

The blackwidow's sensors detected the incoming threat, incandescent flares streamed from the underside of the helicopter, lighting up the yard. Chaff bloomed to the left and right in glittering, silvery clouds.

The blackwidow's technically advanced defenses were optimized to deal with smart weapons with sophisticated seeker warheads. The 40mm grenade heading toward it was a 'dumb' weapon that relied on the skills of the person firing the launcher to aim it accurately.

The grenade sailed through the flares, ignored the chaff and slammed into the lower left side of the helicopter. Its warhead exploded, sending a molten copper whip slashing through the armor and into the body of the machine.

Blurring to his left, Justin leaped from the roof to the top of a steel water tank next to the house. Mini-gun fire immediately cut through the tank, water sluicing around him. He dropped down to the yard, blurring forward with his right hand holding the MGL outstretched toward the helicopter. He pumped the trigger, the barrels rotating as he ran. Grenades looping toward the blackwidow.

The Helicopter turned on the spot. The mini-gun on the near side and the main cannon chasing him, 7.62mm and 20mm rounds stitching their way across the yard. A stray tracer round nicked the side of a diesel bowser next to the farm's working barn.

It blew up, fire and black smoke fountaining into the air. The blast wave struck Justin from behind and blew him over, the MGL rolling from his fingers. He turned over onto his back. The Helicopter was about fifty yards above him, rocking to the side as the same blast hit it, brilliant flares and glittering chaff steaming from its sides. The first grenade scored a great slash across the nose, the second slammed into the middle of the near engine which promptly started sparking and giving off great puffs of black smoke. The third grenade missed it entirely, looping harmlessly away.

"Fall, you bastard, fall," Justin growled.

The helicopter stuttered. Vents on the second engine opened, the far-side turbine suddenly roaring at full power – all pretense at stealth dropping away. The blackwidow righted, backed and pivoted, turning nose down toward him. Its main armament – the 20mm cannon lining up on him.

Justin scrambled back to his feet, diving back into silence, the Ramp flowering within.

A big, Red Empire Assassin smashed through the front wall of the house. Taking out the rail around the porch, he landed on his back in the front yard. The MGL was three feet back from his right shoulder, within reach if he saw it.

The assassin shook his head once. Blurring upright, staring fixedly toward the house. He pulled a pair of sais from his belt and flourished them, poised to attack or defend.

Anton blurred out, the Green and Blue Dragons in his hands.

Justin rushed forward, scooping up the MGL.

The gunship's cannons remained silent, smoke and a dark fluid leaked from a rent in the armor just above them. The pilot grimaced, the blackwidow sliding to the left. The near side minigun pivoting around toward Justin cued to the gunner's helmet – it pointed where he looked. The crew on the helicopter focused on him alone. They ignored the others brawling in front of the house, it was the man with the MGL that was the immediate threat.

Justin blurred again, firing another round at the middle of the blackwidow's cabin.

The gunner in the helicopter stared at the incoming grenade. The mini-gun on the same side swiveled around and up. Fire burst from its spinning barrels. A golden stream of tracers lit up the night sky, intersecting with the grenade, which promptly exploded twenty yards short of the target.

"Shit," Justin hissed between clenched teeth.

He had one grenade left.

Justin blurred through the space where Anton and the big assassin fought. Dodging past them, he fired his last grenade vertically up through the floor of the blackwidow. The grenade disappeared through the armor into the middle of the cabin.

A bright flash lit the interior of the blackwidow. The inside of the canopy immediately painted with a dark crimson wash.

The second engine died, and the helicopter dropped like a stone.

Justin, Anton, and the big assassin scattered.

The shadows of the night lurched forward as the blackwidow crashed into the yard before fleeing as the helicopter erupted into a huge fireball.

* * *

Marcus Drake and Justin had vanished.

The flaming wreckage of the blackwidow gunship burned in the middle of the yard. Unspent ammunition randomly exploded. A Hellfire missile cooked off, the front half of the helicopter evaporating in a blinding glare.

The edge of the blast knocked Anton flying into the wall of the training barn. He fell forward onto the ground. Sparks fell all around him. Several sizzled through his shirt, burning his chest and shoulders.

He jumped to his feet, patting himself off. The barn was on fire, flames leaping through it. It was already half gone. The hay bales lining the walls burning like dry kindling. The air lay thick with smoke.

Two more blackwidows flew concentric circles around the safe house. They were bearing in on the yard at the same time from opposite directions. Mini-gun fire opened up from the left and right, golden streams leaping along the ground toward where he stood.

Anton blurred backward into the barn and hit the deck.

The heat in the barn hit him like a sledgehammer. The smoke enveloping him and stinging his eyes, he could barely see. Bullets ripped through the side of the barn, whizzing over his head. He hugged the ground. He held his breath. He had to do something about the helicopters – no one was getting out of this alive while they were still flying.

Scrambling to his feet, he blurred to the armory door. It stood shut, waves of heat washing through the air above it. Anton ripped off his shirt, and wrapped it around his hands. Grabbing the door handles, he ramped and dragged the armory door open. It fell to the side with a reverberating clang.

Smoke immediately curled down the first step.

Anton dashed down the stairs into the darkness.

* * *

The room was a riot of colors. The Truther coursing through Li's veins was in full effect.

Without being able to Ramp it was almost impossible to follow what was happening around her.

She was desperate to tell someone the truth. Anyone would do, but no one was asking any questions. It was a horribly uncomfortable sensation.

Li shook her head. Anton had run off after some assassin. What was he thinking? She didn't need Truther to tell him precisely what she thought of his priorities. Thankfully Peter was steadfast, staying close – no one had even tried to come near them.

A spray of blood jetted across her face.

One of the Order guards fell to the floor, blood gushing from his headless neck.

A second guard stumbled to the side, three blades converging through his body. They were gone again in a flash. He fell to the ground, his eyes catching Li's for a brief moment before they glazed over.

The line of guards was breaking.

Luther blurred from the side. Scooping up one of the fallen katanas, he leaped into the fray.

The two assassins who had been probing Francis' defenses without success backed away, turned and rushed toward Peter and Li. Francis repositioned to best protect Juliette. His sword held defensively in front of him, ready to gut the first assassin to come near.

"About bloody time," Peter declared grimly, his axes flashing through the air. In moments, he was a whirl of silvery metal as he clashed against the assassins.

Li lay exposed on the other side where Jay, Yvette, and Chiara fought against three opponents, including one from the core group who Justin had wounded with a chair.

Jay swept with his left foot, unbalancing the nearest assassin. Yvette attacked high with a flashing kick across the man's chest. He fell back hard, sliding across the floor toward Li.

Ramped or not, Li's physiology was ramp conditioned. Her bones, muscles, and nerves were harder, stronger and faster than any normal human could hope to match. She leaned forward, grasping the man's head and with a quick, simple motion – snapped his neck.

He immediately went limp.

"Swords?" she asked, indicating with a nod.

Jay and Yvette grabbed another fallen blade each. Jay stayed to assist Peter, while Yvette rushed toward Chiara.

"That felt good," Li declared with a smile, sitting back within the circle defended by Peter and Jay.

After all, she could only speak the truth.

* * *

The Raven fought in tandem with another Mirovar force team member against a pair of Red Empire assassins.

They were horrified by the attack. What were the Red Empire doing here? The only other person who knew about the safe house outside the Order was Shabbah al Ahmar's other agent. The voice on the other end of the calls. The one who had asked them to bug Ramin Kain's phone.

The one who could be a rogue agent?

But the Red Empire never moved in numbers this great without authorization from the Red Ghost.

The Raven blurred, artfully defending against a flurry of attacks. They knew their team mates well, having trained with them for years. Fighting in tandem with any of them was a seamless process.

The floor was becoming treacherous with the blood and bodies of Order and Red Empire dead. The Raven fought for their life and their mission. The Red Empire assassins in the room were either ignorant of or indifferent to, the presence of a Red Empire spy within the Mirovar force team. The Raven considered the former to be the most likely option. They fought blindly against their own colleague, and if they died by the Raven's hand, it was for a good cause.

A large Red Empire assassin appeared at the door.

Reinforcements?

The man's cowl had fallen away, his face veil hung in tatters. He held a pair of sais. His fair skin stood out, his blue eyes flashed, his blond hair lay cropped short next to his scalp.

The Raven almost died as memory flooded through their Ramp. Red Empire blades slashing past their throat. Years of childhood training and dedication to the craft of edged weapons just barely managed to save their life.

It was Marcus Drake.

Their instructors had schooled the Raven on every important opponent, and the chief lieutenant of general Chloe Armitage was near the top of the list.

Sheathing his sais at his belt, Drake picked up a fallen katana, leaping into the fray in front of the table. A pair of Order guards and Luther were fighting like madmen against the main strength of the Red Empire troop.

Beyond them, Francis waited with Juliette, the White Dragon a vision of lethal stillness in his hand.

Kain, his eyes darting left and right, stood with his back hard up against the wall.

The Raven threw themselves back into the fight. Their soul raged. They had been deceived beyond their worst nightmare. The Red Ghost had allied themselves with the hidden voice in an act of supreme treachery. The secret voice, the killer of the praetorians on the water tower, the agent who was not of the Red Empire. The one who had played the Raven for a fool. The pieces of the puzzle clicked neatly into place; the voice could only belong to general Chloe Armitage.

Shabbah al Ahmar was in league with the vampires.

Interposing themselves between their team mate and the assassins, they struck with all the righteous fury of the betrayed.

Nothing could withstand the full force of their true faith.

The Raven burned with a horrifying light, and their opponents burned before them.

* * *

Peter blurred forward, Yvette dove into the fray, and Chiara launched a ferocious attack.

. . .

Peter's left axe caught an assassin's right sword. His right axe trapped the man's left sword. He pushed outward, spread-eagling his opponent. Stepping in close, his head jerked forward, his forehead crashing into the assassin's face.

The assassin went limp on his feet. Blood fountaining from his smashed nose, he started to fall.

Peter's axes flashed in and across each other. The man's head sailed away. His body, jetting blood from the severed vessels in his neck, crumpled to the floor.

. . .

A dozen feet away, Yvette's left foot lashed out catching her opponent's hand, his blade spinning away.

The assassin lunged forward with his remaining sword.

Batting the blade to her right with her left hand, she stepped within his strike as it went past her shoulder. Her right hand flashed up, her blade disappearing under the man's ribcage. The point erupting in a spray of blood at the base of the man's neck.

He shivered on her blade, his eyes bulging from his head.

Yvette hissed through clenched teeth. Twisting the blade, she ripped it up and out of his chest, slashing through his ribcage, heart, and lungs.

The assassin fell at her feet, dead before he hit the floor.

...

Chiara flew through the air, her feet blurring into her opponent's face.

He blurred away, taking at most a glancing blow.

Another assassin, his face slashed and bleeding blurred forward to replace the previous one. He carried a single sword, the twin of her own. Grimacing with rage, he attacked furiously.

She feinted aside, then ducked under his strike, before driving her sword up and under the man's chin. The point sliced up through the assassin's skull and he shuddered for half a second before she pulled the blade free.

She stepped aside as he fell to the floor, blood pumping from the wounds beneath his chin and on top of his head.

...

Peter dashed back into guard position next to Li and Jay. His axes dripping gore. His face speckled with blood and random flakes of bone. His eyes filled with deadly intent. Yvette, flicking her swords clear of blood stalked the room like an angel of death. Chiara, her face a mask of avenging fury joined her.

* * *

Suddenly three assassins died.

Ramin Kain's heart leaped with hope. The tide was turning; he may yet survive this catastrophe.

Sam fought with the Order Guards, his last line of defense. Good Sam, loyal Sam, perhaps Sam would save him, he could certainly fight.

A large, Red Empire assassin, his cowl thrown back, revealing close-cropped blond hair, and wielding a stolen Order katana pushed into the battle. His sword flashed forward just as one of the Order guards defended himself from another strike. The blade shot through the gap, ripping open the man's chest and he fell backward against the table before slumping to the floor.

The leader of the Red Empire troop lunged forward, the point of his blade beating past the deflection of the last Order guard. A line of red appeared across the guard's throat. He reflexively reached for it. Before his hand could land on the wound, a pair of blades gutted him. He gurgled, blood sluicing past his fingers as he fell forward over the bodies of his comrades.

Two elite Red Empire assassins stalked Luther, who backed away toward Francis.

The blond assassin and the troop leader grinned at Ramin and leaped across the table toward him. Two more assassins, one sporting a broken nose followed after them.

Enough was enough. Clearly, the tide had not turned.

Ramin blurred to his right, fleeing past Francis, Juliette, and Luther. Leaping through the broken window, he disappeared into the night.

Six assassins followed after him.

* * *

Justin picked himself up from where he lay on the gravel next to the porch.

He'd been a fraction too close when the Hellfire missile had cooked off and had been dazed for a few moments. A pair of blackwidows rumbled overhead. The clash of blades rang out from the house. A smoky haze mixed with the sharp tang of burning metal shrouded the air. Both barns and the haystack were alight, the flames turning the yard from night into day. Cannon fire had blown half the safe house away.

There was no sign of the big Red Empire assassin or Anton Slayne.

His MGL was empty, all the rounds expended taking down the first blackwidow. He looked around. He needed a weapon, anything would do. Half his motorcycle lay a couple of yards away. On the edge of the wreckage was the drive chain, one end lying in the gravel.

The helicopter gunships circled overhead – currently ignoring him. He assumed their crews hadn't yet seen him move. He didn't expect that to last and had no desire to tangle with them again – especially without weapons.

Justin was brave, but he wasn't suicidal. He blurred forward, stripping the chain from his motorcycle wreckage in a single smooth motion. Turning, he rushed back into the house toward the briefing room.

Passing through the doorway, the room resembled an abattoir. Blood and bodies littering the floor. A Red Empire assassin advanced on Peter. Beyond Peter, Li looked up at Justin and smiled. Jay circled past her, and Yvette and Chiara advanced toward Francis' position. Beyond them, a knot of Red Empire assassins rammed past Luther, Francis, and Juliette toward a broken window.

Ramin Kain had vanished.

Justin leaped forward, whipping the chain with all his strength through a diagonal slash across the nearest assassin's back. The rugged metal blurred forward, faster than anyone could follow. The chain ripped through the assassin's body from above his right shoulder to the top of his left hip. Everything in between, in a strip an inch wide, reduced to bloody pulp.

The man slid apart as he crumpled to the floor.

Justin stepped forward, looked at Peter and Li, and said in a low rumble, "What did I miss?"

* * *

Ramin Kain had disappeared through the window and into the night.

The Red Empire assassins followed after him.

Francis knew that he would have to rescue the head of the Order. There was no way they could allow Kain to fall into the hands of the Red Empire. He knew too much about the operations of the Order of Thoth.

The last of the Red Empire assassins, his nose still bleeding from an earlier crushing wound delivered by Justin with a chair, headed for the window – his attention focused on pursuing Kain.

The White Dragon blurred out. The man didn't have time to register surprise as the blade passed effortlessly through his neck. His forward momentum took both his body and his head through the window, and onto the porch where he fell in a heap, his head rolling out onto the gravel of the yard.

One less opponent to thwart Kain's rescue. They'd cleared the room of assassins. They needed to evacuate the house immediately. With no 'friendlies' on site, there was no reason for the helicopter gunships not to flatten the property with a pair of Hellfire missiles.

Francis commanded urgently, "Juliette, Li, Yvette, Chiara, run for it out the back and head for the western tree line. The rest follow me."

"What about Anton?" Li asked.

Francis shook his head. "There's no time – move it."

Francis blurred toward the window in pursuit of Kain and the Red Empire assassins. A half second later the room was empty; except for a set of lamps, a number of guttering candles, and the dead.

* * *

Chloe pivoted the nightfalcon.

Ramin Kain fled from the safe house, pursued by Marcus Drake, Nasr al Dam and the three surviving members of the elite Fist team. She was not surprised to see that only the strongest had survived the encounter with the Mirovar force team.

She signaled the blackwidows and commanded, "Cover the escape of those men heading south and meet me at the tree line. Expect immediate pursuit from ground forces."

"Yes, Ma'am," answered the pilots.

She opened a second comms link directly to James Haley, operating as a gunner on the helicopter gunship swinging around behind the safe house. "James, you will need to eliminate these crews. They've seen too much. See to it after this engagement."

"Yes, Ma'am," James answered flatly.

There could be no witnesses.

Chloe dropped the nightfalcon like a stone, diving down to a position well in front of Kain.

So far, everything had proceeded to plan. She frowned. Now was the critical moment where success or failure hung in the balance. She'd done everything she could to ensure the former, but there was always a chance of something unexpected occurring.

She scanned the horizon, the only potential threat to her objectives was from the Mirovar force team. She extended her senses, favoring them over the high technology of the nightfalcon.

Four members of the team were heading slowly toward the western forest. The rest were in close pursuit of the Red Empire assassins and Kain.

There was no sign of Anton Slayne, his distinctive Ramp signature was absent.

"Where's Anton," she murmured.

It had always been a risk that he would not survive to become the weapon that she desired.

There was nothing she could do but wait and see if he turned up.

* * *

Ramin Kain sprinted across the field.

His feet barely touched the ground. Arms pumping, knees lifting high, head still, eyes focused on a tree line a mile away. He ran like the devil pursued him, and he wasn't far wrong.

He glanced back over his shoulder. Five figures blurred behind him, silhouetted against the burning farm. Their faces hidden in shadow, they sprinted after him, their blades faintly reflecting distant fires. Above the farm, two blackwidow gunship helicopters wheeled about, setting a new course toward him.

They were coming for him. Everyone was chasing him. Ramin centered himself in his running. If he could make the tree line, he could disappear into the forest. The Red Empire assassins would have been ramping at maximum during the combat in the inquisition chamber. He'd stood back, waiting for his opportunity. He remained rested. There was a good chance that he could out run them. After all, vampires were not chasing him.

He glanced back again.

A second set of figures pursued the assassins. Sam, and the rest of the Order. Brave Sam would save him. He just had to stay alive long enough for them to catch up.

The Red Empire assassins would be looking over their shoulders soon, and they would discover the hunters had become the hunted.

Hope flared in his heart.

A sleek, black nightfalcon emerged from the night sky. It swooped down, hovering a dozen feet off the ground in front of him. The canopy reflected the distant fires raging at the farm. It rested a hundred yards before the tree line, like a great black insect or predatory bird waiting for him and him alone.

Ramin zigged to the right.

The nightfalcon slid in the same direction.

He zagged to the left.

The nightfalcon moved again, blocking his path.

A shiver shot up his back, his anal sphincter puckered and shrank. The assassins were surely making ground as he attempted to evade the black helicopter. He couldn't tell without looking, they'd conducted their pursuit in near silence.

He didn't dare risk slowing down for another look back.

The blackwidows rumbled louder as they approached from behind.

"Damn it, Sam," he snapped in desperation. "Where are you."

He was running out of time.

* * *

Anton emerged from the burning training barn.

He wore a thick, gray blanket like a cape, pulled tight over his head. It smoked, tongues of flame struggling to consume it in a dozen spots. He shrugged it off, and it fell at his feet. He lifted a pair of Milkor MGLs, one in each hand. A bandolier of high explosive armor piercing grenades ran across his naked chest. The Green and Blue Dragons lay strapped in an 'X' across his back.

Half the available Order team members were blurring over the fields in pursuit of the Red Empire and Ramin Kain. A pair of blackwidow's converged toward a spot near the south tree line. A black, nightfalcon hovered there blocking Kain's path.

"First Drake, and now Armitage," Anton said, his eyes flashing. He sank into his Ramp. Power surged through him. He blurred forward at maximum speed. The nearest blackwidow was still within range of his MGLs. He lifted his right hand, pumping the trigger as he ran. The final shot was 'chuffing' away on a trail of gray smoke as the first of the grenades triggered the helicopter's automatic defense systems. Rows of brilliant flares jetted to the left and right, clouds of chaff bloomed above the flares, reflecting their light like so much silvery confetti.

The first of the grenades sailed past the blackwidow, which began to frantically turn away. The second, third, fourth and fifth grenades stitched a line of explosions across the rear of the helicopter. The nose dipped down. The tail broke away. The body of the machine began spinning wildly as it continued to lurch toward the tree line.

The fuel ignited. The helicopter exploded into a huge fireball. Secondary explosions disintegrated the blackwidow into a rain of flaming debris.

Anton dropped the empty MGL, blurring toward the hovering nightfalcon.

The last blackwidow flew in from the far side of the field. Its cannons and miniguns blazing, tracers slashing across the field. The Order team members took evasive action, scattering before the firestorm.

Anton ran on.

The Red Empire caught up with Kain. He disappeared behind their bodies as they converged on the nightfalcon. They leaped up the dozen feet necessary to reach the helicopter's cabin. The nightfalcon roared into the night sky.

Anton shouted, "No." He strove to his utmost. Swinging his second MGL up toward the nightfalcon, he pulled the trigger. The first grenade zoomed away. Anton kept pulling the trigger until the MGL clicked on empty.

Turning away to the east, the nightfalcon disappeared into the night as the grenades all fell short of the target.

"No, damn it, no." Anton dropped the MGL, fell to his knees, hiding his face with both hands. After a moment, he sighed. Picking himself up, he retrieved the MGL at his feet and headed toward the Order operatives. They were already returning from the field, heading for the remains of the safe house. There would be another chance.

While he was alive, there would always be another chance.

* * *

Marcus Drake moved forward to take over the flying of the nightfalcon.

Chloe Armitage moved into the main cabin, she wanted to meet her guest. Ramin Kain lay on the floor of the cabin, bound with chains. There were plenty of empty seats along the walls of the cabin. She took one where she could easily look into his face.

Someone had hit him hard; he was unconscious. His eyes flickered once, and then again. He woke up with a start.

"What the hell," Kain swore, his eyes darting around the cabin at Chloe and the four Red Empire assassins.

222

"Hello Ramin," Chloe stated airily, unable to hold back a smirk of delight. "Do you know who I am?"

"Crane's whore," Kain snarled.

Chloe's eyes went flat, her hand flashed out, and Kain's head rocked to the side. He shook his head, staring at her with naked hatred flashing in his eyes, the outline of her hand a red print on the side of his face.

"Who am I?" Chloe asked softly, just loud enough for him to hear over the helicopter's engines.

"General Chloe Armitage."

Chloe smiled, but her eyes remained flat.

"That's better," she observed evenly. "Now you've found a civil tongue in your head."

"What game are you playing at?" Kain demanded. "Crane would not have sanctioned this. You're completely out of bounds."

"Indeed."

Recognition flashed across Kain's face. "You're the other player – you killed Crane's vampires on the water tower. You called me that morning months ago to warn me of Anton Slayne – you played me!"

Chloe studied him silently.

Kain leaned his head forward, his gaze darting over the four Red Empire assassins, then it flicked back to Chloe. "What strange bedfellows? I see you needed help to capture me. What? Couldn't do it on your own?"

Chloe smiled, her eye's twinkling. "If you're expecting a 'gloat speech' where I reveal the details of my plan to prove how superior I am." She lashed forward with her fist, catching Kain on the chin, his head snapping back hard against the floor.

He quivered momentarily before his eyes glazed over.

"… You're talking with the wrong girl."

Chloe patted Kain's pockets, found his smartphone and fished it out. It was still fully operational. She went back to the front of the nightfalcon and sat in the co-pilot's chair. She plugged the phone into an available charging socket.

It wouldn't do to have it run out of power.

She looked across at Marcus. "Call Logan Airport and get our aircraft ready. We'll be coming in hot. There is no time to waste."

The Order was sure to follow, and follow hard and fast. They couldn't afford to leave the Head of the Order in the hands of their enemies. Their pursuit was a certainty.

Chloe was counting on it.

Soon Anton, Li and the rest would be in the middle of her trap.

It was inevitable.

* * *

Francis picked up the White Dragon's scabbard from where it lay taped underneath the briefing room table. Once it was free, he slid the White Dragon home and returned it to the belt at his hip. He fished around under the table for a second and stood up with a Glock 9mm in a holster. He attached the holster to his belt on his right hip.

All the survivors had returned, the house lay damaged beyond recognition, but it still stood. It hadn't caught fire the way the barns had. They were still burning, but the peak of the fires was over as they had collapsed in on themselves.

"Two minutes, just the essentials," Francis commanded.

Peter walked into the room, shaking his head sadly. "John and Mary are both dead. Caught by cannon fire."

Francis nodded grimly. The farm family had been loyal Order helpers all their adult lives. They knew the risk and had volunteered anyway. Brave, kind people, he vowed never to forget them.

"Quickly now. Shadowstone will return to eliminate any evidence," Francis directed. "We don't want to be here when they arrive."

"Why not?" Anton asked grimly, Li at his shoulder. She was holding the Green Dragon in its scabbard at her side.

"We don't have time. We have to rescue Ramin Kain."

"What the hell for."

"He's the Head of the Order," Luther spat.

Anton snapped back, "He's a traitor."

Luther shook his head, stepping in close to Anton. They stared at each other, a few inches apart.

Francis pushed between them. "Stand down. There is no time for this. Anton – we have to get Ramin Kain back before whoever took him pumps him for everything he knows."

Anton blinked and nodded, stepping back.

Luther sneered silently and stepped back as well.

Anton looked at Francis and declared loudly, "It was Armitage and Drake."

"What?" Francis asked in surprise.

"It was Armitage and Drake who took Kain. I recognized him tonight. He was the big, blond assassin. I kicked him through the damned wall."

Luther snarled, shaking his finger at Anton. "You're still running with this insane conspiracy crap."

"It's true. It was Marcus Drake. I'm sure of it."

Luther implored Francis, "Why are we listening to this crazy kid?"

"I know exactly what I saw," Anton insisted.

"And what did you really see?" Luther sneered. "Just another man."

Anton spread his hands wide and snapped, "What do you want from me? I'm telling the truth."

"What does that mean when you're a Slayne?"

"Enough!" Francis commanded, stepping between the two men. "Enough of this bickering. It would be safer to assume Anton is correct until proven otherwise."

Luther started to speak, then stopped himself.

"Marcus Drake wouldn't be working with a Red Empire troop without Chloe Armitage's permission," Juliette observed calmly, putting the strap of her laptop satchel bag over her shoulder. "Vampires, Red Empire assassins and Shadowstone all working together. Chloe Armitage must be running her own operations behind Crane's back."

Luther shook his head once, his eye's narrowing.

Francis and Juliette exchanged a glance.

"We need to move," Francis declared. He waved his hand around his head and called out, "Everyone, listen up. We're heading for rendezvous point number one. We'll split up to make sure they don't catch us as a group on the way there. Jay, please take Luther, Yvette, Justin and Chiara. Peter, take Anton with you. First hit the demolitions and then follow after us. Li, you'll come with Juliette and me."

Everyone nodded.

"Let's go."

The team streamed away from the house.

Anton turned to Peter with a quizzical look on his face. "Demolitions?"

Peter shrugged his shoulders and nodded. "Yeah. I've got the place wired. It'll only take a minute to arm it."

"Right," Anton noted, following after him as he tracked through the site.

Three minutes later they were at the south tree line. Peter looked back at the safe house, frowned for a second and then pressed a stud on the top of a silvery cylinder in his right fist. The safe house erupted. A fraction of a second later the first explosion was dwarfed by the armory under the training barn going off. The ground shuddered. The northern horizon over a mile away darkened and then a bright flash ripped away the night. Six seconds later a thunderous boom rolled over them.

"What the fuck was that," Anton asked in awed tones.

"A fuel-air explosive," Peter answered glumly. "The only one I had."

Anton wasn't entirely sure what saddened Peter the most, the loss of the safe house or the loss of the bomb.

"I'd plans for that one," Peter whispered as he turned to the forest. He looked across at Anton and grinned ruefully. "Follow me."

Anton ran after him.

Chapter Nine

THE METEOR THAT NEVER WAS!

August 21 | Permalink | Comments: 87

By **Chief Tinfoiler**

Categories: Secret Government, Aliens, Extra-terrestrials, Signs

Well, Tinfoilers, gather around and listen up. This is big. No this is HUGE! No, this is **GINORMOUS!** I know it's all over the corporate-state owned "mainstream media." The Meteor, the Star Rock, The Sky Hammer. The fake news of the rock that fell just short of the sleepy hamlet of White Hill in western Maine – well, there was no rock.

I REPEAT – THERE WAS NO ROCK.

Read on to find out how a secret government agency destroyed a nest of extra-terrestrials using advanced tactical weapons not available to our military. That's right, the extra-terrestrial menace is lurking out there and hiding in sleepy hollow.

– Blog post snippet on the Internet

* * *

South of White Hill, Maine, August 21st, 20:37

Light flashed at the horizon behind them. Fifteen seconds later a thunderous detonation washed over them from the north.

Francis led Juliette and Li into a clearing. There was just enough moonlight to navigate the paths through the forest. He suddenly stopped and swore in harsh French, "C'est un foutu bordel!"

He turned to Li, held out his hand and demanded, "The Green Dragon, pass it to me."

Juliette, her eye's wide, asked, "Francis?"

Li stared at Francis for a moment and then handed her katana to him.

Francis whipped his Glock 9mm out, putting the barrel against Li's temple.

"Francis!" Juliette shouted in alarm.

"Merde! Mon amour. I must know."

Juliette, her eyes flashing, declared earnestly, "Francis. You don't need to do this."

Francis ignored Juliette and asked, "Li, are you a spy for anyone?"

Li shook her head and stated hoarsely, "No."

"Are you wholeheartedly committed to the Mirovar force team."

"Yes."

"No reservations?"

"None."

"What of the Order of Thoth?"

"It has its problems."

Francis sighed and frowned.

"Do you know of anyone else who is a spy?"

"No."

Francis jerked the gun away from Li's head. "I'm sorry Li."

He holstered the Glock and gave the Green Dragon back to her. She took her sword and stepped back, her face pale in the moonlight, her eyes glistening as she stared at him.

"Satisfied?" Juliette asked in annoyance.

"The sensor array was bypassed. There must be a spy in our team!"

"Well, it's not Li."

Francis glanced back at Li; anguish flitted over his face. He turned back to Juliette and declared, "The only person above suspicion is you. If you are the spy, then the team is already dead."

"I could have told you it wasn't Li."

"Your mind palace is a powerful tool, but it couldn't predict this attack, nor tell us who the spy is. I had to take action."

Juliette grimaced. "Li, you're on the inside of this now. Your training with me means it's inevitable that you will know. There is a Red Empire spy within our team. It's one of Peter, Yvette or Chiara. Lamar's arrival two days ago indicated it and tonight's attack confirmed it."

"I had to clear you as well," Francis addressed Li. "To make sure you hadn't been co-opted in any way."

Li stared at him.

"I have to defend this team."

In a voice filled with shock, Li asked incredulously, "By putting a gun to my head?"

Francis dragged his right hand down his face and looked at Juliette. Naked panic threatened to overtake him. Juliette was unarmed in the middle of a fight against a superior force. It was a miracle that so many of his team had survived. If the Red Empire dedicated themselves to killing them, rather than capturing Ramin Kain – they would all be dead. Someone had completely compromised the security of the safe house. The Order was in disarray, and the Mirovar force team was hanging in the wind.

The situation was intolerable.

"Yes. Yes, absolutely," Francis declared wholeheartedly, his eye's glistening in the moonlight. "And you, you wonderful, loyal young woman with a true heart passed with flying colors."

He bowed low. "My sincere apologies. The Order has horribly abused you in the last few hours, and it tears my heart that I've added to your burdens. But know this, I will declare for you at the next Order conclave, and you will always have a home in the Mirovar force team should you desire it."

Li shut her eyes for a long moment. The clearing seemed to hold its breath. Something indefinable flitted across her face.

Stepping forward, she put her hand on his shoulder, and said softly, "Apology accepted." She glanced once at Juliette before staring into his eyes and whispering, "We all must serve unto death and death will claim all who we love."

Francis' breath fled. He stood up; his heart filled with horror. He nodded once, glancing at Juliette and directed in devastated tones, "Follow me."

Juliette, her eyes wide, whispered. "Of course, mon amour."

They ran from the clearing toward the rendezvous point.

* * *

Anton followed Peter through the doorway and into the log cabin.

Everyone else was already there. Justin loomed in a corner talking quietly with Jay. Yvette had just finished suturing Chiara's shoulder, and they were comparing combat moves. Juliette had her arm around Li's shoulders and was talking with her in quiet tones. Francis and Luther were standing apart, apparently lost in their thoughts.

There was a bucket of water just inside the door filled with wet towels. Peter grabbed two and handed one to Anton before scrubbing dried blood from his face.

Francis looked up as Peter and Anton arrived and declared, "Good, everyone is here now."

Luther looked up, lifting his smartphone to show everyone else in the room. "Look here. I have a track on Ramin's phone."

Everyone stared at him for a second. Juliette moved to stand next to him. Luther turned the phone to show Juliette. "See."

"That's incredibly lucky."

"He's trying to help us find him. He's managed to turn his phone into a GPS beacon."

"Or Armitage is trying to lure us into a trap," Anton snapped.

"Not this again?" Luther snarled, pushing past Juliette to stand in front of Anton.

"ENOUGH!" Francis roared.

Everyone stopped and stared.

"Samuel Luther, stand down," Francis ordered. Whipping around he pointed his finger at Anton and commanded, "And you be quiet."

Anton blinked and stepped back.

"It's clearly a trap," Juliette observed knowingly.

"They could've wiped us out with missiles," Francis said. "Instead, they took losses to snatch Ramin Kain."

"We have to get him back," Luther demanded.

"Of course," Francis agreed. "We can't allow him to remain in the hands of our enemies. He knows too much."

Francis looked at Justin. "Will you join us for this mission?"

"No. I have to leave," Justin advised with a frown. "I have to prepare the next conclave ... most likely we need to elect a new Head of the Order."

"Don't be so sure of that," Luther snapped. "Ramin is a living genius and a hero of the Order. Mark my words, I'll be proven right in the end."

Anton glanced at Peter, who shrugged his shoulders. He held his tongue.

"Be that as it may," Juliette conceded without a trace of sarcasm in her voice. "We will proceed on this mission as if it is a trap. We do not know the agenda of those who abducted Kain. But it is obvious they would expect us to pursue him. The availability of Ramin Kain's phone as a GPS beacon to follow is too convenient. They want us to follow him. Soon we'll know where he is going. As to why?"

Juliette left the question hanging and flipped open her laptop.

"We'll have to find out – the hard way," Francis answered directly. "We have two SUVs parked here and ready to go. Juliette, do we have a track on Kain's beacon."

Juliette scanned her screen. "Heading directly to Logan Airport. They'll arrive in ten minutes. From there, they can go anywhere."

"We're three and a half hours away from the airport. Three hours at best," Jay advised.

"Five minutes, everyone," Francis directed. "Peter and Jay, you're driving. We're heading to Logan Airport as soon as possible."

Anton nudged Peter with his elbow and asked in a whisper, "Will Kain reveal what he knows?"

"He'll squeal like a pig," Peter whispered back.

"Peter, your hands are idle – prep the vehicles," Francis ordered

"Yes, Boss. Anton give me a hand."

"Sure."

Anton followed Peter out, and around to the back of the cabin, where a carport shielded two late model Ford SUVs.

Peter declared, "Let's get to work."

Anton nodded. He helped Peter get the cars ready. In minutes, they would be on their way.

* * *

Samuel Luther stepped out of the log cabin and walked about twenty yards into the forest.

He looked around, making sure no one had followed him. He pulled out his smartphone and dialed a number from memory. The phone rang twice before it was answered.

"Samuel?" A voice asked.

"Calvin, we need to talk."

"What the hell is happening over there. There's talk of a major meteor strike all over the media."

"That's just fucking Shadowstone PSYOPS. The Red Empire with help from Shadowstone have abducted Ramin."

There was a long moment of shocked silence on the other end of the line. "This is a disaster."

"Tell me about it. Mirovar is incompetent and a coward. There was a full-on battle. He just stood around on the fringes of it like he didn't want to get his hands dirty."

"That's disgusting."

"It's well known he is a liability who has risen far above his actual ability."

"So, what are you going to do."

"I'll be leading the rescue mission to get Ramin back."

"Is he still alive?"

"He has to be. He's turned his phone into a GPS beacon to allow us to follow him."

"A stroke of genius."

"Absolutely. God only knows what he's going through at the hands of those fiends."

"We have to get him back. He's central to our movement."

"Oh, we'll get him back. Even if I have to sacrifice every member of the Mirovar force team to do it."

"Good approach, they're expendable."

"Completely. By the way, Blake is on the move."

"Blake? What?"

"He'll begin organizing the next Conclave – he wants to unseat Ramin and put Mirovar or himself in charge."

"God help us. What a nightmare."

"We'll have to block any initiative either Mirovar or Blake put in place. You'll have to look after it. I'll be too busy making sure Mirovar doesn't fuck this up."

"Don't worry about it Samuel, the rest of us will look after the political end – just get Ramin back."

Samuel nodded and declared vehemently, "I'll get him back or die trying."

"Good luck."

"Won't be necessary," Samuel promised, hanging up the call.

He walked back to the cabin, and whispered to the night air, "Hold on Ramin, we're coming to get you."

* * *

Outwardly the Raven appeared calm and focused as they helped the team prepare to leave the cabin.

Inwardly, their world was chaos. They were almost ready to make a run for it. To slip away, escaping into the forest. To leave everything behind until they worked out what the hell was really going on and what they really wanted to do about it. But they couldn't leave their friends on the eve of a battle. That was beyond the pale.

The very same loyalty that would have seen them obey a direct order from the Red Ghost to kill everyone in the Mirovar force team now worked to bind them to the team. The link to the Red Empire lay broken. Loyalty could not remain in the face of betrayal.

The foundation of the Raven's world had been torn away the moment they understood the Red Empire had allied itself with vampires. Such an act was unforgivable.

The Raven smiled briefly at something one of the others said. They turned back to their work, cursing Luther for discovering Kain's GPS beacon. The beacon the Raven had managed to put in place with a Red Empire bug on Kain's chair.

If they had been able to stop the beacon, they would have. They wanted nothing more to do with 'the plan' instigated by the Red Empire's other agent – none other than general Chloe Armitage of the Vampire Dominion.

A light switched on inside them. Armitage didn't know the Raven had unmasked them. She still expected the Raven's loyalty. The Raven grinned. They could secretly work against her plan.

A thrill flushed through them, wiping away their distress. They had a new mission – same as the eternal mission – defeat the vampires.

Armitage was in the Raven's sights, and they would do everything within their power to thwart Armitage's trap.

That will be the first step. And then my father, Shabbah al Ahmar, I will bring you to justice.

* * *

Chloe's smartphone pinged.

It was a message from the Raven which read, 'They have taken the bait. The team is pursuing the GPS beacon.'

She continued up the stairs into her Spike 512, supersonic business jet. Marcus Drake, carrying the limp form of Ramin Kain, followed her.

Back on the tarmac, James Haley and the surviving blackwidow pilot walked up to Nasr al Dam, and the rest of the Fist. A second later, the pilot slumped to the ground. Nasr al Dam turned to the side, cleaning a dagger with a black cloth.

Reaching the top of the stairs, she paused, glancing out through the main hangar doors at an Embraer business jet taxiing toward the runway. It had a single passenger. A well-charged smartphone that was behaving exactly like a GPS beacon. The plane's manifest defined a charter by a New York businessman named Ramin Kain, bound for London.

Chloe smiled briefly; events were tracking to plan. James would stay behind with the surviving Red Empire assassins. They still had work to do tonight, especially James to manage the content of the Panopticon. There would be well-constructed video footage of Kain boarding the Embraer business jet and the battle site would need to be cleansed of any remaining evidence. Although it appeared, the Order had done much of Shadowstone's work for them by detonating a fuel-air explosive at the safe house.

She entered the cabin, checking her phone as she took her favorite seat at the front of the luxuriously and stylishly appointed cabin. It was 21:30, she was at least three hours in front of the pursuing Mirovar force team. But there was no time to waste; they would be traveling east toward the sunrise and needed to beat its arrival over the northeast of England. The Spike 512 could fly to the UK in three hours, which would put the local time at 05:30 on landing. A couple of minutes short of half an hour before sunrise.

Soon, she would be back at her ancestral family home – Armitage manor.

She would take off after 'Kain's' Embraer jet. She would honor Crane's command to keep him safe by traveling to the UK after him, 'just to keep a close eye on him.'

Shadowstone had delivered a victory against the Mirovar force team by destroying an active, safe house, albeit at the loss of two blackwidow helicopters and three crews. The battle provided its own distractions.

Already Shadowstone were spinning a web of deception over everything that had happened.

James Haley was proving invaluable.

There was plenty of time to sow doubt and muddy the water of the evidence trails. By the time James completed his work, the only narrative Crane would be able to find would be the one she was in control of.

She hit the intercom button. Her family retainers piloted the plane. Loyal humans who knew precisely what she was but didn't care. Another little secret carefully kept from the view of Crane.

"Home, Derek. There is no time to waste."

"Yes, Ma'am," The pilot responded.

The outer doors closed automatically, and within a minute the plane was taxiing out of the hangar.

Chloe relaxed back in her seat, closing her eyes. Anton had survived the fight. He had even tried to shoot her down with grenades at the end of the battle. She'd recognized his Ramp heat signature as he ran across the field.

She was pleased he'd made it, and Li as well.

All the pieces were falling into place to drive home his belief in revenge.

So much was happening, it was a thrilling time to be alive.

Soon, in less than forty-eight hours, her plan would take another major step forward.

She was sure of it.

* * *

The Day Guard lab facility sat on the third underground level beneath Fort Dix.

The two levels above it were also pure Shadowstone. The US army operated the entire above ground site, and the US taxpayer funded everything. The Shadowstone facility seamlessly integrated with the military base as a para-military government/private contractor partnership under a framework agreement signed by a US president several decades in the past.

When a relationship has been in place long enough, everyone forgets how it came to be, and no one questions it.

Unless, of course, you're Louise Wesson. She stood in front of a line of twenty fit young men dressed in simple white slacks and T-shirts. All volunteers, recruited from a diverse cross-section of US special forces teams for a 'special assignment.' Apart from their common backgrounds, they also shared very high levels of native physical ability and had proven themselves under combat conditions.

They were natural warriors. They were the first batch to receive the Phase V Day Guard serum. She'd selected these men personally. She regretted the fact that ten of them would be dead within two days and they didn't know it.

Louise had worked hard to find the best men, not just to fill Crane's quotas, but to maximize their individual survival rates under the serum. The research notes provided to her were crystal clear about the effects. Full physical transformation would normally complete within three hours, but it took one to two days to be sure the subject would survive. The symptoms of failure were specific and consistent; berserk rage, rapid aging, catatonic depression, and death. Once the rage started death was inevitable.

Four lab techs walked in front of the men. The first handed out mouth guards. The second carefully injected a specially encoded RFID chip with a microcapsule of TEF-4 neurotoxin next to their brain stem. The third injected a measured dose of the Day Guard serum into the side of their necks. The fourth guided each man to a low stretcher on the floor behind them.

Louise noted the date and time on a simple notepad, '21:31, Monday, 21st August.' Underneath a penciled in and thickly underlined heading, 'Super Hero Program Day 1.' It had been two months and ten days since she'd woken up to the existence of vampires and their secret rule over humanity.

She watched calmly as the first of the subjects began to quiver on their cots, biting down hard on their mouth guards.

Rule by vampires didn't sit well with her oath to '... defend the Constitution of the United States against all enemies, foreign and domestic; ...' and the rest. The idea of the subjugation of humanity to a tribe of blood-sucking predators revolted her on a deep level.

The situation was intolerable, and she was not going to put up with it.

The vampires had ordered her to build them an army. She would do that. The next step was to wrest control of that army away from the vampires and use it to kill them.

The trick was in staying alive long enough to do it.

She needed to stay hidden while watched by apex predators with super-sensory abilities.

It was the biggest challenge of her life.

A slight smile curled the edges of her lips.

Where else would you rather be?

Epilogue

An infamous historical figure discovers the Vampire Dominion ruthlessly enforces their laws.

Greifswald, Northern Germany, May 1st, 1945, 23:05

The former *Führer und Reichskanzler* of the Third Reich, Adolf Hitler stared at the passing streets of Griefswald as he made his way through the town toward the docks.

Adolf seethed with rage. The Red Army occupied the city. *Gifted to the communists intact by that ridiculous traitor Petershagen. The sniveling coward who gave the city away without a fight.*

Turning to his companion. Adolf's rage retreated into the background, replaced with something akin to adoration. Dieter Franz, his savior, his mentor, a beautiful Aryan god he'd first met on the blood-soaked mud of Passchendaele in 1917 – his youthful blond hair and blue eyes unchanged in twenty-eight years.

An immortal who had admitted him into the ranks of the divine the night before in the bowels of the *Führerbunker*.

On the night of the 30th of April, Adolf admitted to himself that all had been lost. He'd written his last will and testament. Then it was to have been a poison pill and a 9mm round from his own Luger. Better honorable suicide than the humiliations the Slavic hoards of the Red Army would visit upon him.

Then, against all hope, Dieter had arrived. A colossus towering over the other men within the bunker. He'd locked the door behind him, knocking Eva Braun unconscious with a slap and then attacked him.

Adolf felt ashamed of his display of primal terror, whimpering as Dieter bit deeply into the side of his throat. The pain of having his throat slashed open and feeling his blood draining away in seconds was nothing compared to what came next.

Dieter laid his forearm open with his gleaming fangs. Pressing the gushing wound directly against the holes in Adolf's throat, his divine Aryan blood had mixed with Adolf's own. The excruciating agony of the ravenous fire of Dieter's immortal blood cleansing all human weakness from his body. While his flesh writhed in torment, his mind exalted in triumph over death, and victory over time.

As the pain ebbed away, Adolf had been surprised to discover how the overwhelming lust for blood had a deeply familiar feel to it. He realized he'd felt this need all his life and only after this divine transformation could he fully embrace his deepest predatory need with immediate frenzied feeding.

Eva Braun awoke just long enough to register terror on her face as he lunged at her. Pinning her to the ground with hands like iron. Latching hold of her throat with an unbreakable grip. His fangs lacerated her arteries, blood pouring into his mouth. He drew on new internal muscles, creating a vacuum effect, accelerating the flow and in seconds she ran dry.

Leaning back from Eva's limp body, Adolf sat down on the floor. Drunk with blood, his head whirling, exhilarated beyond measure.

Dieter dragged him to his feet and declared, "Time to go."

Rage suddenly flared, *how dare he touch me*, then immediately settled back to a quiet hum as Adolf followed Dieter from the bunker.

Of course, no one stopped them, he was Adolf Hitler, and the tall, powerfully built Aryan god marching in front of him added an extra layer of intimidation. In moments, they cleared the bunker, striding together through the ruins of Berlin. Fires lit the horizon, smoke tinged the air, and shells whistled and crumped in the distance.

Adolf looked up at Dieter and asked, "What of the Russians?"

"We will go through their lines. I have transport waiting north of Berlin, follow me to safety," Dieter instructed. He threw his coat to the ground, revealing a longsword belted at his waist. He drew the blade, the razor-sharp metal gleaming with a crimson hue in the light of the surrounding fires.

Adolf's mouth twitched incredulously, halfway between a snarl and a smirk. "What use is a sword against tanks?"

"Have faith – it will be all we need. Now make sure you keep up."

Adolf watched in wonder as Dieter rushed off through the ruins of Berlin with superhuman speed. He followed after, wonder giving way to exhilaration. He reveled in the speed and power of his new divinity.

Dieter cleared the way before them. None could stand in his way; he was too fast for the Russian soldiers to react. Blurring through their ranks like a scythe through a field of wheat. He steered Adolf past rows of advancing tanks and together they broke through the Red Army lines. They quickly covered nearly eight miles to an abandoned house surrounded by ruins.

Waiting in front of the house were a dozen heavily armed young men dressed in civilian clothes. They jumped to attention and saluted as soon as Adolf approached. Their youthful faces lit with pride to be part of the mission to save the *Führer*. Discarded uniforms of the 1st SS Panzer Division littered the front yard of the house. The men were members of the *Leibstandarte SS Adolf Hitler*, his personal bodyguard.

Adolf smiled, pleased to see these young flowers of Germanic youth. He knew they would do their utmost to serve him and he was certain he would require nothing less.

Across from the house brooded three powerful armored saloons. The exclusive Mercedes were the color of night and stood ready to fly down the roads. The men piled into the first and last of the cars, with one of the men sliding behind the steering wheel of the middle car and the last man holding open the passenger door for the *Führer* and his companion.

"Our transport," Dieter stated calmly, indicating the middle car with a nod of his head.

Adolf climbed into the plush accommodation of the rear seat of the saloon, and Dieter followed him in, storing his sword and scabbard on the floor well. The last SS man got into the front of the car and the powerful engines of all three vehicles fired into life. Moving forward as a column they disappeared into the night and escaped Berlin.

Morning arrived as they reached the outskirts of Greifswald, and Adolf discovered why thick black curtains covered the middle vehicle's windows. He was intensely disappointed to discover this weakness. This terrible vulnerability to sunlight and his expression remained sour until they had taken refuge in a barn.

Dieter quietly explained while they waited that when evening came, they would enter the port town of Greifswald, making for the docks and a waiting submarine. The Type IX U-boat would take them through the Baltic Sea, then across the Atlantic to South America and a new life in Argentina. The twelve unsuspecting young men of the Waffen SS would join the submarine's crew – as additional food – to sustain them during the weeks of travel. By the time they reached South America, the submarine would be a ghost ship without a crew, but the two immortals on board would survive and flourish in a new land.

The sun had fallen and they'd left the barn. The way into Greifswald had meant crossing the paths of units of the Red Army. Adolf had joined Dieter in combat. Using his bare hands, he'd fallen upon the Russians as a wolf amongst sheep, reveling in bloodlust and death. Not a single soldier they encountered had survived their divine wrath.

Adolf reflected on his new abilities. *A new base of operations to create a foundation for a new Reich, superior to the third Reich, an amalgam of the irresistible alloys of the Aryan race and yes, I must admit it – vampires. I will rule forever. None can resist my power; I am a true Übermensch.*

Suddenly the first car pulled to a halt, and Adolf's mind returned to the present with a jolt. There was a roadblock, four of the Waffen SS exited the front Mercedes, more men came out into the street from the car at the rear. One of the men at the front shouted commands, the men started firing their 9mm submachine guns. In moments, the guns at the front fell silent, their harsh voices replaced with swishing sounds and wet thuds.

Adolf struggled to see what was happening from within the confines of his armored saloon. The men at the back of the column started firing wildly into the air. He thrilled to the rising panic of men beset by terror as something leaped over his Mercedes.

A terror that would never touch him again. *I am the new god of death – all will worship me and die!*

"There is a problem," Dieter declared, grasping his sword and blurring away. The car door spinning into the street, torn from its hinges as he exited the vehicle.

Adolf followed him, flushed with his new powers and supremely confident that whatever the challenge, victory would be his. He blurred out of the saloon and onto the street. Dieter stood twenty yards away. The Waffen SS men lay about on the ancient cobblestones – all dismembered, all dead – their blood pooling in the gutters.

Opposite Dieter stood a tall, young woman of exquisite beauty. She was clad in loose black clothing, carrying a long gleaming sword with both hands like one of the occult assassins that Himmler had been so fond of. She flicked her head, her long dark hair flowing across her shoulders. Glancing past Dieter, she stared directly into his eyes and something passed between them – a recognition of inevitable destiny.

A shiver of dread raced up his spine, his confidence evaporated as his guts curdled and suddenly cramped. Without thinking, he took a step back, raising his hands as if to ward off an impending attack.

Turning slightly toward Dieter, a slight smile curled her sensual lips as she chastised him in sardonic tones, "You have been a very naughty boy."

"He is under my protection. You have no authority here!" Dieter declared.

She laughed coldly. "There are standing orders from Crane himself, you know what must happen now."

"I know no such thing, witch!" Dieter thundered, blurring forward.

They clashed in a shower of sparks. Even with his new abilities, Adolf could not follow how quickly they fought as their flashing blades rang out through the night. He took another step back, a dreadful foreboding freezing his heart.

Suddenly, Dieter's sword shattered into half-melted shards. The dark-haired woman's sword passing through it to cleave off his right arm above the elbow. She blurred again, taking off his legs above the knees. Dieter flopped to the ground in a jumble of separated limbs and spraying blood.

The woman immediately turned to him. Their eyes locking on each other for the briefest of moments before she leaped over Dieter's writhing torso toward him.

Adolf didn't wait for her to land. Turning, he fled down the street. Becoming a dark blur in the shadows. Hurtling toward the docks and the sanctuary of the waiting submarine.

If I can only get inside, I can get away from her. She cannot follow me into the open sea.

The buildings whipped by. Adolf strained to hear the sounds of pursuit, but there were no noises discernible as his pursuer. There was the drip of dank water in nearby gutters, the scuttling of rats lurking in the sewers, the murmurs of frightened townsfolk accustomed to staying inside if there was trouble on the street.

He lamented silently. *Why am I alone? Why is there no one left to die for me?*

He darted into an alleyway and came to a halt. He backed himself up against a wall, looking, listening – his heart beating rapidly – even for a vampire. His head swiveling left and right. *Where is she? Where is the witch?*

There was no sound of pursuing footfalls. There was only a slight whistling. A shadowed hint of a breeze. A glint of reflected moonlight from somewhere above him, and then her sword, an ancient Japanese katana made by a 17th-century genius slicing through his neck.

Adolf felt his head topple from his shoulders. It bounced painfully off the cobblestones of the laneway before rolling into a filthy gutter. He was still conscious, a ring of agony engulfing his throat, an even two inches below his jaw line.

Something smeared over half his face. Stinging his eye, squishing into his nose, seeping into his mouth which soundlessly opened and closed like a beached fish. Its horrid taste magnified by the superb acuity of his vampire senses. It was unmistakable for a man who loved German Shepherds more than he loved people. His mouth brayed silent words, *Dog shit! I have dog shit in my mouth! And its been ill! Mein Gott! What has it been eating?! It's in my eye!*

The experience of life began fraying around the edges. A finely leathered boot tilted his face up slightly. He saw the woman peering at him as a scientist might stare at an obscure butterfly pinned to a corkboard. She wrinkled her nose in physical disgust, her beautiful blue eyes narrowing as hidden emotions bloomed behind them.

"I loathe wannabees," she declared fervently.

Suddenly, she stepped away. He rolled back into the wet dog shit; which again seeped into his mouth and pushed up into his nose.

She called out, her voice betraying her exasperation, "Dieter! Stop trying to escape – or do I have to take your remaining limb as well?"

The darkness closed in. His senses left him one by one, sight, hearing, touch. The last two lingered for a long moment, smell and taste. The most ancient senses and the last to go as his vampire vitality ebbed away.

Adolf's mind echoed a single pungent word repeatedly as it finally collapsed into oblivion, *shit, shit, shit—*

* * *

The End

The story will continue with the next instalment of The Metaframe War.

"The Dragon's Den."

IT'S A TRAP!

Anton Slayne knows it's a trap. One laid for him by his most powerful opponent – Chloe Armitage, rogue general of the Vampire Dominion.

The chase is on. Agents of the Red Empire and the Vampire Dominion have abducted Ramin Kain, the Head of the Order of Thoth. Anton and the Mirovar force team are the only ones in a position to act. They know Ramin is bait, but have to rescue him before he's forced to reveal the secrets of the Order.

Will Anton and his friends in the Mirovar force team rescue Ramin Kain, or will Chloe Armitage discover the secrets of the Order, destroy the Mirovar force team, and enslave Anton to her will?